The Piper's Price

By:

Audrey Greathouse

The Piper's Price

ISBN: 978-1-63422-223-5
Cover Design by: Marya Heiman
Typography by: Courtney Knight
Editing by: Cynthia Shepp

For Alison—
Because if Peter had ever come for me,
I would have made him stop at your house,
too.

For more information about our content disclosure,
please utilize the QR code above with your smart phone
or visit us at

www.CleanTeenPublishing.com.

CHAPTER 1

Gwen lurched forward like a wounded bird. She struggled to stay afloat as she grappled with the air. Only halfway up the small mountain, she gave up and landed. Ever since she returned to Neverland three weeks back, she'd had trouble flying by herself. When she was with the other children, she derived a vicarious confidence from them. Alone, her mind had no playful distraction from its self-conscious apprehensions.

Dillweed zipped up to give her another sprinkling of fairy dust, but she gently batted him away. "It's no use. I'd rather walk." He glanced skeptically at the last steep mile of trail. "It'll be good for me," she announced. After all, if she didn't have Claire and Katie dragging her to yoga classes, how was she going to get exercise?

The green fairy glowed indignantly at that grown-up line of logic, but settled on her shoulder as if in solidarity with her decision not to fly. "Just don't tell the others," she said, sighing as she began the strenuous climb.

She knew he wouldn't tell. Dillweed had kept her secret for weeks now, and Gwen had at least stopped feeling self-conscious around him. When they'd first gotten back to Neverland, she'd worried he would be mad at her for letting him nearly die of alcohol poisoning when he was trapped at Jay's house party. On the contrary, he seemed grateful she had saved him and returned home to Neverland. Like many small tragedies and terrifying near misses, it had served as a bonding experience. She'd begun to learn the fairy language, too. The impatient fairies had only taken time to teach words to Blink, Bard, and now Rosemary. For the most part, they weren't interested in educating the lost children, but Dillweed cared enough about Gwen to teach her and stay glued to her side.

Although part of that was due to the drones.

As they reached the mountain's crest, the trail began to level out. It was the highest point in Neverland. Gwen was sure it had a name, but she couldn't get a straight answer out of any of the lost children. She took to calling it Mount Neverest, and in a few days everyone seemed to have forgotten it had ever had any other name. They rarely flew up it, except for chores.

At the peak, Gwen and Dillweed stood above the jungle-forests and could see all the way to the ocean. The beauty of the panoramic view was lost on most of the children, but Gwen enjoyed the sublime feeling of looking over the entire magical island. She pulled a borrowed spyglass out of her satchel and surveyed the horizon with it.

Nothing was in the sea or sky. She collapsed the wooden telescope and put it back in her satchel. It almost disappointed her that she would have nothing to report back to Peter—no approaching hostile forces or missiles to give him a sense of impending adventure. Since meeting Antoine at the airfield, Peter had buried himself in his puzzling papers. The riddling hints within had consumed him—the only clues he had to the Piper's whereabouts. It was a slow process, and quiet deciphering was not a becoming activity for Peter.

Her lookout duty taken care of, Gwen followed Mount Neverest's trail a short distance farther to the rocky nook on the other side of the mountain. Although she had completed the first of her chores, she still had to deal with Miss Daisy.

The Never Bird sat in a massive nest of straw, twigs, and large, curling leaves. It barely contained her plump, white body, and her stately, blue-tipped feathers contrasted against the cobbled-together nest.

"Hello," Gwen cooed, hoping for a pleasant interaction this time.

The Never Bird squawked threateningly.

She never knew whether to call the creature Miss Daisy as Jam and the others did, or try to win its favor by referring to it by the title of Never Bird. It might have been a moot point—she didn't know whether the bird could understand her at all.

"Peter sent me for an egg. You know, Peter." The bird squawked, but not as loud. It didn't budge. None of the other children had any trouble fetching things from the Never Bird, but crabby Miss Daisy was never kind to Gwen.

She took a step closer to the bird. It cawed, its stork-like beak opening wide. Miss Daisy did not seem to comprehend Gwen was a lost child, and all she wanted was one of the sterile, sloshy eggs filled with milk. Gwen tried not to get frustrated with herself for failing to negotiate with an imaginary animal for bird's milk.

She reached out slowly, thinking maybe Miss Daisy would be more amenable if first petted or allowed to smell her hand. The Never Bird was not a dog and resented being treated like one. It stood up and snapped at Gwen, catching her hand in its beak.

"Owww!" She recoiled and nursed her hand. Once again, Miss Daisy settled her feathered rump over her eggs.

At last, Dillweed intervened and began buzzing at the bird until it waddled off the nest. With its begrudging beak, it gently nudged one of its large eggs out of the nest. The milk-filled egg rolled unevenly toward Gwen's feet. She picked the pale blue offering up with both hands. It was too big to fit in her satchel, so she tucked it in the crook of her arm like a football and forced herself into a polite curtsy for the Never Bird. It squawked once more at her, still hostile and unpleasant. Gwen hurried away, happy to leave it behind and return to those who accepted her legitimacy as a lost child.

Gwen flew in short spurts down the mountain. Having procured Miss Daisy's milk egg, she felt more confident, but she now worried she might fall and break the egg if she flew too high. This precaution didn't stop her phone from falling out of her dress pocket. Gwen gasped and cringed as she heard the phone smash against the ground. "Please don't be broken, please don't be broken…" she muttered as she dropped to her feet and picked it up.

There was a crack in one corner of the screen. It would still be usable, but Gwen wondered why she even cared. The battery must have absorbed ambient magic from Neverland because the device never died, but it wasn't as though she got cell phone reception. She'd only been using it to look through old pictures earlier. Gwen stuffed it in her satchel and hoped it would be safer there as she continued.

She was down Mount Neverest and back into the thick of the jungle when Dillweed shot up and yanked a lock of her hair in panic. She looked where his tiny finger pointed when he buzzed, *Drone!*

Without the sound of her footsteps, Gwen could hear the malicious hum of the device's four rotors. Like a tiny helicopter, the boxy metal contraption hovered through the forest in a steady and methodical search. A red laser light scanned the space ahead of it, helping the device adjust its flight and avoid trees while it searched for fairies.

It was not heading for them, but if it kept on its course, it would cross the path they had just cut through the forest, and instantly identify the fading trail of pixie dust Dillweed had dropped. As soon as it did, it would switch from its search function to its capture one. Any sudden flight from the fairy would send a fresh cloud of dust into the air and trigger it even faster. Gwen set the Never Bird's egg at the base of the nearest tree trunk, and then reached into her pack with the same slowness. She pulled out her tiny bag of emergency fairy dust and hurried to tie it to the longest stick in reach. Standing upright, she whispered, "Ready?"

Dillweed buzzed *yes*, and then leapt into the air, sprinting on his wings as fast as he could. As he did so, Gwen took off running in the other direction.

The drone sensed this activity and engaged in an immediate chase. Its rotors turned tenfold as it began whizzing toward the cloud of fairy dust almost as fast as a fairy, and with a mechanical perseverance that would be sure to exhaust and capture even the swiftest pixie. Fortunately, Gwen's diversion worked.

Dillweed's head start left a trail of pixie dust, but Gwen's simple decoy dropped a much more obvious stream of magic for the drone's sensors to follow. She ran as fast as she could with the stick propped over her shoulder, taking long leaps that turned into quick bursts of flight. She headed *weast* and tried to keep as much distance between her and the drone as possible, even though she knew it would eventually catch up to her.

She didn't know how long her pixie dust supply would last. The whirling menace was still behind her, so she knew she hadn't run out yet. Trying to stay focused, Gwen told herself she'd already succeeded. Dillweed had gotten away and was safe from the scouring drone. That was a small victory, though; if she didn't manage to destroy the device, it would continue combing the island for fairies to capture and return to the Anomalous Activity Department in reality. The next fairy it stumbled onto might not be so lucky.

Her breath grew short and a stiff pain settled in her lungs as she continued to run. This was an unfamiliar part of the forest for Gwen, and she couldn't gauge how close she was to the creek until she nearly tripped into the water. She took an immediate turn to follow it downstream, and then continued to run. She desperately wanted her chest to stop burning and to take a moment to recuperate. Her initial spurt of adrenaline was wearing thin, but the drone had no bodily constraints. It was still flying with wicked determination.

Whenever she could, Gwen took to the air. It wasn't much

faster, but at least it didn't require the same physical exertion. She was too nervous to sustain flight, and she wished someone could take over for her. Batting her way through a canopy of vines, she had a brief opportunity to rush ahead while the drone went the long way around the entangling vines. Feeling a small fire kindling in her lungs, she decided to pretend. She pretended she wasn't in any kind of pain as sweat began to run down from her brow. It surprised Gwen how much that helped. The stress of exertion faded as she imagined she was an Olympic medalist merely running track. She was always startled that such tricks worked in Neverland.

At last, she came to the tributary she was looking for. The slender offshoot of water led only a little ways before dissolving into a muddy swamp. Previously used only for mud pies and other baking endeavors, the swamp had become a graveyard for drones. Hopping along rocks out to the sticky depths of the sweet muck, Gwen suspended her bag of pixie dust an inch away from the mud and stood as far off as she could. In seconds, the drone came sweeping down, and Gwen jerked the bag back with a quick twitch of her stick. Too late to adjust its course, the drone drove itself straight into the mire, smothering its thin rotor blades in mud. It tried to churn through the thick goop, but all it managed to do was make the mud bubble around it as the machine overheated.

Trapped among half a dozen dead drones, it suffered a gloppy fate. Gwen hurled a rock at it as hard as she could, but it didn't so much as dent the impressive war device. It was already doomed... but she watched it overheat and savored her victory, all out of breath and bitter in her joy. The drones were less destructive and easier to avoid than newsprint bombings, but they were just as terrifying in some ways.

Once the drone had short-circuited itself and she had caught her breath, Gwen packed the remnants of her depleted pixie dust bag back into her satchel and meandered away from the swamp. She retrieved the Never Bird egg from the tree she'd left it under, and then leisurely made her way back to the grove, trying not to think about how frequent drone attacks were becoming.

CHAPTER 2

On her way back to the underground home, Gwen found Bard, Spurt, and Jam aboveground and weaving. Or rather, Bard was weaving. Spurt was running on his hands and knees pretending to be a werewolf, while Jam insisted Spurt was a dog and attempted to train him. Bard was the only one who had the attention span to continue work on the project they had started earlier that afternoon.

The spider-silk yarn she was working with moved fluidly between her tiny fingers. The task did not require precision—the net didn't need to be tight—but her net's holes were all identical in size and shape anyway. She was almost done by the looks of it. Finished nets already hung on saplings around the island. By dinner, Bard would have another to drape over some little tree and the fairies would come with their domesticated spiders to spin finer webs between the net's holes, creating another small haven away from the drones. The machines could not track magic when it was enclosed in these protective spiderwebs. The enchanted spiderwebs of Neverland could hide anything magical and stop it from radiating beyond the cover of the web.

Spurt came galloping toward Gwen and pawed at her leg ferociously before pretending to gnaw on it.

"BAD DOG!" Jam yelled. "*STAY!*" She came chasing after, blonde pigtails bobbing, and the freckly younger boy howled as he dashed away.

Gwen didn't mind them. "Hi, Bard. Nice net."

"Thank you. Is the egg for dinner tonight?"

"I think so? I don't know how to… uh, prepare it?"

"Jam makes a very nice egg and flower soup. Maybe she'll start that when she's done training her puppy."

It occurred to Gwen that Bard was unusually alone with the spider-silk. The fairies that brought the spider-silk tended to stay with their benevolent weaver and encourage her or bring her berries, sweets, and trinkets for her efforts. "Where are the fairies?"

"Some others came and got Foxglove and Hollyhock a few minutes ago. Blink followed them out to the blackberry bushes."

Gwen noticed a knot in Bard's clump of spider-silk yarn. She sat down cross-legged and began untangling it for the girl. "Did Dillweed come back here?"

"No—did you lose him?"

She wasn't surprised—she assumed he went to find a stiff drop of mead to calm his nerves after their frightening run-in with the drone.

"He must be back at his hollow with the others. We found another drone."

Bard looked up, surprised and worried. "There's so many." She cast her gaze back down at the net she was making. "I didn't think they were ever going to find Neverland again."

"When was the last time drones came?"

A blank look settled on the girl's face. She had no means with which to measure time. Gwen dropped the subject. "Where's Rosemary?"

Bard thought about it, but didn't have an answer. "I haven't seen her since Blink left with the fairies. She might be with them."

Gwen wandered back into the forest. It wasn't far to the blackberry bushes—just beyond the grove, a towering mass of them grew in what appeared to be one giant clump. Not deceived by its appearance, she plucked aside one of the largest thorny branches to reveal an opening low to the forest floor. Crawling through, she emerged in the blackberry theater.

She didn't fear interrupting anything since she could hear the fairies from the other side of the brambles. They continued to trill words and conversation beyond her comprehension. Dark little Blink sat in the middle of the bright enclosure, quiet and unblinking. Hollyhock was there with her usual fiery-gold glow, as well as the purple and twinkling Foxglove. With them in discussion was Hawkbit, a fairy unfamiliar to Gwen. He had a pale yellow glow and seemed to be wearing armor made of tree bark.

From what she could gather, the gentleman was giving the girls bad news, and was not even particularly sorry about it. She caught only a few words: Peter, danger, children, grown-ups, drones…

She decided to wait until the conversation was over to ask about Rosemary. Soon enough, Hawkbit prompted a fitful outburst from Hollyhock, and he flew off… away from the swarm of unhappy words she cast at him. In a huff, Hollyhock departed in the other direction and went to seek solace with her beloved Peter. Only Foxglove remained, and she floated over to hug Gwen's finger as if in apology, but muttered fairy curses as she did.

"What was all that about?" she asked Blink.

The girl shook her head, her black hair slipping like silk across her shoulders. "The fairies are worried that the bombs and drones have found Neverland again… some of them are scared they'll never stop coming as long as there are kids here."

Gwen held her arm, remembering the scar the newsprint bombing had left her with. The burn had healed completely, but the careful eye could still see a few grey words on her arm. "Don't they realize that it's Neverland's magic they're after, not the kids? Even if we weren't here, they'd still come for it. At least now we can help destroy the drones and make spider-silk havens for them."

"Hawkbit thinks it would be harder for the grown-ups to find if children weren't keeping the pathways open. He thinks that the more kids that fly to Neverland, the easier adults can track it and send drones."

It seemed like a reasonable concern, but Gwen never knew what to believe about the nature of Neverland. She wondered if tracking and accounting pathways was part of her father's job, or if the task fell on someone else in the strange agency he worked for.

"Hawkbit might be right," Blink continued. "I understand why he's sad. He doesn't want us all to leave, but he says there are some fairies who blame Peter for this… and Bramble's death."

"Ah," Gwen sighed, "that's why Hollyhock flew off." The impish fairy never could stand to hear Peter insulted and was still a tempest of grief whenever someone mentioned Bramble.

She cupped her hands and let Foxglove sit in her palms. The fairy's wood-shaving dress felt funny against Gwen's skin. She looked up at the girl, her big eyes almost as dark as her short, crooked hair that jutted out in all directions.

"But Foxglove is on our side. Lots of them want to help. They know we love Neverland and want to stop the adults as much as they do," Blink informed her.

Foxglove burst into a rant, denouncing the horrible adults who sent the bombs and drones. For all the vices for a fairy to have, wrath was sometimes the most inconspicuous. There was very little that could incite wrath in a fairy, but the newsprint bombing had boiled Foxglove's hot blood and pushed her to the forefront of this unusual war.

Gwen could imagine how an issue like this would polarize the fairies. It made sense—more fairies had been wandering into the grove and keeping company with lost children. They were showing allegiance. They wanted Peter's help fighting this.

"Have you seen Rosemary?" Gwen asked.

Blink shook her head again and somersaulted in the sun, her red overalls collecting yet another round of grass-stains in the process. Foxglove became excited though, and tugged on Gwen's finger.

"You know where she is?"

Rather than answer, she floated back out of the bramble, and Gwen scrambled to crawl out too. She followed the fairy back to the grove, and soon saw Foxglove was leading her into the underground home. They flew up to the top of the tall oak tree—the one flight Gwen had mastered—then descended through the darkness to the warm light of glow flowers and a fire in the hearth.

"Rosemary?"

No one seemed to be home.

She looked at Foxglove, but the fairy shrugged her pea-sized shoulders, surprised by this as well.

A boy's voice came from afar. "Hello!"

Gwen crossed the room and pulled aside a curtain tacked against the wall. A deep, dark tunnel greeted her. "Hello? Is Rosemary with you?" she called.

A light appeared as Newt crawled toward her with his miner's cap on. He looked blindingly happy under an almost uniform layer of dirt. "Who?" he asked.

"Rosemary!" Sal answered from much farther down the tunnel.

"Oh," Newt responded.

"Is she *with* you?" Gwen reiterated.

"I can't hear you," he yelled back.

Gwen padded toward Newt on her hands and knees, but only got a few feet before the tunnel gave out. She gave a startled scream as she tumbled a few feet down into a gaping hole.

"Watch out," Newt told her. "That's our tunnel to China."

"It's not finished yet," Sal added.

Gwen pulled herself up and decided Rosemary was neither with the boys nor any part of their plan to dig a complex series of tunnels under Neverland for emergency escape purposes. She wondered where all the dirt for this project was going.

"If you're looking for Rosemary," Newt announced, finally

helpful, “she’s probably with Peter.”

“Where’s Peter?”

“Same place as always.” Sal called, still a disembodied voice in the darkness. “In the house.”

CHAPTER 3

FOXGLOVE WAS DISTRACTED BY THE BUBBLING SOUP JAM HAD STARTED cooking in the grove, so Gwen wandered through the woods alone. She had not yet memorized the subtle natural reference points that led to the house, so finding it meant craning her gaze up until she was sore in the neck, looking for the house among the trees.

She spotted it eventually: its walls made of branches glued together with reddish sap, except for where craggy windows were formed. Roses and brambles had taken root in the old weathered and greying thing. It had a tiny chimney—despite the fact that no fireplace existed in it—which only smoked when Peter was inside.

Gwen began climbing the tree in which it was situated. There was a rule of etiquette against flying into the house; it had to be climbed into.

The house was an odd landmark in Neverland. No one referred to it as a treehouse. Peter insisted it was merely a house that had blown into the trees during a savage windstorm. When he first began using it again, it was a novel discovery for all the lost children. It had sat dormant in the trees for years, if not decades. Peter claimed to have forgotten about it.

Since their return from reality, weeks had passed Peter by

unnoticed. The children were left to their own devices when he hermitted himself away inside. The wonders of Neverland kept them amused. In their own time, each child would wander off to spy on their reclusive leader, never comprehending what his quiet withdrawal meant.

Gwen didn't understand either, but not for lack of trying. She saw too many possibilities for why he might be shutting himself away for long hours, studying his notes and old journals. The house had little in it but old books full of chicken-scratch shorthand that documented all the important details of this war that his childish mind could not be bothered to remember.

As she climbed up to the house, she heard Rosemary and him volleying a conversation back and forth.

"But how will figuring out the riddles help us find the Piper?"

"The riddles point to his payment," Peter answered. "The price merely to meet with him. If we figure out what those objects are, we'll be able to pay for his attention."

"But we'll just have *stuff*."

"No, no, no... that's why we need someone who has heard his song. Someone who has heard his song will know how to find him and deliver these tokens."

Gwen poked her head into the conversation and went effectively unnoticed. She climbed up to one of the platforms and joined the scenery for Rosemary and Peter's discussion. The house's floor was more holes than floor after being blown up and away from the ground. Branches poked through up into the house from all the holes and windows, and scavenged floorboards were nailed to those to create steps, tables, and seats. Below the house and outside its many windows, other platforms littered the branches. Inside and outside were not helpful terms when describing things. Books, journals, and a ragged globe a hundred years out of date stayed on mismatched end tables safely under the moss roof, but Rosemary leaned against the tree trunk on one side of a window, while Peter perched on a branch nearer to the ceiling than the floor.

"Won't the Piper want money? Gold or something?"

"Of course," Peter scoffed, "but first... this is a test for anyone who would make a deal with him, to make sure it isn't a trap. Only someone magical will be able to figure out and find the mark of the first debt, the melody of lamb and death, and a patch fit for a prince."

"Oh, I see." Rosemary's glee spread across her face as she crawled forward on her branch, back in through the window. Leaves and flowers had collected in her voluminous hair, over the course of hours or days Gwen couldn't hazard to guess. In a dress she had all but decimated from thorn snags and mud splatters, Rosemary looked more comfortable than she had in anything Mrs. Hoffman had ever dressed her in. "I don't think we can find the Piper. I think we have to make him want to find *us*."

Peter considered this, striking a thinking pose by dropping down off his branch until he was only hanging by his knees. Upside-down, he put a thoughtful hand to his chin. Casting his glance at their visitor, he asked, "What do you think, Gwen-dollie?"

"I think Jam's making an egg-flower soup and dinner will be ready soon."

"Flower soup?" Rosemary asked. "I should take her roses!" She twisted around, looking for roses at the window, before realizing the only one in reach was already in her hair. She plucked it out and scaled back out of the tree one-handed. Gwen didn't have the heart to tell her egg-flower soup didn't actually have flowers in it. With any luck, something lovelier would distract her little sister before she stumbled onto that reality.

Peter was packing his notes and maps away. Gwen returned his spyglass to him, but he didn't say anything as he took it back from her. She waited for him to say something, but he seemed to possess no desire to break the silence. Was he frustrated that she derailed his conversation with Rosemary? She couldn't get a read on his emotions. He functioned so much like a child, but he had grown just enough to hold a mood quiet and hidden. "Will you join us for dinner tonight?"

"Perhaps," he nebulously answered. Peter was infamous—even before this obsession with finding the Piper—for skipping meals and imagining his hunger away. She didn't know how he did it. Pure willpower and strength of imagination, she presumed. It seemed super-human.

Gwen climbed over to a branch nearer Peter. He seemed lost in the wild labyrinths of his mind. She turned her back to him, but hung tight to the branch with her knees as she fell back. She looked at him, her hair trailing down from her head. They hung upside-down and shared a silent moment. The blood rushed from her heart to her head, but Gwen just stared at Peter within the tiny forest house.

At last she spoke, broaching thoughts that had been simmering for too long in her own head. "Before I came to Neverland, I heard adults talk about the Invasion of '08... the Piper was part of that, wasn't he?"

Peter smiled at last. "Aye, he was the linchpin in it. He found a key for his song that not only didn't affect grown-ups, but that they also couldn't hear at all."

"I would have been eight when that happened." She looked at him and floated an idea that had only recently surfaced in her own mind. "I think I remember it."

His smile dropped, replaced by shocked interest. Peter bolted upright, flying over to Gwen's branch and grabbing her hand in his. He pulled her right side up, and it happened so fast that Gwen felt her blood-addled head spin with dizziness for a full minute afterward. It didn't help that Peter began hurling a zealous line of questioning at her.

"Really? You were there?"

"Do you remember where it happened?" she asked. "Was it by my house?"

"I don't know exactly where. I was waiting out at Lake Agana for his signal."

This encouraged her. "That's half an hour from my house.

Did it happen in the evening? Just before sunset?" Although she had little memory from the night, what details she did have were clear in her mind. She had been outside, and music from a flute had started playing. Her mother made her leave her dolls outside, and she tried to open her window after being tucked into bed. The most potent aspect of the memory was her desire to find the source.

"Yes, right at the end of the day," Peter affirmed. "Then *you* heard Piper's song! *You* can help us find him."

At last, he let go of the hand he had pulled her up by, and somersaulted back to the ancient globe. He pulled out a mathematical compass from the end table's drawer and stretched it from Germany to the United States. Gwen could not discern the purpose of this gesture and could not imagine how any information was derived from it. She suspected he was only mimicking behavior he had witnessed from adults too long ago to recall.

"There's just one thing," Gwen said, interrupting his joy. "I don't remember the song."

The energy faded from his posture, and the compass dropped from his hand, clattering against the globe and then falling through a hole in the floor to the depths of the forest below. He had completely lost interest in it. "What do you mean, you don't remember? How can you not remember the most magical thing that ever happened to you?"

His accusatory tone flustered her. Peter had barely spoken to her the past few weeks, and now she had initiated a conversation for the sole purpose of raising his hopes and then dashing them. "I just don't remember the song. I remember that I liked it. I thought it was fun and wanted to follow it, but then my mom took me inside and tucked me into bed. When I told her I heard music, she locked my window shut and turned on my music box."

Peter listened with a dissatisfied expression, but it lifted as soon as she finished. "Could you hear the music after she shut the window?"

"No, my music box was playing over it."

"But before your mother woke up the music box. Could you hear it through the window?"

"I… I guess so. She turned on the music box to drown it out, I think."

Peter paused, taking only one excited and apprehensive breath before asking, "Do you still have her?"

"My mother?"

"Your music box." Peter's intense expression and silly questions seemed to contradict each other.

"Oh. Yes, I suppose so… what would an old music box matter?"

Peter's face gave way to a sly smile and victorious little joy. "Your music box," he declared, "might have a much better memory."

CHAPTER 4

DINNER WAS AN EGG AND FLOWER SOUP, NOT AN EGG-FLOWER SOUP. The Never Bird's egg was stewed in the pot with lilacs, orange blossoms, and roses. The broth was a beautiful and luminescent pink color. They pulled the egg out, its blue shell bleached white and the milk within ready to drink. Jam recruited Gwen to hold the heavy egg while she pricked a hole in it, and Bard laid out a collection of cups, mugs, glasses, and a brass goblet to pour the milk into.

The first squirt of milk shot straight onto Jam, soaking her ruffled pink shirt. To her dismay, Spurt began trying to lick her clean. Bard fetched Newt and Sal from their tunnel. They surfaced looking like subterranean mole boys. As night fell, Blink wandered into the grove, right as dinner was served.

"You can't come to the table looking so dirty," Rosemary objected when she saw the tunnel diggers.

"What table?" Sal asked.

"It's a matter of principle," Rosemary insisted. Gwen watched her little sister struggle with understanding her own precepts. Talk of principles seemed alien when espoused from a child as young as Rosemary… the little girl did not seem to remember that these were her mother's words she was regurgitating. It concerned Gwen to see that thoughts and memories of their mother only arose for Rosemary in sputtering intervals, always devoid of context. She was forgetting. The little girl remembered everything about their mother when prompted, but Gwen was worried by how cohesive thoughts of their mother never organically occurred to her sister.

"Jam's dirty too!" Newt objected. He followed Sal's lead, taking off his shirt and wiping his grimy face and hands with it.

"Yeah, she's all covered in Spurt's slobber."

"She can't take her shirt off. She's a lady."

"*I'M NOT A LADY, I'M A PRINCESS*," Jam screeched, flinging her shirt off and almost into the fire.

Gwen sat in the grass a ways off—far enough from the fire that she could just barely discern what flowers were floating in her soup. While the children slurped their soup from bowls and danced shirtless around the fire, she retreated to that cusp of darkness, feeling even more isolated than she was. Even Peter sat on the other side of the fire, staring at it as if unaware that Hollyhock and Foxglove were puckishly plucking the flowers from out of his soup for themselves.

The evening felt as though it carried a chill no one else noticed. Neverland was never cold, even at night. The bare-chested children were evidence of this. The weather bent to one's desires, which was why only Gwen felt cold. She pulled the oversized grey sweatshirt tighter around her. She played with the zipper and rolled back the cuffs each time they unrolled and swallowed her hands again.

Her mind wandered back to Jay's room with the wistful thought of her left-behind sweater. Did her cardigan still smell as much like her as Jay's sweatshirt smelled like him? She hadn't meant to leave her sweater behind—or steal Jay's, for that matter—but now that she had, she wondered if he took as much joy in the accident as she did.

Peter and she had fled the party with urgency. Did Jay wonder what had happened to her? Was he happy she got away or angry she left him behind with the cops? Her musings were fruitless things. She couldn't even decipher her own emotional impulses… let alone make sense of someone else's.

No one remarked on the sweatshirt. It was absurdly big on her, but all the children wore silly clothes and thought nothing of it. She was certain that none of them understood it was a boy's coat or the fluttery connotations that came with wearing it. She didn't know what Peter thought of it. He never remarked on it, but brief anxieties struck her whenever she considered that he might comprehend the nature of her attachment to that other world.

Fireflies blinked by, gravitating toward Gwen as if hoping to illuminate her confused mind for her. Rosemary came running to her.

"Gwen, are you going to tell us a story tonight?"

The other children's ears pricked up. She didn't know why anyone ever asked for a story. It was only a matter of minutes before the rest of the children flocked over and began outright demanding a tale.

"Oh yes! Please, Gwenny?"

"We haven't had one in so long!"

"The fairies want one too!"

They crept forward like inchworms, scooting their bottoms across the grass and closing in on Gwen. Hollyhock and Foxglove drifted over, but theirs was only an idle interest. Peter pushed his bowl aside, but lay down where he was by the fire. He was not out of earshot, but it was unclear whether he was listening.

"Make it romantic," Jam sighed.

"No, make it scary," Newt demanded.

"Yeah!" Spurt agreed, before qualifying, "but just a little scary, okay?"

"No! Stop it! I want it romantic," Jam insisted.

Blink broke her pensive quiet to suggest, "Maybe you could do a scary romantic story?"

Gwen sorted through the haphazard collection of story ideas and plot points that had been rattling in her head, and began to draw a suitable story from these varied elements. "Alright. This is a story about two people who loved each other very much… and the horrible thing that happened to them." Gwen folded her legs into lotus pose and ignored Foxglove and Hollyhock as they began eating the lilacs out of her bowl like popcorn at the movies.

"Once upon a time, there was a boy and a girl who were very much in love, and had been for a number of years. One day they decided to have a picnic at the beach where they first met. It was a long drive through the mountainous country, so they left early and walked along the beach until it was time to have their picnic dinner with the sunset. Afterward, they watched the full moon rise over the mountains in the east. They had never been at the beach for a full moon before though, so they did not know what that meant. As the tide went out and the night got cold and dark, they decided it was time to go home. It was easy for them to find their way back to the car by the bright light of the full moon, but as they began driving the long way home, the sky began to cloud over.

"Despite the glowing moon, black clouds rolled over the sky and covered it so thoroughly not a single star could peep through. All they could see was the short stretch of road ahead of the car's headlights. Tired and unable to see well, the boy took a wrong turn down an old dirt road and became lost in the dark countryside. He kept going, looking for a place to turn around, but the narrow road just kept going into the black woods, farther and farther…"

She watched Spurt's anxious eyes start to dart around. For safety's sake, he climbed into Bard's lap. She held him protectively in her arms, but kept her own wide eyes on Gwen.

"At last, the boy pulled off and got turned around, but to make up for the time he had lost, he began driving faster to get back to the main highway. It was very late, and the tired girl was almost falling asleep when suddenly—"

Rosemary preemptively gasped, and the fairies momentarily forgot to chew their lilacs.

"A dark creature swooped by, rushing in front of the car… or at least trying to. As the boy saw it, he slammed on the brakes in an attempt to avoid it. It happened too quickly though, and the dark form thudded against the hood of the car as the vehicle struck it.

"The girl screamed and clutched at her heart. 'It must have been a bird,' her love said, but she didn't believe it. What they had hit was much bigger than a bird, and in the moment of impact, it had looked almost human.

"'But it flew in front of the car, didn't it?' he asked, and she could not argue. There was no denying that it had appeared to be a giant, black raven of some kind."

Jam made a fussy face—unamused but not scared of the eerie bits in the story.

"He told her to stay in the car, but she was too afraid to let him look at the creature on his own, for fear it was still alive and dangerous. When they stepped out of the car, however, they found an old woman wrapped in a black cloak, collapsed on the ground. The boy reached out and touched her shoulder, fearing that the collision might have killed the ancient woman. Her wart-covered face and crooked nose wrinkled in pain at his touch, and she began to moan. 'Oh you horrible children,' she cried, even though the boy and girl were very nearly grown up. 'You've killed me, and I'll curse you for it.'"

Newt and Sal were giddy with this twist. They could think of nothing more terrifying than a witch's dying curse, and they delighted in it.

"She began muttering a frightening spell, and the couple began to feel horribly wrong, as if their bodies were no longer their own. The girl looked to her love and saw that he was turning an awful, ghostly white and shrinking away to almost nothing. However, before the old witch could finish her curse, she died on the ground. She shrank away into her cloak, and then the cloak turned into a dozen ravens that all flew off into the night."

"So they were okay after all?" Spurt hesitantly asked.

"That's what the girl thought as her body started to feel her own again, and she realized that the nightmarish encounter was over. But when she looked over to her love..."

"Oh no," Bard muttered, burying her face in Spurt's dark, rumpled hair.

"...she saw that in his place, there was only a little white dove. The boy was gone. This so terrified her, she began to scream, which in turn frightened the dove away. On white wings, it flew off, disappearing into the forest beneath the clouded night sky. Overwhelmed and alone, the poor girl fainted.

"In the morning, a farmer from the other side of the woods came along the road and saw the stalled car on his way to the highway. When he saw the girl lying in front of it, he immediately got out to help her. Afraid she was dead, he was glad that she woke up as soon as he started shaking her. She couldn't remember what had happened to her—at least, that's what she told him. She couldn't bear to mention the bizarre and horrible reality that a dying witch had turned her love into a dove. Once she had assured the farmer she was all right—which she wasn't, but she had to pretend—he helped her back into her car and watched as she drove back to the city that morning.

"When she got back to her home, she crawled into bed and cried. For days and days, she stayed in bed, heartsick for her lost love and distraught that she would never see him again."

"This isn't romantic—it's just *sad*," Jam pouted.

"Until," Gwen announced, instantly hushing her, "one day, she heard a tapping at her window. A strange rapping noise, as if someone was gently knocking against the glass pane. She drew the curtains, and found a little white dove sitting on her window ledge, peering at her with curious eyes. Excited with an impossible hope, she flung open the window. The dove flew in and began tweeting a cheerful tune. She watched it, and then held out her hands for the bird to land in. As she held him she asked, 'Is it really you?' and he tweeted so happily, she knew that it must be. Her happiness gave way to grief as she confirmed her beloved was now trapped in the body of a bird. Miserable, she declared, 'Oh, I wish that awful witch had turned *me* into a bird, not you!'

"As the words left her lips, she began to feel a tremendous change in herself. She was shrinking down, closer to the ground, and the dove began to feel immeasurably heavy in her hands. She let go of him, but he could only flutter his wings for a moment in the air before he lost them, growing back into her beloved boy at the same time that she morphed into a white dove herself.

"The boy immediately panicked. 'Why would you ever say such a thing? I flew for days in the woods to find my way back home because I wanted to see you safe. I would spend my whole life a bird if you could be fine,' but as he spoke the words, the transformation began again, so that once more, he was a tiny dove and she was a human girl. This was how they discovered the strange result of the witch's half-cast curse. The cruel witch had died before she could turn them both into birds, so now they existed in a middle ground in which one of them would always be a bird.

"They were happy that neither was hurt and they could both be human at least sometimes. The girl went out, bought a beautiful birdcage, and filled it with all the things that she would find most comfortable and enjoyable while in avian form, and from then on, they lived together and took turns being a bird. At night, she would sleep in her bed with the birdsong of her love like a lullaby, and in the morning, she'd wish herself the bird. Her boy would then go out and work, eat lunch, and go about the town as a human until he came home and became a bird again in the evening for her.

"A bird is not a person who can hold you though, and the girl began to feel very alone even though she had the boy she loved still beside her. They would never be able to hold hands, to have a conversation, or go on a date together again. Although they still loved each other, she feared that this would ruin either of their chances at a full life. One day, while the boy was home and the girl was a bird, a pretty neighbor lady came over to borrow a cup of sugar.

"Why?" Next asked.

"She was baking a cake, and so the boy let her in and took her to the kitchen for sugar. She thanked him and invited him over for a slice of cake when she finished baking. She looked around at the big home and asked him if he lived alone. He told her he wasn't alone, as he had his dove. She thought it must get very lonely living with just a bird for company.

"At this remark, his beloved began chirping furiously and squawking in distress. It was very obvious that the pretty neighbor lady liked the boy. The girl shook her cage until it rattled open, and then she flew straight out. The boy tried to calm her and tell her that it wasn't true—he was very happy with her even if she was a bird—but before he could catch her, she went to the window and flew away. His love did not return.

"He waited days and nights, but the girl never flew back. First, her body had vanished in the form of a bird, and now, she had vanished all together. Days passed, months passed… in time, years passed. Out of necessity, the boy moved on. He met another girl who he eventually married. They had three darling children who grew up, went to school, and then got married and had children of their own.

"One day, when the boy was an old man made of wrinkles and grey hair, he sat down by his window to read. His children were grown and his wife had passed away. He lived all alone and led a quiet life. While he was reading though, he heard a tapping at his window. When he looked, he saw a beautiful white dove pecking at the glass. Amazed and astounded, he hobbled over to the window and opened it. The bird flew in and right into his hands. His wrinkles folded up as he smiled. 'You've come back!' he said. It had been sixty years since he last saw his beloved, and he had been sure the bird had died long ago. He whispered, 'I wish I was the bird,' and watched from his shrinking body as the dove blossomed back into his beautiful young love. She had not aged a day in all her time as a magic dove, and as soon as the old man had feathers and wings again, he felt light and young himself.

"He was wonderfully happy that now he could leave and let

his first love live out a full and rich life of her own. He would fly away, not an old man but a bird capable of soaring anywhere in the world.

"But before he could fly away, the girl caught him in her hands. He struggled to free himself, but he could not lift his tiny wings out of her grip. As she held him, she began to speak in some strange and ominous language that he had only heard once before, when the witch had first cursed them. The girl had spent sixty long years traveling the world as a bird and learning the mysteries of magic and the language of spells from far corners of the globe. She could not undo the witch's black magic, but as she spoke, she finished the curse and turned herself into a bird as well.

"A neighbor heard the boy's frantic chirping and came knocking to see what was the matter, but when she arrived, all she found were two beautiful white doves that took off flying out the window to spend their lives together at last."

Jam *aww*'ed with wistful satisfaction, and Spurt seemed to have completely forgiven the scarier elements of the story in light of its happy ending. "So they're just *birds* now?" Newt complained.

Bard answered him, "Yes—it's very nice."

"*I* wouldn't want to be a bird," Newt grumbled.

Sal thought briefly on this. "I'd be a bird if you were a bird."

Newt mumbled, incomprehensible and disgruntled, before admitting. "Well, yeah, I guess if *you* were a bird."

The fairies buzzed around, creating a whirling and disorienting spasm of purple and gold between them.

Gwen saw Peter looking over at her, still lying on the grass near the fire. He leapt to his feet and wandered over to her. She waited for him to pass judgment on the story. She knew it was more important to make all the other children happy, that all their joy counted for something, but she could never shake her desire for Peter's approval. The children always loved her stories, but Peter was much more of a connoisseur.

The only one standing, he towered over Gwen and cast a tall shadow over her as the fire danced behind him. "That was a good last story," he told her.

"Whadya mean 'last story?'" Spurt objected.

Peter looked at him, but then back to Gwen. His eyes on hers, he announced, "She's leaving tomorrow."

CHAPTER 5

ONCE THE FIRE WAS OUT AND THE CHILDREN STARTED FLOODING BACK down into the underground home through their various tree trunk passageways, Gwen grabbed Peter by the shoulder and turned him to face her before he could take off flying. The glowing embers of the fire cast little light, but between the fireflies and fairies, she had enough light to see his face… not that she could make sense of it.

The children had devolved into a frenzy of complaints, questions, and demands for more warm milk. When Peter announced that Gwen was leaving the next day, she hadn't had a chance to get a word in edgewise. She was not going to let the announcement go undiscussed. "Why am I leaving tomorrow?"

He didn't seem to think it merited discussing. "Because you need to find Piper."

"*Tomorrow?*" She had anticipated something of this nature would follow once she admitted to having heard the Piper's song, but she never thought it would incite a trip to reality so soon! Granted, she'd been in Neverland twice as long as she had following her first arrival, but leaving this time carried different connotations. Last time, she'd flown to reality with the intention never to return. Coming back had been a solemn commitment to standing by Peter's side. Or at least, she thought that was what it had signified. Now he wanted her to *leave*?

Peter paused in consideration. "You can wait until the day after. You probably should, on account of the supplies you'll need to collect first."

A day. He would delay her departure a day. "I don't want to have to fly to reality again with you!"

"Oh, you won't." Peter sounded reassuring, and he seemed not to understand that he was utterly destroying her when he added, "I'm not going with you."

"I have to go alone?" Was she even capable of making the flight? She could hardly stabilize herself well enough to make trips around the island. Gwen was struck by a vision of herself falling out of the sky and drowning in an ocean that may or may not even exist between Neverland and home.

"Hollyhock will go with you," Peter offered. The golden fairy made a violent objection to this idea, tweaking Peter's nose. "Foxglove will go with you," he said, as if the previous remark hadn't even been uttered.

Foxglove nodded, more with her body than her tiny head, trying to encourage Gwen toward this civic duty that was being thrust upon her.

"How long will I have to stay in reality?"

"Until you find Piper."

Having spent more than a month with him and the children now, Gwen couldn't imagine what it would be like to spend entire days back in a world that penalized her every thought and action for the inbetweeness of her age. She couldn't bear the idea that she would be abandoning Rosemary either. She tried to pull Peter's plan apart in order to escape a role in it. "Where will I stay? I can't go home. Do you realize how much trouble I'd be in?"

"You only have to go home to get your music box."

"I hate to break it to you, but I don't think my parents will let me just run upstairs to get something out of my room when I've been gone for a month and effectively dropped out of school."

"School never did anything good for anyone worth their snowsalt." The fairies floated into his hands, and he began casually half-juggling them as they flew back and forth.

"You're missing the point. I can't go home. Not go home and come back, that's for sure."

"Don't go home, sneak home. At night." Peter gave all his instructions as if they were the easiest tasks. It galled Gwen. He couldn't wrap his mind around anyone else's challenges.

"I didn't exactly bring my house key with me when I flew to Neverland."

It was apparent that Peter was painfully bored of explaining what he had already figured out in his own mind. "Go through the window."

"I'm not about to smash a window to steal my own music box."

"You won't have to smash a window. Your bedroom window will be open."

"My parents never keep windows open at night in the winter."

"They will now," Peter answered, returning his gaze to Gwen. "Parents always do… the first few years, anyway."

She didn't know whether to be glad she was finally getting him to show some emotion, or frustrated that she still didn't understand whatever was going on in his head.

"Alright," Gwen ceded, "but where do I stay while I try to find the Piper? Which, by the way, I have no idea how to do even once I have the music box. I can't live underground in *real* life."

Peter's brief emotion evaporated off his face, and she regretted patronizing him. "I know that." The words seeped out in a bitter tone. "I have a friend you can stay with."

She thought of Antoine the aviator, and wondered how many adults were in league with Peter. "Another ally?"

"No, a friend," he insisted. He walked behind Gwen and began pushing her to the tall oak tree. She plodded along with his shoving—it was either that or flop to the ground in an attempt to resist him. "And as for how to find Piper, leave that to me. I'll figure it out by the time you need to know."

"Are you really so clever?" The sarcasm cut its way out of her mouth.

"I am."

Gwen tried to let that assurance sink in, but she knew that she would never be as confident in Peter as he was in himself.

"Once I've figured it out, I'll send Rosemary to take over. If you can teach her the song, you can come back afterward."

Rosemary to take over? She wanted to balk at the idea, but it left her with too strong and unsettling a sense of powerlessness. Peter was serious. He had more faith in Rosemary.

They got to the bottom of the oak tree and Peter rose into the air, flying up to the top. Gwen wasn't going to let him get away that easily. As he took off, she linked her arm in his and continued with her questions. "Why don't you come? Shouldn't *you* find the Piper?"

From directly underneath, they had to ascend to the top with caution as they dodged dozens of thick branches and passed through layer after layer of leafy coverage. "I think Rosemary is right—I had the idea myself earlier," he said, as if to convince her of its validity. "We're going to need to make Piper want to find us… and he's not going to want to find me." An ominous silence followed that Gwen didn't dare break until they had reached the hole into the oak's hollow.

They landed on the last sturdy branch, and Peter unlinked his arm from hers. Before he could get away and bound down to his young comrades, Gwen grabbed his hand. Grasping for straws, she still tried to find fault in this plan that took her so far from what she wanted to be so close to. "What about your friend? How will I find him?"

Peter stopped and chewed his lip. She felt like she was antagonizing him, and wanted to apologize for how she was acting… but Peter never apologized, so why should she? It was part of the childish code by which he lived.

"I'll fly with you, and introduce you to my friend. You can fetch your music box that night. Once you have it, I'll send

Rosemary. You'll be fine." He jerked his hand from hers. It did not feel unkind, but Gwen suspected he would resent any further questions.

"How can you be so sure of it?" she squeaked.

Peter turned, his face a spotty mesh of shadow and moonlight. "Because I'm certain of you." He climbed into the tree trunk and gave her one last instruction before he fell into the darkness of the hollow tree. "Don't doubt yourself so much, Gwenny-Lyn—it's horribly grown up."

CHAPTER 6

Rosemary woke up with ease and was much more eager to greet the day than her sister. What was Gwen's last day in paradise was Rosemary's excuse for a grand adventure across the island with her sister. While the other children hurried off to smash and dissect the awful drones trapped in the marsh, Rosemary was honored to escort her sister on a supply run. Peter was, again, holed away in the house and pouring over his notes from the aviator. Gwen was uncertain what supplies she needed, so she was glad she had someone to take the lead.

Before she left the underground home that morning, Spurt had given her a square wicker picnic basket with closing flaps. It was a large, awkward object for the children, but Gwen could carry it with casual ease. Jam soon after approached her with the first of her supplies.

"It's from Black Sun," she announced, handing her something wrapped in a small weaving. Gwen unfolded it, and a smiling face with painted features greeted her. The papery substance of the cornhusk doll looked fragile, but the fibrous material was strong. Her starchy skirt was crinkly, but the little black eyes and sweet mouth gave the doll a soft expression.

"What is this?" Gwen asked.

"It's a redskin doll!" Jam answered, unhelpfully. "Chief Black Sun said something about why it was important for you to have it… but I forgot."

Spurt came running by and snatched Jam's headband off her head. She howled at this injustice and took off running after him. Rosemary was already at Gwen's side, trying to pull her along to go hunt for other supplies.

Gwen bundled up the cornhusk doll and stuffed it in her picnic basket. *I guess I'll just have to figure it out once I'm there,* she thought.

She went with her little sister on an expedition across Neverland, collecting everything they deemed necessary for a trip back to reality. Following Rosemary's confidence through the forest, she felt powerfully out of her element.

"What are we looking for now?" Gwen asked, her picnic basket already heavy with bottled tree sap, a hand-carved flute, assorted bird feathers, gemstone marbles, emergency reserve pixie dust, and a spider-silk lined jewel bag that would function as a covert hiding place in the event Foxglove needed one.

"Fruit!" Rosemary declared.

"There will be fruit in reality," Gwen reminded her sister. She didn't want to pack any heavier than she had to. "You do realize we could get mangoes at the grocery store, right?"

"I don't remember any mangoes."

"Well, Mom didn't pick them up often… and they weren't always in season…"

Rosemary didn't react. An alienating silence followed, warning that Rosemary had nothing to contribute or recollect about reality. Her older sister fidgeted with the basket, perturbed by this. "But Mom did get a lot of good food… do you remember all the nice things she used to cook?"

Rosemary rolled her eyes up, but it was not apparent whether she was searching her mind for memories or the trees for fruit. "Um, rainbow rice?"

Gwen's heart sank. "Bard made that last week. That's a

Neverland food."

"Oh. No, I don't remember." She shrugged, and then plucked some mushrooms off the ground. She stuffed them into her dress pocket, unconcerned with her inability to recall anything from the life in suburbia she had spent eight years living.

"What about her cheesy dogs and noodles?" Surely, Rosemary hadn't forgotten the way she demanded her macaroni plain and her hot dogs slathered in cheese sauce.

"Oh yeah!" She bounced happily at the memory, but it moved through her with the fluidity of something that had no bearing on her life.

Leaves crunched under Rosemary's gleeful feet. The day had a summer's blue sky, a spring's gentle breeze, but a thin, autumnal layer of crispy leaves rested beneath everything else green and alive. There was even a magical coziness in the air that Gwen had only ever associated with winter. The environment was overwhelming, the best of all moments and seasons, and Gwen saw how it was all joyful white noise painting over Rosemary's memory. She, however, was lost in it.

"Where are we, Rose?"

"I don't think it has a name."

Few places in the jungle did. She hadn't been paying attention, and now she realized she would be lost if not in Rosemary's tow.

"But we're almost there."

They trudged along, Gwen weighed down by the picnic basket and Rosemary enviably light. She decided to test her little sister again, this time direct and to the point. "What do you remember about Mom?"

Rosemary stomped down hard on a patch of moss that was as springy as a trampoline.

Giggling as she fell back onto her feet, she answered, "I don't know. She was nice."

The young girl came to an abrupt stop. Gwen noticed a caterpillar in her wild hair and plucked it out. She tossed it to the ground, but midway down it turned into a butterfly and flew off.

"Do you hear it, Gwen?"

There was a noise like a hundred birds all in a hapless chorus. The random cawing and cooing united in a blur of syncopation and counter-melodies that blended into something chaotic but musical. She couldn't imagine what a flock of birds was doing knit so tightly together in the middle of the jungle. Gwen rarely got lost in Neverland anymore, but she couldn't begin to imagine where they were right now.

Rosemary laughed and took off running. "Rose, wait!" Gwen called, but it fell on ears that were deaf to all but Neverland's noise of joy and the magic song of the bird flock. She struggled to keep up, the picnic basket banging against her knees with every stride. She kept Rosemary in her peripheral vision and watched her footing, until Rosemary disappeared behind a curtain of vines. Gwen had no attention to spare on where they were going as she parted the thick wall of foliage. At the exact moment that Rosemary came to a stop, Gwen tripped over a root, dropping her basket as she put out her hands to break her fall.

The ground was hard and cracked, like a dried-up marsh. Dizzy, her first instinct was to look for Rosemary, who had gone quiet. She was safe and sound, staring ahead, so Gwen pulled herself up and repacked the marbles that had rolled out of her basket. She found one butted up against the root that tripped her, and examined the root with more careful awe.

It was scaly and bony, rimmed like a bird's claw. Where it dove into the dirt, the root was as dark and sleek as a talon gripping the earth. As her eyes followed it through a long mesh of roots to its source, she saw the raven tree.

Rosemary swayed to the sound of the hundreds of chirping beaks that littered the trunk like bark. She looked so at home and had navigated them to this secret tree without any effort. All afternoon, Gwen had been trailing her sister, wrestling with the feeling that somewhere along their adventures in Neverland, Rosemary had become the knowledgeable and competent big sister.

Getting to her feet, she approached with reverent caution. The raven tree had been a thing of her imagination, an odd little plot device in a homemade fairy tale. How was it that her own fantasy was so alive and real here, and that only Rosemary had known where to find it? The tree's intricate root structure choked out all other trees for several yards, and it held its proud branches out unhindered by any competing vegetation. Black eggfruit hung in ripe and heavy abundance, every shell—or peel—dotted with a glittering starscape.

"It's just like in your story about Margaret May." Rosemary stepped closer to the tiny snapping beaks of the trunk, and extended a little finger to pet one. "Do you remember the story you were telling me the night before we left for Neverland?"

Gwen gave her a morose smile. The only thing Rosemary remembered from home were the fantasies they had carved out while stranded in reality.

Rosemary ran back to Gwen and squeezed her in the biggest hug a little sister could give. "You never finished that bedtime story. You have to tell me how it ends… and if Margaret May gets back in time for Prince Jay's coronation."

Gwen blushed, remembering how shamelessly she had woven her fantasies into the ones she gave Rosemary. "But the other kids don't know the start of the story. I'll have to tell you the rest sometime when it's just us. Maybe when we go back home."

Rosemary made a face, implying sheer insanity on Gwen's part.

"We have to go home, someday, right?"

Rosemary shook her head, and another caterpillar fell from her hair only to transform mid-fall into a beautiful blue-and-yellow butterfly. It flew right back into the girl's hair, and stayed there like a living barrette. She didn't even notice. "I don't think so."

What was Rosemary's plan? Gwen had committed to playing this game with her, but games only lasted so long. It was still a game, wasn't it? She refused to believe Rosemary was looking at this in Peter's strange terms of war and ideals.

"Maybe when I come back to reality to help you find the Piper, you can tell the rest of the story." Rosemary floated up to one of the branches and began judiciously feeling the egg fruits, picking only the ripest. She looked to her sister for an answer, and could not tell that Gwen was desperately trying to keep her face expressionless.

Rosemary *was* going to return to reality with her. They would be back in the real world together, very soon. It was possible, she thought, that her little sister's memories of home might return. Maybe even her desire to be home. It wouldn't be betraying Peter or his cause if they just went home. "That sounds good," Gwen answered, her mind elsewhere.

Rosemary waddled back to her sister, her arms full of egg fruit. "Margaret May needed her music box to find the raven tree, but I found this one all by myself!"

The raven tree's squawking had calmed. It was exactly as Gwen had described it, but it still wasn't quite as Gwen had imagined it. She didn't realize that Neverland's raven tree was born not from her whimsical story, but from Rosemary's powerful imagination. The land bended to the wills of those who believed deeply in the contents of their fantasies, and this was the great advantage Rosemary had over her sister.

She unloaded her armful of fruit into the open flap of the picnic basket. Her excitement fell away into timid optimism as she continued, "Peter thinks your music box can help us find the Piper, too. If that's so, it might help to have some egg fruit."

She smiled wide, and Gwen wondered if her missing tooth would ever come in so long as she was in Neverland.

7

AFTER A LONG DAY OF GATHERING SUPPLIES, GWEN AND ROSEMARY were on their way back to the underground home when they ran into Bard.

"There you are," she exclaimed, finally stumbling onto the sisters in the last of the twilight. "I've been looking everywhere for you!" From the looks of her muddied, wet, and grass-stained dress, she *had* been everywhere.

"What's going on?" Gwen asked.

"I have something for you," Bard chimed, digging into the ragged pockets of her calico dress. She pulled out a dark iron key, heavy and wide. Handing the Edwardian artifact to Gwen, she told her, "I think this might help you with your mission."

Gwen felt the weight of the huge metal key in her hand before Rosemary's grabby fingers took it from her so she could ogle it for herself. "What does this key go to?" Gwen asked.

"Everything!" Bard exclaimed. "It's a skeleton key. There aren't many locks in Neverland though, so I think it'll be more helpful to you. Margaret gave it to me when she left Neverland and stopped being our mother."

"Margaret?" Gwen asked, but before she could get an answer, a blue light came buzzing furiously by.

"Hello, are you alright?" Bard asked. The girls all knew how unusual it was to see fairies this far away from their clustered home at the heart of the island. With all the drone attacks, it wasn't safe for the fairies to wander so far from any of the spider-silk nets that could shield them from the invading magic probes.

The fairy grumbled, his voice like pebbles pelting into water, and Gwen did not get the sense that he was in a pleasant mood. "Are you trying to get home for the night?" she asked, tucking the skeleton key into her basket of supplies and preparing to help the unhappy creature.

"It's not safe for fairies alone out here! Did you get lost?" Rosemary asked.

The pebbles struck harder as he made some flustered noises.

Bard translated. "He says his name is Oxalis and he does not get lost."

"Then what is he doing all the way out here? Would you like us to walk you back to a fairy hollow?" In response to Gwen's question, Oxalis pinched her. "Owww!"

Gwen took a step away, but the fairy just continued to jitter in his blue glow. Remembering what Hawkbit had said yesterday, she began to suspect this was one of the fairies who thought the lost children were to blame for the drones. "Do you not like kids?" she asked.

His buzzing made it clear that he did not. This fairy, prideful Oxalis, was not happy to feel in danger simply because he had flitted to the other side of the island.

"The offer stands. Whether you like us or not, nobody deserves to be snatched up by a drone," Gwen told him.

Oxalis remained disgruntled, but the fairy was swayed by this logic. As Gwen marched on with Bard and Rosemary, he flew close behind and they all kept their eyes peeled for the red glow of any lurking drone's scanner.

CHAPTER 8

THE GIRLS HADN'T BEEN WALKING LONG BEFORE A RUSTLING IN THE jungle caught their attention. It sounded low to the ground as it slowly rustled in the distance. Rosemary took a hesitant step toward it, and the noise amplified as the creature scurried away. Bard grabbed her friend's arm and pulled her back. "I think it might be the crocodile," Bard muttered. "What would he be doing so deep in the jungle? Do you think he's lost, too?"

Oxalis buzzed in objection.

Gwen, duly cautious, was filled with the exact opposite urge to investigate that Rosemary and Bard had.

"We'll go check, just to be safe!" her sister declared, bounding into the air with Bard.

"Wait, Rose, no!" Gwen cried, wanting to explain checking on a crocodile was the least safe thing they could do.

"It's okay, Gwen," Rosemary assured her. "We'll fly out of reach. I'll make sure it's safe."

The little girls darted off before Gwen could convince them otherwise, and she sighed as she considered the odd reality that her sister had just taken off to keep *her* safe. The blue fairy pitched a fit at this delay, which didn't subside until Gwen resumed their trek toward the safety of one of the fairies' spider-silk hollows.

Oxalis buzzed ahead of Gwen, dissatisfied with her pace no matter how fast she walked or jogged. After a while, she gave up trying to please him and went at her own pace. The fairy was in a flustered fury for a moment after, but had no option but to put up with it. They didn't see any drones, which was good since she didn't know whether she could have run all the way to the swamp in this darkness.

Once they were in sight of one of the spider-silk-covered hollow trees the fairies congregated in, a fairy beelined for Oxalis's blue sparkling and began fussing at him. She escorted him the rest of the way to the tree, thanking Gwen profusely for bringing him home safely. Oxalis continued to brood.

That taken care of, Gwen toyed with her thoughts as she walked home. She considered searching for Rosemary to make sure she'd not fallen into a misadventure with the island's dangerous crocodile, but it was a futile thought. She could go charging into the jungle on this noble impulse, only to get herself lost or entangled in a worse fate than capable young Rosemary would be in. Looking after her sister would be responsible and mature of her, and Neverland never favored the responsible or mature.

Oxalis had led her to the fairy tree nearest the shore, and she was not far from the beach. Gwen wasn't ready to head back to the underground home yet. Just because the night was dark didn't mean it was not still young.

She veered off her course to the underground home and headed out toward the water.

Navigating was hard without Oxalis. The jungle floor was treacherous when wandering in the dark. A fairy companion provided the perfect amount of luminosity to light the way, but Gwen wouldn't have wanted one anyway, considering whom she was going to go meet.

She could see a fragment of the moon through the crooked branches and odd trees of the forest, but it was still low to the horizon. She lifted off her feet to avoid tromping on strange plants or stranger creatures, and hovered through the forest for a moment to get back in the swing of flying before she shot up into the treetops. She reached the other side of the canopy in one swift motion before she had time to question herself. Leaping to the tallest branch that could support her weight, she paused. Taking in the nocturnal landscape, Gwen saw little lights flickering where fairies gathered for the night, and could still see the last of the redskins' fire glowing in the darkness. The moon, easing toward fullness one night at a time, was steady in the sky even as it danced in the water. She imagined that she could feel the breath of the island as she stood on one of the many trees that created its splendorous fresh air. In the moonlight, there was no color to the forest beneath her feet, only the texture of leaves like carpet.

Gwen felt a noise inside of her trying to get out. Was she scared? Was her body telling her to scream, to call for help? Was the sadness of knowing she would be leaving in mere hours demanding she cry?

She bounded forward to the next branch, but it was not strong enough to support her adolescent body. It didn't matter. As it snapped beneath her, she pushed off it and shot as high as she could into the sky with that momentum. She came down on the next branch but didn't even put her full weight on it. Half skipping, half flying, she touched down for the token sensation of feeling something under her feet as she raced over the top of the forest… running on the leaves as easily as solid ground. She felt miraculous, as if she were walking on water, and the noise inside of her finally choked itself free. She laughed, loud and unrestrained. No one was there to hear her. She was so used to using laughter as a social queue and communicative expression, she had forgotten how good it felt to laugh for sheer joy.

As the ground became sandy and infertile, the trees grew sparser and shorter. She could have flown down to the ground, but Gwen descended the treetops in the smallest steps possible. She walked down the tree branches as simply as she would have a staircase. Once on the shore, she kicked her bare feet and sent sand flying with every step. In fantastic spirits, she plopped down at the edge of the waves. Her toes dug into the wet sand and the moonlit waves lapped at her feet while she searched her purse. The warm air was pleasantly still. Back in reality, it would be November… or was it December now? Time had a funny way of standing still and slipping by in Neverland.

The scale was in its usual place in her satchel, and she dropped the thin, coin-like token into the shallow waves and watched it dance under the water… bright enough to retain its multicolored sheen even in the strictly silver glow of moonlight. A forceful wave pushed forward, sending Gwen scooting back to avoid getting her dress wet. The mermaid scale vanished. A moment later, the mermaid appeared.

"Hello there," Lasiandra called, out where it was deep enough for her to tread water. "Fancy meeting you this late." She held her scale out of the water and chucked it back to Gwen.

She caught it easily; Lasiandra always had deadly aim. "It's been a busy day," Gwen told her, "and I'm leaving tomorrow." She wiped the scale dry on her dress and tucked it into her purse again. The mermaid had explained to her how the scale would scream in the water, calling her to the shore of whatever body of water it landed in. The mermaid always returned the noisy enchantment back to human hands as soon as possible.

"Leaving again?" Lasiandra teased as she swam closer and pulled herself up to the shore. "How do you suspect that will go for you this time?"

"I'll come back after a few days," Gwen assured her, but even she could hear the hesitation in her voice, trying to chisel away her good mood. "It's just part of Peter's plan to find the Piper."

Lasiandra lay on the sand, propping herself up on her elbows and letting her tail rise and sink on the slight waves that washed in. Her curiosity and confusion were muted by her dispassionate face. "Peter's planning to spend *days* on the mainland?"

"No, he won't be staying. Just me."

A slender expression of amusement pricked up a corner of

Lasiandra's mouth. It still made Gwen uneasy how the excitable mermaid tried to obscure her feelings. She wondered if Lasiandra would ever get comfortable enough around her to respond with candid emotions. They had been meeting every few days like this, often rendezvousing away from the lagoon. None of the other mermaids gave Gwen any reason to trust them, and she did not want word getting back to Peter that she was regularly visiting a mermaid.

"Why would Peter want you alone in reality?"

"I won't be alone; he's taking me to some sort of ally he has."

"Who?"

Gwen traced shapeless lines into the wet sand. "I don't know. He hasn't told me."

Lasiandra brushed her hair over her shoulder to keep the sopping blonde locks from falling back into her face again. "And so you're just going to go linger in reality until he lets you come home?"

"The aviator told him the only way to find the Piper is if he has someone who has heard his song. He needs me because I'm the only one he knows who has heard the Piper's song."

"Eelgrass!" Lasiandra exclaimed. Following that expression or expletive—Gwen could not tell—the mermaid explained, "Piper got his song from the mermaids. It's an old melody from the ancient sirens. Every mermaid knows it. If that's all it takes to find Piper, why, I could manage it."

She knew it wasn't a lie, but she also felt Lasiandra was trying to shepherd her to some duplicitous conclusion. Mermaids couldn't lie, but they could ask all the questions they wanted. She considered this before figuring out what question to follow with. "Does Peter know this?"

"Certainly. We might not be able to sing it the convincing way sirens do, but mermaids knew it well enough to teach it to Piper."

"Mermaids taught the Piper his song?" In Gwen's mind, the mermaids didn't intersect with anything but Neverland. "Why?"

"He made a deal with a mermaid for it," she answered.

The Piper seemed so powerful to Gwen; she couldn't imagine him divorced from his musical magic. She couldn't imagine what price such a gift came at, either. "What did he have to give in exchange?"

"That's between Piper and the mermaids," Lasiandra responded, her tone dark as if Gwen's question had been inappropriate. Her voice lightened as she continued, "He's lucky, though. If he hadn't had mermaid magic, he would have been done for when they caught him the first time."

The moonlight sparkled on the shore as much as it did on the glassy water, but it was a broken sort of light as it reflected off rippling waves and specks of sand. "What do you mean?" Gwen asked, unsure as to whether she even wanted to know.

"The mainland is after magic, and they'll take it however they can. They would rip every plant and creature from Neverland if they could. Whatever their process is, it can kill a fairy, or turn a myth into a man. A great many battles have already been lost, closer to reality than Neverland is. If you're heading to reality, I'm sure you'll see their handiwork for yourself, soon enough." Lasiandra threw her hands up in exasperation, and they splashed back down into the water as she declared, "But no one should need to venture to reality and risk that. The mermaids knew the song well enough to teach it to him, and well enough to send for him with it… so why would Peter want to send you away? Vanda's magic still binds him to us."

"Who's Vanda?"

"The mermaid who made that mediocre musician a magnificent myth."

While she didn't know how old the myth or reality of the Piper might have been, Gwen knew it originated hundreds of years ago. "How old is Vanda?"

"Oh, she's naught but seaform now," Lasiandra replied. "She died at three hundred years, same as all mermaids."

"Mermaids live three hundred years?" Gwen didn't know, in the scope of Neverland, whether to regard that as a long life or not.

Lasiandra laughed. "I suppose that sounds like a long time to a human, but it's really not so long, considering our circumstances."

Gwen didn't want to be insensitive, but everything Lasiandra said just prompted more questions. Hoping it wasn't a socially awkward thing to do, she asked, "What do you mean about your circumstances?"

Lasiandra shrugged, water still rolling off her bare, moonlit shoulders. "Just that we are so soon forgotten by our kind, and mistaken for fish-tales by mankind. There are no books underwater, no scribes or any inks to write with. All we know about our ancestors is what little the stars tell us…" She gazed off at the horizon, where the night sky and dark sea met but never mingled. "But we tell stories. We remember songs. We know how to find the one Peter seeks."

Gwen didn't know what troubled her most out of all this new information. Her stomach churned and she answered, "Peter's been very distant lately. Ever since we returned from reality."

As her spirit sank, Lasiandra's compassion seemed to rise. "He's been very busy. You said the aviator gave him riddling instructions for how to find Piper… Do you think it is something more?"

She took a deep breath and looked to the stars. If the stars trusted the mermaids enough to whisper their secrets to them, surely Gwen could at least share her apprehensions. "Promise you won't mention it to Peter?"

"Of course. I've promised you I won't tell anyone—Peter or otherwise—about our talks."

Gwen hated to doubt her friend, but the guilt was small in contrast to the relief she got from hearing Lasiandra give her word on these important matters. She was so grateful for Lasiandra. Neverland was full of comforts and joys, but so few of the things that made Gwen feel at home. Having another girl she could talk to made Neverland's other failings seem inconsequential. None of the children would be able to understand the finer points of social relationships and hormonal mis-logic. Somehow, Lasiandra had no trouble wrapping her mind around Gwen's problems, even when it involved concepts as foreign to the ocean-dweller as school and boys. Halfway between human and fish, Lasiandra was familiar with in-betweens and the limitations that came with occupying an unusual middle ground.

"I think he's disappointed in me," Gwen confessed. "When he found me at Jay's party… it was like I wasn't just going home for Mom and Dad. I think I betrayed him in a way that he hadn't been betrayed before. I didn't go back to some nebulous sense of future and comfort… I went someplace with loud music, alcohol, and boys."

"But you came back! Doesn't Peter appreciate how important Neverland must be to you that you abandoned the man you love?"

Gwen winced. That sounded so over the top and cliché. She had a crush on Jay. She doodled his name in her notebooks and tried to think of witty things to say around him. They'd kissed, but what had that done but confirm that the infatuation was at least mutual? Love was a word so strong it couldn't help but sound silly when applied to her indecisive heart. Besides, she didn't want to believe Jay was a man. He was just an older boy. That was part of the reason she liked him. He just wanted to play football and video games, draw and make jokes with everyone. He was as childlike as a young man could afford to be.

All that was irrelevant to the conversation. "I've never mentioned Jay to Peter."

"Why not? Are you worried he'd be *jealous*?" Lasiandra seemed scandalized by the thought.

"No. I mean, it's Peter. I don't know that he'd understand, and either way, I don't want him to think my alliances are based on who I'm kissing. There's so much more involved in my decisions."

"Clearly." Lasiandra flopped over onto her back to enjoy the feeling of the little waves flooding around her. "Do you make any decisions without agonizing over them?"

Her question hit too close to home for Gwen. She was painfully aware that she gave her important decisions a level of scrutiny the lost children usually reserved for deciding whether they'd rather be a rock star or race car driver, or where to tuck themselves away during a game of hide-and-seek. It was the inconsequential decisions that deserved attention. When they faced important issues, the choice was always clear for them.

"No," Gwen moaned, "and I'm worried I never will."

Lasiandra sighed and let the stars fill up her blue tide-pool eyes. "You're never going to be happy until you figure out what you want."

Gwen scooted back another few inches. The tide was coming in, washing away the meaningless scribbles she'd left in the sand. "Actually, I think I'm fantastically happy." It was counter-intuitive, but it was true. "If anything, if I ever figure out what I want, it'll probably disrupt the balance and just make me miserable wishing for it." Gwen was full of desires, but there was an unexpected blessing in that. When they all finished canceling themselves out, she never found herself pained by longing for anything.

"You forget that you don't have to pine for your heart's desire," Lasiandra told her, reaching over and patting her leg. "You've got a friend in a mermaid. As long as that's true, you can know that things will work out for you. Someday, we'll get our hands on a sky glass and have everything we could wish for. Reflected starlight contains secrets only mermaids can read, and once we find one, we'll get the last of the magic that stars usually hold back from us. Sky glasses can't be as rare as Peter says they are."

Gwen didn't react to Lasiandra's comments about mirrors—much less let her know that she had a compact mirror sitting in her purse at that moment. She only trusted her friend so much. Lasiandra had exacerbated Gwen's irrational fear that Peter might be sending her to reality as a sort of banishment, but she had unintentionally led Gwen to another idea. Peter might be sending her because—unlike the mermaids—he trusted her.

Lasiandra sat up on her tail and stretched her arms. "I should go. You caught me at a bad time—I don't want to miss the star chatter in Orion tonight."

"Oh, I'm sorry, I didn't realize." Gwen wished they had a better system for meeting than just screaming into the water until Lasiandra came.

"Don't be sorry, silly girl," she laughed. "I'm happy I could come talk to you for a bit. I hope we can spend more time together soon. Don't be afraid to call for me, no matter where you are."

"Yeah—I'll definitely catch you later."

She wiggled her way back into the water until it was deep enough for her to begin swimming again, but before she left earshot, she made sure to give Gwen some parting advice. "Good luck finding Piper... and if he gives you any trouble, Gwen, just mention Vanda. If you tell him you know us, that'll stop him in his tracks." She laughed with cheerful malice and bobbed under the water, sinking like a stone into the dark waters she called home.

CHAPTER 9

FLYING BACK IN GOOD SPIRITS AND A FLUTTERING SUNDRESS, GWEN didn't even entertain the thought she might be unstable in the air. Such concerns seemed beyond crossing her mind after this encouraging evening. The stars were winking at her as she glided over the treetops. Her flight was perfectly stable, until an unexpected stimulus interrupted her.

"Gwen!"

Her name shot her down. She was no longer a force among the sky, but sixteen-year-old Gwen Hoffman. She twisted around in time to see Peter's face before she began her unglamorous descent.

She fell like a rock sinking through water, but not so fast that she could not compartmentalize the awkward stages of it. First, she cut through the leaves, and then the twigs snapped. A stronger branch broke under her, and she thrust her hands into the patchwork darkness, reaching for anything that she might be able to grab hold. She knocked her head hard against one branch, and then slipped further down.

In the course of those short seconds, Peter had already zipped into evasive action. She felt his hand on her elbow, and then another at her opposite arm. With this leverage, he pulled her awkwardly until he had counteracted the pesky force of gravity and could get a better grip on her. He set her down on the nearest tree branch. The position was not comfortable for either of them. She rubbed her sore elbow and watched Peter hover in front of her, his arms crossed.

He wasn't mad, but she thought she would have preferred anger to his flabbergasted disbelief. "You are the worst flier I have ever seen in my life." The insult stung harder when Gwen realized just how long Peter's young life had gone on for. "I didn't *know* people could be this bad at flying."

"You surprised me." She didn't realize how meek she felt until she heard the pitiful tone of her voice.

"Flying is all about surprises! That's why grown-ups don't do it. It's too surprising for them. The way you fly, it's like you forget you're not one of them mid-flight. I've seen kids worry they might be getting all grown up, but never in the middle of *flying*!"

"I'll get better," Gwen promised. She didn't say *I promise* to Peter, but she said it in her head. She had to. It was either that or get older.

"I hope so." Did he say that in earnest, or was he mocking her? Did he want her to get better, or did he just want to be done with her? His voice gave no hints. "Can you at least get back to the grove? I don't want to have to carry you." He made a face, as if the thought was repulsive the same way carrying a slug would be. "Foxglove and Hollyhock will be there for pixie dust before we go. You're not allowed to fall into the ocean while we're flying back, or get struck by lightning, or anything. I can't have you dying right now."

"Believe it or not," Gwen announced, launching herself off the branch and leaping back into the air, "I'm not planning on dying, and it has nothing to do with what *you* want."

"Just so long as you stay alive."

"I will."

The conversation was curt, and then it was over, but only until Gwen thought to ask, "Were you looking for me?"

"Of course. We have to leave," Peter slowly rolled onto his back as he flew, bobbing on the air and playing in it as he went through it, as if it were not some invisible, intangible thing.

"Wait, right now?"

"Well, we're going to stop by the grove first…"

"But it's the middle of the night!"

Peter rolled his eyes, and then flipped back onto his belly. "Not where we're going."

"People will see us flying if we arrive in the day… what kind of plan is this?"

"The kind that requires espionage-levels of stealth, clandestine operation, and covert maneuvering." He sounded so happy uttering the phrases.

She laughed, and her flight stabilized. "I'm going to try to be stealthy with you in tow?"

"Don't worry," he assured her. "We'll have disguises."

The prospect of dressing up for a stealth mission with Peter took her smile and bolted it to her face. Just like that, she started looking forward to this absurd adventure back to reality.

In the grove, Bard and Jam were waiting with armfuls of clothes. Rosemary was on the ground with them, taking the contents of the picnic basket and loading them into a more durable backpack. Hollyhock and Foxglove had subjected themselves to Spurt's will, which dictated that he hold them and use them for signaling Peter and Gwen like an air traffic controller. He had always wanted to be an air traffic controller, ever since the idea occurred to him several minutes earlier. The patient fairies let him wave them in gibberish instructions as the older children landed.

"What is everyone doing up so late?" No one ever complained about bedtimes—there weren't any—but the underground home collectively went to bed on a schedule that sometimes ran far ahead of Gwen's own rhythm. It was unusual to find them out like happy nocturnal creatures so long after dark.

"Right this way, Miss Dolyn," Jam announced, ushering Gwen forward with a hand as soon as she had landed. "Here are your clothes."

"We got them from real people!" Spurt exclaimed.

"How long ago?" Gwen asked, holding the heavy felt skirt out in front of her so she could get a good look at it.

"Umm, last week?" Spurt asked.

"No, we haven't flown back since, like, a month ago," Jam announced, proving that her sense of time was almost as perturbed as his. Gwen didn't know what decade the skirt was from, but certainly some point in the twentieth century.

"We got it in case of an emergency," Bard told her. "In case we ever needed to spy on real people, we wanted real people clothes."

"Why are they so big?" She pulled on the skirt; it fit her fine, but came down to an awkward length just beneath her knees.

"I thought it was a dress," Jam pouted. She handed her a blouse that was straight out of the seventies. "This one too. It was hard to tell. We took them off their clothesline at night and didn't want to get caught." She laughed. Gwen wondered if she'd ever seen a clothesline, aside from the one the girls strung up on laundry days when they were playing house or pretending to be old washerwomen. She pulled the paisley blouse on over her dress. Although Jam tried to insist Gwen had to take off the dress she'd been wearing, she was neither going to take off her clothes in front of everyone nor explain why she refused to. She kept her back to Peter though, uncertain whether he'd reached a point in his maturity where he would share her sense of discretion.

She felt like she must be wearing her grandmother's clothes. The skirt was nondescript from a distance, but the blouse was ostentatious and outdated with its bright pattern and billowy cut. Retro was in though, right?

"Okay! Enough," Peter announced, sending the little costume designers retreating and finally drawing Gwen's eye.

She stifled a laugh but could not get her hand over her mouth fast enough to cover her smile.

"What?" Peter asked, standing in acid-washed jeans—the cuffs rolled up—and a windbreaker that was equal parts sunshine yellow, hot pink, and turquoise. If he had a mullet, the look would have been complete.

"Your clothes are old. Suspiciously old." She walked over to him and tried to imagine how Claire or Katie would do "damage control" on an outfit this outrageous.

She unzipped the jacket—he had the zipper all the way up, which she was pretty sure hadn't been trendy since the eighties. He had a polo shirt underneath with a popped collar.

"Okay. If you don't want to attract attention, you're going to need to get rid of the jacket." He took it off, and Gwen creased his collar back. She knelt down and started unrolling his pant cuffs.

"It's cold where we're going," he warned.

"Trust me, you don't want to wear that jacket… although… I'll be right back."

She sprung up, and Peter finished unrolling his pant cuffs while she dove back into the underground home to grab a better jacket. She returned a minute later. "Here," she told him, "put this on."

The sweatshirt was a little big on him—Peter was neither as tall nor as broad-shouldered as Jay—but the bagginess was fashionable. The acid-washed jeans were a bit of a statement, but at least they were jeans. He could pass for a modern teenage boy, and that disturbed her. Peter Pan in denim seemed so false that it was inherently wrong.

"That looks good," she told him.

"Don't forget shoes," Rosemary exclaimed, running up to them with five socks of all different colors and two pairs of sneakers that were almost peeling apart. Gwen was glad for the reminder. She was so used to going barefoot that shoes probably wouldn't have even crossed her mind until she set foot on the frosty ground of reality.

By then, the other children had come up from the underground home. Sal and Newt had been hard at work in their tunnels with Blink's assistance, but they knew Gwen's departure was imminent once she had come down to grab her sweatshirt.

Her shoes laced up, the backpack full of supplies, and her nerve feeling like it would only be worked up for so long, she asked, "Which way are we flying tonight?"

Blink dumped a black ball in Peter's hand. Its surface looked like cracking asphalt, but something glorious and golden was glowing inside. He smiled, the way he always did when he was about to share something wonderful. "We can't be spotted," he reminded her. He tossed the ball in his hand and caught it as it came back down. "We're going to go through the storm."

CHAPTER 10

HOLLYHOCK AND FOXGLOVE PREEMPTIVELY TUCKED THEMSELVES into the spider-silk purse Gwen was bringing specifically for concealing fairies. They did not want to leave even a hint of pixie dust on the wind, but the bag was also waterproof. Hollyhock grumbled about the close quarters, but Foxglove dragged her in and they got comfortable cuddling together in the safety of the bag. They insisted Peter carry them, however. Gwen couldn't blame them, but she resented they were starting to doubt her flying, too.

"Goodbye, Gwenny!"

"Come back soon, okay?"

"I want to meet the Piper!"

The children were a chorus of requests and desires that could not be addressed at the moment. Rosemary was the odd one out, quiet and content. Gwen felt perturbed by how happy her little sister was to see her leaving. Before she took off, she gave Rosemary a big hug. The little girl whispered to her, "I'm so proud of you. I'm so glad you're my sister."

Her concerns eased, but did not disappear. Gwen felt full of mush and melted-down emotions. "You stay safe and come find me soon, okay? I'm going to need your help."

Rosemary stood, poised and beaming. "I know."

"I love you."

"I love you too!"

Gwen ruffled Rosemary's messy hair for good measure, and then took off as Peter called to her from the sky.

She tried not to look back. It would be dark. She wouldn't be able to see. She couldn't help herself. Glancing over her shoulder, she looked down but could not distinguish which of the funny, shadow-shape children was her little sister.

The stars seemed to get bigger as they flew higher, but Gwen didn't trust her eyes as they left Neverland. An uneasy feeling clung to her as she and Peter headed for reality. She had a bad feeling about this mission.

"Are you ready for this?" Peter yelled to her.

"Ready for what?"

"For the storm!" he declared. "I don't know how much farther we can go before it hatches."

Gwen zoomed forward. She couldn't figure out a way to maintain good flying posture while weighed down with the backpack. Peter had started to glow though—an act of illumination usually reserved for fairies—and Gwen wanted to know why.

The orb in his hands released a light so startlingly bright it burned the pattern of its golden cracks into her eyes. Peter didn't look directly at it, but Gwen didn't know where else she was supposed to look.

Her eyes darted back to the ball again, but she knew to look away faster this time. It still hurt her eyes, but the glance served its purpose. She could tell the cracks were getting deeper, longer, and more volatile. Peter's terminology was perfect: it looked as if it was about to hatch. She realized that the low roar she was hearing came from within the egg-like object.

"What's inside of that?"

Peter gave her a sly look. "A thunderstorm."

"Is it dangerous?"

"How could it be dangerous?"

"That looks like an awfully small container for a whole thunderstorm. What if it explodes?"

"Oh, don't worry—it will." Peter's confidence was contagious. Despite the alarming facts he gave her, she found it easy to trust his nonchalant attitude. "I'm going to hold onto it until the last possible moment, but when I drop it, we're going to have to stay as close behind it as possible. As long as we're above it, we'll be fine."

"Okay."

"We're going to have to fly fast."

"Okay."

"It'll be a hard landing."

"Okay."

"Can't you say anything besides okay?"

"No," Gwen replied, sticking her tongue out at him.

He laughed. "For a second, I thought your voice puppet might have gotten stuck."

The thunderstorm in his hand rumbled again. It shook, and bits of the black rock flaked and fell away. In the darkness, she could not see that they were expanding like popcorn into ominous clouds below.

It took both hands for Peter to contain it. Hollyhock and Foxglove still huddled in their pixie purse, securely strung around Peter's belt. Soon, it sounded like they were actually caught in a storm. The air stayed as still as the silhouetted horizon, but the sound of thunder engulfed them. As the contents of the orb reached their brightest, they began pulsing with unsustainable flashes of near-blinding light.

"You ready?" Peter yelled.

Gwen's reply could not be distilled to a single-syllable answer, but anything else would be lost in the fury of noise. Fudging her feelings, she shouted back, "Yes!" She thought she would have just a moment more to brace herself, but before she had finished the word, Peter dropped the storm.

As soon as it left his hands, it was free. There was nothing to hold it back. Even Peter had relinquished the pretension that he could contain it… and the wind knew.

An invisible wave crashed down on them. A furious force flew toward the storm. Every violent wind and mischievous current for miles around came as instantaneously as light. The storm sucked clouds toward it like stars to a black hole. It was summoning them, so it would have a clouded sky to explode into. It needed a stage, so it dragged everything in the sky with it, including Gwen and Peter.

Her mind shot back to the reality bombing that had struck a few weeks ago. Her arm had finished healing little more than a week ago, and some faint lettering was still visible to the discerning eye. She could not bear to endure that hellish experience again, yet she was in the midst of a wind totally out of her control. She realized she was screaming only when her throat began to hurt. She couldn't hear herself over the sound at the heart of this storm, the ball just out of reach. It was not a question of trying to keep up with its swift free-fall, but rather keep control of the speed it forced on her.

Peter grabbed her hand and clamped down on it. She knew he wouldn't let go; he wouldn't lose her. She tightened her grip and tried to give herself over to his instincts—hers were no good in this fury. If she was going to survive, she had to suspend her sense of panic and trust in Peter.

Sparks of lightning sputtered out of the orb, breaking their way through the surface and decaying what remained of the storm's rocky, black containment. They weren't bolts, not yet. They stretched out like uncertain fingers grasping for some unknown object. They were not as fast as proper lightning. Shorter in reach and longer in duration, the proto-lightning shot in all directions, creating a crisscross of slender, electric obstacles. Peter didn't blink. Tears poured from his wind-ravaged eyes, but they stayed as steady as his grip on Gwen's hand. They could not lose sight of the orb and risk drifting from the heart of the storm to be caught exposed in the sky.

Up, down, left, up, right, down, left, down, left... there was no pattern to the sputtering electrical outputs. Peter responded to each with extraordinary reflexes that jerked Gwen in random directions, yanking and shoving her so they traveled as one entity through the chaos.

As they got closer to the ground, the storm clouds caught up. The ball was disintegrating and becoming harder to follow through the thick clouds, but the lightning was getting stronger and faster. The openings in clouds and passages between shocks of lightning were getting slimmer. A spark flashed out and struck Gwen's loose hair. It crackled and singed, but the wind put the flame out. All Gwen noticed was an instantaneous flash of fire in her peripheral vision and the brief smell of burnt hair. She grabbed onto Peter's arm with her other hand, pulling closer to him and praying she was near enough as she pressed against his arm.

Peter jerked her back in the opposite direction. Gwen felt some parts of her slowing, and other parts continuing down at terminal velocity. Her bones—particularly those in her hands, crushed in Peter's grip—were feeling this force. Her stomach and assorted other vital organs felt like they were hurtling toward the storm.

She joined him, fighting against the pull of the storm and strength of the wind. Together, she and Peter made a desperate effort to escape the force of the storm, which was shrinking down to a mere marble of light that would, at any moment, explode in the meteorological equivalent of the big bang. Gwen realized with horror that they would not escape it, that they could not get away in time. As the clouds gave way to a thick fog, she saw how close they were to the ground and how fast they were falling toward it. She screamed—this time loud enough to hear herself over the screeching of the squall.

Peter flung himself around her. He wrapped his arms around her neck and back, trapping her arms against him. She felt tucked into him like an infant swaddled in covers. The monolithic storm that surrounded them was so loud, her thoughts seemed quiet and calm in contrast. She was going to die on impact, but at least she felt safe in Peter's hands.

Tossed around and uncertain of anything with her stomach gone and her bones squeezed to a pulp in Peter's grip, Gwen only knew which way was down because the wind was still blowing her hair in the opposite direction, away from Peter.

They were no longer vertical. She was on top of him, and he was about to take the brunt of the impact. Was he trying to save her? Didn't he know it would be impossible for either of them to survive?

Whether it is impossible is irrelevant, he'd told her once.

She could feel even as he gripped her how calm his body was, how little tension there was in his muscles. He was free falling like a dead man. He was not afraid. He was relaxed, because there was nothing he did better than the impossible.

Gwen could not unglue the fear from her body. Her muscles braced for a collision her body knew she couldn't survive, but she gently closed her eyes. She forced her lungs to breathe at a rate ten times slower than her frantic heart was beating.

Through her closed eyes, a golden light exploded into being all around her. The first strike of true lightning touched down on the earth, and the flash overpowered the dark of the clouds. She was falling through a sky made of light. It was beautiful, even if it was all on the other side of her eyelids. She knew what came next. She knew what always followed lightning.

An earth-shattering roar of thunder broke as Gwen and Peter slammed against the ground with the full force of their bodies. She felt the earth through Peter's body as the shock of impact reverberated through him and shook her.

They skidded, and she felt dirt and grass thrown up around her, pelting the parts of her face that she couldn't press against his chest. For a moment, she forgot that it was really Peter she was clinging to underneath that sweatshirt.

At last, it stopped. All of it. The thunder was in the distance, and the lightning could not be seen through closed eyes. The storm was elsewhere, and the air was still. There was no more motion—neither gravity nor friction. Gwen rolled over and felt the grass underneath her. She pushed her head over to look at invincible Peter. He was smiling at the sky. He didn't bother with his hands as he rocked back, and then threw himself onto his feet. He dusted off his pants before striking a proud stance. His chin turned up and his boyish chest puffed out, he looked to be basking in his extraordinary glory.

"That is the most remarkable storm landing you will ever see. That is, unless you ever see me land in a storm again."

She knew she shouldn't humor his ego, but Gwen couldn't help her awe. "That was impressive."

He extended a helpful hand and unhelpful remark. "I knew you'd be terrible at it. Girls never get it right at all the first time."

"I would have died by myself," Gwen admitted. She wasn't entirely clear on how Peter's force of flight had stopped them from reaching a lethal velocity, but she was certain she wouldn't have been able to do the same.

Peter's lithe hands untangled the ties of the pixie purse on his belt and let Hollyhock and Foxglove rush out of it like cats out of water. They flew in swooping circles, kissing the air. How they survived the fall was just as much a mystery to Gwen.

"No," Peter objected. "You're not allowed to die without my permission. I need you, and falling to death isn't an acceptable way to die anyway." He extended a hand and pulled her to her shaky feet.

"You say that like there are acceptable ways to die."

"Of course. Most of them involve pirates though."

They started to walk. The storm was moving away, and they had managed to avoid any rainfall. The grass was still wet and the trees were dripping around them, but Gwen could see that the nearby lake's surface was still.

"So if I got locked in mortal combat and died, would that

work for you?"

"Well, not *now,*" he complained. "I need you now. But yes. Providing your adversary was sufficiently nefarious."

Peter pulled an eighteenth-century compass from the pocket of his disco-era jeans. It only took him a second to check it before they started walking northeast, away from the lake and into the forest.

"Where are we?" She couldn't imagine where in the world the thunderstorm had taken them. What country was she in?

Peter whacked through a bush and pushed on with intrepid enthusiasm. "Lake Agana."

"What?" Gwen stopped, and waited until he paused. "Your friend is here?"

"About two miles northeast of here. This was just the closest open space we could land in without being spotted."

"How is this possible?" she demanded. "We're an hour away from my house. How is it that the aviator lands in the closet airfield, the Piper invades my neighborhood, your friend—whoever that even is—lives beside the nearest lake… Why is all of this happening in my backyard?"

Peter gave her a dull and dissatisfied look. The fairies were also staring at her. "I'm not going to stand around and answer all your dumb questions." He started stomping through the brush again.

"But—"

"So keep up and listen."

Gwen dashed to his side, and didn't interrupt him as he began to explain.

"Magic is kind of… magnetic," he told her. Hollyhock chimed in, but the vocabulary and concepts she was using didn't have English translations. "Exactly. It is like a magnet with a limitless range. But the further away you get from it, the slower it moves toward more magic."

She thought back to the day Rosemary disappeared, and what she had heard from the police officers while eavesdropping through the heater vent. Her father worked with magic—Anomalous Resources, they'd called it—to help funnel power into the economy. They thought that had something to do with Rosemary being targeted. They could track magic to find it, and they thought Peter Pan could too. It wasn't a tactical strategy though… it was just the draw of magic to magic.

"A lot of magic has gathered here in the past decade," Peter told her. "It's impossible to know what started it."

Chicken and egg, Gwen thought. Did Peter Pan visit this place on a whim and leave a trail of magic that drew others to it, or did he come because something was already pulling him toward it?

She tried to imagine the ramifications of this as she stomped down a thorny nettle bush and soldiered on through the brush. "What happens when too much gathers here? Is that going to happen?"

A smile ripped into Peter's face with devilish delight. "We're counting on it to find Piper." Without elaborating on that thought, he launched into another explanation to give her context. "That's how Neverland works. It started out with just a little magic, but it has collected so much more. It's powerful now. That's why they want it. Grown-ups never let magic grow. They redirect it and use it up. They treat magic like a scarce resource, so that's what it becomes for them. They don't give back and put their hearts into it to keep it going and growing. If they ever got to Neverland, they would strip it clean."

She couldn't imagine a Neverland deforested of its magic. "How are we going to stop them from getting there?"

"That's the one good thing—we don't have to. Neverland is exerting such a magical pull… nothing can get in without ample magic."

"But how do the bombs and drones make it?"

Again, the pixies tried to answer, eager to explain their homeland, but Gwen was not proficient enough in the fairy language to understand their intricate trills.

"It takes less magic to send a thing than it does to send a

person. They use some of their refined technology-magic to attack, but it's the magic that finds Neverland, not them."

Peter pushed a sapling's branch out of his way, then let go of it. It thwacked Gwen almost before she could get her hands up to shield her face. "But what's to stop them from someday compiling enough magic to make it there themselves for a real invasion?"

"Neverland is smart, Gwen-dollie. It knows its own magic. No one can reach Neverland's horizons unless they have a native inhabitant guiding them… That's why I keep Holly around." As soon as he said that, Hollyhock zipped down and pinched his ear. He clapped his hand at his ear to cover it, but she was already out of his way. "One of the many reasons I keep Holly around," he corrected himself, smiling.

She considered this information as she felt a fungal patch squish under her foot. She was glad she was wearing shoes… mushrooms in reality were neither colorful nor enchanting, just white and goopy.

"Is it possible, if one of the drones did capture a fairy…" She didn't have the heart to finish the thought.

Foxglove and Hollyhock settled in the hood of Peter's—Jay's—sweatshirt. His expression became grim. "We don't know. That's certainly what they're trying to accomplish. Last time drones found Neverland, back before you showed up, they did take some fairies, but the grown-ups never came. It isn't enough to have a fairy—they would have had to convince them to take them to the island—but things might be different now. Something must have changed that they're spending their limited magical resources to send drones to catch fairies again."

She didn't want to think about what happened to the poor fairies who refused to cooperate with the Anomalous Activity Department.

"What could have changed?"

Peter picked a golden dandelion and went to stuff the bloom in his buttonhole, but he was in strange clothes without buttonholes. He flicked it aside, losing interest in it all together.

"They might have some new device or technology they're working on that they think will bypass the magical laws of Neverland."

"What—do they think they are just going to be able to teleport to Neverland?"

"I don't know," he answered. "That's why we need Piper. Whatever his price, he's the only one who can help us reach the kids we need to build a resistance and defend Neverland. With enough kids, Neverland will be able to hide itself for good. Then we'll be safe, and there'll be no way to find us or any reason for us to return here ever again."

They didn't talk much for the rest of their trek through the woods. They could still hear the low roar of the thunderstorm in the distance. Soon, they were close enough that the fairies had to hide again. Gwen was afraid for them since they had been out so long, but Peter assured her that the grown-ups wouldn't be scanning for magic in daylight, especially so far away from suburbia. Even if they were, by the time they tracked it out to Lake Agana, the dust trail would be too scattered by the wind to follow.

They found the forest's hiking trail moments before breaking the tree line. "Where are we going, Peter?" He was heading toward a mobile home community next to the state park.

He continued to walk with confidence. His usual cocky stride looked surprisingly like the swagger of an ordinary teenage boy. "My friend lives here. Don't worry. Don't look like such a stranger here."

She didn't want to appear conspicuous, but Gwen was too baffled to help it. The unkempt lawns were boxed in by chain-link fences covered in varying degrees of rust. They passed a lawn littered with bicycles; on the other side of the gravel street, two different cars were parked on the lawn, clearly non-functional. Satellite dishes were on every trailer home. Despite all being painted differently, the track housing still managed to present a uniformity of depressing color.

Multiple houses had motorcycles out front or a dog

milling around their yard. When she and Peter passed a pack of Rottweilers, the dogs ran up to the fence and began snarling until all the other dogs in the neighborhood were barking too. "Ignore it," Peter advised her.

She was scared. This was not the sort of place she ever expected to visit with Peter. She didn't trust his ability to protect her here. This wasn't his world, but it wasn't hers either. They were both out of their element. Peter just didn't have the sense to realize it.

Winding down the gravel road, Gwen matched Peter's pace almost step for step. They approached a blue-and-grey house. Like the others, it had wooden latticework around the bottom to help obscure the fact it didn't have a foundation in the ground. The square house reminded Gwen of how she would take shoeboxes and try to turn them into homes for her dolls by decorating them. It was hard to fathom that she was walking up the plastic steps of the porch to knock on the door.

She waited, feeling her heartbeat in her throat, her toes, and everywhere besides her chest. Even the predictable noise of the door opening startled her.

A woman with a long, black braid and beige cardigan stood in the doorway. Gwen looked up at her, and then watched as the sharp features of her dark face dissolved into unadulterated shock.

"Peter?"

CHAPTER 11

THE STARTLED WOMAN USHERED THEM IN. SHE WAS JUST AS uncomfortable with their presence in the trailer park as Gwen. Once inside, they stood in a living room full of old furniture, facing a kitchen with old electric appliances. There was no unity or romance to the orange recliner, chipped mixing bowl, off-white blender, dull toaster, and sunken couch. It was a bunch of old stuff that looked like it represented several decades of objects abandoned at Goodwill. The chingadera and bric-a-brac wasn't any more cohesive: porcelain angles, an antique pot, a vase full of bird feathers, and a stopped clock made the place confusing and strange in the same way her grandmother's house had been.

"What are you doing here?" the women hissed, pulling her cardigan close and tossing her thick braid over her shoulder and out of her way. She had a shapeless housedress underneath the beige sweater, and a pair of black leggings insulating her legs as she stomped around, heavy-footed in her leather slippers. She looked comfortable, except for the unexpected guests who were putting her so ill at ease. "You shouldn't be here."

"I need your help," Peter said.

"They're still keeping tabs on me."

"That's why I came in disguise."

"You're being irresponsible. You're jeopardizing us both, and Neverland to boot."

"I took all the right precautions. This is important." Hollyhock and Foxglove wrestled their way out of the pixie purse and came twinkling out now that they knew they were safely inside.

"You brought *fairies* here?" she exclaimed. She leaned down and grabbed a hold of his arm, forcing him to look her dead in her dark eyes. Gwen wanted to leave. This wasn't a friend, not anymore. This was a grown-up, and unlike Antoine the aviator, she was not amused with Peter's wartime antics.

"What happens if they figure it out and come to question me?"

Peter scoffed. "You won't tell them."

"What if they threaten to arrest me? They could put me away forever until I told them what they needed to know, and nobody here would stop them."

Peter broke free of her hold with ease; she wasn't actually trying to restrain him. "Preposterous," he declared. "If they did that, you would sit, stone-faced and silent in your cell until they all died."

"What if they beat me?"

"You'd take the blows as though you were made of rock, and you would not speak." Peter seemed to disregard the question.

"What if they tortured me and stuck blades under my nails?" she demanded.

"Then you would not even scream, but stay silent as a stone!" Peter insisted, hopping up onto a wooden kitchen chair at her dining table, looking down at the woman.

"What if they bring knives and cut off my fingers, one at a time, until I told them how to find you?"

Peter yelled right back, "Then you would steal their knives and scalp them all like the redskin princess you are!"

Her anger slunk off her face and out of her shoulders. She shook her head, frowning as a sad laugh escaped her. She clung to her sweater, blinking back tears, until, at last, she flung her arms around Peter. Still on the chair, he had to bend down to return the embrace.

"Oh, Peter," she muttered, unaware of the tears slipping off her smiling face. "Oh, Peter."

"It's good to see you, Tiger Lily."

Her smile was wide, but tightly closed-lip. Gwen recognized the feeling that was fighting to get out—that beautiful sense of joy that she was trying not to foolishly indulge in. The shock and excitement had reduced the woman to non-functionality. "I—I'll make some sandwiches," she offered.

12

PETER AND GWEN SAT AT THE KITCHEN TABLE TOGETHER WHILE TIGER Lily shuffled around the kitchen to make lunch.

"How did you get here without anyone seeing you?" she asked, glancing out her blinds as if she thought Anomalous Activity officers would be pulling up to her door at any minute.

"The thunderstorm that passed through, that was us."

She nodded. "I heard the storm earlier, it raged all morning. It reminded me of Storm Sounds…" Gwen wondered how the storm had lasted so long and started so early. The bits of lightning they had witnessed had moved slowly enough to dodge while flying through, so maybe she wasn't entirely clear on how time behaved in the middle of a hatching thunderstorm.

"It was the cleverest way to come in daylight." Peter sat on his chair backward, draping his arms over the arching wooden back.

A look of mild amusement swept across Tiger Lily's face as she layered deli meat on sliced bread. "So I suppose you thought of that all by yourself?"

"Of course!" He seemed to take offense at the implication that anyone else could have.

She laughed and sliced a tomato. "Peter, you haven't changed at all." Gesturing to Gwen with her paring knife, she pointed out,

"You haven't even introduced me to your friend yet."

Gwen would have been happy to remain a piece of scenery for this conversation. Something about Tiger Lily intimidated her, even though the woman was much more amiable now than she had been when they first arrived.

"This is Gwendolyn Lucinda Hoffman."

She was taken aback by the introduction. Aside from the night he had swept her off to Neverland, she had never mentioned her middle name. At this point, she assumed Peter had forgotten what her actual name was anyway, what with all the Dollie-Lyn and Gwenny nonsense. Stammering, she told Tiger Lily, "I'm Gwen. It's a pleasure to meet you."

"Good to meet you, Gwen," Tiger Lily answered, getting the peanut butter and jelly out of her refrigerator. The appliance hummed happily as she sorted through its various prepared foods. "What brings you to Neverland—or back home, if that's the case?"

Tiger Lily didn't directly ask what a girl as old as Gwen was doing running around with Peter Pan. Thinking about her own age spurred her to wonder how old Tiger Lily was. She looked to have aged into her thirties, but her face and dark skin retained a youthful glow. The way her hair cascaded into her braid was beautiful too. "Peter found my little sister a few months ago, and when I couldn't convince her to stay home, I went with her."

"That is an admirable loyalty to your little sister."

"Gwenny's our storyteller now," Peter interjected.

Gwen fidgeted on the stiff kitchen chair, doubly uncomfortable when she couldn't think of what to say next. Tiger Lily approached with an assortment of sandwiches and announced, "Any friend of Peter is a friend of mine. Make yourself at home, Gwen."

She set down the sandwiches and took a seat at the round table with them. Gwen couldn't think of the last time she'd been in the company of an adult that wasn't a teacher or parent. Tiger Lily acted as if they were all on equal footing. She said *make yourself at home*, but every other time Gwen had ever been told that, she'd sooner or later gotten in trouble for wearing shoes on carpet or touching some dusty old antique. She had a feeling Tiger Lily meant it though.

"Old Willow has christened her Lily on Fast Waters," Peter told her, his mouth full of a ham sandwich already half devoured. Gwen reached out and took a peanut butter and grape jelly sandwich. It was on white bread, and she'd rarely had the pleasure of sweet bleached bread in her mother's health-conscious kitchen.

Tiger Lily's delight was apparent, but her face remained fairly inexpressive. There was a muted, stoic nature to even her most passionate expressions. "So you are a Lily, too, my friend?"

Gwen felt like she was blushing, and took tinier bites of her sandwich as she began to feel tinier. She was rediscovering the unpleasant nature of social dynamics with unknown adults. "That's what Old Willow thought, when she threw my bones."

Tiger Lily's eyebrows raised, but she suppressed any questions she might have wanted to ask. She picked up a sandwich of her own and began eating. Peter reached across the table, still sitting backward on his chair, and tore into another sandwich. An odd silence lasted far shorter than it seemed to before she quietly asked, "Why are you here, Peter?"

"We're going to call for Piper. I need your help."

"I don't know where Piper is, and you should know better than to be looking for him. I don't know how to find him."

"We do."

"Then what do you need from me, Peter? They're watching me." Tiger Lily set her sandwich aside on the edge of the plate, and ignored it from that point forward. "It isn't often, but they come by every few months. I think it has to do with when you come back. Two Anomalous Activity officers showed up in October, asked me all sorts of questions, and searched the house. They don't trust me."

"I know you're on their radar, but that's how much I need you right now. If we find Piper, he'll be able to rally children for our resistance. We'll be able to defend Neverland well enough to keep grown-ups away from it altogether."

"You really think that final fight is coming?" Tiger Lily was skeptical, but not unwilling to believe it.

"They're sending drones again," Peter told her. "They've got bombs coming through. If we don't do something soon, they'll figure out how to incapacitate us and harvest what's left with their technology… and that's if they don't manage to capture and manipulate a fairy into leading them there."

"How is my tribe?" Her voice stayed steady, but her eyes were compromised by a look of concern.

"Safe and in peace. Captain Rackham is gone, but so is the strength and fire of the redskin people. Their numbers have fallen, and without adversaries to fight, their spirit slowly dwindles."

She nodded. Taking this in, she then ventured, "My father?"

"Dark Sun is in good health."

"My father?" She blinked back a sad confusion.

"Oh," Peter exclaimed. "Yes—Dark Sun. He goes by no other name since you were taken. The sun clouded over that day, into darkness as it sometimes does, even on the clearest days."

"But he is well?"

"Yes."

Tiger Lily didn't ask for any more elaboration.

"How are you fairing?" Peter asked. "How are the redskins here?"

She shook her head, the thinnest traces of amusement on her face. "They are not redskins, Peter. And now, neither am I."

"Snowsalt!" he burst. "Of course you're a redskin."

"I'm a Native American." She spoke it like an apology, as if she were informing him of a death in the family. "I'm real now."

"I don't understand," he grumbled. Gwen didn't think she had ever heard Peter admit that before. It wasn't a concession though; it was an end to the conversation. He didn't understand and wouldn't be made to. Peter was not someone who changed, or grew, or knew what was once unknown to him. Tiger Lily knew better than to challenge that. "What, exactly, do you need from me, that you are willing to risk both of our wellbeing by coming here?"

"Gwen-dollie has heard Piper's song. She'll be able to find him, but she needs a few things, first and foremost a safe house to operate from. Her sister will be along shortly to help."

"You're not staying?"

"I can't afford to."

"Of course."

Both took a slow breath.

"I have a guest bedroom," Tiger Lily said. "You'll be comfortable enough there, Gwen, but I don't think it is advisable for you to go out in the daytime. Whatever bidding you have to do, I'm sure it will be better for us both if you do it under the cover of night."

Gwen nodded, agreeing with the logic while also feeling horrified by the prospect of being cooped up with this strange woman, an old childhood friend of the eternal child.

"If anything goes wrong... if they catch you using magic and trace it back to this house... I won't be able to protect you. I'll be lucky if I'm able to save my own skin." Her tone became severe as she warned, "I will not forfeit Neverland for anyone. You must know that now."

"Yes," Gwen agreed, wishing she had the unwavering force of will to say the same... If not about Neverland, than at least about something.

CHAPTER 13

PETER PAN AND TIGER LILY DOVE INTO CONVERSATION WITH THE intensity of hawks on the hunt and the playfulness of dolphins in warm water. They talked faster than Gwen could have kept pace with, even if she were familiar with the stories and subjects they volleyed back and forth. Her discomfort only eased when she grew comfortable being a third wheel. She never would have imagined that Peter could make her feel like such an outsider, trading their dynamic to throw himself into sociable antics with an adult. The fairies delighted in the conversation and ate jam by the handful.

As the afternoon wore on to evening, Gwen began to better understand the gravity of this reunion. After Tiger Lily had been captured by Captain Rackham and his pirate crew, she was never seen again by the denizens of Neverland. Peter's tongue let slip more information than he seemed to intend as he asked Tiger Lily about various aspects of her life on the Agana Reservation. No one acknowledged how obvious it was that he had been keeping tabs on her, despite the risk.

They told decades worth of stories, leaving Gwen severely confused about how time passed for redskins even after they had crossed the threshold of reality and been assimilated to the culture theirs was based on. Tiger Lily was eager to hear the details of Captain Rackham's demise. Peter went into great detail, painting a fantastic picture of how a blinding fog had rolled into Cannibal's Cove one morning and set the stage for an epic battle in the hull of the ship once it had run aground in the impossible weather.

Tiger Lily had few stories. She tried to keep Peter talking and the fairies buzzing, which was an easy task. He needed little convincing to spew story after story that highlighted his adventurous spirit, and the fairies corroborated everything. What little Tiger Lilly said about her life on the reservation was about the Native American children in her community and their humorous, endearing adventures.

Gwen was intermittently roped back into the conversation, but these solicitations only gave her a chance to contribute the occasional awkward statement before fading again into the background like just another piece of mismatched furniture.

When they spoke of Piper, she was at least able to follow their thoughts and engage with what she was listening to. Peter rattled off everything the aviator had told him, and brainstormed with Tiger Lily in order to make sense of his instructions.

"The melody of the lamb and death?" Tiger Lily asked, taken aback by the phrase.

"We're not sure what that is," Peter told her. His shoes removed long ago, he now had his feet kicked up on the kitchen table. "'The mark of the first debt' was easier to figure out… I'm certain it means a guilder, and I aim to gather a few of those before returning to Neverland tonight."

"What's a guilder though?"

"A golden penny. You know, a guilder."

Tiger Lily clearly did not understand, but shook her head. "Why would Antoine give you such riddling instructions? It doesn't seem like him at all."

"They're not his instructions. He got them from accounts of people who had found the Piper. Someone sees him every few weeks in some part of the world, but doesn't recognize him or otherwise finds themselves led away from wherever they were when they spotted him. They're always left with one of four clues. The mark of the first debt, the melody of the lamb and death, the tune of his enchantment, or the patch fit for a prince. The one I'm stuck on right now is a patch fit for a prince."

"Well, he is the prince of pipes…"

"But what prince patches clothing?"

"What I don't understand is why he's giving his calling card out in piecemeal." Tiger Lily brooded over this reality with healthy apprehension. "It's suspicious. If he doesn't want to be found, why leave these notes with anyone?"

Peter flashed a knowing smile. "Piper doesn't want to stay hidden. He just doesn't want to be caught. He's waiting for someone who can put it all together. It's a trial. He won't waste his time or take a risk on anyone who isn't prepared to pay the price of a meeting."

"But even you haven't figured it out yet. I don't like this, Peter. He made a deal with mermaids for his song, and now he makes deals like they do, too."

"It'll be alright," Peter promised. "Once Gwen-Dollie has her music box, I'll send her sister with everything else. You forget I've dealt with the fellow before."

Slumped in her chair, Tiger Lily put her hand to her chin. Her braid was slowly coming undone, her silky black hair seeping out in strands like tributaries off a narrow river. "I don't think you're going to be able to find a patch fit for a prince." Pursing her lips, she ventured, "But I think I know who might."

Peter leapt up with great joy. "Then I put it in your hands, Tiger Lily. I will gather the guilders and make sense of the melody of the lamb and death. Gwen will find her music box, and we will manage this."

"I can't make promises," Tiger Lily said. "They will not be happy with me for bringing it up. They might not be willing to help at all."

"I have the most star-shattering faith in you," he told her, as if that alone would dismiss any challenges she suspected in the task.

"I hope you know what you're doing, Peter. This is not a moment in which we can make it up as we go along."

"Tiger Lily, when have I ever been wrong?"

She didn't answer.

Gwen didn't know what time it was. The stopped clock, antique and broken down, gave her no sense of how long they had been there, eating sandwiches and talking in the kitchen. Twilight had rolled by like a boy on a bicycle, the darkness at its heels.

Peter glanced at the window. Tiger Lily had long ago shut the blinds so that it would not be obvious she was entertaining two unfamiliar teenagers in her home. Still, the darkness crept in at the edges. The bright yellow kitchen light and the twinkling of the fairies was all they had.

"I need to leave now," he announced, no emotion in his voice.

"Already?" Gwen asked, afraid to be left behind so soon.

"Be careful," Tiger Lily warned him, standing up. "Don't leave a conspicuous trail of fairy dust out of here."

"Don't worry," he assured her, peeking out between the narrow blinds. "There's enough wind tonight it'll scatter instantly. I'll walk back to the forest before I take off, too. It's still early."

Tiger Lily walked over and folded him into her arms. He hugged her as she planted a kiss atop his ruffled hair. "Take care, Peter," she told him. "Take care of my home."

He whispered something back to her, but Gwen couldn't hear. They let go of each other, and Peter went to the door. He didn't put his shoes on. The shoes remained ignored in the corner he had kicked them off. "I will," he assured her. "Even if I have to scour the globe to find Piper myself." He unzipped the grey sweatshirt and threw it aside on the depressed couch beside the door, then stripped out of his acid-washed jeans and down to his usual mud-and-grass stained shorts. He pulled off his polo shirt and chucked it as well, ready to head out bare-chested and barefooted into the night. In a way, Gwen was glad to see him looking so much more himself before he launched out into the cover of night.

"Goodbye, Peter," she told him, afraid if she didn't he might wander out without a word.

He stared at her, a sublime focus in his eyes. Hollyhock flitted to his shoulder, and he threw open the door. A breeze blew in, feeling like a great wind inside the still air of the house. "Find your music box and get her to remember Piper's song," he told her.

Then the door closed and he was gone. The wind was outside, he was with it, and the stopped clock on Tiger Lily's shelf did not tick.

CHAPTER 14

TIGER LILY STARED AT THE DOOR STANDING BETWEEN HER AND EVERY world beyond it. Peter had vanished, and Gwen, too, wondered when she would see him again. The magic of the evening was gone without Peter to animate it. Even Foxglove seemed muted after the parting, and Tiger Lily and Gwen felt equally stranded in reality, once again.

"Oh, is that the time?" Tiger Lily asked. Gwen didn't notice what clock she looked at. "I should make dinner. I'm sure you're hungry if all you've had to eat are those sandwiches. I think I have some fish fillets in the freezer or chicken soup…"

"I'm not actually hungry," she replied, "but thank you."

"Neither am I…" Tiger Lily began clearing the table. Little remained on the platter but crumbs and the crusts of Peter's sandwiches. "Whenever you get hungry, help yourself to anything in the kitchen. Would you like a cup of tea?"

"No, thank you." Gwen looked at the pile of clothes Peter had cast off before leaving. They were clumped in a sad heap on the couch.

Tiger Lily filled a kettle and put it on her electric stove anyway. "So, you've heard Piper's song?"

"A long time ago," Gwen admitted. "I don't remember it now,

but Peter thinks that when my mother turned on my music box… This sounds absurd, but he thinks the music box might remember."

"Not as absurd as you think. Come take a look at this."

Gwen got up from the table and followed Tiger Lily into a dark bedroom. She flicked on the overhead light, and Gwen was overwhelmed by what greeted her.

The bookshelves and wall shelves were filled with redskin knickknacks. None of it looked like actual craftwork by Native Americans; it was all kitschy trinkets that seemed like props out of a low-budget western film. A colorful feather headdress sat decked over a vanity littered with more face paint than makeup. She had bracelets and necklaces made of bright plastic beads and painted bone, cheaply imitating Native American jewelry. Her collection of carved figurines looked like miniature cigar-store Indians, and a little cloth tee-pee was surrounded by toy dolls made of red cloth skin and black yarn braids. There were books and CDs collected on shelves, sage incense, and a tapestry on the wall that depicted a buxom woman in leather and feathers riding a wolf under a full moon.

Tiger Lily went straight to a treasure chest jewelry box on her vanity. It was painted with romanticized pictures of natives wandering through wide, grassy plains. When she opened it, a figure inside started spinning like a ballerina, only it was a dancing man with a bow and arrow in his hand. Tinny music began clicking out of the music box to the tune of "One Little, Two Little, Three Little Indians."

"Music boxes were one of the first integrations of magic and technology," Tiger Lily explained. "The legend says a watchmaker built a clockwork watch with fairy dust in the gears that then played music when wound instead of telling time. It was only when another watchmaker without magic attempted to imitate his creation that a purely mechanical solution was discovered."

Tiger Lily set the music box in Gwen's hands. "But that must have been hundreds of years ago," Gwen argued. "Modern music boxes wouldn't be magical at all." She felt the weight of the mechanisms inside, and watched the little archer spin in a victorious dance, powered by a simple spring.

"Magic is harder to get rid of than you think," Tiger Lily told her. "Music boxes were conceived with magic, and that lingers in their nature. You're right; they aren't magic. But they're still receptive to it. So when an ordinary music box is exposed to an enchanted song, something magical just might happen."

Gwen closed the jewelry box and handed it back to Tiger Lily, who set it aside on the vanity. "Why do you have all this… *stuff* collected in your room?" She refrained from calling it junk, but that was what it looked like. It was just corny decorations that tried to make Native American culture looked exotic and mysterious.

"If I kept it out front, it would perturb most of my guests," Tiger Lily replied. "But if you're asking why I collect it in the first place… It reminds me of home." She touched the feathers of the vibrant headdress with an odd sort of longing.

"This doesn't look like your tribe though… not really. It isn't nearly as real." Gwen remembered the beautiful leather headband Dark Sun had given her, and the turquoise pendant Old Willow had gifted to Rosemary. Those things were not tacky decorations.

"This is true," Tiger Lily admitted, "but I'm not nearly as real as I used to be either. This stuff all came from the same vision of Native Americans that imagined my tribe into being. There's an echo of home in anything that portrays the mythical red man instead of Native Americans. I have to go out and be a Native American every day now, but I still like to fall asleep with reminders of what I used to be."

Gwen thought on this for a moment before announcing, "I think I have something for you." She dashed out of Tiger Lily's room and back to the couch where she had set down her backpack.

She rooted through the pack, but as she did so, Tiger Lily came out and told her, "I have to make a phone call first before it gets any later."

Tiger Lily made no attempt to obscure her conversation, so

Gwen didn't feel guilty for listening and trying to figure out what was going on.

With her phone, Tiger Lily paced around the kitchen waiting for someone to pick up. She continued to meander, nervously playing with a note-taking pencil in her hand. It looked like a good outlet for her apprehension—there wasn't any sound of distress in her voice. "Hi, Irene… I'm good, how are you? … Glad to hear it. I'll keep this short. I know you're scheduled to host tomorrow, but I was wondering if we could swap. … I can call the others and let them know. … It's a long story, I can tell you tomorrow, but I don't think I'm going to be able to make it out to your place. … Well, bring the pie over and I'll bake a loaf of huckleberry bread when we meet at your house. … Okay, great. No, no, I appreciate it. Okay. See you tomorrow. Say hi to Curt for me."

Tiger Lily hung up as the teakettle began to wail through its tiny steam hole. She set the phone aside and got the kettle off the burner. "Are you sure you don't want a cup of tea? I've got fresh honey. My friend Chayton keeps bees."

Gwen reconsidered. "Actually, that would be nice."

Tiger Lily pulled out two ceramic mugs. "I've got ginseng root, blackberry leaf, rose hip, and chamomile."

"Chamomile, please."

Tiger Lily plopped tea bags into the cups and dumped the steaming water in to start them steeping. "Are you going to go try to get your music box tonight?"

"No, not tonight. I'm pretty sure it's already like three AM Neverland time. I'll worry about that tomorrow, when I'm not so jetlagged."

"Sounds wise," Tiger Lily told her. "It will probably be best to get a good night's sleep and stay out of sight during the days. I don't mean to coop you up in the house, but I don't think it is a good idea for you to go out in the daylight… Also, as I'm sure you just heard, I'm having some friends over tomorrow."

"You think they can help us find the Piper?"

"I know they can, I'm just not sure if they will. Whatever you do with your sleep schedule, you'll want to be up before they get here at ten tomorrow morning." Tiger Lily brought the mugs over and set them on the table to finish steeping. A pink bunny was glazed onto the cup she set in front of her.

"I'll set an alarm on my phone." Gwen had found what she was looking for in her backpack and brought the cloth-wrapped bundle to the table.

"What's that?" Tiger Lily's eyes locked on the familiar geometric patterns of the beautiful weaving.

"I think I'm supposed to give it to you."

She handed over the bundle, and Tiger Lily took it, her hands betraying more excitement than her face did. As she unfolded the weaving and found the cornhusk doll inside, her eyes began to smile even before her mouth did. "Oh, little Singing Robin," she sighed. "Oh…"

She seemed unable to articulate a response beyond that. Gwen could tell she had just done a very good thing by reuniting a girl with her doll. "It's from Dark Sun."

Tiger Lily brushed the crinkled folds of Singing Robin's dress and smiled. "You are a good girl, Gwen. Any friend of Peter's is a friend of mine, but anyone my tribe trusts is someone I trust. I'm glad you're here, and I hope I'll be able to help you."

As Tiger Lily picked up her tea and started drinking, Gwen stirred some honey into hers. "That might be hard… I'm rarely able to help myself. I can't imagine it will be easy for anyone else."

"How did you come to find yourself here?"

"What do you mean?"

"You point to your little sister as your reason for being in Neverland, so why have you come here without her?"

"I'm not sure," she answered, taking a first sip of her tea as it continued to steep in a rich, floral flavor. "Peter asked me to. He needed me."

"You're growing quite fond of him, aren't you?" Tiger Lily leaned back in her chair. Gwen didn't know how to feel about this friendly interrogation.

"It's hard not to share his excitement," Gwen answered. "He makes me feel good about everything, including myself. He seems to have more faith in me than I do sometimes. I feel like I don't really know who he is though… all I know is that when I'm with him, it's like I'm looking at the whole world with rose-tinted glasses." She swished her tea around, a dark ocean inside of a small mug. "What do you think of Peter? You know him better than I do."

Tiger Lily gave a slight smile. "No, I don't. I've just known him longer and grown more attached. That's the thing about Peter… what you see is what you get. There's no surface to break beyond. He's got a dirt-covered and ivy-sprouting heart. He isn't hollow or shallow the way so many people are… he's just the same all the way down to his soul."

So full of layers, emotions, and contradictions, Gwen couldn't imagine someone having such a solid character. "I keep thinking there must be something going on inside his head I can't see. I don't understand why I feel so magical just being around him."

Tiger Lily propped Singing Robin up against the teakettle and admired the doll as she recalled Peter's nature with a sad fondness. "That's because when you're with Peter and you feel like you have the whole world inside of you… it's because when he's with you, you are the whole world to him."

CHAPTER 15

After their tea, Tiger Lily showed Gwen the spare bedroom. It was tidy and neat, with two twin beds and a baffling amount of toys and books for young readers. "Do you have guests often?" Gwen asked.

"Not often, but kids from around the reservation come around, especially in the summer when I keep my front door open in the day. Sometimes on the weekend, they show up too, and everyone around here knows they can leave their kids with me if they need babysitting. Sometimes though… kids spend the night here. Some of these kids… their houses can get pretty loud and rowdy. I like them to know they can always come here. I should warn you, if any kids show up at night, you'll get demoted to the couch."

"Of course," Gwen replied, looking at a mobile hanging in the corner of the room. Tiny jungle animals were spinning in slow motion.

"Do you have pajamas?" Tiger Lily asked. Gwen pulled her polka-dotted pajama bottoms out of her bag. "Very nice. If you need anything else, feel free to poke around or come wake me up."

Gwen was eager to call it an early night. As soon as Tiger Lily left, she got out of her felt skirt and paisley blouse in order to pull on her pajamas. She nuzzled into the bed nearest the window, but it was cold in her camisole. Almost tired enough to fall asleep anyway, she got up and grabbed Jay's sweatshirt. She wrapped herself in the oversized hoodie and curled back under the covers, but now the sweatshirt smelled like Peter.

She fell into sleep, wading into it, and then dropping off into the deep. Exhausted by everything that had happened since she woke up that morning, Gwen let sleep claim her without a fight.

While she slept, strange and unfamiliar dreams moved through her mind. She felt aware she was asleep, yet still caught in a dream she had no control over. She tossed and turned, always surrounded by sleep and the boyish smell of clover and spice that Peter had left on the sweatshirt. When Gwen's stressful sleep finally stirred her back awake, she checked the cracked screen of her phone. The time was little past one in the morning.

It was so novel to have a functioning cell phone again. She loved that the battery did not drain while she was in Neverland. As soon as she came back to the real world, her phone behaved as if she'd never been away. There were several texts and chat messages waiting for her, but they were all from the first few weeks of her disappearance. Her inbox was overflowing with emails from colleges, peers, and websites that were aware she had stopped visiting them. She didn't want to read through any of it.

She felt surprisingly awake considering the time. She couldn't remember exactly when she'd gone to sleep, but it had been little past eight in the evening. Five hours later, she was feeling ready for an adventure. It was probably morning somewhere in Neverland. Peter, Rosemary, and the others would be stirring now, too. Gwen was with them in spirit and consciousness, somehow unwilling to latch onto the reality that she was stationed far away from their haven.

It was depressing to wake up alone in a spare bedroom on an Indian reservation so far—and yet so close—from her home. Foxglove's purple glow was dim with sleep as she cuddled into the pincushion pillow Tiger Lily had provided for her. The wind-chime whistling snores of the fairy signified a heavy sleep. Glancing back at her phone, Gwen realized how much power she had in her hand.

She opened her texting app and began drafting a message. She only had a hundred and sixty characters to work with, and Gwen knew what she wanted to communicate wouldn't take nearly that many. Still, she wrote and rewrote with her thumbs, feeling electrified with every tiny buzz of haptic feedback her phone gave. Her rising heart rate should have warned her against sending the text, but it only egged her on:

Can you keep a secret?

It took a minute, but Jay texted back:

GWEN? Holy shit!

Where are you!?

Gwen didn't respond as these messages came in—she just waited. After a moment, the text she was waiting for came through:

Yes.

CHAPTER 16

SHE HADN'T THOUGHT THIS FAR AHEAD. EXCITED BEYOND MEASURE, SHE texted, *I still have your sweatshirt.*

His response was instantaneous: *I've got your sweater too.*

Her fingers tripped over the screen as she tried to type the simple phrase, *We should trade.*

Do I get to know where you are? he asked.

It was Friday night according to her phone—Gwen wouldn't have known otherwise—so she dared to ask, *Can you meet me out at Lake Agana?*

In a moment, she got a response: *Yeah, in like forty minutes.*

Ample time to get from Tiger Lily's house back to where she had landed earlier that day. She could meet with Jay, and then get back home in time to finish an eight-hour night of sleep before Tiger Lily's company arrived in the morning. As she threw on her clothes, her phone buzzed again. *Are you doing OK?*

She smiled, her face illuminated by the glow of her phone screen as she absorbed his concern. *Definitely,* she typed back. *Can't wait to see you.*

She felt silly getting ready to go see Jay in these outdated clothes, maybe even sillier than she had when she flew to reality in them. The felt skirt and paisley blouse didn't look like anything someone her age would wear. Then again, hadn't Jay praised her for being so strange and unbelievable when she showed up in her sundress to his house party? For as well as he did in the shallow perceptions of their peers, he seemed to give little weight to appearances. Gwen tried to remind herself that Jay had kissed her mere days after turning down Jenny Malloy. This man had the girl's swim team captain throwing her blonde, manicured self at him and he was *still* more interested in her.

She tried to use that to force perspective on the situation—what could go wrong if he actually liked her for who she was? Still, Gwen's nerves wanted to take her through a thorough examination of all the ways in which she could come off as an utter idiot.

She snuck out of her room with Jay's sweatshirt, being careful not to disturb Foxglove, who was sound asleep on her pincushion bed. Tiger Lily's door was closed and her lights were off, so Gwen had no worries as she laced up her shoes and grabbed her satchel. She left the front door unlocked behind her as she stole away, making sure she would be able to creep back in before the morning light started inching over the horizon.

She walked back the way she came. At least, she appeared to. No bystander who might have seen her would have realized that Gwen was flying just barely above the ground. She swung her legs to imitate her own gait, but avoided crunching on gravel and waking any of the dogs in the neighborhood. Once she made it to the forest, she took more liberties with her flight.

Aside from a few camping trips back when she was still in scouts, Gwen had never spent much time in the wilderness after dark. Neverland didn't count. She knew there were no foxes, coyotes, spiders, or rats creeping the jungles of Neverland and threatening to surprise her. Gwen wasn't so sure about the forest surrounding Lake Agana. She hovered four feet off the ground, which she imagined was high enough to avoid any animals on the ground, but not so high that she would risk running into bats and owls. She comforted herself thinking the animals of this forest would be inclined to avoid anything as big as her that could fly.

She knew she could walk two miles in forty minutes, so she was confident that even with the deterrent of the dark, she would still be able to make it flying. Retracing the steps she and Peter had taken was impossible, but she had her cell phone and its GPS at her disposal. She tried to set up navigation to plot a course for Lake Agana State Park, but "flying" wasn't a transportation option. It was too dark to find the walking trails, so she settled for watching her little blue GPS dot move across the screen's map as she headed toward the lake.

Once she was confident of her direction, she glided through the trees like a bird of prey on holiday. She was more excited than she'd been in months, knowing she zoomed toward Jay. She was sneaking out to see a boy! Gwendolyn Hoffman, of no reputation at Polk High School, was flying through the forest on her way to meet with an attractive senior boy. It didn't register in her giddy mind that the flying should have been what felt impossible and exciting. She managed to reach the lake without running into any major tree branches, and then flew around the edge of the elongated lake much faster without the trees to dodge. She wasn't brave enough to cut straight across—should her flight give out, falling into the bitter cold of the lake water would be disastrous.

As she approached the grassy bank of the eastern shore, she fell onto her feet and jogged the rest of the way toward the maple tree where she was almost certain a young man leaned against the trunk. She felt fearless. If it wasn't Jay, she knew she could fly away.

She passed a picnic bench and watched as part of the maple's shadow peeled away. Jay walked over, her cardigan sweater in his hand.

"Hey," he called.

Gwen's heart stopped, and it almost stopped her feet with it. "Hey, Jay."

He held out his arms—a noncommittal invitation for a hug. She was happy to walk into his arms. First and foremost, they were friends, weren't they?

"How have you been?" he asked, his voice full of curious excitement. "What's happened to you?"

"I've been great," she gushed. "How are you? What happened at the party? I'm so sorry I bailed on you."

She pulled out of his arms a little, just to see his face, but Jay took it as a signal that the hug was over. He let go of her and was empathic as he told her, "No, don't think twice about it. I'm glad you got out. That was some scary shit." He shook his head, recalling the traumatic night.

"What happened after I left? What did the cops do?"

"You're not going to believe this," Jay explained, "but they left."

"They just left?"

"They didn't even confiscate the alcohol! They didn't ask for any names or make any threats… except for when you vanished. They wanted to know who you were."

This was discouraging news. "Oh."

"We didn't tell them," Jay insisted, wanting to make sure she knew he hadn't ratted her out. "When they asked me where you went, I told them you must have gone out on the roof and down to the porch to get away. I said I didn't know who you were, that you had said your name was Sarah, and I thought you were a friend of Troy's. He had no clue who you were, but then everybody got the drift and pretended to realize you were some weirdo who had just crashed our party."

"And then what happened?"

"They told us to knock it off and sent everyone on their way home, but that was it. Just a warning. When the officer who found us first came back down, they grilled us really hard about some missing kid. I guess they had bigger fish to fry. The other one went up and searched, but neither of them could find anything. They didn't care about anything else."

Gwen wandered closer to the tree and sat down against it. "That actually makes a lot of sense," she told him. Remembering how much trouble Jay, Claire, and everyone could have gotten into, she shuddered and apologized. "I'm so sorry."

Jay looked confused, and Gwen regretted even broaching this conversation.

"What do you mean? Do you know who they were looking for?"

She grimaced and admitted, "I think they were looking for me; they just didn't expect me to be so old."

His eyes narrowed, and his tone became cautious and serious. He hunched down beside her. "Are you in trouble, Gwen?"

"I didn't do anything wrong," she burst out. "I just might have aided in the abduction of my little sister… or run away with her, depending on how much autonomous decision making you attribute to children."

"You have a sister?" Jay sank down, sitting beside her under the maple tree.

"Yeah. Rosemary is eight. She's adorable. So when my decision was to let her run away or go with her, I went with her."

"So you've just been on the lam with a fourth grader all this time?" He picked up her arm and examined it. Gwen almost shuddered to feel his fingers on her skin. "It looks like that bad burn you had healed up pretty well. I had no idea what happened to you, but I didn't think you were just sick. Apparently, your parents have been telling people you have mono." He looked amused. "I'll give you credit—you've got guts to bail on school."

Gwen hadn't stopped to look at it in that light. "It just kind of happened. I mean, nothing's more important than school, and I know I'm supposed to be sending out college apps next year, but…"

"Family is more important." Jay was adamant. "It sounds like your sister's got some serious issues with authority, and she's dragging you along with her. Of all the reasons I've heard for dropping out, I think that's the best."

"I don't know. I'll go back." Wasn't that a reality? Sooner or later, everyone wandered home from Neverland. She'd heard one of the officers say that himself. Had she really abandoned high school? Was she going to have to be one of those weird GED kids when she got back to reality?

"Okay, taking a semester off then. That's more reasonable." He laughed. "I have to admit, when Gwen Hoffman drops out of school, that's cause for alarm, right?"

She thought he was trying to convey she'd had an admirable commitment to school, but her inner insecurities pushed the idea that he was somehow laughing at her.

"So, tell me," he continued, "what's with the dress? You look like my grandma."

The insecurities of her nervous mind lurched forward like a transmission switching to a higher gear. She reminded him of his grandmother. She never should have shown up, not in clothes like these.

"Take out your hair," he requested. Gwen took it like an order. As she shook out her ponytail and let her long, ash-brown hair down, he laughed and ran his fingers through it. "Yeah, my grandma was a total hippie. She's got this picture from high school that looks just like that."

"Thanks." She didn't know if she should be grateful for the remark. Thanking him just seemed like the least awkward response.

"She was really pretty when she was young. When I knew her, she was this finicky old lady, super worried about how fast dust collected on her furniture… but when I saw that picture, I could see how my grandpa ended up falling in love with her."

He smiled, and Gwen knew that nothing was wrong with her in his eyes, and his eyes were the only ones that mattered. Uncertain how to respond, she handed his sweatshirt to him. "Here's your hoodie back. Sorry I stole it."

"It's all good. I hope it kept you warm." He handed her the cardigan she'd left with him, and they traded garments without breaking eye contact.

"So how was homecoming?" Gwen asked, pulling her sweater on.

"Eh," Jay shrugged, "it was alright. I ended up going with

Ashley Richards. I don't know if you know her. She lives like three houses down from me, so we've known each other since kindergarten. Anyway, neither of us had dates so we just decided to go together. The game was a lot more fun. We beat Clinton High 28-20."

She was happy and satisfied with this answer—primarily because it did not contain the name Jenny Malloy. Gwen didn't know Ashley, but it was obvious she was some childhood friend unworthy of envy. "I wish I could have been there to see you play in the big game."

"I wish you could have been there for the dance," Jay responded, lighting up all the right parts of her heart. "It would have been a lot more fun with you there. I kind of thought you might show up... I mean, you weren't at school, but I figured it wasn't totally out of the realm of possibility you would just show up like you did at the party."

She imagined an alternate reality where she had come home in the knick of time and whirlwinded off to homecoming, still smelling of magic and glittering with pixie dust. The enchantment of it would have been lost on her peers, who were in no way trained to recognize real magic, but Jay would have seen her and laughed openly, full of kindness and joy.

"So, are you going to tell me what happened after I left you upstairs at the party, or are you going to try to maintain this alluring air of mystery?" Jay asked. "I have to warn you, if you pick mystery, I'll still try to figure you out, and I'm not too bad with this brain of mine."

"Okay, I'll tell you what I've been up to... but you have to promise not to get mad when you don't believe me."

Jay looked both skeptical and amused. "I can promise I won't get mad, but I can't promise I won't believe you. I'm sorry to inform you, but I've already started believing in some of your unbelievable things."

She giggled. He was using that word again—unbelievable. She was unbelievable. "Like what?"

"Like how you got out of the house from upstairs when there's no way in hell you could have gotten on the roof and down off the porch." He gave her a severe look, conveying he was onto her impossibilities, even if he still had no idea what those impossibilities were.

"You say that like you think I just flew away."

"At this point, that's looking like one of the more reasonable explanations. For a long time, I thought you were still upstairs, hiding somewhere. Once everyone left, I called for you and expected you to come out… but you were just gone."

"I'm sorry I didn't have a chance to explain," she whispered.

"It's fine. I enjoyed the puzzle, wondering how this beautiful, mysterious girl had disappeared. So correct me if I'm wrong, but I think this has something to do with it…"

From out of the letterman jacket he was wearing, Jay pulled a small sandwich bag that was empty but for a little bit of sparkling substance in its corner. A mix of green and gold, Gwen recognized Dillweed and Hollyhock's pixie dust.

She was impressed with him. There wasn't a lot of pixie dust collected, and she knew the fairies would have left little more than what he had managed to scrape up. He'd caught her red-handed in something she wasn't ashamed of—the sensation was unfamiliar. "You're really bright, Jay. You sure you want to know all this?"

"Whatever is going on with you, I want to know." He reached out and took hold of her hand. "I told you, I can keep a secret."

She thought about all the ways she could begin this explanation, but they all seemed equally infeasible. In her silence, she heard the croaking of frogs amid the cattails, prompting an idea. As foolish as anything she could have said, Gwen sprung up and crept toward the lakeside, muttering, "Stay there a second," to Jay. Her eyes were well adjusted to the darkness by now; it was easy to watch for motion on the swampy edge of the lake. When she saw something bound between the cattails, she pulled out her cell phone in order to blast the screen's light at the poor bullfrog.

Stunned and blinded by the light, it stopped croaking and

froze, giving Gwen just the opportunity she needed to reach down and grab the slimy creature. At this point, the frog began croaking in distress. She held it by its back legs so that she wouldn't risk squishing anything but its rubbery limbs. It was just like she used to do when she was little, and unlike so many of her friends, Gwen had never fallen out of practice with frog catching because as soon as she would have tired of the activity, Rosemary had been old enough learn.

Jay could not quite see what was happening, but he was aware that the croaking was coming toward him as Gwen returned to the maple tree. "Do you have a frog?"

"A big old bullfrog," she informed him. Tucking her cell phone back into her satchel, she plopped down beside him again. "Hi."

"Hi." He laughed. "What are you planning on doing with that ugly thing?"

"Don't call him ugly!" Gwen feigned offense to keep him laughing. "You can't even see him. I think he's very handsome. Maybe even as handsome as you."

"I'm flattered," he sarcastically replied.

"Dump the bag," she commanded.

"The what?"

"The bag full of magic. Dump it on him."

His curiosity allowing no other option, Jay complied. Gwen was impressed with her own confidence and how willing he was to follow her instructions. As he shook the sandwich bag, the green and gold dust danced out and came to life in the moonlight. "This isn't going to hurt him, is it?" he asked.

"I thought you didn't like him."

"I didn't say that. I just think he's ugly. I wouldn't want him to get poisoned or anything."

"He'll be fine. I wouldn't hurt him."

The bullfrog was the only one who was seriously worried. He continued to croak, his low rumble like a broken brass horn. The fairy dust did not just catch the glow of moonlight, but began to actively glitter on his amphibious skin. Gwen eased her grip and felt him lift out of her hand a second before Jay could see that the frog was flying.

"Whoa." His wide eyes spoke volumes. He reached out and poked the bullfrog, pushing it through the air and waiting for it to fall back down. It kicked its webbed feet as if it thought it was swimming, but could not manage much motion until it attempted to jump. Leaping through the air, it landed even higher up, still perched on nothing. Uncomfortable with this height, it was more successful when it attempted to swim back down toward the ground. Intermittent leaps and strokes back down kept it busy while Jay and Gwen watched it.

"Oh man," Jay muttered. "I do not envy that thing."

Gwen looked at him; his eyes were transfixed on the now glowing frog. "Why not?"

"He looks so out of his element. All of his life, he's been learning to swim and jump, and now he's in the air where neither of those skills are useful. What do you think he's even trying to do right now?"

She stared at the frog, his buggy eyes scanning the darkness for something familiar a solid yard above ground. "Probably trying to make his way to Neverland."

When she looked back at Jay, he was staring at her with far more interest than he had even given the flying frog. "Is that where you've been?"

"What do you want to know?" she asked, smiling.

He looked happy to hear the question. "Everything."

CHAPTER 17

GWEN DIDN'T TELL HIM EVERYTHING. SHE WAS ACUTELY AWARE THAT she was in the middle of a war and she had clandestine information she shouldn't be revealing to anyone who couldn't fly. Even still, there was more to say than she could have fit into a single night. As she spoke, she melted into Jay's arms. The bullfrog leapt away toward the lake, and at some point, they heard a distant splash when the fairy dust finally gave out and he returned to the water. Sitting against Jay with his arms wrapped around her, Gwen's hands were free to gesticulate with the wild intensity that her stories deserved.

She told him about Rosemary and the tales she would tell her little sister, and how those bedtime stories motivated Rose to return for her the night after she vanished. She told him, in length, about the officers who had shown up to her house and how they belonged to the same mysterious Department of Anomalous Activity as the cops who busted the party.

There was definitely a point at which Jay started believing her. His face contorted in confusion as he listened to everything she was telling him, but as he pieced together all the strange details, he started to fathom the reality of her story. Prior to that moment, Gwen suspected he had only been playing along with some imagined game, trying to playfully goad a real answer out of her to explain everything about these events that was causing him such violent cognitive dissonance.

He nodded along, amazed and disturbed whenever he could confirm some aspect of what she told him. He found himself agreeing that the police car had lacked any insignia, and that the glitter he'd found did cause a light numbing feeling in his hand when he'd touched it.

She avoided discussing her father's work with the economy and skipped the subject of the Piper altogether. She was careful not to speak of Tiger Lily, or bring up Peter's plans for a new invasion. She did mention the Invasion of '08, but Jay had no memory of it.

Her throat became dry as she chattered away, telling him all sorts of inconsequential details about Neverland. She came to an abrupt stop and tried to turn around to face Jay. She was still leaning against him, and he didn't let her move. "What time is it?"

"Does it matter?" he asked. "I want to hear more about this Neverbird… why doesn't it like you?"

"I have to get back before… well, before morning." She checked her phone. It was minutes to five. She'd been out here for four hours, and it was only another five until Tiger Lily's friends arrived. "I need to go. I've got a big day tomorrow."

"Doing what?" Jay pried. "Catching leprechauns?"

"I'm not sure yet, but I want to have some sleep for it."

"Let me give you a ride," he offered, letting go of her and getting to his feet as well. "Where are you staying?"

"That's classified information." She kissed his cheek. "Besides, it'll be faster to fly."

He kissed her back, on the lips.

"Are you going to be around the next few days?"

"Yeah, a few days. I'm not sure how long."

"So I'll get to see you again?"

"I think so." The words slipped out from behind her smile. "I hope I didn't take you away from a fun Friday night."

"Nah, the guys and I were just hanging out and playing *Call of*

Duty at Michael's when I got your text. Don't worry—I didn't tell them I was going to meet you."

Gwen didn't respond. She knew she trusted him, and her attention was so much better focused on the grey color of his blue eyes in the dim of moonlight.

"I guess I'll see you later." Jay pulled her into one last hug.

"Yeah. See you later." Gwen took a deep breath, savoring the smell that had clung to his sweatshirt for so long, and longer still in her imagination. Jay was so much more potent than his sweatshirt. In person, he smelled like his usual, charcoal-covered self.

He kissed her, and Gwen felt his tongue in her mouth, all alien and wonderful.

They parted like static, like a video that couldn't load fast enough and was rendered in jerky, pixelated frames. She was too excited to move seamlessly. Her emotions were going so much faster than her body and mind could load them.

"Bye, Gwen," Jay said, backing away and starting toward the trail to the parking lot.

"Bye, Jay," she called back, trying to fidget less with her body than she did inside herself. She turned around, trying to maintain her cool, but then dashed off and took to the air, wondering if Jay saw. She couldn't bring herself to look back. She feared it would break the spell that was now filling her with the bubbly happiness she needed to fly.

She hurried back through the forest without the aid of her GPS. Arriving at the edge of the woods, it became apparent that her calculations were off. Breaking past the wall of the forest, she dropped down to the ground almost half a mile away from the gravel road that led to Tiger Lily's house. Now comparatively conspicuous in the moonlight, she resigned herself to walking the extra distance without the cheating use of magic.

Away from Jay, her fatigue washed over her like a series of waves, at last dragging her down with a powerful undertow of exhaustion. The cold December air was biting at her, and her feet couldn't keep pace with how tired she'd become. She remembered to hover along the gravel for fear of waking the dogs, but aside from that singular burst of awareness, she felt non-functional. Slinking back into the pale blue trailer house, Gwen closed the door behind her. She didn't breathe easy until she was back in her pajamas and cozy in bed. It took her a moment to warm under the covers, but as soon as she did, her mind allowed her to thud into sleep as hard as her head had thudded to the pillow.

Her rustling did not disturb Tiger Lily, however, fairies kept very different sleeping rhythms than people. Tossing and turning in the midst of vengeful dreams, the slight stimulus of Gwen returning woke the fairy. In a groggy haze, it occurred to Foxglove that the girl was returning from somewhere, but this knowledge seemed inconsequential. Unlike her friend Hollyhock, curiosity was not woven into Foxglove's being. She turned over, frustrated only that she had been woken. Too tired to act on her contempt, she nuzzled against the pincushion and went back to her furious and powerful dreams with her clenched, sleeping body and her gnarled, dreaming face.

But Gwen was already sound asleep, dreaming in bright colors and forceful glee where she could have everything, and all without consequence.

CHAPTER 18

GWEN WOKE THE FOLLOWING MORNING WITH TIGER LILY'S HAND shaking her shoulder. In her exhaustion last night, she'd forgotten to set an alarm on her phone. Tiger Lily had already opened the blinds, and she seemed to be only an extension of the unwanted daylight to tired Gwen.

"I'm sorry to wake you," Tiger Lily apologized, "but the girls will be here in half an hour. I made eggs and toast. You should eat breakfast before they get here."

Foxglove was already awake and raring to go. She flitted into Gwen's face with far more assertive energy. Pixie dust fell into her eyes, creating an alarming feeling of numbness that she tried to blink away as she got up.

She shuffled through the clothes in her backpack—all frilly and feminine dresses from the chest in the underground home. Tiger Lily saw, and, before she left, offered, "Would you like to borrow some clothes? I just worry you'll stand out in those."

The idea of wearing actual, modern clothes appealed to Gwen. After so long in play dresses in Neverland, jeans and a T-shirt sounded like a luxury.

Tiger Lily brought her just that, as well as a belt to make sure the jeans stayed up. Gwen liked the red stallion on the metal belt buckle. She hoped it distracted from how many times she'd had to fold the tan jeans' cuffs in on themselves to roll them up. Tiger Lily was much taller than she was. The dark T-shirt had a bear printed on it in red, white, and black. The Native American design was so much nicer than all the tacky objects Tiger Lily had collected in her room to remind her of the redskins.

In the kitchen, Tiger Lily served the eggs. She was dressed much nicer today. She was in a short, cream-colored dress and tan leggings. From what Gwen could tell, Tiger Lily clung to earthy tones and leathery colors even now that she was forced to dress like a modern adult. Gwen thought it was sweet how she had done her hair in two tight pigtail braids. She could imagine her, years ago, the young and proud daughter of a redskin chief.

As Gwen ate her fried eggs and white bread toast, Tiger Lily finally explained exactly what was going to happen that morning.

"They'll be here in fifteen minutes," she announced, glancing at the stopped clock. "We have a book club. We take turns hosting. It'll only be a few women, but they have a… similar background, in a sense. It's hard to explain, and I don't want to gossip about them right before you meet them."

Her mouth full of food, Gwen covered it as she spoke. "But that's what gives them the resources to help us find the Piper?"

"Yes, the resources," Tiger Lily answered, "the willingness… I'm not sure about. They might need some convincing."

"Is that something I can help with?"

"Hopefully, but I'll have to warm them up to the idea first." Tiger Lily began taking the dishes out of her drying rack and towel drying them. "They can't see you when they get here. I can't have their guard going up as soon as they walk in."

"Okay." She tried not to take it personally, although she did wonder what about her made her so dangerously repulsive. "What's the plan then?"

"I'm going to try to feel them out and figure out if they'll help us. That's a best-case scenario. If not though… I'm not going to broach the problem if I don't think they'd be willing to assist. I'm just going to try to get as much information out of them as I can without letting on that I need something from them." Tiger Lily put her spatula and frying pan away, and Gwen suspected she was anxious beneath her calm surface. "In that event, you should be privy to our conversation. I can hide you in the coat closet. It's not ideal, but I think you could definitely sit in there and eavesdrop for two or three hours while they're here. You could just go out or stay in your room if you preferred, but I think it would be better for you to hear exactly what they say."

"Yeah, totally," Gwen agreed, mopping up her egg yolk with the last of her toast. "I want to hear them. I'll be fine in the closet."

"And, hopefully, you won't even have to be there the whole time. Between the four of them, certainly one of them will be in a position to help."

Tiger Lily cleared Gwen's spot at the table while the girl moved the vacuum cleaner and all the shoes from the closet to the guest room. Once there was room for her to sit, Gwen situated herself and closed the slatted wooden door. She pushed all the coats aside and made herself comfortable so that she would not have to rustle anything while hiding inside. She was excited to eavesdrop. She'd never done it in good conscience before, but Tiger Lily was explicitly instructing her to listen in on this conversation. Through the slats in the door, Gwen had a perfect view of the couch and the chairs Tiger Lily was moving into the carpeted segment of the room. Her view of the door wasn't quite as complete, but it would work.

She had only been in position for a few minutes before she heard a sharp knock at the door. Gwen refrained from checking the time on her phone, on the off chance that the glow would be obvious from the other side of the door.

Tiger Lily answered the knock, and Gwen heard more than she saw as the women came in.

"Lily," a shrill voice cried, "it's *so* good to see you."

"How have you been? How *are* you?" another asked, her voice breathy.

"I'm doing well. It's good to see you both."

Gwen saw the women take turns drawing Tiger Lily into hugs. The angle of the slats made it impossible to see their faces or figure out which voice belonged to which body. They both clutched identical books, but one woman was deathly thin and had a tiny, boxy purse while the other carried a massive black shoulder bag and extra weight.

"Irene's parking now; she'll be here in a minute. Are we the first ones here?"

"Yep, right on time," Tiger Lily told the shrill woman.

"Oh, I'm sorry we're early."

"No, I think it's ten o'clock to the minute. You're perfect."

The shrill woman laughed, "Oh, I try. I try."

"Come on in, make yourselves comfortable. Elisa can't make it today."

"She can't?" The breathy woman sounded devastated. "I thought she was bringing the wine."

"I think Bella is bringing the wine." The shrill woman came into full view as she sat down on the couch directly across from the closet. Her dirty-blonde hair was pulled tight in a bun on the back of her head; it reminded Gwen of the pincushion Foxglove had spent the night sleeping on. Her naturally sharp chin was an unfortunate companion to her bony frame. She looked like one of the poster girls for anorexia that Gwen had seen in health class… but she was so old in contrast to the troubled teens pictured in those warnings. Her mouth was wide, and her teeth were bared in a smile that was unnaturally white.

"But she's not here either!"

"She's probably just running late," Tiger Lily announced. "Does anyone want tea?"

A new voice emerged at the door. Irene, Gwen assumed. "Tea? At this hour of the morning? I think I'll stick to the wine." The women all laughed at this.

"No, no, we should have tea, in the spirit of the book." The breathy woman sat down on the couch beside her slender friend.

Her chubby body was packed tightly into her modish black-and-white dress. Her hair was long, but looked frazzled from hard bleaching and hot iron curling. The summery southern California look was fighting for a chance to shine through the reality that her body was slipping into the autumn of her life.

"What do you mean?" the skinny one asked.

"The hero, he was English, remember? Christ, Cindy, did you read the book?"

"Of course I did!" Cindy defended. "I just forgot he was from England."

"Wales," Irene corrected. "Percival wasn't English, he was Welsh."

"Oh, whatever," the bleached hair replied.

"I don't get why authors write foreign men. The whole attraction of a British lover is the accent, and you don't hear the accent in a book," Cindy announced.

"You didn't like *Tryst on the Thames*?" Irene asked, taking a seat on a chair where Gwen could see her profile. Her short, full hair and long nose were both distinctive. It was hard to tell whether her hair was dyed. The gingery red was bright, but could have been her real hair color. Gwen was more distracted by the thick and colorful layer of makeup on her face.

"I liked it. I just wish it could have been a movie so I could hear the sexy accent."

"Why, Cindy, you have to use your *imagination*."

They all laughed again, as if there was some remarkably funny joke in that statement. Gwen noticed that whenever the women laughed, Tiger Lily's voice was absent from the chorus.

The final guest arrived, her high heels making a racket as they clicked into the house. "Sorry I'm late. Traffic was beastly."

Tiger Lily started to tell her it was fine, but the breathy blonde woman was louder and quicker. "You would know."

"It didn't help that the kids threw a fit and made us late to school."

"Little monsters," Irene remarked.

"Kids are wonderful," Cindy shrilly objected. "You'll get it, one of these days, when you and Curt finally have some of your own."

"I've got nothing against kids," Irene remarked, crossing her thick legs. "It's Bella's kids that scare me."

"They take after Harry's side of the family." Bella sighed.

"Clearly," Irene agreed.

"Where's Elisa?"

"Not coming," Cindy told her. "She's in charge of the country club's big Christmas party this year. I haven't heard a word from her since she started the project. Between that and her knitting, I doubt she had time to read the book."

"Oh, but what a *book*," Irene announced. "Didn't you just love the romance between Sarah Lynne and Percival?"

"Did you bring the wine?" the heavy blonde asked.

"Yeah—Lily, do you have a corkscrew?"

"Let me grab it."

"Don't start drinking *already*," Cindy warned. "You know it only ever makes you sleepy, Dawn."

Bella came into view with the wine, sitting in the chair opposite Irene, on the other side of the couch. Tiger Lily had strategically arranged the available seating so that Gwen would be able to see everyone's faces. She dragged the last kitchen chair over to complete the circle and sat with her back to the spy in the closet. She handed the corkscrew off to Bella, a short woman in an ostentatious black-and-yellow suit dress. Her face seemed disproportionately fat compared to the rest of her body.

"I'll get some glasses," Tiger Lily offered.

"Did anybody else read the book in one night? I couldn't put it down," Dawn announced.

"That," Bella replied, struggling to get the bottle open, "is because… you don't have… children." The cork popped and startled Cindy. "I read the whole thing in ten-minute bursts over the course of a month."

"That also explains the condition of your poor book."

"Reginald spilled grape juice on it…"

"Those children of yours, Bella," Irene remarked.

"That's nothing." Cindy was empathic, but it was hard to take her seriously when she was using the same high and excited tone she'd used for the entire conversation. "Priscilla found my copy and started *reading* it."

"She *didn't!*" Dawn gasped.

"She did!"

"That's not appropriate for her age at *all.*"

"I know!" Cindy agreed. "You think once you get past the preschool years, you're in the clear, but you've only got four or five years of reasonable childhood before they turn into precocious little preteens. I swear, I have to watch Priscilla and Angelica closer now than when they were still sticking crayons up their noses."

"And then Harry has the gall to come home and ask me what I've been up to all day," Bella groaned.

"As if herding children isn't a full-time job."

Dawn chimed in, "I think men are under the impression that our houses clean themselves."

"Oh," Irene exclaimed, "bless his heart—you wouldn't *believe* Curt. The other day, I mentioned that I needed to clean the oven and he told me I didn't have to… it was self-cleaning!"

They all laughed and poured rich, red wine into the glasses Tiger Lily handed out. They tossed their books on the coffee table and ignored them from that point forward.

"Makes you miss the old days, doesn't it?" Tiger Lily added, her voice even and calm, especially compared to her guests' expressive tones.

"Oh heavens, don't remind me about how good we had it," Bella sighed.

"I wouldn't mind it, if only Curt understood." Irene swirled her wine and shook her red hair. "He's got that blue-collar background… he thinks living in Birch Haven means we've made it somehow."

"We're comfortable," Cindy announced, "and the girls are happy. Considering everything, we all ended up in nice places." No one responded, and she admitted, "Albeit, the magic isn't really there anymore."

"That's putting it charitably," Irene scoffed.

"The magic hasn't been there since the honeymoon." Dawn groaned. "Everything else… that's just collateral damage."

"Are they still watching you?" Cindy asked.

Bella laughed and her neck jiggled with the motion. "They're watching all of us. They're just subtle about it."

"I don't know," Dawn remarked. "They check in, I'm sure… but they know we're not going to do anything."

"If you hadn't put up such a fuss, you'd probably be in the same boat, Lily," Irene added.

Tiger Lily addressed Dawn, "You're really not doing anything?"

The woman seemed taken aback. "What do you mean?"

"Oh, come on," Cindy goaded. "Do you mean to tell me that red velvet cake you made last meeting was baked with only Betty Crocker's help?"

"I learned to bake! Is that so hard to believe?"

"Don't be so defensive. Nobody's going to blame you for it."

"So I suppose your pumpkin pies are just squash and sugar?"

"You're cute, but I don't eat pie." With her figure, Gwen could believe it. Cindy continued, "But when it comes to the girls' dresses… there's only so much a sewing machine can do, and they shouldn't suffer just because I never learned to sew as well as my godmother."

"I don't believe this," Bella announced. "There isn't a speck of magic in our house—Harry wouldn't have it. *Our* kids are growing up without magic."

"No wonder they're such a mess," Irene muttered, sipping her wine so quickly after that it almost seemed that she hadn't said anything at all.

"Well, no one expected us to go cold turkey," Dawn admitted.

"They're not going to fuss over a little household help. I gave them all my spinning supplies, and they never asked questions after that."

"You were smart," Bella told her.

Irene nodded. "The only reason they're still keeping tabs on you, Lily, is you haven't given them any help or reason to trust you."

"It's not the same," Tiger Lily told them. "I can't just hand over a pumpkin or spinning wheel. They want Neverland."

"With all the grief Peter's giving them, you can't blame them," Bella replied, reclining in the kitchen chair and trying to make herself comfortable… an impossible task, from the looks of her tight suit dress.

"You lost the fight, Lily," Irene announced. "We all did. If you can't beat them, join them."

"At the expense of the entire island? Don't tell me you would have them wipe Neverland off the map."

"It's not *on* a map," Bella grumbled.

"Cindy, Bella," Tiger Lily pleaded. "Do you mean to tell me you've never told your kids about Neverland?"

"Of course, I did," Cindy answered, "but they were going to hear about it somewhere. Better from me than Disney."

Bella and Dawn shuddered.

"I made damn sure they knew it was imaginary before they ever got a hold of the story," Bella insisted. "It doesn't matter if Neverland exists or not—legends work fine either way."

"Dawn?" Tiger Lily asked.

"What?"

"What do you think? Do you really think there's no good in Neverland existing?"

"I can't imagine it matters what I think."

"It doesn't matter what any of us think," Cindy added. "There's nothing we could do either way."

Irene's eyes narrowed. "What's all this about, Lily? Why did you need to have us meet all the way out here today? What's really going on here?"

Tiger Lily looked over her shoulder to the closet. The women's eyes all followed. Gwen swallowed a nervous lump in her throat and stepped out.

CHAPTER 19

"WHO..." BELLA BEGAN, HER PUDGY FACE SLACK-JAWED. "NO. Never mind. I don't want to know."

No one was happy to see her, and Gwen felt the cold and vicious disapproval of the adults weighing on her. It seemed unfair. They didn't even know her, and already they didn't like her. Irene eyed her skeptically, and Dawn gave a dramatic sigh as she put her hand to her face. Cindy was in pure shock, an expression that fit her tiny facial features in an odd, cartoonish way.

"Lily," Irene began with cautious contempt, "what are you trying to do here?"

"It's just a girl," Bella announced. "We don't even know her name."

"I'm Gwen."

"I don't even know her name," Bella insisted, louder. "I think I left the stove on. So sorry I can't stay longer."

"Oh, pull yourself together," Dawn snapped.

"I don't have to deal with this." Bella picked up her bag and backed away from the group. "Harry would throw a fit if I got involved in something like this."

"You can't live your whole life in fear of him, you know," Tiger Lily told her.

"You don't even know what Lily's getting at here," Dawn added.

"And I'm not going to find out. I've got *kids* to worry about. I'm not going to start pulling magic back into my life and into their reality. They're going to grow up and live normally ever after."

"So… unhappy?" Tiger Lily asked.

"You should get out of here too, Cindy." Bella was already at the door. "I'll drive you home."

All eyes refocused on the slender woman fidgeting on the sunken couch. "I… I think I want to know what is going on. This isn't a lost boy, Bella. It's a young woman. I've no reason to think Lily would expose us to anything that would jeopardize us."

"Think of Priscilla and Angelica!" Bella exclaimed. The other women gave her fish-eyed apathy. As frustrated as they were with the unexpected appearance of a teenage eavesdropper, they were too intrigued to walk away. Bella appeared more shocked by her peers' reactions than Gwen's presence. "Well, I'm leaving, and I don't want to hear another word about any of this magic nonsense."

"You won't tell anyone, will you?" Tiger Lily asked, but she seemed confident she already knew the answer.

"And risk having them investigate *me*?" Bella cried. "No, I'm going to go home and make sure the stove is off. Have fun with this young lady… who is perfectly ordinary and not at all magical as far as I know."

Almost as mad as she was unnerved, she shut the door hard behind her as she left.

"At least she left the wine," Dawn joked, no hint of a smile on her face.

Everyone looked at Gwen again.

"Well, come here. Let's have a look at you," Irene demanded, waving her over. "Your name's Gwen?"

"Yes. It's a pleasure to meet you."

She didn't blink. "I sincerely wish I could say the same, young lady." She reminded Gwen of a teacher, with her strict tone and matronly expression. Irene surveyed the others' faces and then decided, "I guess the rest of us are staying. Long enough to hear what this is about, anyway."

Cindy nodded. Gwen felt uncomfortable in the company of someone who seemed so much older, yet so much frailer. Dawn was the first to formulate a question. "Is this one of Peter's girls? Is he here too?"

The question was demeaning, but Gwen did not sling back any hostility of her own. These women were reactionary and excitable, so Tiger Lily answered, "Gwen is Peter's emissary. I wouldn't jeopardize you by bringing him here."

"Public enemy number one, I hear," Irene casually remarked.

Cindy had an adverse reaction to this news. "Emissary? For what? What does he want from us?"

Tiger Lily paused, seeming to struggle with how to word her answer. In her hesitation, Gwen spoke up. "He's trying to unriddle the Piper's whereabouts."

A painful dread passed over her audience's faces. "Oh no. No, honey," Dawn told her. "I don't know who you are or how he roped you into this, but you need to get out. You don't want to find the Piper."

"Nobody wants to find the Piper," Cindy muttered.

"Peter does," Gwen assured her. "He's the only chance we have of rallying a resistance large enough to defend Neverland."

"Defend Neverland?" Dawn scoffed. "The war's been lost, young lady. Neverland is just a post-bellum battle."

"Neverland is still vibrant and strong," Gwen argued. "It has a rich fairy population and the prophecies of the mermaids guiding its strategy. It just lacks the manpower—or child power, I suppose—to hide it from the grown-ups' radar."

"Did she just say grown-ups?" Cindy asked.

"What about the redskins?" Dawn demanded, her voice cutting over Cindy's.

Tiger Lily kept a stoic face. "Still stronger than you ever gave them credit for."

"You're pretty grown up yourself," Irene remarked. "What

interest do you have in the fate of Neverland?"

As usual, Gwen's mind buzzed with an assortment of answers, many of them contradictory. "My little sister is there, and I want to know she'll be safe as long as she is."

"If Peter Pan comes anywhere *near* Priscilla or Angelica—" Cindy erupted.

"He won't," Tiger Lily assured her. "This isn't about you or your children. It's about the greater issue of children's autonomy and Neverland's right to exist."

"Well, good," Cindy grumbled.

"We're not going to hunt down the Piper for you." Dawn spoke with authority; she spoke for everyone. "We don't know where he is, and I, for one, would rather spend the holidays with my ogre of a mother-in-law than come within spitting distance of that awful man."

"I don't need your help finding him. We know how to find him. We're just missing a piece of the puzzle."

Tiger Lily crossed her arms and explained further, "Piper left riddles for how to find him."

"It's always riddles," Cindy muttered under her breath.

"One of the things Gwen needs in order to find him is—in his own words—a patch fit for a prince. Peter doesn't know I have you all here, but if anyone can figure out what Piper means by that, it'd be one of you."

The women got quiet. Gwen had a much better view of them now that she was not spying on them through the slats of the closet door. Irene had a nose that sloped the way magazines said noses were supposed to slope. It was one of the few things about her appearance that still looked at its peak. Little lines crept up around her eyes, as well as bags underneath them she barely managed to obscure with a liberal use of makeup. From a distance, she still could have passed for a twenty-something.

She could not say the same for Dawn, whose bronze glow was an artificial thing that existed only on her face. The rest of her skin was pale, and starting to sag with the combination of extra weight and age. Her bold bangs were clinging to the nineties' vision of youthfulness.

All she noticed about Cindy was how prominent her clavicle bone was at the collar of her V-neck sweater. She wore a long glass pendant around her neck, but it just drew the eye to her flat chest. She had a ridiculously small slice of Irene's pie on a plate in front of her, but she had not taken a single bite out of it.

"I don't want any part of this," Irene announced. "I understand you're doing what you think you have to, and I'm not going to stop you, but I'm not going to help you."

Cindy and Dawn exchanged looks, and Cindy asked, "Just a patch? If we gave you a patch, you'd leave us alone and go do… whatever it is you think will save Neverland?"

"It'll cost them more than that," Irene huffed.

Gwen ignored her. "The patch is all we need. Peter and the lost children will be able to manage the rest from there."

Tiger Lily, knowing Cindy better, thought to add, "We won't even need to tell Peter that you helped. Nobody outside of this room will ever know."

Cindy glanced at Irene for direction. Her mousy eyes begged for approval. "I won't stop you." Irene reclined into her seat and finished her wine with one final sip.

Dawn animated all at once and sprang into objection. "Cindy, no, Bella's right. You've got kids. You shouldn't be getting mixed up in this."

Cindy spoke quietly, as if afraid for what response her words would prompt. "It seems there ought to be at least one place left… if we let it all disappear, won't the stories get old and die too?"

"Stories don't die the way places and people do," Irene replied.

"But they do die," Cindy insisted, "and I don't know what we're going to do when all we have is the Frankensteins that Disney resurrected. Priscilla was amazed when she found out that *Peter Pan* was a book, a play, a movie… anything other than a cartoon. That's all she has, for all that we lived and did. A bunch of cartoons."

"Some of us don't even have that," Irene admitted.

"Don't make this about the kids," Dawn complained, once again burying her face in her hand.

"I don't know." Cindy looked like she was on the verge of tears, but her expression hadn't changed. She just perpetually looked like life was about to overwhelm her emotionally. "We chose to hand over our magic and assimilate. Nobody forced us to, not like this."

Irene pursed her lips, her eyebrows raised. The motion almost turned into a shrug. "That is a fair point."

"For God's sake," Dawn exclaimed, throwing up her hands. "Fine. If that's the consensus, who am I to argue?" She sounded like she wanted to argue and hash it out considerably more. "You're not doing this, Cindy. I'll go get her the patch. You've got your kids to think about. You shouldn't stretch your neck into this."

Cindy's stiff shoulders hunched back down, relaxed and submissive. "Thank you."

"That's real good of you, Dawn," Irene told her. She then looked at Gwen with harsh eyes. "You're very lucky."

"Thank you very much," Gwen told Dawn. "I hope it won't put you too far out of your way."

"It'll take some rooting around in the closet and a trip to the mall. As long as the black coats don't catch us at anything, it should be pretty painless."

"But that's a disastrous *if*," Irene insisted. "So mind your manners and reflect on how lucky you are, young lady."

Gwen was getting tired of being referred to as *young lady*. She sensed she would have to put up with a lot more patronizing before this affair was over.

"I vote we reschedule the meeting for next week to talk about the literary significance of Percival and Sarah Lynne hooking up in a flat just west of London," Dawn announced, standing up and then facing Gwen. "If you want the patch, let's just get this done with now."

"Next week is good for me," Irene agreed.

"I'll have to double check Priscilla's dance schedule, but I'm sure we'll find a time." Cindy got up and tried to stuff her paperback book into her boxy purse. It wouldn't fit.

Tiger Lily looked delighted; her slender smile spoke volumes. "Thank you, Dawn. I am in your debt."

"Yeah, yeah, yeah." Dawn waved a dismissive hand at her. "Come on, Gwen."

This command caught her by surprise. "I'm coming with you?"

"I sure don't want to get this mission of yours wrong, and if anyone catches me at it, I'm blaming you."

Gwen was reluctant to work with someone who exhibited such an unlikable mix of vapidness and conniving, but knew it was her best—if not only—option. "Should I bring Foxglove?"

"I don't know what you mean," Dawn replied, "but certainly not."

CHAPTER 20

Irene left to unblock Dawn's car in the driveway, but not before she slipped Dawn something out of her own purse. Gwen pretended not to see what was obviously meant to be a clandestine hand-off. The redheaded woman then drove Cindy home, and Gwen admired how odd their sleek cars looked in the environment of the reservation where trucks with rusted fenders were the norm. Gwen plopped into the luxury sedan's passenger seat and watched Tiger Lily wave goodbye. She felt like she'd just been taken as a prisoner of war.

Dawn was quiet until they were shut in the car and out of earshot. "We meet for our club every month and take turns hosting at our houses," she explained. "So every few months, we all drive out here when Lily hosts at her trailer. We wouldn't want her to feel self-conscious."

Gwen marveled at the awful sentiment, and the ludicrous thought that Tiger Lily could be made to feel self-conscious. Choosing to ignore the remark, she asked, "Are we going to your house to pick up the patch?"

"Yes, and we'll stop at the mall afterward. The patch is currently attached to one of George's jackets and will have to be removed." Dawn watched her rear view camera on screen as she backed out.

"At the mall? I don't think I should go to the mall..." Gwen tried to imagine just how bad it would be if someone who knew her saw her there.

"Don't worry about it," Dawn insisted. "You're with me. You'll be fine."

"Couldn't we take it off ourselves?"

"No can do. I gave up spinning, stitching, and fabric work as part of my deal with the Magic Relocation Program."

"Your deal with the—what?"

Dawn drove slowly and huffed at the gravel road as she heard it crunch under her tires. It was a bumpy drive off the reservation, but the car dulled the sensation. Strapped into the large leather seat, it occurred to Gwen that she hadn't been in a car since she drove home from school and found out Rosemary was missing.

"The MRP. It's what's going to be responsible for finding your friend Peter a family and—God help us—a school to go to."

While Dawn drove toward the highway, Gwen picked up the copy of *Tryst on the Thames* jammed between the cup holders in the car. There was a picture of two people on the cover who looked constipated and scantily clad. "So what's the book about?"

Dawn reached over without looking at her and snatched the book out of her hands. She flung it into the backseat. "It's a love story. It's not appropriate for you."

"I'm sixteen."

"If you're still playing house with Peter Pan, you're not old enough for it."

She was snide, but she had a point. As soon as they got back onto a paved road, Dawn punched the gas pedal and sent them rocketing along the highway.

"I appreciate your help," Gwen said, wondering if friendly gratitude would put Dawn in a more amenable mood.

"I can't imagine why you want it," she answered. "What on earth is a girl as old as you doing with Peter Pan?"

"Keeping my options open," Gwen answered.

"Ha!" The single laugh sounded mean spirited. "You're smarter than you look, but not nearly as bright as you think you are. You're so young. You can't see how many doors you're already closing. Do the black coats know you're in league with Peter?"

"You mean the Department of Anomalous Activity?"

"Yes, of course. Who else?"

"I'm not sure." Jay said the folks at the party hadn't ratted her out, but what had her parents told officials when *she* went missing too? "My parents have been telling my friends that I'm just really sick."

"I'm sure they reported you a runaway, for legal reasons, but normal cops would have dealt with it since you're not exactly in the target age range for the black coats to take note," Dawn told her. "But the officers will certainly figure you out if you summon the Piper. Then you're just like the rest of us—magic on your record."

"You make it sound like flying is a felony." Gwen tried to move her seat back, but there were too many buttons to figure it out. She tilted it back, moved it up, and even shifted it a little to the side before she discovered how to give herself more foot room.

"It doesn't show up on normal legal documents, but believe me..." Dawn craned her neck, watching for the street they needed to turn onto. "It follows you your whole life."

Gwen wasn't concerned with the future as Dawn saw it. Even in a worst-case scenario, she couldn't imagine ending up like this woman. In the silence that followed, Gwen only wondered why her parents had told her friends she was sick if they'd been legally obligated to report her as a runaway.

When they reached Dawn's house, she sloppily pulled into the driveway and turned off the car. Unbuckling and jumping out of the car, she said, "Stay put. I'll be back in a minute." Gwen felt like an antsy child, left in the parking lot in front of a dry cleaner. While she waited for Dawn to return, Gwen entertained herself by trying to spot differences between all the cookie-cutter McMansions on the block.

Two minutes into her wait, Gwen heard an electronic, crystalline chime—her phone notifying her of a new text.

Please be Jay. Please be Jay…

The desperate and excited prayer circled in her head as she scrambled to get her phone out of her purse as if it were a bomb she needed to defuse within seconds.

She sat in the car, smiling at Jay's simple text:

Hey :)

As the initial delight wore off, she began to overthink what the correct response would be. Before she could get too caught up in her misplaced analysis, Gwen shot back the exact same six characters to him.

It worked; he responded with something of more substance:

Just thinking of you. It was good to see you last night.

Gwen giggled out loud.

Ditto :) What are you up to?

Her cracked phone screen didn't even have time to go dark before he answered. She had his full attention.

Homework. I go to school :P

Another text arrived immediately after:

What are YOU up to, Miss Unbelievable?

Gwen felt her confidence spike. *Sorry*, she answered, *that's classified right now.*

The car beeped, startling Gwen out of her infatuated daze. She jumped in her seat, but the seatbelt restrained her.

Maybe you can tell me about it tonight? :)

"Who are you texting?" Dawn asked, an innocent and genuine interest in her voice.

Gwen hurried through her response, relying on shorthand to make her meaning clear: *maybe. g2g but ttyl*

"Don't tell me Peter has a cell phone," Dawn asked, peering over to satisfy her nosy curiosity.

"No." She shoved her phone back into her purse. "It was just a boy."

Dawn chucked a black-and-orange letterman jacket into the

backseat and strapped herself in. Starting the car, she turned on the radio where top-forty pop hits began playing at an elevator music volume. Gwen recognized Katy Perry's voice, but the song was one she'd never heard. An electrifying sense of disconnection grabbed her. She didn't listen to pop music often, but her teenage insecurity had demanded she at least be familiar with the hits that rose to the top of the charts.

"A boy?" Dawn asked, vicariously excited. "You looked awful happy staring at your phone there. Who is he?"

"He and I were in math class together at the start of the semester before I, you know, ran off with Peter."

"Oh," she replied. It made Gwen uneasy how much attention Dawn gave the conversation when she should have been checking mirrors as she backed out of the driveway. "I bet he didn't take kindly to that."

"He missed me," Gwen admitted, smiling. "He's glad I'm back in town."

"Does this young gentleman have a name?" Dawn's voice had some pep in it now, as if this was a topic she'd just been dying to fall upon.

"Yes," she answered, not wanting to go into the details. If magic was as damning as Dawn seemed to think it was, she probably shouldn't be actively adding people to her own list of associates.

"Oh, come on, Gwen," she chided. "I'm sticking my neck out for you and this silly patch of yours and you can't even tell me his name?

"James," Gwen answered. It was a common name, and not what he went by.

"Is he cute?"

"I think so." Her voice was noncommittal, but there was no way to say that without conveying the strong bias she had in his favor.

"Let me see a picture of him." Dawn's smile perked up like a puppy's ears. Her excitement was genuine, but Gwen couldn't help but notice how even when her mouth was full of straight, smiling teeth, her eyes stayed low in a sunken, sad expression.

Gwen fished her phone back out of her purse and was surprised by how much she was enjoying this conversation and the chance to show off her crush. She'd had no such opportunity in Neverland, and adults in reality had never taken an interest in her romantic life. Dawn may have dismissed the importance of Neverland, the Piper, and magic, but at least she understood how captivating a handsome boy could be.

At a stoplight, Gwen showed her Jay's best profile picture—one taken by his previous girlfriend on a camping trip last spring, short weeks before she left for college and they broke up. Gwen liked the picture because it captured his best expression—the way his eyes could be more happiness than blue, how his smile was always so earnest but mellow.

"Oh!" Dawn exclaimed making a dramatic, desirous face. "He *is* cute."

"The light's green." Gwen pointed to the traffic signal. The car behind them honked. She tried not to let on how validated she felt by Dawn's reaction.

"So tell me everything—what's he like?"

She proceeded to explain the menagerie of interests and traits that made Jay the wonderful and attractive person he was. Dawn was full of questions, but the nature of her questions revealed the startlingly shallow nature of her interest. It didn't matter to her that he was a gamer or a wonderful art student, but she was thrilled to hear he was homecoming king, and eager to know what position he played on the football team. There was a melancholy satisfaction to sharing her excitement about Jay with someone who had a functioning understanding of high school and boys—as opposed to dear Lasiandra—but Gwen had to wonder how much of what she was telling Dawn was really registering.

Dawn's planned community was not far from Franklin Square, the biggest shopping complex in the area. Gwen had spent plenty of long afternoons milling through the myriad shops in the commercial mall with Claire, Katie, and other peers. Those memories were all a silly blur of bra purchases, fur-lined boots, the occasional movie, and caffeinated beverages. Most of the things Gwen had bought at the mall were token investments in sociality. Bikinis and statement jewelry migrated to the back of her dresser drawers, never to be worn.

They pulled into the parking garage, but Gwen made the mistake of trying to get out of the car once they parked.

"Wait!" Dawn objected, adjusting the rear-view mirror. "I need to fix my makeup."

Gwen pretended to be patient.

Once Dawn's lips were an even shade of Coral Perfection, she grabbed the letterman jacket from the back and they headed into the mall. She led with a powerful stride, gripping her sagging black purse to her side and seeming to derive satisfaction just from hearing her uncomfortable high heels click against the tile of the floor. On a Saturday morning this close to Christmas, the mall was hopping. A potpourri of greasy, salty smells radiated from the food court, and seasonal music blasted over the speakers only to be drowned out by the chatter and clamor of the shoppers.

"I'm not sure I should be here," Gwen told Dawn, trying to keep pace with the woman who was plowing her way through the crowds. "What if someone recognizes me?"

"Don't worry, you're with me." They narrowly dodged a frantic mother driving her stroller forward like it was a cow catcher. "Nobody sees what they aren't expecting to see. The MRP makes sure of that. Hold onto this if it makes you feel more comfortable."

She reached into her purse—almost elbowing a man heading in the other direction—and pulled out her keys. She dropped them into Gwen's hands for inspection. The key chain was incredibly heavy. A glossy, black metal disk the size of a half-dollar hung on the keys and read: *MRP Anomaly Reduction Device, issued to Dawn Charleston 1.16.97 certified by the Department of Anomalous Activity.*

"I don't get it," Gwen replied, turning it over and trying to make sense of it. "How does this thing keep people from seeing us?" It felt like a painfully ordinary trinket.

"It's an intensely magical object that focuses all its magic into appearing non-magical and preventing anomalous activity."

"So it attracts any magic nearby..."

"And sucks it up like a black hole," she finished. "Everyone can still see you, but if anyone who would think it was *really weird* to see you pass by, they won't notice."

Testing the odd device, Gwen tried to fly an inch off the ground as they passed a pretzel shop and a stand selling a dizzying array of cell phone cases. She couldn't even manage that much while she held the metal disk. "So you just carry this thing around all the time?"

"Yep. Part of the deal with the Magic Relocation Program."

Gwen looked at the key chain, and then handed it to Dawn. "You can have it back."

CHAPTER 21

THE TAILOR OPERATED OUT OF A TINY SHOP WEDGED BETWEEN A department store and a service corridor. Gwen wasn't sure she'd ever noticed the shop before; she'd never needed to get anything altered or adjusted. The store's name, *A Stitch in Time,* hung in simple, blocky letters over the storefront. The left window was covered in a similar font, listing out all the services the shop provided: zippers replaced, pants hemmed, clothes adjusted, darts added, tears mended, girdles made, embroidery stitched… The list encompassed everything Gwen could think of doing to clothes.

As they walked in, the door detected their presence and responded with a perky chime. While they waited for someone to come out of the back, Gwen ogled the purses and dresses hung up on the walls of the tiny shop. The whole room wasn't much bigger than her bedroom. She was staring at a rack of thread and sewing kits when a short man came to the counter.

He had an impossibly bushy mustache and hair almost long enough to be pulled into a ponytail. His hair was a darker brown than his muddy eyes, which Gwen could easily see since he was almost exactly her height.

"Ah, Mrs. Charleston!" he exclaimed, setting aside a piece

of jam-covered toast and wiping his mouth with the back of his hand. His mouth disappeared under his mustache when he was not actively talking. "How are you?"

"Doing well, Mr. Schneider."

"How are you sleeping these days?"

"Not as well as I used to," Dawn admitted.

"Ah, who does at our age?" He had a kind smile, and a vest embroidered with leaves and vines that fit him snuggly. "I'm afraid I haven't finished the adjustment work on your gown yet… I didn't expect you back so soon."

"That's alright. I've come with a more pressing project."

"Is your husband's jacket tearing?" he inquired.

"No, no," she answered. "It just needs some… special attention."

The shopkeeper had a tape measure draped around his neck, giving him the quaint look of an old tailor. He raised a bushy eyebrow and glanced at Gwen before asking, "How special?"

"I need the fencing patch removed and replaced." She laid the jacket on the counter like a wounded animal. Mr. Schneider put on a tiny pair of square, rimless glasses and examined it as though he were a vet dealing with a critical patient.

"The patch is in good shape." Mr. Schneider mused. "I take it you have other plans for this?"

"Yes. My friend here has been looking for a patch, and we think this might be what she needs."

Mr. Schneider folded his glasses up and stared at Gwen with an almost frightening intensity in his eyes, like a mad scientist. "That would depend greatly on what purpose this patch is for."

Dawn looked to Gwen, signaling her to explain.

She coughed, realizing her throat was dry only as she went to speak. She had no idea who this man was or how magical he might be. "I need a very nice patch—one fit for a prince. It's going to be part of a gift, of sorts."

He nodded along with this explanation. "For a prince?"

"For someone who does a lot of patching," Dawn cut in.

Mr. Schneider did not look happy about this. "Am I right in assuming this project of yours is of such an unusual nature that anyone found assisting you in it would face rather unfortunate repercussions?"

"It's possible," Dawn announced, aggressively apathetic. "But I don't know what my friend wants to do with this patch, and you don't know who my friend is, so certainly it isn't unreasonable to expect a tailor to take a patch off for an old client without asking questions."

His smile turned mischievous as he told her, "I've known you to touch a needle but once in your life—who would I be to question that you are bringing me such a simple sewing job?" He turned the jacket inside out and felt the patch, shaped like swords crossing. "I can take it off without hurting the patch and get an identical one on… it will take at least two hours, however. As I'm sure you're aware, we are not dealing with an ordinary patch."

"That's fine. We can run some errands while you work."

"Good, good," he replied, putting his glasses back on and bundling up the jacket in the other hand. He reached for his jam toast, but thought better of it. "I'll see you this afternoon then, Mrs. Charleston."

"Thank you, Mr. Schneider," Gwen announced.

He looked back over his shoulder, his bushy eyebrows raised. "Ah, miss… do not thank me now. This will buy you so much less than you want, and so much more than you have bargained for."

22

When Mr. Schneider announced they would have two hours to kill in the mall before he finished with the patch, Gwen braced herself for a boring afternoon with an unlikable woman twice her age. She was not prepared for Dawn's giddy excitement and unlimited, consumerist imagination.

She took Gwen to the pretzel shop, where they had a light lunch of fluffy, salty pretzels, and some complicated drink from Dawn's favorite coffee stand. Gwen was expecting more from the drink after hearing how many special instructions were given during ordering. It turned out to be sugared milk with coffee flavor, whipped into a strange consistency.

"We should go to the salon," Dawn announced, looking dainty but sounding obnoxious as she slurped her latte. "I didn't want to be rude and say anything about your hair, but as long as we're here, we really should get it fixed."

"My hair?" Gwen asked. "What's wrong with it?"

"Darling, I don't know what you did with it—and I'm sure I don't want to—but it looks like you lit it on fire."

Gwen had forgotten about the bolt of baby lightning that had lashed out at her and sizzled half her hair in the storm with Peter. The damage wasn't so obvious when she had it pulled back in a ponytail, but Dawn's critical eyes had seen the split ends and frazzled strands tucked away among the healthy bulk of her hair.

Before she was even done with her low-fat vanilla, something-something latte, Dawn dragged her to the other side of the mall, promising she'd take care of Gwen's hair.

The trendy salon was busy and bustling with half a dozen women in chairs that faced a long, silvery mirror. The lights were colorful, and the shop played a strange style of upbeat techno music that Gwen couldn't place. A woman with streaks of blue and pink in her white-blonde bob cut was overjoyed to see Dawn, and somehow got Gwen seated at once, even though she didn't have an appointment.

Dawn paged through magazines and talked to Rochelle, the hairdresser. They swapped tidbits of celebrity gossip like trading cards and discussed the wide variety of hair products for sale in the salon. Gwen listened to it like it was white noise in the background, grateful she didn't have to make small talk with the hairdresser. She only had to answer the intermittent barrage of questions about what she wanted. Dye? Perm? Blowout? Highlights?

The answer to all was no. Gwen's experience with haircuts was eighty percent her mother trimming a few inches off and twenty percent going to the same barber shop the rest of her family did.

However, Rochelle gave Dawn a terrifying veto power over Gwen's instincts. Consequently, her hair was shampooed, blow-dried, and layered by the time they were done. Rochelle also gave Gwen her first asymmetrical haircut.

Although skeptical at first, Gwen was pleasantly surprised with the end result. Rochelle had cut off all the burned hair, but rather than lop off the majority of Gwen's long hair, she cut down at an angle. On her right, the hair barely passed her shoulder, but it ran fluidly down, increasing back to its original length on her left side. With layers too, Gwen felt like her freshly washed and dried hair was a stream trickling down her back. When Rochelle finally asked about the burned hair, she told her it was due to a freak accident with an old straightener.

Dawn was clearly satisfied as they left. Her smile broadened, stretching her Coral Perfection lips to happy lengths, even as her eyes remained inexpressive, almost sad.

"Your hair looks absolutely *wonderful,*" Dawn gushed. "Rochelle is a *genius.*" Her smile started to falter as she took in the whole picture. As she looked at the Native American bear shirt and long jeans, it at last occurred to her, "Are you… wearing Lily's clothes?"

"Yeah."

"Oh, that's a *relief.* I didn't want to be rude and tell you how drab those clothes are. I'm glad they're not yours."

Gwen suppressed the urge to bite back at her shallowness for the umpteenth time that day. "I just got here from Neverland. I didn't have a chance to pack normal clothes."

"Oh, well, we *have* to get you some new clothes then!" The thought made Dawn so happy Gwen was loath to question it. Still, she felt awkward with this stranger spending so much money on her. She didn't know what her haircut had cost, but she was certain the stylish salon was expensive.

"That's really not necessary. I appreciate lunch and the haircut. You've done so much for me today. You really shouldn't take me shopping too."

"Nonsense," Dawn was now beelining for the nearest clothing store. "George doesn't work all day so I can worry about a few dollars here and there."

"What does your husband do?"

"He owns a landscaping company. Now come on, let's find you some cute clothes!"

It was apparent to Gwen that Dawn was doing this not out of some benevolent impulse, but for her own satisfaction. They visited three different stores, and in each one, Dawn went through the racks all but foaming at the mouth in her enthusiasm. Gwen stood by and held onto the clothes she pulled out, then marched off to the dressing room to model them and give minimal input.

Somehow, the process was still enjoyable for her. It was like immersion learning of a language. She started using fashion terms, echoing them without fully understanding. Dawn had a keen eye for trendy pieces, and a sixth sense for how to build cohesive outfits out of disparate garments. Gwen was, for all her childish quirks, still a teenage girl, and couldn't help but enjoy the novelty of a shopping spree. Two dresses, a jacket, two blouses, a pair of pants, and some colorful leggings later, Gwen was in a happy daze, carrying bags of brand-name clothes and waddling like a baby duck behind Dawn as she sauntered into a cosmetics department.

By the time the makeup artists were done with her, and Dawn had thrown a fistful of beauty products into their bag, it was time to head back to Mr. Schneider's shop. When she got there, he didn't even recognize Gwen at first.

"Well! You look like a regular princess now." There was a neutrality to his voice that kept it from sounding like a compliment. He handed the jacket back to Dawn, seemingly unaltered, and then slipped the original patch across the counter so Gwen could tuck it away in her satchel—one practical aspect of her image she hadn't let Dawn update.

"Thank you, Mr. Schneider," Gwen said. This felt like the first real victory toward finding the Piper. Peter probably had found the guilder coin by now and maybe even made sense of "the melody of the lamb and death," but Gwen was making progress of her own.

"Be careful with that," Mr. Schneider warned. "Not that I have any idea what mess you're trying to get yourself into with it."

Dawn looked comfortably happy with the way her day had gone. "Yes, thank you... you're a brave little tailor to help us with this."

His mustache twitched as a smile formed on his obscured lips. "I try," he answered. "I still try."

Dawn drove Gwen home, chattering on about how beautiful

all the new clothes were, and what fantastic taste the girl had—as if unaware that she had picked everything out for her, with the exception of one blue party dress that had captured Gwen's eye.

In the passenger seat, Gwen fiddled with the patch and waited for a break in Dawn's conversation to ask, "So what's so magical about this patch?" It seemed like an ordinary felt patch.

"Not much, now that we ripped it off, but that pack rat isn't interested in more magic," Dawn scoffed, glaring at the road. "He knew it would be hard to get and inconvenience someone, so he demanded it. The Piper isn't interested in his own gain as much as others' loss."

As they turned back onto the reservation and neared the gravelly road, Gwen attempted one last time to share a serious feeling with Dawn. "Thank you so much for helping me today."

"Oh, of course—I had fun shopping with you, too."

"I mean with the patch," Gwen clarified. "I understand that it puts you at certain risk, and I'm glad you still believe in magic enough to help Peter and the rest of us."

"Now look here," Dawn announced, bristling in her pudgy skin. "I didn't do this because I believe in magic or think that somehow having Neverland around makes the world a better place. And I certainly didn't do it because you deluded me into thinking a bunch of lost boys stand a chance against the black coats." She stared Gwen in the eye, but only for a second before she put her eyes back on the bumpy road.

"Then why are you helping us?" She wished Dawn had at some point, just once, given her a reason to like her other than taking an interest in cute high school boys and buying her things.

"Nostalgia." She spat the word bitterly. "You'll know it someday… when all this is over with and the last battle is lost… you'll find yourself compelled to help doomed causes, just because it looks like something you used to know. Nostalgia, that's all."

Gwen didn't believe her. She didn't think she did, until she realized that she was afraid.

"And speaking of," Dawn took one hand and half her attention off the steering wheel to dig into her purse, "if anybody catches you with this, you *stole* it from Irene."

It was an empty spool of thread. She dumped it in Gwen's hands while she was still confused.

It didn't feel like a bare spool.

Gwen ran her fingers over the surface, smooth and wooden to the eye but wound with thick thread to the touch. She felt the invisible end of the thread and found she could unwind it and rewind it with ease. "Tell her I said thank you," Gwen replied, a little mystified as she wondered how such an object could aid her efforts.

"No," Dawn insisted. "You *stole* it."

"I stole it," Gwen repeated, appeasing the woman. "I'm grateful anyway."

Dawn didn't stop the engine or get out of the car. She pulled up to Tiger Lily's house and said her stilted goodbyes to Gwen, neither one ever anticipating seeing the other again. Gwen thanked her for the haircut and clothes, because that was what the woman wanted to be thanked for.

The dark luxury car drove away for the second time that day, back to the McMansion suburbia where it belonged. Gwen tromped up the squeaky stairs and knocked on the door to the trailer house before testing the knob and realizing it was unlocked. She walked in and found Tiger Lily cooking in the kitchen, listening to the radio. She didn't hear her guest until the door closed behind her.

When Tiger Lily turned around and saw Gwen—haircut, new jacket, smoky makeup, and all—she burst into laughter. Gwen couldn't help herself—she laughed too. Foxglove came out from the spare bedroom at this jubilant sound, but she was unamused.

"Oh, goodness," Tiger Lily finally said. "Come tell me all about it. I've got peanut butter celery sticks."

CHAPTER 23

Tiger Lily made fish for dinner, and Gwen kept her company in the kitchen, crunching on celery while the fish cooked. Foxglove listened too, eager to hear what she had missed and bored to tears after spending so long cooped up inside. She had a glob of peanut butter in her hands and munched on it as she followed their conversation. Tiger Lily had cleaned up from the book club and was happy to hear things had gone so well for Gwen, even if she did come home looking like a poster girl for twenty-first century fashion.

"You don't look bad—not at all," Tiger Lily told her. "You just don't look like yourself."

They ate dinner, and then lingered at the table. Irene had left her boysenberry pie behind, so Tiger Lily put on a pot of tea and they had a quiet, conversational evening over dessert. Foxglove picked berry pulp out of Gwen's slice of pie while they chatted, and then tore open a tea bag so she could eat the dried chamomile flowers like candy.

Gwen felt validated, breathing in Tiger Lily's candid conversation and discussing Neverland with a grown-up who loved it. Her expressions were muted, but genuine, and Gwen appreciated her relaxed demeanor.

As the evening wore on, conversation became harder. Gwen was only avoiding the inevitable. "So," Tiger Lily finally asked, swirling her tea mug as if anything was left in it. "Are you going for the music box tonight?"

Gwen nodded and stared at the blinds, wondering how long ago the night had reached absolute darkness. "I don't see the point in putting it off another night. If I can get my hands on it tonight, we can send Foxglove back to Neverland to inform Peter we've got both the patch and the music box. It'll probably be afternoon there or something."

"Sounds like good logic," she agreed. "It's getting close to my bedtime… Unless you need something else, I think I might just head to bed."

"I'll be fine. I think I'll do some reading until it's late enough to head out. If I go too early, my parents might still be up and hear me creeping around."

Tiger Lily cleared the tea mugs from the table and put them with the other dishes on the counter, to be washed in the morning when she had energy. "I hope it doesn't have any bearing on your evening… but it's worth mentioning again—if anything goes wrong, if anyone finds you or tries to follow you, there's no way you can come back here. I don't know where to tell you to go if that happens. I would hide you if I thought there was any chance I'd be able to, but as soon as they catch sight of a flying child, they'll probably investigate me again, even if they don't follow you back."

Gwen pulled her legs up and sat with her feet on the kitchen chair, making herself cozy and compact as she took in this dismal fact. "I know. I won't come back. I can fly anywhere. If they start to follow me, I'll run until I lose them."

This speculation triggered a temper in Foxglove, who began sputtering all the horrible things she would do to anyone who attempted to apprehend them. She trilled so quickly, neither Gwen nor Tiger Lily could understand a single fairy word out of her tiny mouth.

A smile crossed Tiger Lily's face. "I'm glad you're braced for that reality. I have confidence in you though. Fly high until you get where you're going and keep Foxglove hidden in spider-silk."

On an affectionate impulse she didn't question, Gwen leapt up from her chair and dashed across the room to hug Tiger Lily.

"Oh!" Tiger Lily exclaimed at the sudden embrace, but she reflexively reciprocated. Gwen felt herself pulled closer and cherished the warmth of her hold. She felt the woman plant a fond kiss on the top of her head. "Stay safe tonight, Gwen, and have a good adventure," she whispered.

After Tiger Lily went to bed, Gwen and Foxglove prepared to take off. Gwen made sure the patch was zippered away in a secure pocket of her satchel, just in case she didn't have a chance to return to the house. Foxglove kept herself busy punching a hat like it was boxing bag, psyching herself up with her violent energy before they left.

Again, Gwen hovered an inch above the gravel and pantomimed walking to avoid crunching until she was far enough away from any of the dark houses to feel comfortable springing high into the air. Foxglove tucked herself loosely into the spider-silk jewel bag, and Gwen secured its ties to the strap of her purse. In her hand, she watched her phone's GPS dot. She knew which direction her house was, and she knew how to get there on the roads, but she was too high to gauge the route in the dark.

She felt like the trendiest girl who had ever taken to air. In dark blue pants and a cropped trench coat, she was an unlikely candidate for whimsical flight. The shopping trip had her confidence boosted in an unusual direction. Anything was possible. She could have a normal day at the mall and enjoy herself in a typical teenage fashion… somehow, that gave her a sense of power that translated into steady flight. Somewhere in the back of her mind, a thought rustled that suggested if the happiness she needed to stay afloat was derived by a shopping spree, she shouldn't be flying. It stayed in the far pocket of her brain, and she was smart not to bring it forward and give it any credence while suspended in the air.

Foxglove buzzed much along the way, which kept Gwen's mind off the particulars of her own thoughts. She didn't understand too much of it, but Foxglove was patient and happy to teach Gwen a few new words. By the time Gwen reached her house, she had figured out the fairy words for star and night, and had to shush Foxglove.

It surprised her how strange her house looked from an aerial perspective. She'd seen a satellite view before online, but that hadn't seemed real. It took her a minute to find it, and she grew paranoid as she descended. All the lights were off in the house, and she had no idea how she would break in. As fast as possible, she got to the porch's awning and hovered over to her second-story bedroom window. She tried to trust what Peter had told her, but she found it hard to believe that her parents would still have her window open in December. How many times had she been scolded for leaving it open while the heaters were on, needlessly inflating the energy bill? They wouldn't leave a window open through the night.

Yet, they did. The window to Gwen's bedroom was open and welcoming, waiting for her to climb back in as if she'd never left. Rosemary's window was open just the same.

She floated in and landed on her old carpet. It was an eerie sensation, visiting her room like a ghost. It was how she thought she would feel when returning from college—it was the only thing she could imagine comparing the feeling to. She didn't live here anymore. She'd forsaken this room, and now it was as cold as the December night just beyond her open window.

Still, it was home. She gave her desk chair a slight swirl and paged through the math composition book still on her desk. A draft of her persuasive speech for Mr. Starkey's class sat beside it. How foreign this all was! When was the last time she had even written anything? Did letters on the shore of Neverland count, when she played hangman with Rosemary, racing against the incoming tides?

She lay down on her bed, neatly made—not at all as she'd

left it. Her ancient stuffed lion was propped up on the pillow, his cotton compressed and body sunken from years of cuddling and squishing. He smelled like home—old cloth, her mother's laundry detergent, and maybe even a bit like the house's citrus-scented air fresheners.

The house creaked and Gwen froze. She lifted back into the air, afraid that any little sound might wake her parents. She was on a mission and needed to keep her focus. Foxglove, now safely inside, was conducting a rapid search of the room. Although Anomalous Activity Department's scanners wouldn't pick up on her magic inside the confines of a house, she needed to keep in motion. If she was in one place for too long, she risked her trail of fairy dust compiling enough to be noticeable to the human eye.

Gwen drifted to her closet. She hadn't used the music box in a long time, but she knew she wouldn't have ever gotten rid of it. Opening the folding closet doors as slowly and quietly as she could, Gwen then pointed to the top shelf and sent Foxglove up to illuminate it. Flying up, she had a view of her closet that she'd never had without a chair. "Aha," she whispered as Foxglove flew past the ceramic carousel. Foxglove objected to the sculpture. It wasn't a *box*. Gwen picked it up in both of her hands and turned it over to show her fairy the familiar crank on the bottom. Two of the horses were chipped and the device was covered in dust, but it was just as magical to Gwen as it had been when her mother gave it to her on that long-lost day of her fourth birthday. More magical, if Peter and Tiger Lily were right about music boxes and the effect the Piper's song might have had on it.

Gwen grabbed it, and then shuffled around until she found her spare cell phone charger as well. Her phone's battery was wearing down quickly now that she was back in reality. She stuffed it in her purse, and then took the music box with her back out the window. Flying up further, she sat on the black-shingled roof and examined the music box. Foxglove, halfway tucked back into the spider-silk purse, cheered her on as she turned the crank.

As it unwound, the four horses began their motion around

the base of the carousel. They slid up and down as they circled, just like a real carousel. Gwen immediately recognized the song from her childhood, although she had never been able to name it. On a dozen different occasions, she'd sung made-up, gibberish lyrics to the tune, all as long forgotten as her childhood dream of being a pop star.

Older now, she recognized the song was a waltz, but there was nothing special about it. She watched the porcelain ponies follow each other: the white stallion, the chestnut mare, the black beauty, and the pale pony. Foxglove, peeking out of the purse, hummed her disappointment. "I don't know," Gwen answered, only understanding her sentiment, not her words. "I know this is the music box, but maybe it needs some kind of prodding."

As the gears stopped churning and the music came to a stop, she thought back to what Peter and Tiger Lily had told her about music boxes. She decided to see what would happen if she added a little magic of her own.

She turned it over and wound it again, this time with four hard cranks. As the music started, she asked Foxglove, "Can you dance to it?"

The fairy wiggled out of the spider-silk bag and complied without question. She began waltzing through the air, spinning and twirling in a dance style unique to fairies. Like a ballerina, she glided and leapt, but stayed rooted in the space above the carousel. Gwen tore her eyes away from the enchanting dance to watch the glittering specks of fairy dust fall onto the music box. Those that touched it disappeared with a little flash. She hoped the magic was flooding into the gears, absorbed by the music box, but it was unclear whether it was working.

The music slowed, and Gwen watched with disappointment as the horses' mechanical prancing came to a stop. She sighed, announcing, "I don't think it's going to—"

Foxglove flitted back into her spider-silk, sorry her dancing had achieved nothing, only to discover what was happening.

The music box began to reverse itself. By Foxglove's faint purple light, Gwen saw the carousel moving backward. It began just as slowly as it had spun to its end. Stray notes chimed in intervals of whole seconds, but the poles to which the horses were fixed began to twist, too. The horses spun counter-clockwise and started moving in the other direction.

Not just moving, but prancing! The ceramic figurines, once glued into motionless poses, filled with life as their little legs stretched and reached for new ground. As they settled into a natural pace, so did the music.

Gwen had a sudden desire to cry. There was something about the tune that moved her as she listened to the music box, chiming with a sweeter sound than the notes had carried before. This new song was no waltz, but an alluring, enchanting melody. Full of bright excitement, it remained calm enough to fall asleep to. It was an impossible mix of unadulterated joy and soothing tranquility. It agreed with what little she knew about the Piper—the sound begged her to dance and adventure off, but had her in a wistful, hypnotic daze.

"It worked," Gwen whispered in awe.

The ponies came to a stop and resumed their solidified poses. They still faced the opposite direction. Carefully, Gwen slipped it into her satchel with the prince's patch and the invisible thread from Irene. Foxglove cheered at this triumph, bouncing in the purse with glee. "*Let's go,*" she exclaimed.

"Wait."

Foxglove's jubilant excitement came to a halt.

Gwen cast a nervous glance back into the house. She could see her wall clock. It was nearly one in the morning, and with all the lights off in the house, she knew her parents were certainly asleep. They would both be in bed. Her mom might wake up to use the bathroom, and it was within the realm of possibility that her dad would tromp downstairs for a midnight snack, but neither of them would have any reason to be in her father's office.

Her father's office, where he kept all his boring financial documents and work papers that Gwen had never had any reason to wonder about as a child.

CHAPTER 24

FOXGLOVE WAS AFRAID OF SNEAKING DEEP INTO A HOUSE, PARTICULARLY one that had no children inside. Gwen offered to tuck her into the spider-silk bag and let her sit outside, hidden in the gutter, but that did not suit her either. The desire to find information that would help them avenge the attacks on Neverland was too powerful a draw for the vengeful fairy to say no to. She stayed tucked in the purse, tied to Gwen's satchel.

Gwen closed her bedroom door behind her, but other than that, she did not touch her house. With Foxglove's diffused light from the purse, she flew through the hall and down the stairs, slow and silent. Eerie nostalgia crept up her spine as Gwen floated by, an intruder in her own home.

A moaning mew startled Gwen, and she almost fell out of the air before she caught herself. Out of the darkness, a tabby cat came padding toward its estranged owner.

"Hi, Tootles," Gwen whispered, reaching down to pet the orange house cat. He purred as she scratched him behind the ears. Foxglove stayed safely in the pixie purse, out of the feline's reach. Gwen shushed the purring cat, but felt as though she should apologize for her absence. Poor Tootles probably had no idea what had happened to the two happy girls who used to shower so much love on him.

Gwen continued downstairs, but didn't put her foot down on the carpet until she had closed the door behind her in her father's office.

She clicked the light switch on, acknowledging Foxglove's buzz of concern. "If we don't find something in five minutes, we'll get out." Her voice stayed hushed. "He works for the Anomalous Resources division. He might have information that's valuable to us."

At no point in her life did Gwen think she would ever steal from her parents. However, whenever she conceptualized the idea, it looked like sneaking money out of her mother's purse or raiding the wine shelf for an experience getting drunk. She had never imagined she could—much less would—try to steal information about fairylands from her father's office.

She scanned the papers on his desk for anything of significance, but didn't dare touch them for fear of adjusting them in some noticeable way. After that, she went to the file cabinet between his two massive bookshelves. If he had brought anything interesting home from work, it would be safely tucked away.

She opened a metal drawer and started paging through the folders, most of them organized by date. After a minute of this, it became apparent that magic was a very small part of her father's job. Magic was just another line item integrated into adult reality for him. Nothing interesting in his work folders appeared until she came across a file with a single document: a fifteen-page report titled *Proposed Distribution of Neverland's Resources.*

Gwen pulled it out and laid the unstapled pages on the floor. Too excited and apprehensive to read it, she only noticed a variety of keywords that seemed pertinent to her interests. She whipped out her phone and began snapping pictures of the pages, effectively scanning the document to read through later. Foxglove snickered from the purse, thrilled with this find. She tucked it back in its unmarked folder and continued searching to the back of the file cabinet. She found another document, *Planned Resource Use for The Invasion of Neverland*, and snatched it out of the file. Before she could start photographing it, the office's phone started to ring.

CHAPTER 25

Foxglove screamed; it was a tiny noise, overpowered by the phone's ring. Gwen shoved the document back into the file cabinet and closed it, less worried about noise now that the phone was ringing. She turned off the office light, trying to figure out where she could hide. The office was right underneath her parent's bedroom… they would certainly hear the phone. They still had a home line and a telephone console capable of conference calls for when her father telecommuted. This was a work call, at three in the morning.

She heard groggy footsteps hurrying down the stairs. Where could she hide? There was no furniture that could effectively cover her from any angle.

The door opened, but Gwen was already above it, her back pressed against the ceiling. The light clicked back on, but as her father rushed into the room, he didn't glance directly up. The phone created a sense of urgency that allowed her to hide in plain sight. Her father didn't close the door behind him. By the time he reached the phone, she had already shot out of the office and into the short hall downstairs. Foxglove stayed silent in the purse, and Gwen stuffed it deeper in the satchel so the fairy's glow would be even less obvious in the dark. Banking on the hope that her father would stay in the office while he took his call, she lingered just outside of the room and listened to the conversation.

"Hello? … It's alright. Is something happening?"

He sounded frantic and disoriented.

"Are you sure? At this hour? … I suppose they wouldn't be expecting that… yes, I saw the data this morning, too. It's probably nothing. The MRP has an individual out by Lake Agana. You know how that screws with the readings… The radar probably picked up a minor anomaly related to them. I saw it… the anomaly wasn't even radiating as much magic as a standard fairy."

He was quiet a long moment. Gwen wasn't going to move until she heard him hang up the phone and step away from his desk. "Oh. *That's* who they relocated out there? … Yes, I see your point. … Are you supposed to be telling me this, Harris?"

Another silence, and then, "Do you think it has something to do with the girls? … I don't know… off the record? … Yes. I saw Officer Armstrong's report. His description of the girl at the party sounded like Gwendolyn to me."

A shudder snuck down her spine as she heard her father use her name. A childish impulse told her to run into the room, to hug and surprise him. She suppressed it and kept listening.

"I reported her as a runaway to the local authorities. We told the school she had mononucleosis. She'll come home soon, and we want it to be easy for her when she does. I don't want her to have a record with your department if it can be avoided. She's just upset with us, concerned for her sister. She's sixteen."

Gwen's stomach sank.

"So this is a standard investigative run? Do I even *have* clearance to accompany you, Harris? … Okay. I'm not going to get my hopes up. It's not half the signal Gwen had heading to the party. But if there's a chance. … I'll be ready to go in ten minutes. … Alright, see you then."

The phone clicked down, and Gwen shot over to the laundry room, tucking herself into a half-shut linen closet. Foxglove was still in the spider-silk purse, stashed in her satchel. She patted the purse as a gesture of reassurance, but could not gauge Foxglove's feelings when the fairy was stone quiet. She made herself comfortable in a nest of spare pillows, waiting for her father to leave so that she could sneak back out of the house.

He went back upstairs to dress and came down a few minutes later. She heard him pacing in the living room before he left out the front door. Once she was sure he had gone, she got up from the cozy pillows and crept into the living room. Afraid to go upstairs where her mother might still be awake, she slunk over to the door. It was locked but not dead-bolted now, so she walked out and left it in the same state.

Music box in her satchel, fairy in her spider-silk, and a fifteen-page document from the enemy on her cell phone, Gwen felt like a real-life spy. Well, she was filled with the same sense of accomplishment and ambition that had once existed in her childhood dreams of espionage.

She didn't want to leave a trail of magic away from her house, so she kept Foxglove in the purse and started walking down her street. There were no lights on in the houses and no cars on the road. She was chillier than she'd been in a long time and kept her hands stuffed in her pockets. Her brisk pace helped warm her, but she had bigger problems in front of her.

As she walked, she talked to Foxglove. "You should get out of here. If they're looking at whatever little trail we've left since we got here, then making more magic tonight is probably a bad idea. If they go investigate Tiger Lily, we'll probably be okay as long as we're not actually there. We didn't leave anything incriminating in her house, right? A little bit of dust, but I doubt that will be enough to register on whatever they're measuring magic with."

Foxglove buzzed in objection. She didn't want to leave. She wanted to beat the officers back to Tiger Lily's and set awful traps for them. She wanted to get back at the officers. Gwen talked her out of this vengeful impulse and continued to think.

"If I can't go back to Tiger Lily's, I need to find someplace I can stay until I'm sure that they're done searching tonight. Wherever I go, it'll be easier for me if I don't have a fairy with me—no offense. Besides, you can go back to Neverland now and let Peter know I've got the patch and the music box to play the Piper's song. He'll be happy to hear that, and he'll know what to do next. Barring any run-in with my dad's friend in the Anomalous Activity Department, I should be clear to go back to Tiger Lily's tomorrow."

Her fairy came out of the spider-silk purse. The trail of pixie dust she left was no matter—no one would be able to follow it to Neverland. Foxglove picked up Gwen's pinky finger and pulled on it, lest Gwen not understand when she said, *Why don't you come with me?*

"Peter told me to stay in reality," Gwen told her. "I'm not going to let him down." If she went back to Neverland tonight, she'd just have to come right back, possibly through another storm, and her first storm landing was traumatic enough. "You don't have to worry. I have a plan."

Foxglove made a tinkling-rattling noise. Gwen understood her word of caution. "I'll be careful," she promised. Foxglove planted a tiny, tingling kiss on her forehead as a final goodbye, then zipped off toward the stars. Her glittering form turned to a purple smudge in the sky before disappearing altogether.

Gwen sighed, alone again. She was beginning to enjoy these brief spurts of time where she had no one—human or otherwise—watching her. She looked up and saw heavy, grey clouds blundering forward and swallowing stars as they encroached on her spot of sky. She wondered if it would snow tonight—it certainly felt cold enough for it.

While she strolled through the dark suburban landscape, Gwen paged through the pictures on her phone, zooming in to read the tiny text of her father's documents on her cracked screen. She tried not to feel guilty as she took advantage of her father's secret work files.

Most of it read like bureaucratic gibberish, detailing the need for "anomalous resources" in the Anomalous Activity Department and Research and Development. Gwen began to gather that structure of this strange organization, and suspected it might not even be as large as she once thought. The Magic Relocation Program was mentioned as a subset of the Anomalous Activity Department, and she saw that her father's job with Anomalous Resources placed him in some clerical subset of Research and Development. The two branches of this strange Illuminati seemed to function only in a dozen other locations where strange and magical things culminated into something worth investigating.

What intrigued her more was the report's description of Neverland. In particular, the "Essential Capital" which was a resource they valued above all else they might find there:

The Essential Capital represents the most powerful anomaly known. References to it as "Etz Chaim" date back over two millennia, and it is suspected to be one of, if not the only, actual physical trees of its species. If extracted from Neverland, the Essential Capital has the potential to advance medical technology and longevity research past all existing boundaries. The ability of this "Never Tree" to conceal itself and the host land it is rooted in is an equally anomalous, although less promising, aspect of the Essential Capital's nature.

As interesting as the following description was, there didn't seem to be any information that would be of practical use to their resistance against the adults, and she doubted the grown-ups knew anything about Neverland that Peter didn't. She tucked her phone away, watching her breath fume like smoke in front of her. She wished she'd had a chance to look at the *Planned Resource Use for The Invasion of Neverland* document, but she tried not to worry about that ominous title.

She kept walking, keeping herself warm and mulling over a plan. She couldn't return to Tiger Lily's, and without a fairy, her options were further limited… but her feet swung forward and carried her along deserted streets for a few miles until at last she came to a familiar house on Park Street, where all the lights were off except for one—in an upstairs bedroom where a glowing computer screen was a sign of a still-conscious teenager.

CHAPTER 26

Gwen picked up some stray bits of gravel and pebbles as she approached Jay's house so when she flew to his roof, she had something in hand to make a tiny noise. She didn't want to startle him, so she sat beside his window, just out of sight, and tossed the rock flecks at the glass. Each one made a tiny plink noise against the window. Finally, Gwen saw the light shift in the room, as if someone was moving a laptop. Jay came to his window and peered out, a curious smile on his face. It widened with delight as soon as he saw Gwen sitting on his roof. She gave him a meek wave but matched his smile as he opened his window.

"Hey!"

"Howdy." Rubbing her near-frozen fingers, she asked, "Mind if I come in?"

"Yeah, no, of course," he answered, throwing the window up all the way and allowing her to climb in before he closed it and shut out the wintry weather that was trying to come in with her. Gwen didn't involve flight at all in the process. It didn't seem appropriate—plus, she was wearing pants from her shopping trip earlier that day. For the first time in weeks, she didn't have to worry about moving in a ladylike fashion. Neverland was too playful for pants.

"Wow, you look good," Jay remarked.

Gwen remembered that she was also still wearing a face full of makeup from her superficial adventure with Dawn, artfully applied by the mall cosmetologists. Gwen laughed a little, keeping her voice low. She didn't want to wake his parents any more than she had wanted to wake hers. "Thanks. I got dragged to the mall to day and doted on."

"By who? Wendy Darling?"

"You're closer than you think," Gwen whispered, raising her eyebrows and realizing the truth was so ludicrous, she wouldn't dare explain it.

"You don't have to keep your voice down," he told her. "Troy and Sean were over until about an hour ago, so when my mom went to sleep, she put her earplugs in. We were kinda making a racket."

"What about your dad?" she asked, raising her voice to a natural volume.

"He's working a night shift—he's not here."

"Your dad works night shifts? What does he do?"

"Not usually. This week is just a weird schedule for him. He works in electrical maintenance. Basically, he gets paid to be a really smart guy who stands around in case something goes wrong. Anyway, you don't have to worry about my parents. What are you doing all dressed up and out tonight?"

Gwen laughed. "Nothing glamorous."

"Well, you're sure making me feel under dressed."

Up until that moment, she had been doing everything in her capacity not to think about what Jay was wearing. Or rather, what he was not wearing. After his company had left, Jay had trudged upstairs and gotten ready for bed. When Gwen had arrived, he had been cuddled down in his warm bed in a pair of flannel pajama bottoms. She'd seen him shirtless at the beach in a few of his photos online, but it was a much more intense experience in person.

"Sorry," she apologized. "I shouldn't have shown up

unannounced."

"Don't worry about it."

"I should have shot you a text—I'm out of habit with that."

"No cell reception in Neverland?"

"None," Gwen laughed.

"Well, I'm glad you came by." He leaned over and stole a kiss. The motion was so quick Gwen was surprised for a second before she realized she should be happy. He looked proud.

"I have some time to kill. Some of those officers are on their way to search the safe house right now."

"Where you're staying out by Lake Agana or whatever?"

"Yeah. I can't go back until I'm sure they're done scanning the area. I figured I'd drop by here first and see if you were still awake."

"Oh man, that's wild," Jay replied. "I guess I'm aiding and abetting your escape now, huh?"

"I'm not doing anything *illegal*," Gwen answered.

"But the mystery cops are after you."

The selfishness of arriving at his window occurred to her with the full weight of its unpleasantness. "I can leave; I just thought—"

"It's all good," he cut her off. "You are just a lot to take in, Gwen Hoffman." Her name sounded so good when he said it. "I'm just still trying to wrap my mind around how unbelievable you are."

He gave her a look that made her insides as melty as her outsides were freezing. "Okay. I don't want to keep you up."

"I'm pretty sure I'm officially nocturnal after how late you kept me up last night. I still had to drive home after you left, you know." He was complaining, but poorly. He looked far too happy for Gwen to take his grievances seriously. "I woke up at, like, three this afternoon."

"I had to get up at nine-thirty this morning."

"You must be exhausted."

"I really am," she chuckled.

He leaned in and gave her a hug, but shuddered as he did so. "You're so cold." Gwen tried to form words, but being pressed against Jay's bare chest short-circuited several portions of her brain, including the part used for structuring coherent sentences. "Do you wanna go downstairs and watch a movie or something? You can sleep a while too if you want... my dad gets off work at six though, so you'll want to fly off before he gets home."

She rubbed her eyes, at last coming to terms with how tired she was. "A movie sounds great."

They stripped the blue-striped comforter off Jay's bed and took it with them to the media room downstairs. The Hoeks owned an impressive collection of DVDs, shelved like library books beside the television. For almost half an hour, Jay and Gwen just went back and forth discussing movies and swapping stories about their favorite films, during which time he convinced her to watch one of his favorite animated movies.

Aside from *Sailor Moon* reruns and a few Hayao Miyazaki films, Gwen was unfamiliar with anime. As he put the movie into the DVD player, Gwen cuddled into the blanket on the leather couch and waited for her body heat to warm it up. Jay had pulled a shirt on—it was colder downstairs—but he still looked so handsome. She listened, not wanting to interject anything as his warm voice explained how nerdy and into manga he'd been in junior high, and how he hung out with the kids from Japanese Club now just because nobody else wanted to watch anime with him.

He sat down beside her on the couch, excited to share something he loved with someone who had never seen it before. Gwen slumped against him, and he took hold of her hand as a plot about a sci-fi mystery in a virtual reality started to unfold, full of characters with colorful hair and an imaginative blend of Asian culture and internet memes.

She thought for a moment that she was tired, but her happiness infected every inch of her. Her eyes did not even feel heavy; they were buoyed by such contentment as she sat hand in hand with Jay on his couch in the wee hours of the morning.

27

To Tiger Lily's surprise, Gwen walked in the door minutes before dawn.

"Hello there," she announced, instinctively getting up to put the kettle back on the burner for more tea. "I thought you must have headed back to Neverland."

"Foxglove did," she answered, yawning. "Did officers come around last night?"

"That they did." Tiger Lily caught her yawn and it lifted out of her lips like a roar. "I hardly got any sleep after they woke me up and did a brief search."

Gwen brushed her hair back and tried not to appear as nervous as she felt when she asked, "What officers came by? I mean, what did they look like?"

"Oh, I don't know… they looked like adults," she responded, as if momentarily forgetting she, too, was an adult. "Only one of them was in uniform. The other must have been undercover. He didn't say anything, just let his partner do the talking. He looked… really worried."

Gwen's gut knotted as she imagined her father here, talking to Tiger Lily in a fruitless attempt to find his daughter. She remembered the look on Dark Sun's face when he had discussed his own daughter's disappearance to a foreign world.

"I was worried about you," Tiger Lily continued. "It was a good thing you didn't come back home while they were here."

"I stayed at a friend's house."

"Is that going to cause problems, if one of your friends knows you're back?"

"No, he's chill. He won't mention it to anybody. He knows I'm kind of in trouble," Gwen mumbled. "I didn't get much sleep either..."

After their movie, she'd talked with Jay for another hour or so, a discussion of the movie segueing into a discussion of life, future, and the universe as best they could speculate on it as teenagers. At some point, she'd fallen asleep on the couch for a few hours, and woke up to her cell phone's silent alarm vibrating in her pocket. She had unwound herself from the blanket and slipped off the couch, trying not to wake Jay as she did so. He was handsome awake, but gorgeous in his sleep. Somehow, it was better remembering his eyes' vibrant blue color while they rolled around, dreaming under his eyelids. She had found her satchel—music box still tucked in it—and put her coat back on. Before she left, she had kissed the top of his head. He took a deep, sleeping breath and rolled over, sprawling more comfortably on the couch now that she was no longer on it with him. A peaceful smile spread over his face.

There was just enough of the night left to take to the sky and be invisible in the darkness as she flew back to the reservation. She landed along the deserted highway, walking the last mile to Tiger Lily's trailer park. Vigilant though sleepy, she watched for any car or soul that might have been associated with the Anomalous Activity Department. No one was out at that unnatural hour of the morning.

"If it's alright... I'm just going to go to bed."

"Very reasonable." Tiger Lily took the kettle off the stove, topping off her own cup of tea instead. "I might go back and get a few more hours myself. Was the mission successful though?"

Gwen smiled and pulled the music box out of her satchel.

Tiger Lily's lips lifted and uttered the single, happy word, "Wonderful." Gwen trudged off to the spare bedroom, but before she could close the door behind her. Tiger Lily asked, "What comes next?"

"We wait for further orders." Gwen shrugged. "Foxglove returned last night to tell Peter we have everything we needed to gather. He promised to send my sister once it was time to begin the search for the Piper."

"Sleep well then," Tiger Lily advised. "It sounds like this adventure is just getting started."

Gwen didn't need to be told to sleep well. Exhausted and delirious, she collapsed on the bed. It took effort to crawl under the covers. She couldn't be bothered with changing into pajamas—she fell asleep in the alien apparel Dawn had bought for her. Her sleep-deprived flight home melted away in her memory until she felt she must still be at Jay's house, cuddled against him on the couch. She fell in and out of the dream through the early hours of the morning, and then dipped into a heavy sleep that lasted until the afternoon gave way to evening.

She awoke, again, with a tiny hand's ecstatic shaking and whispered excitement. "Gwen, Gwen!"

There was no use pretending not to notice. Too much energy was launching itself at her. Gwen stirred, flailing in an attempt to deter the stimulus. In response, her awakener climbed on top of her.

"Ooph." She groaned, feeling winded as a child sprawled out on top of her.

"Gwen!" Rosemary cried, her voice no longer even trying to be quiet. She knew her sister was awake. She'd seen this trick before.

As Gwen opened her eyes and met Rosemary's overwhelming stare, she heard laughter in the doorway. "I tried to let you sleep," Tiger Lily apologized. "But after a while, she just couldn't be contained."

"Tiger Lily made me spaghetti—only the noodles were all

curly!"

"There's still some warm on the stove if you want dinner," their hostess offered.

Gwen ignored these details, if she even heard them. "Hey there, Rosemary." She slumped the girl aside on the bed as she sat up, and then gave her a big hug, burying her face in her voluminous hair. She smelled like sun-warmed mud and dandelion milk. Their mother would have had a heart attack if she saw the dirt-smudged girl who was once her pristine little daughter.

It felt good to have Rosemary back. It was easier to feel comfortable when her little sister was safe and in sight. "Did Peter come back with you?"

Rosemary shook her head. "No, but I brought Foxglove and Hawkbit."

Hearing their names, the two fairies flew into the room—abandoning the tea leaves they'd been chewing together—corkscrewing through the air and blurring their purple and yellow streams of fairy dust.

"They're going to help us. Peter and I figured everything out—I know how to find Piper!"

Foxglove and Hawkbit began explaining all the intricacies of the plan, their words all running together as they rushed out of their mouths. Tiger Lily listened to their trills, slumped against the doorway. She knew the fairy language backward and forward. Gwen, however, had to wait for Rosemary's version in English.

"You have the patch and the music box that plays Piper's song, right?" She didn't even wait for her sister to get a full syllable out of her mouth. "Great! Then we can start tonight. Right now!"

"Right now?" she echoed, skeptical and groggy. "How long is this going to take us?"

"Three nights," Rosemary told her, holding up three fingers for clarity's sake. "So we should definitely start tonight."

"Okay," Gwen announced, rubbing her eyes. "Let me get some dinner and we can head out."

Eating by herself while Rosemary talked was one of the subtler pleasures of life for Gwen. When they ate together, Rosemary was distracted by her meal and spun back into the conversation on different tangents, intermittently playing with her food. Worse, she expected Gwen to keep pace with her conversation. When she had nothing in front of her, however, Rosemary found the longest and most ridiculous stories to tell, expecting little more than mumbled affirmations and intrigued face expressions. While Rosemary recounted every inconsequential thing that had happened to her the past two days in Neverland, Gwen made faces and nodded, enjoying her pasta.

Tiger Lily had already heard the whole story, but mixed chocolate milk for the girls and listened to it all again. As Rosemary wound down, she had the presence of mind to request, "Tell her about the melody of the lamb and death."

"Oh yeah," Rosemary announced, happy for the reminder. She leapt out of her chair, her energy making it look like she was flying even when she wasn't. From the picnic basket she'd brought with her, she pulled out a translucent coiled cord. "It's from a harp!"

She handed it to Gwen, and the older girl held it taut, feeling the strength of the amber-colored string as she wound it around her fingers like floss. Her sister reached over and plucked it. The noise was muted and dim, but there was a musical quality to the sound it made.

"We had to talk to the mermaids," Rosemary told her. "We couldn't tell them what we needed it for. I don't know why. Peter pretended like he wanted a harp, just for playing. They went down to the bottom of the ocean and found one aboard a sunken ship! Most of its strings were all broken and rotted, but we got one!"

"I don't understand." She looked closely at the twisted substance of the string. "What would the Piper want with this? What does a harp string have to do with lambs or death?"

Rosemary pouted and made sad eyes. Tiger Lily answered for her. "Sheep's gut—it's what they used to make all music strings from."

"Poor little sheep," Rosemary mewed, before continuing, "Peter said Piper was famous for making music even more pretty than harps. I don't know why it was harps. There's lots of pretty things he could have been better than."

Gwen held the string up, looking at it against the kitchen light. "So now it's part of his calling card." Rosemary had already shown her the round, golden guilder Peter had fetched, and so this was the last piece of the puzzle.

The sheep's gut string was a different feel than any nylon or metal string she had ever encountered. It was undoubtedly a rare artifact, to be fetched from the ocean floor by mermaids. If they could get it in the Piper's hands, he would know that someone had begun a serious search for him.

28

THE GIRLS WAITED UNTIL IT WAS LATE ENOUGH THAT ALL THE SHOPS IN the town center would be closed. Rosemary was emphatic about this. They had to start the hunt there. As was the norm these days, Gwen followed her little sister's bigger sense of confidence.

With Foxglove and Hawkbit tucked away, the girls shot up into the sky until they were high enough not to register on any officer's radar. Gwen was confident that after her father and Officer Harris had investigated Tiger Lily's home that any trace amounts of magic they left behind would be attributed to standard anomalous fluctuation surrounding Tiger Lily and her home.

They made it to the town center, a tiny outdoor mall with Spanish architecture, landing on the synthetic clay shingles of the red roof. Checking first to make sure there was no one in the shopping plaza, they dropped down to the ground in front of a dry cleaner and scampered over to the fountain in the middle of its mock courtyard. "Are you sure this is where we want to be?" Gwen asked, watching a rat scamper away from a trash bin by the light of one of the few old street lamps.

"This is the best place," Rosemary announced. Foxglove and Hawkbit hummed in agreement, darting out of the concealing pouches and dancing over to the three-tiered fountain, still bubbling and gurgling in the night. They stayed hovering over it, where their fairy dust would dissolve into the water. Gwen let go of her fears and embraced the odd setting. Everything from the mission-style roofs to the brick ground felt like an homage to something older. Maybe that was exactly the sort of place to coax a man from fairy tales back into the world.

"Okay," Rosemary announced, taking a fighting stance against the darkness and unknown. "First, we need the song."

Gwen pulled the music box out of her satchel and sat down on the edge of the clay fountain. She wound the ceramic carousel, and then set it down beside her. It was obvious from the first few notes that the song had reverted back to the original, unremarkable waltz. "Foxglove, can you come sprinkle some dust on this again?"

The fairy was happy to comply, and Gwen wound it further before setting it down and letting Foxglove dance over the contraption. Hawkbit joined her in this prancing fun, neither of them worried about the dust they dropped as it was absorbed by the music box.

As they had the previous night, the horses reversed and came to life in their porcelain forms. As they pranced around in the opposite direction to a new tune, Gwen was about to ask, "What now?"

Rosemary was faster to react. "Why didn't the song change?"

"What?"

The younger girl crouched down and stared at the music box inches from her face. She was enchanted by the animated pony figurines, but on the whole disappointed in the music. "It's still the same song. Doesn't it need to change?"

"It did—can you not hear it?"

"Nope," Rosemary answered. "What does it sound like now?"

"I don't know… Like the Piper's song."

Her sister scanned the courtyard, looking in all directions for any sign of life, magic, or motion. "I don't think it works like that. Peter said you'd have to do the song."

"What do you mean—do the song?"

Rosemary shrugged. "Like play it on an instrument, or sing it I guess. The music box is only reminding you, Gwen."

The older girl buried her face in her hand. Her, sing? She'd lasted a whole of two weeks in junior high choir. This was not going to be a fun experience, and she didn't know what would happen if she butchered the melody. "I can't sing it," she countered. "There aren't lyrics."

"Make some words up," Rosemary suggested. "They don't even have to be real words." The fairies gave her words of encouragement, which only worsened the pressure she felt. Everyone in high school knew you didn't make people sing if they didn't want to sing. There were some unspoken rules like that. If someone didn't sing, you let it go. It was so ingrained in her that it seemed shocking Rosemary's naivety could not fathom the inherent humiliation.

Rosemary was a child though, unaware and uncritical in many social and aesthetic regards. She gazed up at her sister with adoring eyes. Swallowing her pride, Gwen knew a foolish display would do nothing to diminish her from her sister's perspective. "Okay," she agreed.

She listened for a moment more, waiting for the tune to loop back to its starting point on the music box. Hawkbit bobbed up and down with her voice, trying to encourage her. She sang gibberish, the way she used to when she had wanted to give the music box's original song lyrics.

Tepper tepper yolen and teaming tull,
Swanning sing-swim and afterall again,
Gilly groat and vinder much wrote annul
Addle pie, perfect sky, pota po hunch.

She continued, growing more precise as she attempted to hit the notes of the song circling through the music box. She felt like a fool and her face burned with the absurd embarrassment her voice caused her. As the music box wound down, Rosemary picked it up and spun the crank again, whispering, "Keep going," to encourage her sister. A moment later, she squealed, "It's working!"

Gwen almost screamed when she saw the first rat. Instead, she only overshot one note, and continued singing to the best of her ability. She pulled her legs up off the ground and onto the fountain seat, as if that would keep her safe from the rats on the bricks two feet below.

Rosemary was not afraid of them. They drew closer with a steady, plodding gait of their paws. Once her initial shock wore away, Gwen could see how strange and mesmerized they behaved. The rodents paused in intervals and rose on their haunches, standing in spellbound attention to her before meandering even closer. By the time the music box came to a slow finish, there were six of them, waiting with patient and tiny eyes, at the foot of the fountain.

They stared at each other, the Neverlandians and their audience of rats. The fairies stayed high in the air, leery of creatures with claws, despite their hypnotized state. Gwen was at a loss, but Rosemary's startling adaptability kicked into gear. Reaching into her sister's satchel, her motions slow as to not disrupt the spell, she pulled out the ancient, coiled harp string.

Trying to reach down and lean back away at the same time, she held the loops of twisted string with two fingers and extended it toward the largest of the rats. He took it in his mouth, his two minuscule front teeth trapping it in place. "Take this to Piper," Rosemary told him.

The rat gave no sign of acknowledgement, but her instruction seemed to break the enchantment. The rats went scurrying in every direction, fleeing from the girls. The largest of them kept the string tight in his teeth and dashed off, galloping on short legs into the night.

CHAPTER 29

THE HANGING MOBILE SWUNG OVER ROSEMARY, THE SAVANNA ANIMALS seeming to race across an invisible landscape. The little girl murmured and sighed with dreamy aspiration as she pushed through unconscious adventures in one of Tiger Lily's spare beds. Gwen was still wide awake.

With her pillow propped up against the wall, she slouched back and waited for something to strike her. She had no feeling of accomplishment from handing off the harp string to the rat earlier in the night. She didn't even feel sleepy after spending the whole day in bed recovering from her night with Jay. While Rosemary was still falling asleep, Gwen had hidden under her covers and surreptitiously texted Jay. They'd gone back and forth, each new text lighting up her phone and smile in equal parts. He had spent his day sleeping late and finishing homework. Gwen's heart constricted with joy as he told her how much fun he'd had last night, and asked, *Do you want to meet up tonight?*

Gwen had hesitated before responding. She wasn't the least bit sleepy and had no intention of staying trapped in Tiger Lily's guest bedroom listening to her little sister dream. However, she felt a new rush of nerves concerning Jay. The past two nights she'd seen him had been fantastic, but had left her head spinning.

Sorry, she wrote, *there's somebody else I have to see tonight.*

They exchanged adorable goodnights, and she set her phone aside. She paused, staring out into the darkness of the room and feeling her heartbeat's subtle thumps in her chest. She didn't know if she'd meant that, or if it was just an excuse. She wanted to see Jay, desperately in some ways, but she couldn't account for the nagging intimidation that drew her away from that desire.

Not committing one way or another, Gwen pulled on real clothes again and laced up her shoes, careful not to make any noise that would disturb the sleeping fairies or her little sister. She slipped out of the trailer as quietly as she had her first night, and started on her way to Lake Agana. The night was peaceful. After a few days of successful sneaking around, Gwen experienced no apprehensions about being caught. She was even bold enough to fly over the very tops of the forest's trees and skirt through the air in half the time it would have taken her to weave through it. She hovered down to the edge of the still lake, digging through her satchel even before she'd landed. In the dark, she depended on her fingers to find and recognize the glossy, cool feel of the mermaid scale. She chucked it into the water like a stone and waited.

In a moment's time, a head bobbed to the surface and shattered the still surface with minuscule ripples. Eyes, colorless in the moonlight, peered upward as Lasiandra approached the shore. At first Gwen, thought she was looking to the treetops, but it soon occurred to her Lasiandra was watching the stars. "A very long way from home tonight, Gwen," she announced.

"Actually, closer than I've been in a long time."

She didn't take her eyes off the sky. "Such strange stars you grew up under. No wonder you are such an odd girl."

"What makes them strange?"

"They're full of old constellations. The constellations in Neverland and over the sea never stay constant so long. But look there, that is still Orion, as he has been in this world for thousands of years. It must be so tedious to live where stars cling to the names they've been given by men so long dead." She at last unlocked her gaze from the sky and looked to Gwen, her eyes twinkling as if they'd swallowed the stars. "But they look after you. They tell me Piper is on his way to you now."

"Already?" Gwen asked. "Rosemary says we still have two more nights of summoning him."

"Oh, that's true," Lasiandra admitted, finally handing back the scale. As Gwen tucked it in her satchel, her fingers found the spool of invisible thread and began nervously playing with it while Lasiandra continued, "He won't be here soon. He has thousands of miles to go first. But he is coming." There was a sharpness to her grin that possessed her eyes as well.

"You look so happy about that. Everyone else I've talked to is scared by the thought of calling the Piper back."

"Is it so strange to think that I might have confidence in you?" Lasiandra announced, as if defending herself. "Mermaids aren't afraid of Piper; why should you be? He's powerful, but like all land-bound, he has his weaknesses."

She was prodding Gwen to a question, pushing her to ask about the Piper and his weaknesses, but she wasn't interested in that. The remark pushed her to another train of thought.

"Don't mermaids have weaknesses, too?"

Lasiandra splashed onto her back, relaxing, but also bracing herself for a more defensive role in the conversation. "Doesn't everyone?"

"You're avoiding the question."

"But giving you an answer."

"Don't mermaids have weaknesses, too?" Gwen repeated.

Cornered, Lasiandra's options were to directly refuse the question or give an honest answer. On almost every issue, she would sooner tell the truth than alienate her landmaid friend with secrets. Gwen sometimes felt bad for bullying her friend into talking like this, but it was not a potent guilt when it was clear what lengths Lasiandra went to in order to obscure the meaning of her words.

"Mermaids aren't so different from one another, the way

people are," she answered. "We're simpler for it. This idea of conflicting desires… there's no such thing in the dark of the ocean. There is only survival and death, swimming and stagnation, desire and disregard. What we desire… we desire it to the same depths that we swim."

"And what do you desire?"

"That's where we differ. Different mermaids have different passions."

"What do *you* desire?" Gwen pressed.

Lasiandra had a sly and melancholy look in her eyes, which she refused to show to Gwen directly. Staring back at the stars again, she admitted, "I love it too much to betray it to you."

"You don't trust me?"

"I didn't say that," Lasiandra said, denying nothing. "But if you wanted something with the same desperation, you would understand." She looked back to Gwen and smiled. "Maybe someday you will, and we'll finally be able to bend the stars' magic in a sky glass and help each other."

Gwen giggled as the thought of Jay flashed into her head. "I think I might be getting closer," she whispered.

Lasiandra leaned in, her body slinking forward with her interest. "Do tell."

The mermaid floated flat on the lake, only one ear out of the water as Gwen lay down on the grass beside the lake. Gwen talked until her throat felt dry, telling her friend everything she could think to say about Jay and the wonderful world in which he—and she—lived. Explaining her suburban reality to a mermaid and looking at it through her curious eyes, she saw a new sort of magic in what she'd had before Peter had whisked her away to Neverland.

She liked talking to Lasiandra. She spoke freely and excitedly, watching as her friend melted into candid and enthusiastic reactions. When Gwen was in control of the conversation, there was none of the clever obfuscation that Lasiandra instinctively applied in order to avoid being too revealing. As she explained falling asleep on Jay's couch and in his arms, Lasiandra reached out and clutched Gwen's hand, holding it tight with delight. "That's so wonderful," she declared. "He really does care for you, doesn't he?"

Gwen held Lasiandra's hand back, squeezing it to communicate all that she couldn't as she smiled at the stars.

CHAPTER 30

GWEN RETURNED TO TIGER LILY'S WELL BEFORE DAWN. HER BODY fell like a rock into bed and into sleep. Most of the morning disappeared while she slept, but Rosemary's jangling laughter in the other room woke Gwen up before noon. This felt like a definitive victory to her. She was getting up early, compared to the past few days.

Rosemary was as disappointed as the fairies to be regulated to the trailer in daylight hours, but Tiger Lily was used to entertaining children. Her arsenal of manufactured toys and library of picture books were a novel treat for a lost child like Rosemary, who derived a happy satisfaction from reading to Gwen and telling stories to her storyteller. Tiger Lily also had an impressive collection of familiar cartoons on DVD, and Rosemary wanted to watch all the old shows she'd never seen before.

It galled Gwen to think these staples of her childhood had never reached Rosemary. It felt like her little sister belonged to a different generation altogether. When they were both old ladies after half a century in the same millennial era, the cultural intake of their childhoods would seem a trivial thing… but right now, the difference seemed just as massive, if not more, than their age gap.

Tiger Lily left in the afternoon to run errands and have a coffee date with a friend, but returned in persistent good spirits midway through an episode of *Kim Possible*. Gwen helped her unload groceries from her car—a dented, grey sedan that looked like it had been running shoddily, but reliably, for the past twenty years. While they filled the fridge with food, and shooed the fairies away to keep them from getting trapped in the refrigerator, Rosemary's attention remained glued to colorful action and cartoon dialogue. Mrs. Hoffman would have had a fit about so much TV in one day, but it seemed natural to binge in front of a screen after literal months of nothing but playing outside.

Gwen's mind wandered as she unloaded apples and oranges into the fruit drawer, and curiosity prompted her to ask, "Tiger Lily... do you have a job?"

"No," she chuckled, shuffling frozen foods around her freezer to make space for boxes of pot pies, "I never saw the attraction of those."

"If you don't mind me asking," Gwen continued, "where do you get your money?" It was an impolite question, but she knew Tiger Lily wouldn't take offense.

"Reparations," she answered. "They give me enough to stay comfortable."

It didn't occur to Gwen until much later that she should have asked whether the reparations came from the Bureau of Indian Affairs or the Magic Relocation Program.

The rest of the day dwindled away in front of books, TV, and toys. The music box and other magical items stayed tucked away, but Gwen fidgeted with the invisible thread Dawn had given her from Irene. She kept it on her at all times, but couldn't tell if the artifact was reassuring her or feeding her anxieties.

As much time as Gwen devoted to thinking about Jay and her own world, she leapt at the opportunity to be drawn into Rosemary's world, where no concerns carried over from one day to the next. Her little sister didn't so much as mention tomorrow, but stayed perfectly present in her afternoon activities until, at last, night fell and broke the childish spell. Purpose seized her spirit as soon as it was dark, and Rosemary was impatient from that moment forward. She insisted she hold onto the mysterious patch, then ran back and forth between the stopped clock and pitch-black window, waiting for it to get either later or darker.

When they finally headed out with Hawkbit and Foxglove, Gwen struggled to keep pace with Rosemary's flight. Stray snowflakes rolled down from the sky, as white as the girls' breath. They had bundled up as tight and warm as possible, and didn't see anyone else out on such a cold and dark Sunday night as they flew to the town center.

They landed inconspicuously all the same, and dashed over to the center of the shopping plaza to continue what they had started the night before. The fountain had been shut off at the end of the weekend in preparation for the chilly temperatures that now threatened to freeze pipes. The fairies stayed in the warm spider-silk purse for fear of dropping dust in the cold. Snowflakes moved down with languid grace, melting on impact with the ground.

Rosemary cranked the music box, and Gwen took a deep breath before launching into her gibberish song. She felt the words vanish from her mouth in the same eerie way her breath vanished in the air, and sensed something was different tonight. Pushing past the feeling, she continued to sing, longer than she had last night. The rats seemed reluctant to venture out from wherever they were hiding from the cold.

Vet mey pollar popping linguid gibber
Tosher lon fet fasten dayton mey tu
Winch toom tapper hashling getly gego
Reser, ebber, vet milday widder roo

The rats wandered toward her on hesitant paws. Their presence concerned her more than their reluctance to come, and Gwen was taken aback when she saw how many more rats had come tonight. It was as if news of this summoning had trickled down their grapevine and drawn even more to come listen to Gwen's nonsense song. Did the tune mean anything to the rats? Certainly, these rats had never heard the Piper's song in person.

Twenty rats lined up in front of the girls, their tiny bodies shaking whenever a chilling snowflake fell on their dark fur. They came so close, Gwen could watch their bodies flex as they breathed. The biggest rat didn't seem to be the same one from last night. This one was even larger. The fairies hid deeper in the spider-silk, not wanting anything to do with the rats. Rosemary's conviction made her courageous, and she didn't even flinch as she leaned over to hand the patch to the master rat. He took the fencing patch from George Charelston's Princeton jacket gingerly between his sharp teeth. Bewitched by the spell, he knew not to tear a single thread of the patch, but deliver it, as Rosemary told him, to the Piper.

As soon as she'd given this order, the rats broke their formation in a frenzy. They had stood on their haunches like soldiers at attention, but they scurried away with their bellies low to the ground. They raced back to whatever cracks and crannies they could find, some even dashing up the adobe style walls. The largest rat, patch in his mouth, bounded without hesitation to the other side of the shopping center. There was nothing frantic in his pace, and he remained under the spell as he hurried away to give the Piper this second, penultimate gift. Rosemary and Gwen were left with nothing but the music box and guilder coin, which would have to wait until the next night.

"How do we know it's working?" Gwen asked. They had no way of knowing that last night's rat had even successfully carried the harp string to the Piper. What if the rats were just throwing away these artifacts or padding their nests with them?

Rosemary knew the answer though. "Because more rats came tonight," she explained, staring after the rodent who would deliver the patch. "Tomorrow, Piper will come."

CHAPTER 31

ROSEMARY AND GWEN WERE SUBJECT TO THE SAME RUDE AWAKENING when they felt fairies pulling their hair early the next morning. "Owww!" Rosemary whined, only seconds before Gwen felt it too.

"Wha—stop!" Gwen shouted, slapping at the pestering fairy. She opened her eyes and saw an unsettling blue glow. Where were Foxglove and Hawkbit? She'd expected something purple or yellow. The blue fairy pinched her ear, and she attempted to bat it away again. Her eyes were too blurred with sleep to see clearly, but she rubbed them and insisted, "I'm awake! Give me a second."

His furious trilling jogged her memory of the blue fairy. As her eyes finally focused, she saw the sharp features and angry face of a fairy she'd encountered once before.

"Oxtail?" she asked. He boxed her in the nose, his tiny fist stinging. "Owww! Oxalis?" He grumbled more amenably, and Gwen knew she at least had his name right.

Hawkbit buzzed like a wasp around Rosemary, but Foxglove paced on her wings near the ceiling. They all jittered with panicked motions, shouting over each other. It occurred to Gwen how out of place Oxalis was. Had the ill-tempered fairy ever left Neverland or sought out lost children? A horrible fear settled in her stomach as she realized just how wrong something must be for Oxalis to come to her.

"What's the matter?"

His fury was indecipherable. She threw the covers off and stood up, trying to catch Foxglove's attention. "What's going on, Foxglove? Why is Oxalis here?" Her speech was just as hurried and flustered. There was no following it. Even Rosemary, much better at following fairy speak, couldn't translate.

Oxalis buzzed into her face. Determined to make his message known, he shouted at Gwen, channeling his frustration into volume not speed.

"Hollyhock?" Gwen gathered.

He buzzed *yes*, and then continued. It felt like an unpleasant game of charades.

"Drones?" she repeated. Foxglove let out a pained cry, and the reality of it dawned on Gwen. "Oh no."

The girls raced to Tiger Lily's room, fairies fast behind. Gwen felt herself lurching back into childhood. *Go get the grown-up. Grown-ups know what to do.*

"Tiger Lily!" Rosemary exploded into the room, wearing a tiny nightgown borrowed from Neverland. Gwen suddenly felt absurd, rushing into Tiger Lily's room, hiding behind the lost guise of naivety as her fear surged forward. Who was this woman to her that she could be a friend or an authority, whichever suited Gwen's needs at the moment?

"What's the matter?" Tiger Lily cried, bolting upright. She wore a large Washington Redskins jersey like a nightgown and had her hair pulled into two black braids. She was already out of bed before the girls could answer. Without any information, she pulled on a pair of jeans and prepared to deal with some unknown disaster. The fairies were faster to explain than the girls. By the time Gwen had sputtered, "It's Hollyhock—she's been taken by drones!" Tiger Lily already understood.

She put a hand to her mouth, covering her inexpressive but expansive grief. Her features stayed like stone on her face as she crossed the room to sit on her reading chair. Folding her legs up, she found a comfortable position on the plush armchair and seemed not to mind the fairies and girls orbiting around her in panic.

"Is she still alive?" Rosemary squeaked. Foxglove wailed.

"Certainly," Tiger Lily answered. "Her pixie dust is too valuable to their purposes for them to kill her."

"How do we rescue her?" Rosemary pleaded.

She was not so quick to respond. Her eyes stayed steady, as if she could physically see the problem in front of her. "I don't know. She'll be nearby. It will be easier to contain and experiment with her magic if they're already in a magically dense environment."

"So she's in some kind of laboratory?" Gwen guessed. "Somewhere under the control of the Anomalous Activity Department?"

"They have a holding facility that they'll be keeping her in." Tiger Lily's distress was barely visible on her face, but a look of intense concentration gave away how troubled her mind was.

"Where is it?" Rosemary demanded, as if she wanted to charge the facility that very second.

"I don't know. I just know they have one. It's where they put magical folks who refuse to join the grown-ups. It's hidden, with a similar magic that hides Neverland."

"How on earth do we find it then?" Gwen exclaimed.

Tiger Lily looked her dead in the eye, her composure regained. "The same way you find Neverland: you find someone who has been there before."

Rosemary's hands tightened into fists. Gwen felt a chill perch on the top of her spine as that night's errand gathered even greater importance.

CHAPTER 32

THE FAIRIES, STILL GRIEVING AND FEARFUL OF THE PIPER, DID NOT GO with the girls that evening. When Rosemary and Gwen showed up by themselves at the town center that night, there were still a few straggling people left. All without children, grown-ups hurried along with packages and presents not yet wrapped. The girls wandered at a meandering pace, as if waiting for a parent or looking at the toy displays in windows themselves. They didn't worry about running into their own parents… they would have no reason to be out shopping for their children this year. It had an odd effect on Rosemary, being so far removed from every child's favorite time of year.

"Was running away to Neverland bad?" Rosemary asked, her voice piercing the silence between them as they stared at princess plushies and marble track gizmos. It was a complicated question, and Gwen didn't know how to answer. Fortunately, Rosemary elaborated. "Will I be on the naughty list this year? I've never been on the naughty list."

Did Gwen dare tell Rosemary what their father had told her? There was no Santa Claus… their parents were responsible for every last inch of mock magic that went into Christmas. Her father had told her, after Rosemary's disappearance, that

Santa Claus no longer existed. He had, once, before the adults determined his job was nothing that they couldn't do, and his magic was more valuable in their hands than his. She watched as a lanky blonde woman passed, her arms laden with bags and her hands holding the glowing screen of the phone she was texting on. The world had cashed in Santa Claus for something more exciting but less enchanting, like a teenager leveraging Christmas to get his parents to pay for concert tickets.

"I don't think Santa Claus will come to Neverland," Gwen answered, steering away from the more complex realities of the situation. "We probably aren't on any list, naughty or nice."

"Why not?" Rosemary asked, finding the simplest way to phrase the hardest questions, as usual.

She watched the people scurry out of the shops threatening to close in the next few minutes. They scampered with the same urgency as the rats. "Well, if nothing else, Santa Claus is a grown-up, and only kids can get to Neverland."

"Yeah. And Santa only visits families," Rosemary decided. She left the conversation at that.

The stream of shoppers seeped away. They might as well have dissolved into the ground like rain into thirsty earth. They were bystanders, unaware of the great and magical crime the Hoffman sisters were primed to perpetrate.

The girls wandered slowly, made invisible to the adults by Gwen's presence. An unattended child would have attracted eyes; a child with an adult would have been noted as a fellow shopper, but a teenager? Gwen was not worth registering. She was a powerless middle ground that needed no attention.

They wandered away from the storefronts, heading back to the fountain, a still sculpture without its water. In the courtyard, they hid themselves from the employees who were locking up shop, and hunkered down on the side of the fountain that faced a tiny Mexican restaurant, long since closed.

"So what happens tonight?" Gwen asked, her nervousness obscured by years of conditioning herself to appear calm and cool in front of her peers.

"Piper comes!" her sister exclaimed as she lifted the music box out of her bag.

"Will there be rats? Are we supposed to give them the coin, or will he come by himself?"

She put a finger on her chin and looked around as if thinking very hard on the subject. "I bet there will be rats," she decided. "A coin is a tiny thing for them to carry. It'll be like the final test. Magic things always come in threes."

"Then he'll appear?"

"Uh-huh."

Gwen remained skeptical, but didn't voice a word of doubt. If belief counted for anything, as it often did with magic, she didn't want to tread on her sister's optimistic appetite for the impossible.

"First, I think we should ask him where they took Hollyhock." Rosemary held up one finger, and then two as she continued, "Second, we should ask him to help Neverland."

Gwen felt the coin in her hand—its reeded edges were worn down to a nearly smooth rim. Strange words—in Latin or German, she couldn't tell—were etched around the cross pattern on the front of the dull, golden penny. "No," she told her sister, "we should talk to him about business first. We need to get his attention."

Rosemary agreed, amenable to anything in her current mood.

The older girl was less confident. She tried to internalize Lasiandra's cavalier attitude toward the Piper. The mermaids weren't afraid of him, why should she be?

But she was not magical. Not inherently. She had no defense against the Piper. She was proceeding on the faith that his greed would make him a predictable, rational entity.

The shops cleared out and the last of the lights clicked off inside. The standing lampposts in the plaza were dim orbs of light in contrast to the totality of the night's darkness. The sky wasn't the star-studded blackness of Neverland, but rather the dark grey of clouded-over reality.

Gwen wound the music box and began their summoning song one last time. Rosemary skittered up to the edge of the fountain and stood beside her sitting sister, scouting for nearby rats. The music chimed, seeming slower. Gwen's heart beat at a similar pace. She felt eerily calm, aware she had no options but this unnerving course of action. As the music played, she sang once more:

Dally gordon apple gongsing dinner
in bellies of better blooming blue bells
Happenstance heroes halv hon blow away
Keppling yellow mouse issn really tells

The rats came creeping slower this last night. They had a cautious and methodical manner to their movement as they drew near. They spilled out from every conceivable cranny of the shopping center's architecture. The trash cans, gutters, pipes, planters, and roof poured the rodents out into the courtyard toward the girls at the fountain. Little ones came up from sewer grates, others poked out of utility boxes and cracks under the stores. From nests in crawlspaces, chimneys, and vents, more than a hundred rats came marching out to confront the girls. They ordered themselves, naturally finding their positions in a vast military-like formation.

The regiment of rats disturbed Gwen, and she cut her song short. There were already too many for her comfort. She didn't know what would happen if she kept singing.

"Wonderful," Rosemary whispered above her, still standing on the fountain's rim.

Gwen drew her feet up, away from the rats gathered beneath her. She still clutched the tiny guilder. She tried to be as impressed as Rosemary, but now her heart drummed in her chest. It had never occurred to her how much she disliked rats until she'd been charged with finding the Piper.

The man himself was nowhere in sight. The girls scanned the courtyard while the rats waited on patient claws. Gwen didn't trust the circumstances. She reached into her pocket and felt about for the end of the thread that Irene had given her. Without looking at her hands, for fear of tripping up her mind with the invisible thread, she wrapped the coin in the magic thread several times, knotting it tight around the gold piece. The rats didn't comprehend what was happening, and although Rosemary stared and tried to make sense of it, she didn't make a sound. She knew when magic was afoot, and she knew better than to speak and break a spell in the making.

The spool still firmly in her pocket, Gwen lowered the coin down to the rat nearest her. Aware of how close the quick creature was to her face, she suppressed the fear she wanted to wince with. "Send the Piper. Here's the first of his payment. Make sure he gets this, and make sure he comes." She didn't know if her words meant anything to the rat, but he snatched the coin between his teeth all the same.

A shrill chorus of squeaking began as the rat militia dissolved into a frenzy. With rabid intensity and frantic motions, they stampeded away from the fountain, tripping over each other in their haste.

The girls lost sight of their courier immediately.

Had there been light, they could have seen the shine of the guilder—remarkably polished for a coin that was certainly hundreds of years old. In the night, it was impossible to discern which of the mad rats was dashing away with their coin. This event didn't feel like the previous nights; the squeaking and squealing of the rats suggested some sort of horrible distress… or betrayal.

Rosemary's eyes went wide. On some frightened instinct, she started to back up away from the rats, all inefficiently fleeing. She started to step off the ledge of the fountain, but Gwen saw the motion and sprung up to grab Rosemary's hands and pull her back to balance.

"What's going on?" the little girl shouted.

"I don't know. It'll be okay."

None of them went for easy hiding places again. The furry monsters ran around buildings and toward the horizons beyond them. The vast rat population that had congregated in the town center's plaza somehow knew, just as Rosemary did, that magic came in threes. The furious flurry died down as the rats again disappeared. The shopping plaza's courtyard became silent and still in a way that indicated the rats had kept running even once out of sight. The event over, they scattered back to whatever lands and nests they'd originated from.

In a minute's time, there was nothing to suggest that anything had ever happened. The girls waited several minutes more, sitting close together for comfort in the cold and uneasy night. There was no sign of the Piper.

"He was supposed to come." Tears started to swell in Rosemary's eyes, and her little nose gave way to a series of sniffles. "Why wouldn't he come? We got all the things he wanted!"

"It's okay," Gwen assured her, patting at the poof of her sister's voluminous hair before wrapping her arm around the girl's small body. "I have a plan. I thought he might play tricky."

Rosemary wiped her eyes. It was a dramatic gesture, since she hadn't actually started crying. "Really?"

"Really. Now follow my lead and we'll see if we can't find him on our own terms."

Gwen pulled her spool out of her pocket, still averting her eyes. *There is thread there*, she told herself. *Don't look down and try to prove yourself wrong.*

The spool had rapidly unwound as the rat dashed away, but the magic thread had neither run out nor tangled. Gwen felt the invisible cord between her fingers and re-wound it as she followed it.

"What is tha—Oooh..." Rosemary cooed as she reached out and touched the silky string. "Oh, I can see it now! It's so pretty and glittery."

Gwen looked down, wondering if moonlight or some other

quality of the night had brought the enchanted thread into view. She saw nothing. What Rosemary could clearly admire once aware of, Gwen couldn't see even as she held it. She took a deep breath and tried to force self-conscious thoughts out of her mind. She was not a child enough to tap into the whimsical beauty of everything, so what? She could still do this. She was the one who thought to track the coin, not just hand it over with blind naivety. She had some strengths unique to her age.

Once Rosemary saw the thread, she was reinvigorated and chased after it. Following Rosemary was easier than pulling at the thread to get a sense of where it went. Gwen pursued, her hands tiring faster than her feet as she jogged after her sister and wound the thread back around the spool fast enough to keep up with her sister's impossible pace.

It twisted between shops, around, and back again. They were running, as if in a wild goose chase, through the complex of retail buildings and restaurants.

Rosemary came to an abrupt stop, just ahead of an uncovered passageway between buildings. A restaurant's emergency exit and an employee's-only door stood on opposite sides of the passage, creating it between their adobe-style walls and arched windows.

The string went taut as they approached, closing in on the coin and the rat carrying it. She thought she saw the creature move in the shadows, but then felt her stomach rise and fall in one movement. In the center of the archway, the rat sat poised at the opening down into the passageway. It was an obvious dead end, and the animal seemed reluctant to dash down and corner itself. The golden guilder was no longer in its mouth. Gwen pulled the string again, but it went slack all at once.

Without a word of discussion, the sisters parted from each other's sides, sneaking left and right as they closed in on the alley. With no sudden motions, they approached the rat. It took a few steps before fear struck him and he urgently darted down the corridor. The thread still ran in the rat's direction, and there was not another creature in sight. Rosemary took off sprinting after him, and her sister followed after.

"Wait!" Rosemary pleaded, but the rat dashed headlong into the dead end and squeezed itself into a chink in the wall. Its body vanished, its twisting tail slipping away like the last stream of water down a drainpipe. The jagged crack was a passageway the girls could not follow down, and they found the end of the magic string on the alley floor. The coin was gone, and now the rat was, too. "But where's Piper?" Rosemary called after the rat, desperate and distraught.

Their efforts appeared fruitless, but Gwen's instinct was to reassure her little sister and keep her calm. Before she could say anything, she felt a large hand clap over her mouth. Everything went black as a dark cloth came down over her, like a curtain engulfing her.

CHAPTER 33

GWEN STRUGGLED LIKE A FISH IN A NET, BUT THE MORE SHE PUSHED, the tighter it got. She could hear Rosemary's stifled screams on the other side. The folds of the fabric swallowed her as if she was trapped in a bag. She felt it under her feet, she felt it against her face. The hand had disappeared as soon as it had forced her into the bag. She was alone and unable to cry out. She pressed the cloth away from her enough to cry, "Rosemary!"

When her confinement let up, it was instantaneous. The pressure and tightness went slack, and she found herself pushing a curtain. It blew away, and she stumbled down, barely managing to break her fall. Braced against the ground, she heard Rosemary shout as she plopped down beside her, rubbing her bottom and pouting at the disorienting experience.

The curtain, still whirling in front of them, seemed to shrink—everything moved so fast, Gwen couldn't be quite certain of what was happening. It froze, and she saw the hand clutching it out, the feet below it, and—at last—the man behind it.

Still sitting where they'd fallen on the floor of the alley, the girls watched as he lifted his head slowly up and dropped the enchanted cape from out of his hand. It fell furiously, as if blown back by a violent wind, or as if it had some strange sentience of its own.

The man glared at them with beady eyes. He looked disheveled in his dark clothing. He wore baggy trousers and a shirt with loose sleeves and tight cuffs. On his head, he had a wide-brimmed hat with a tiny, speckled feather. His waistcoat was almost invisible under its many brass buttons and colorful patches.

"What are you children *doing*?" he snarled, looking almost archetypally villainous with his goatee and thin mustache. Everything this man did seemed to suggest he wanted to be left alone—from the way he hid to the way he groomed his facial hair.

Of course, Gwen knew they had found the Piper, but she couldn't quite bring herself to say it. She propped herself up on her hands, sitting a little higher while he towered over her. "We're looking for the Piper."

He slid forward on his long legs and hunched down, his knees jutting out at odd angles as he crouched to look Gwen in the eye. "But having *succeeded* in that..." He spoke with a hesitation that suggested he was somehow restraining himself. "What then, my *mäuschen*?"

Rosemary piped up, braver then Gwen until Piper put his intimidating gaze on her instead. "We need his help—we have a job for him!"

His eyes narrowed, their darkness disappearing between the slits of his eyelids. "What children would need my services?" He spat the word *children*; Gwen wondered how much of his contempt for the two of them was rooted in their age, and his past experiences with children.

Before Rosemary could say anything with her persistent tone of whimsy and joy—no doubt offensive to this embittered man—Gwen plucked up her courage and announced, "The children of Neverland."

Piper's cape seemed to spring up before he did. "I knew it! That little bastard is hounding me again!"

Rosemary cast an alarmed look at Gwen, shocked to hear a

swear word. It seemed as though that utterance was the trigger for Rosemary's trusting heart to doubt the integrity and kindness of this dark stranger.

"He's smart to send you to do his bidding—I would lead him straight to the bottom of the river if he'd had the nerve to come for me himself. The boy's always known how to look out for his *own* skin..."

He stormed off, back down the alley and away from the girls.

"Wait," Gwen cried, scrambling to her feet.

"Give him my regards," Piper sneered, turning to face them and drawing his cape up. "Or a swift kick to the gut."

"We can pay you!" Rosemary yelled, also rushing to get up.

"I've heard that one before."

There was something about his posture that suggested a total control of the situation. He held his cape like a weapon, and Gwen conceived that he might use the cloth to disappear as quickly as he had appeared. Afraid he would transport himself away into the night in another second's time, she blurted, "It'll be Vanda who finds you next!"

Piper dropped his cape.

"What did you say, girl?"

She backtracked through her mind, trying to recall what Lasiandra had told her about Piper and the mermaids. "The mermaids have long memories, Piper," she bluffed, "and Neverland is their home, too."

He eyed her with grave distrust, but straightened his spine and stood tall. He slid over to the girls, never picking his feet up any more than he had to in order to walk. With fear curdling the edges of his voice, he asked, "Have you made a deal with the mermaids?"

"No," she huffed, taking command of the situation and getting comfortable in her bluff. "We'd rather not involve them, and we figured you'd be willing to listen to reason. Will you discuss the issue with us, or will we have to rely on other persuaders?"

She'd taken that line right out of a book she'd read in junior high. It sounded so villainous, and it got Piper's attention.

"You wouldn't," Piper told her, his voice betraying his alarmed disbelief. He either knew he was right, or he was bluffing too.

"We would."

They stood, frozen and staring at each other. When he wasn't hunched or squatting, Piper stood incredibly tall. He dwarfed Gwen, and Rosemary hardly came up to his knee, even with all her fluffy hair. Still, the older girl matched his eyes. It was easier for her—she didn't fully understand the stakes or the gravity of what she was threatening. Piper knew, Piper feared, and Piper took her unblinking resolve as truthful conviction.

"Shit," he muttered. Rosemary clapped her hands over her own mouth, as if hearing the inappropriate word somehow meant she would immediately be overcome with the compulsion to repeat it. Piper ignored her. He hung his head and stared at the pavement for a brief moment, then crooked his head to look at the girls. "You said you can pay? In what? Fairy dust?"

"Gold," Rosemary said. "Real, pure, pirate gold."

Piper groaned, knowing he had no option between the horrible threat and fabulous reward. "Alright, we'll discuss the issue," he ceded. "But not here. I need a drink."

CHAPTER 34

WHEN HE WAS NOT TRYING TO APPEAR SINISTER AND STRANGE, PIPER walked with a proud, awkward stride. He remained stooped, his body somehow contorted in a way that made him look less conspicuously tall. He swung his legs forward and let his cape blow like a broken sail behind him. Gwen could keep up if she walked fast, but Rosemary had to prance, skip, and jog to keep pace.

He cast a snide look down at Gwen, but didn't slow. "I should have known you were one of Peter's girls. How long have *you* been mothering him in Neverland?"

"I'm nobody's mother," she objected, hating how she burned at the remark. "And it's none of your business how long I've been there."

"Long enough to tangle with mermaids," he muttered.

"Where are we going?" Rosemary asked, her eyes scanning the street with novel delight. It was a profound and grown-up thing to be out in the city after dark.

"Somewhere we can hide."

"We're passing lots of good hiding places!"

"No," Piper answered. "We need somewhere with people."

They had cut out of the town center and down an adjacent

street, almost as well lit as the courtyard, but equally deserted. Gwen kept her eyes open for dangerous-looking individuals, conscious that she had her kid sister in tow tonight. They passed only a few souls on the sidewalk, and none of them was as dangerous—in appearance or otherwise—as Piper.

He took a sudden left, and Gwen scrambled to adjust. On the corner ahead, she saw the glow of neon signs and two men loitering outside of a door, smoking dwindling cigarettes. Piper homed in on it, compelling her to ask, "Where are we going?"

"Somewhere I can get a drink."

Stating the obvious, Gwen tried to catch his eye and force him to acknowledge her with more than cursory answers and short remarks. "We can't go to a bar. Rosemary and I are kids."

"Who?"

"Rosemary! My sister!" she said, pointing back at the gleeful girl.

"Don't fuss. Just stay quiet, the both of you."

Piper approached the doorway, and the two men, snickering at a shared joke, took objection.

"Whoa, hey." The bald man crushed the remainder of his cigarette under his foot and put up a hand to stop him. The other continued smoking. Gwen stared at the flashing LED lights that illuminated drink specials on a black whiteboard. The Dirty Girl Scout and Mexican Midget cocktails listed did not make the bar seem any more appealing than the smell of smoke at the door.

"What?" Piper asked.

"You can't come in here with your kids. Twenty-one and up!"

"I'll catch you later, Mike," the other man said. His friend waved him away, focused on Piper.

"Kids? What kids?" Piper asked.

The conviction left the man's eyes as soon as he looked back to Gwen and Rosemary. An odd confusion began to fill his eyes. Still staring, he opened his mouth to speak, but Piper cut him off and forced him to look him in the eye.

"Didn't your mother ever teach you any better than to stare?

Now will you let me and my aunts in? It's my great-aunt's birthday today, and we're here for a drink." Piper held his gaze, forgoing any blinking as he spoke. "For eighty-two years, she's always had a gin and tonic on her birthday, is that too much to ask?"

"Is that too much to ask…?" the man echoed. "No, no… but…" He looked at Rosemary. "This is your great-aunt?"

"Yes," Piper insisted. He said it with such natural conviction that Gwen felt shaken in her understanding of reality.

"How old is she?"

"Don't you know it's impolite to ask a woman's age?" Piper demanded. The disoriented bouncer hastily apologized before Piper continued, "But if you must know, she's a hundred and two today. She's all shriveled up and shrunk, but she's a good woman."

Everyone stared at Rosemary, who took the opportunity to do her best croaky, old lady voice and tell the bouncer, "Hello there, sonny!"

He seemed thoroughly convinced. He gave Gwen one last look. "And you are?"

Piper didn't give her a chance to answer for herself. "My other aunt, who hasn't shrunk nearly as much with age, but is still as grey and wrinkled as any old lady you've ever laid eyes on. They're very tired, and all this standing around isn't good for their knees. Now you will take us inside and show us to a quiet table."

There was a moment's pause in which Gwen questioned the sheer lunacy of what was happening. Then Piper snapped his fingers, and the bouncer became enthusiastically agreeable. "Of course. We've got a table in the back. It shouldn't be too noisy."

"Whippersnapper!" Rosemary shouted at him.

He laughed it off as the antics of a senile old woman. "Right this way, ma'am."

Heads turned as the three of them entered the bar with the bouncer. Piper in his baggy and colorfully patched clothes was almost more out of place than the two little girls. They were in the company of the bouncer though, so the patrons dismissed the event. Rosemary ogled the bar, but Gwen tried to keep her eyes away from everyone else's. She didn't want to give them away with a guilty look, although that was probably impossible given Piper's profound hypnotic ability.

Towering booths lined the brick walls, their glossy maroon fabric reflecting yellow light from the hanging lamps in diffused blotches. The bartender wore a button-up shirt and slacks, but everyone else seemed to be wearing at least one denim garment.

The room was subdivided by a wall of booths, and the bouncer led them to a table on the other side where they would be out of sight of the other patrons, but not the bartender. All the furniture in the room was made of a wood so dark it looked black. There was no polish or shine to it. As they took a seat at a round table with square-backed chairs, Gwen cast a glance at the bar—a great black juggernaut, behind which rested a library of liquors. The bartender gave them a nasty look, which only intensified as they settled at their table.

"Happy birthday," the bouncer told Rosemary, as the bartender stormed over.

"What do you think you're doing?" he fumed.

"Don't worry," the bouncer said, pulling out another cigarette and heading back out to smoke it. "It's the old girl's birthday."

"What about the little one!"

But the bouncer was already beyond reach, oblivious to his coworker's concerns.

Confused and frustrated, the bartender told Piper, "I'm going to have to ask you and your children to leave. There are laws against minors in bars." He made the mistake of looking him in the eye though.

"No, there aren't," Piper replied, holding his gaze. "You will be happy to serve us."

The tension dissolved out of the bartender's shoulders and brow. His body relaxed as if his split-second progression from angry to confounded was a natural motion. "I'd be happy to…?" He was begging for some kind of direction or confirmation, lost in the mind Piper had so effectively clouded.

"Serve us," Piper asserted. "These two old ladies and I are here to celebrate her hundred-and-second birthday."

"A hundred and two?" He still bore a skeptical expression as he turned to look at Rosemary.

"I'm an old lady!" the eight-year-old declared, amused.

Piper waved his hand with a sharp gesture that brought the bartender's eyes back to his. "She is your best customer, and you will give us drinks tonight, free of charge, to celebrate her birthday."

The bartender was quiet. Still staring into Piper's eyes, he was unable to object but in too much of a daze to react. Piper snapped his fingers, and the bartender lapsed back into his—now adjusted—reality.

"Drinks are on the house tonight," he announced, as if it were his own happy idea. "What can I get for you?"

"A Pilsner—or whatever pale lager you have."

"And what for the birthday girl?"

Rosemary's eyes grew wide like a flower opening up in the sunlight. "Can I have a Shirley Temple?"

"Sure thing." He turned to Gwen. "And you, ma'am?"

"I'm fine," she answered, her mouth barely moving with the taciturn response.

"Can I get extra cherries?" Rosemary asked, aware that she had an enchanted adult in her power and wanting to capitalize on this glorious event to the best of her ability. "Like, five?" She held up her hand with all five fingers to illustrate.

The bartender laughed. "Are you going to want a shot in that or anything?"

Bounding back into character as a hundred-and-two-year-old woman, Rosemary croaked, "No thank you, sonny. My gallbladder isn't what it used to be."

The bartender left and Piper took the guilder out from a pocket on his waistcoat. Gwen hadn't even seen the pocket amid the patches. It looked like an obsessive collection, visible now that he was sitting still in the light, his cape brushed back. There were patches for places, bands, brands, sports teams, a yellow smiley, a green alien, a Coca-Cola logo, an ACDC thunderbolt, the Batman symbol, an Australian flag… and affixed somewhere, Gwen assumed, was a varsity jacket patch for Princeton University's fencing team.

Piper flicked the coin and snatched it out of the air with an animal's reflexes. He darted his eyes to Gwen, and it planted a healthy fear of him in her heart. She didn't doubt he could manipulate her as easily as he had the bar employees. "So what's the proposition? You want to talk about it? Talk."

She felt more comfortable looking at him when he wasn't talking. That would be her strategy for this conversation—only meet his eyes when she was the one speaking.

"Peter wants to recruit more children. Neverland is seeing more attacks than it has in years, from Molotov newsprint to drone invasions, and—"

"Where do I figure in these desires of the brat?"

"Mass recruitment," Gwen answered. "We need a way in which to communicate with the children that will go undetected by ordinary adults."

He rocked back in his chair as she spoke, and then let it fall forward onto its legs. As he opened his mouth, Gwen averted her eyes. "And what about the un-ordinary adults? I've heard this pitch before, *mäuschen,* and it landed me in prison for nearly three years. Why should I think this time will be any different?"

Rosemary watched him eagerly, waiting for him to stop speaking so she could start. Gwen had begun this conversation, but with no idea where it would go. She gave Rosemary the reins, and sat back as she realized how little she knew about Peter's plans, and how passionately her sister had invested herself in them.

"We'll be prepared. We want to do it at night, when the ordinary grown-ups won't wake up. When the officers arrive, we'll be ready to fight."

"We?" Piper's dissatisfaction was pooling on his face. He was a clogged emotional drain, and all his negativity just spilled back out. He looked like a man who had done prison time under surreal and magical circumstances.

"Us kids," Rosemary told him. "The rest of us will be there to defend and get as many of the other kids as possible. We just need you to wake everyone up with your pipe. At the first sign of the anti-magic people, you can leave the rest to us."

This plan of action put him in a moderately more conformable disposition. The bartender returned with his beer, frothy and golden in a tall, bulbous glass. He set it down in front of Piper, and then placed the Shirley Temple in front of Rosemary, who was all but jumping out of her seat in excitement for the elegant sugar water. The cocktail glass looked ridiculous with five waxy maraschino cherries floating in it.

Once the barkeeper was out of earshot and Piper had downed half of his beer, he wiped the foam from his prickly mustache. "What's in it for me?"

"Pirate gold," Rosemary repeated, slurping a cherry out of her soda and chewing it as she talked. "A whole chest of it, if you want!"

He seemed unimpressed with the idea of a trunk full of the greatest relics and riches of mortal men's dreams. "That won't do. Not now."

"What do you mean?" Gwen asked, offended by his pretension. "What do you even need with money, anyway, when you can just hypnotize people to give you your things? There's nothing in Neverland that would have more value in the real world."

"Ah, but there is," Piper told her, nursing the rest of his golden beer. "Hypnosis only works in person, and I don't like people. A trunk full of ancient coins… it would take time to track down the sort of person interested in the full value of those old pieces. They'll be imbued with magic for as long as they've spent in Neverland, and melting them down for the gold would unleash that magic in a way that would be traceable, if not dangerous."

The hum of other patrons' conversations was drowned out by the fog of intensity forming around their table. "Then what do you want?"

Piper had his answer. "First of all, I want the crown of Princess Charlotte of Wales. That I can easily get to an interested party for a great sum of modern money. It was Blood Bone Eddie's greatest steal, and I know it never left Neverland. Secondly, I want a root cutting from the Never Tree."

"What do you want with that?" Gwen didn't dare ask *what* the Never Tree was, for fear of sounding like an idiot when she desperately needed to appear like a knowledgeable negotiator. She remembered seeing it in her father's paper, but she knew little about it.

Piper seemed to sense her ignorance and replied condescendingly, "The same thing Neverland wants with it. I don't want to be found."

"And the riddles, music, and rats aren't doing that well enough for you?"

Piper leaned just an inch closer, and even that motion made Gwen uncomfortable. "No—as you yourself pointed out, the mermaids and the ramifications of their magic can still find me. They collude with the stars, and they can always find me. I want to be finished with them, and I won't until I have something more powerful than them."

"If it's in Neverland, Peter can get it." Rosemary sipped her soda, holding her cocktail glass with both hands.

"Good. There's just one more thing then."

It sounded exorbitant to Gwen, but it was just what she'd been warned to expect from Piper. "You want another thing, too?" Gwen asked. "That's convenient. So do we."

His smug satisfaction dripped away; he couldn't know if he still had the upper hand when this older girl continued to reveal new information. "What else could you possibly want from me?"

Rosemary grew sober, which added to Piper's discomfort. The two girls exchanged a glance before Rosemary told him, "We need to know where they took you when you got arrested."

His beady eyes shrank into dissatisfied slits in his face again. "Why do you need to know that?"

Gwen swallowed her unease and spoke with all the confidence she could muster. "A fairy was captured in Neverland this week. We need to find her. They must have her in a prison or laboratory of some kind, and we suspect it would be wherever you were held."

Piper laughed, which was an unsettling experience. "A fairy? Girl, do you have any idea what forces you are up against? No matter—this will serve both our ends."

"How so?"

"You want me to pipe the children to Neverland? Then there's one thing I'll need in addition to my payment—my pipe."

"Your—what? Don't you have a pipe?"

He shook his head, with a vindictive pleasure in his own misfortune since he knew it would be remedied by others' effort. "They took it. When I managed to mesmerize one of the guards, I didn't have a chance to break it out, too."

"I thought the song was magic, that you were magic… Why can't you make use of a different pipe?"

Rosemary chugged her soda, enthralled with this discussion, and then picked cherries out from amid ice cubes in her glass, one at a time.

"Go ask the mermaids that one," he scoffed. More somber, he added, "Never trust a mermaid." He gulped down the last of his lager. Nothing but a frothy residue was left in the glass.

Gwen took a deep breath and fidgeted with her hands, under the table and out of sight. "Okay. So if you tell us where the facility is, we can make a plan to rescue Hollyhock and get your pipe back. Peter will get you the crown and the Never Tree root, then you'll be on board?"

"Yes—providing I'm paid up front."

"Alright then. It's a deal."

"Shake on it," Piper demanded, standing up and extending his hand.

"Pardon?"

"Shake on it. It's a deal, isn't it?"

"Oh, well, yes. Of course." Gwen got to her feet, but there was a level of commitment signified in a handshake that put her at ill at ease. Why couldn't Peter be here, with his boundless confidence? Why would he send such a nervous emissary? She tried not to think about how unqualified she was—chronologically and philosophically—to be working as the right-hand woman of Peter Pan. She gave him her hand, but his hand was as rigid as his grip. They did not shake.

"What is your name?" Again, he caught her of guard, she stammered, and he repeated, "What is your *name,* girl?"

"Gwen. Gwendolyn."

"Alright, Miss Gwendolyn. If you can look me in the eye and shake on this, we've got a deal. I'll pipe a small army to Peter."

She hesitated. What did looking him in the eye have to do with it? Swallowing her fear and bracing her mind against whatever might come, she stared up at him—so tall, even when he hunched over. She jerked her hand up and down in a stilted handshake that became more fluid only as she realized nothing was going horribly wrong.

"Good," he declared. "This arrangement will be advantageous to all—except for the Anomalous Activity Assholes. What could be better?"

He searched several hidden pockets in his waistcoat until he found a pen. On the back of a drink coaster, he began scribbling instructions. "This will give you everything you need to find my pipe, and presumably your little winged friend as well."

She took a deep breath and flashed a quick smile at Rosemary while Piper was busy writing. This was working. She wanted to take just a second to revel in that success before she powered through the last minutes of this stressful interaction. One last pertinent thought occurred to her. "How will we find you once we have the pipe and your payment?"

Piper finished scrawling his instructions and shoved the coaster into Gwen's hands. He stroked his slender beard once, and then looked around the bar. "Outside. We'll find a messenger outside."

Rosemary spit a cherry stem back into her glass, and Gwen tucked the coaster into her satchel. Piper's swift pace carried them out of the bar almost before the bartender could call out one last, "Happy birthday," to Rosemary, his favorite hundred-and-two-year-old customer.

"Whippersnapper!" Rosemary yelled back. Gwen grabbed her arm and lovingly tugged her out the door.

Outside, Piper began whistling. He strolled now, back in the direction they'd come from. The girls recognized the tune he was whistling, and the enchanted melody carried far into the urban night.

A rat poked out of a dumpster between a teriyaki shop and nail salon, squealing in recognition. With the grace of a snake, it slid out of the dumpster and obediently ran to Piper. He put out his hand and let it bound onto his palm. He stopped whistling only when he had raised the rat to his face and was eye to eye with the rodent. "Go with this girl. Stay by her side. When she tells you to come for me, come."

Gwen thought she saw it nod.

He waited a moment, never blinking, and then snapped the fingers of his other hand. The rat squealed again, bouncing frantically in his hands. Piper held it out for Gwen and dropped it down to her. She scrambled to catch it in her hands, rather than have it land on her. It was impulsive to stop something from falling on her, but she was disgusted as soon as she realized she was holding a rat they'd just found in the dumpster. Fortunately, the creature was calm in her hands and nuzzled her thumb. It was almost cute, now that Piper had tamed it for her.

"Of course," Piper began, "I'll need collateral."

"Collateral? But we aren't asking anything of you yet. We'll pay up front."

"But you know where to find me. You know I'm near. I never break a deal when I shake, but I've learned not to take others at *their* word."

Gwen petted the rat and tried to suppress her repulsion.

The trash-eating pest already had a great deal of affection for her. "What could you possibly want for collateral?"

"You'll come with me."

Gwen didn't like the turn this discussion was taking. She didn't look at him. She kept her eyes on her rat, feeling her best defense would be to feign distraction with this creature. "Where?"

"You'll do as I say. You won't worry."

Gwen dropped the rat. It had the wits to land at her feet. She wanted both her hands to grab her sister, but when she looked to Rosemary and saw her eyes fixed upward…

"I won't worry…" the little girl echoed.

"*No!*" Gwen screamed. She reached for Rosemary, but Piper was faster. He pulled Rosemary out of Gwen's reach, never breaking eye contact with her. Gwen lunged to slap at his spellbinding eyes… but Piper only stretched up and stood tall where she could not reach.

"You will come with me," Piper repeated.

The usual silence did not follow; Gwen filled it with her scream, "*Rosemary, NO!*"

He spoke over her terrified babbling and calmly promised, "When you have the crown, Never Tree root, and pipe, send for me. Our deal is sealed, Gwendolyn."

He grabbed his cape, throwing it into the air. It caught its own impossible wind, expanding and twisting like a storm of silk. It engulfed Piper and Rosemary, and its blackness instantly became the black of the night along an empty street.

CHAPTER 35

TIGER LILY WAS SLEEPING, SOUND AND DREAMLESS, WHEN GWEN BURST into her room… not twelve hours after she'd come running in for help with Hollyhock's sudden capture. This was an even more emotional event. Gwen came in, her face already soaked with tears that had dried and left an invisible salt from her hurried flight back.

She had knocked at the door first, but didn't have the composure to wait for Tiger Lily to answer. She had launched herself into the room, knowing the intrusion would be forgiven in such great emotional distress.

Had there been room for logic in her screaming mind, Gwen would have known that no amount of volume or speed would have any effect on Tiger Lily's reaction or ability to help. The same would have been accomplished with a quiet knock and a heavy, slow entrance. But Gwen was a volatile sixteen, lost in a stew of emotion.

Tiger Lily sat straight up as if her hips were hinges. She tore off her sleep mask and turned on her bedside light. When she saw Gwen hurtling to her, she instinctively opened her arms.

Without hesitation, Gwen ran into her embrace and felt Tiger Lily's arms swaddle her to the best of their capacity. She held the girl close, repeating the question that Gwen had failed to hear when she came babbling in, "What's the matter?"

"Rosemary… he… he took Rosemary!"

Pressed against the woman, Gwen physically felt Tiger Lily's jaw drop. "Piper?"

"Yes, he *took* her!"

Tiger Lily pried Gwen away from her, but held even tighter to her arms as she locked eyes with her. She hunched an inch, making sure they were looking at each other straight on. This alone helped Gwen gather her wits, if only so she would be better able to fully communicate her panic. Tiger Lily was looking—she was listening.

With careful and economic use of language, Tiger Lily gathered the relevant

details. "Where did he take her?"

"I d-don't know—he just disappeared!"

"Did he say why he was taking her?"

"C-collater-ral—he said it was… collateral."

"He agreed to help you and Peter?"

"Yeah, but he k-kidnapped Rosemar—"

"Gwen," Tiger Lily interrupted. The girl fell silent, mid-syllable. With calm authority, Tiger Lilly told her, "She'll be okay. We will get her back. We can make a plan for it right now—but first, you have to understand that. She'll be okay. We'll get her back."

"N-n-no! He—"

"Gwen. It's alright. It's scary, but there's no reason to worry, and once you stop worrying, we can start working on a plan. Piper doesn't want Rosemary. He wants gold, doesn't he?"

"P-princess Charlotte's crown…" she stuttered.

"Okay. Princess Charlotte's crown. That's what he wants. We'll get him that, and he'll—"

"An-and a root from the Ne-never Tree…"

"The Never Tree?" Tiger Lily's confidence seemed to falter.

"What's the Never Tree?" Gwen wept. "He wants it to hide

from the mermaids."

Tiger Lily shook her head. "The Never Tree is the tree at the heart of Neverland. Fairies are born in its hollows, and redskins cut their bows from its branches. It's the magical nucleus of Neverland, but I have no idea why Piper would want any part of it. It won't hide *him*."

"But he thinks it will and—"

Tiger Lily hushed her, firm and loving. "Then Peter will take a cutting and make him give Rosemary back. Peter never leaves anyone behind. I'm sure the tree will survive that. Did Piper tell you when or where he wanted to meet again?"

"He gave me a rat." Gwen held out the creature, which had been shoved in her coat pocket and traumatized by the flight back home. He squeaked, grateful to be near the ground and not in motion.

"Oh!" Already on edge, Tiger Lily was startled by the rodent and jerked back. The rat squeaked again, and she took it on faith that the creature was not feral. "Alright. We'll wake up Hawkbit and send him to Neverland right away. Peter will take care of the crown and the Never Tree, and we'll call Piper back. In the meantime, Rosemary will be safe, and no doubt dazed and happy in his spell."

"B-but!" There were no words in her mind, just abstract fear.

"If he did *anything* to hurt her, he would see the wrath of Neverland, the redskins, and the mermaids, too. He knows that. He wouldn't dream of it, even if he had anything to gain from it."

"Are you sure?" She wanted to have that faith, but her adrenaline-flooded mind wanted her to suffer her fear still longer.

Tiger Lily drew her into a hug again. "Positive. You don't even have to believe it yourself, as long as you trust me. Don't think about it. Just think about how much you trust Peter, Hawkbit, and me."

Gwen lifted her arms and returned the hug. In turn, she was rocked back and forth. Tiger Lily was asking her to stop thinking, to play the child and have faith in the one rocking and assuring her. She appreciated it. For a moment, it made it easier to be an adult about the situation.

"Okay," Gwen agreed, trying to convince her heart with her voice.

"Did he tell you how to find Hollyhock?"

Gwen nodded against her shoulder, and explained everything that had happened while they sat in the reddish glow of her cigar-store Indian lamp. The fairies wandered in after the initial commotion to listen as well. Tiger Lily kept her talking and made her walk through the better aspects of the night. When the fear and anxiety had dissipated enough, Gwen felt exhaustion, pure and simple, flood her system. With all the relevant information, Hawkbit zoomed off to Neverland to report back to Peter. Gwen closed her eyes, certain she would not be able to fall asleep, until the moment that she did. Foxglove dragged her pincushion bed in from the other room, and then helped the rat make a little bed out of a bandana beside her on the nightstand. Tiger Lily continued sitting in her bed, reluctant to move and risk waking poor, tired Gwen. When the girl began to snore, Tiger Lily brushed the hair out of her eyes and turned off the lamp. In the darkness, she snuggled down herself… but stayed in Gwen's hold and kept a comforting hand on the young woman's shoulder.

CHAPTER 36

BLINK WAS WAITING FOR THEM IN THE MORNING. GWEN STIRRED herself awake before Tiger Lily, whose sleep schedule was suffering as a result of the girls and their emergencies. When Gwen pushed herself up and away from where she was cuddled against Tiger Lily, she caught sight of the girl in a blue softball jersey and cargo shorts.

She was surrounded by all the blocks, stacking cups, playing cards, and other building materials she could find in the house, and all the plastic animals, too. She sat in the middle of a small village she had built on the floor of Tiger Lily's room. Happy and silent, there was no telling how long she'd been sitting there, immersed in a world-building game of her own design.

"Blink?"

Tiger Lily stirred.

The girl set down the narwhal figurine and plastic tiger. "Peter sent me. I didn't want to wake you."

"Where's Peter?" Gwen got up out of bed, watching where she stepped. Blink's card-cup-block-and-Lego village spanned over most of the carpet.

"He's coming tonight with the others, once it gets dark. He sent me ahead."

While Gwen appreciated the logic of sending inconspicuous Blink in daylight, she didn't fully understand. "Why?"

Blink stood up and artfully bounded around all of her houses. "So that you'd know that everything is going to be okay." She approached Gwen, empty-handed, and announced, "He wanted me to give you this."

She was confused, but understood as soon as the girl threw her arms around Gwen's waist. Her heart melted a bit, and the words echoed in her head. *Everything is going to be okay.*

She turned and saw Tiger Lily lying awake in bed, watching the embrace with warm eyes. Blink looked at her, too. "I found some worms for my animal town outside in the mud. I put them in a jar with their dirt so they wouldn't get on the carpet. They're the only real animals I brought in. Is that okay?"

Tiger Lily smiled. "Absolutely."

Foxglove had woken up as well, and now wandered through the imaginary streets of Blink's animal town. She was delighted to find Dillweed dozing in one of the card houses. The green fairy had accompanied Blink to reality, despite his fears. His terrifying and drunken experience at Jay's party left him wary of the real world, but Gwen had saved him from that, and he trusted her to watch out for him again if he came to keep her spirits up and help find her little sister. He owed her that much, and cowardice was no vice of his.

Blink wanted to know everything Gwen knew. They went into the living room and listened to bacon sizzle while Tiger Lily cooked breakfast for the young strategists. Blink marveled over the coaster with Piper's instructions for finding the holding facility. It shouldn't have surprised Gwen that Piper's directions pointed deeper into the woods, just past Lake Agana. The lake was beginning to seem the nexus for all the area's magic.

Blink gave everything her full attention and asked occasional, pointed questions. Any other child would have added to the frenzy of Gwen's concerns, but Blink came with a mission. Dillweed and Foxglove stayed at her shoulders like two flitting angels in purple and green.

Piper's rat popped onto the table midway through their discussions and started gnawing on the coaster. Blink took it from him with a firm, scolding, "No," but then gave him half a piece of bacon from her plate. She watched him eat it, vanishing the stiff slice of meat incrementally with his sharp front teeth. "What's his name?"

"I don't know," Gwen answered. "We only met last night."

"Pablo?"

The rat squeaked in protest, and shook his head.

"Rufus?"

The rat shook his head even harder when he squeaked in denial.

"Roscoe? Seymour? Norbert?" Each time Blink mentioned a name, the rat objected. "Leroy?" she tried.

The rat hesitated, then made a low, contented rumbling sound, signaling some sort of approval, as if Leroy was not his name, but would suffice.

"Okay, Leroy. I'm going to need your help today." Looking again to Gwen, she asked, "Do you have some paper I could use?"

Blink proceeded to outline her plan, drawing a map and tactical symbols on a page of the little notebook Gwen kept in her satchel.

"I'm going to follow Piper's instructions to the lab. They probably thought they were smart to put it out in the woods away from the town, but it is actually really close to us if it's just on the other side of Lake Agana."

"It's too far to walk on your own." Gwen told her.

"I can fly," Blink said. "I won't let anyone see me, so long as the fairies don't come with me."

Dillweed assured her he wouldn't. Foxglove wasn't excited about going to the holding facility either.

"What will you do when you get there?"

"Watch," Blink answered. She picked up the rat and held him in both her hands. He looked like a pet when she cradled him—

not the animal Gwen had found in a dumpster last night. "I'll be lookout and figure out as much as I can about it. I'll find a way to sneak in… but I'll need Leroy's help."

Gwen could see the advantage a rat had over a fairy in this instance. The usual charms of fairies, who left their magic and presence undetected by unsuspecting eyes, would be of no use in an environment full of trained Anomalous Activity officers… or whoever guarded such a place. No one would suspect a rat though. Rats were ordinary things, unsavory pests that had no association with Neverland or magic.

Blink lifted Leroy to meet her eyes and asked him, "Are you prepared to do daring and brave things for your countrymen and infiltrate an enemy base?"

The rat growled with a happy and hypnotized thirst for adventure.

"Alright," Blink announced getting to her feet. "Leroy and I will scout and have a full report by tonight. Peter and the other kids will come, and then we can all go save the day together." Gwen admired the girl's confidence as she took her map and tucked it into the pockets of her cargo pants. They looked like boys' pants. Gwen missed having functional, deep pockets in her clothing. Blink pulled her hair into a high ponytail to keep it out of her face and looked like she was prepared for anything.

"Excuse me, Tiger Lily?" she asked. "Would you pack me a lunch, please?"

CHAPTER 37

GWEN BIT HER FINGERNAILS MORE THAT DAY THAN SHE HAD IN THE past six months. It was a nasty childhood habit she had almost completely beat, but it crept back whenever she suffered through an episode of blind anxiety. She wound and rewound Irene's invisible thread around her hands until they went numb. Tiger Lily tried to keep her heart calm and her mind distracted, but there was only so much she could do with card games and work around the house. Gwen appreciated it, however. If it weren't for Tiger Lily's almost apathetic regard for the situation, she probably would have gone to pieces worrying about Rosemary. She tried to remember Peter had sent Blink with a hug and a plan.

The day dragged on like a wounded animal, but when dusk at last came, it seemed to devour the sky all at once.

Gwen sat outside on the porch, the way she had once waited in the yard for her father to come home in the evenings—back when her father coming home from work could be the highlight of her day. Even that happy memory seemed complicated and melancholy to Gwen now. She wished she'd spent more evenings waiting for her father to come home from work—that strange, adult work she was now fighting against.

If she could have snapped her fingers and been safe at home

with Rosemary, she would have. She'd sworn she would watch out for Rosemary, but she'd only enabled the girl to embroil herself deeper into dangerous adventures. Gwen could not escape the feeling that she was at fault for Piper taking Rosemary. The treasures and enchantments Piper demanded from them seemed like small trinkets in contrast to what Gwen suffered in her sister's absence, and she understood, too late, everyone's warnings about what price the Piper would come at. She was paying for what she'd instigated now.

She watched for stars in the sky. A few untwinkling planets emerged—Venus and Jupiter, as Lasiandra had taught her to identify—but it took another minute and much sky scanning before Gwen caught sight of the first star.

Wringing her hands, she started, "Starlight, star bright, first star I see tonight…" As her voice plodded through the words of the superstitious rhyme, Gwen thought of every other time she'd asked favors of stars. Always wracked with indecision, always torn in two by the divided nature of her conflicted heart, she'd never known quite what to ask for. Every wish had left her melancholy in her suspicion she was misusing potential.

As she made her wish tonight, Gwen longed for the luxury of confliction.

Midway through the sky, it adjusted its course by a hair, and her eyes trailed after the fast-falling speck of light until it hit the artificial horizon formed by the towering forest. Half a second after the star left sight, a faint, white aurora surged from the depths of the forest. It was subtle enough that it would have gone by unnoticed by anyone not waiting for the impact.

Nothing else happened.

Gwen kept her eyes on the forest, but backed up and opened the door to the trailer. "Dillweed. Foxglove," she whisper-called. The fairies, eating apricots in the kitchen, came when called. "I think they're here," she whispered.

Tiger Lily came to the door, too. She looked out into the night with wild longing in her eyes. A smile of supreme mischief crossed her face, and Gwen watched as it withered away. "Go," she said. "I'll keep watch for anyone who might track your magic trail back to here. If I suspect anything, I'll light a campfire in the fire pit."

Gwen gave her a hug. "You are a wonderful safe house tender," she told her.

Tiger Lily smiled at the compliment, but there was no mistaking the sadness in her eyes… the desperate wish that she could run, brave and wayward, into the woods with the children to thwart their adversaries. "Go," she said again.

Gwen almost stuck her hands into the pockets of her crop-top jacket, but realized that Dillweed and Foxglove had nestled themselves in those cavities. She dashed over to the woods, careful to stay on foot since the night was still so young and newly dark.

Once she was in the black of the forest, her fairies burst out of her pockets in order to illuminate her way and search for Peter.

He wasn't hard to find.

Hawkbit was with him, much to the delight of Foxglove, who scooped him up and shook him until their yellow and purple glows blurred together. Dillweed dutifully stayed by Gwen as Peter approached, a small squad of lost children behind him.

Newt, Sal, and Bard were in company. Newt and Sal had painted their faces with dark mud and were in the most artfully dirty clothes they could find for camouflage. Bard was in a practical jumper and had her hair in a neat braid, wrapped and pinned to her head. Peter looked like Peter.

"Ready to go?" he asked.

Gwen nodded.

"Where's Blink?"

"She's waiting for us there—scouting the place with Leroy."

"Who's Leroy?"

"Sorry—Piper's rat."

"Good." Peter looked to the other children. "The adventure begins then."

Bard saluted him. Sal and Newt pounded on their chests in

a demonstrative show of proto-masculinity. "Which way to their base?" Sal asked.

Gwen handed Peter the coaster so he could examine it for himself as she announced, "This way."

The fairies led the way, illuminating a path through the forest. Newt and Sal bushwhacked their way through ferns and brush with large sticks, clearing the way for the others. "What's the plan?" Bard asked.

"We'll know when we rendezvous with Blink," Peter answered.

"Stealth attack!" Newt yelled.

"Of some kind, yes."

The children descended into a flurry of thoughts on this matter.

"Sal should cause a distraction."

"The girls should wear camo, too."

"We should have a secret code."

"I think I'm going to need a bigger stick."

While they discussed their options, Peter cast a look at Gwen and seemed to register for the first time that something was amiss with her. "What happened to you?" he asked.

"What do you mean?"

"You don't look so good." The hard winter ground crunched under his feet with fallen leaves and dying shrubbery.

Appalled with his memory, his indifference, or both, Gwen snapped, "My sister got kidnapped last night. I haven't *been* so good."

Peter looked taken aback, as if her bitter tone surprised him. "I just meant your hair. And your clothes. You look weird."

"Oh." A pang of guilt struck her for having attributed such callousness into his immature question. Her temper was flared now, and it was hard for her to push it back down and remind herself that Peter's rude remarks still coexisted with his friendship. "I had to play with princesses in order to get the patch we needed for Piper."

"Hmm," Peter responded. "Well, I'm glad it was for a noble

cause. You look awfully grown-up though. It isn't becoming."

She knew that on another day, she might have agreed with him, but she was too distraught to handle his blunt remarks about her appearance with a level head. She wanted to snap back, *Jay thought I looked nice*, but it was a stupid impulse. What did it matter how Peter judged her appearance anyway? On some shallow level, she could justify seeking Jay's approval, but what did it matter what she looked like to a friend? And yet, because he was a friend, his frank opinions felt full of impartial honesty and greater weight.

"But speaking of princesses," Peter finished his sentence not with words but with an object. He pulled a glittering crown out of his knapsack and placed it in Gwen's hands.

"Princess Charlotte's crown?" She knew it could be nothing else, but she was hesitant to believe it. She'd never held something so valuable before. It was almost underwhelming simply because it was a real object instead of a thing of impossible fantasy.

"You don't have to worry about Rosemary," he promised.

"What about the Never Tree root?" Gwen asked.

Peter's expression turned grim as he pulled a dark, scraggly root out of the pack as well. Tangled and dirty, it looked like strange symbols or runes were seared onto the root. He held it tight in his hand, but did not offer it to Gwen. "The tree suffered for it. The Never Tree is strong, but its roots are important. It'll recover its full strength in time, but I hope I can talk Piper out of this madness. The root can't do anything for him, and we could still graft it back to give it strength."

"We have to get Rosemary back, though," Gwen insisted. She understood now that the Never Tree was no small thing, but her sister remained more important.

"I'll get her back. Sure as snowsalt. You know how clever I am."

Gwen handed the priceless Welsh crown back to Peter. "Yeah. I do."

They tromped through the forest, the most mischievous band to ever pass through those woods. Not so much as a twig snapped under her feet when Blink approached, even though she was avoiding flying and all traceable magic. She startled Gwen, the way she appeared out of the darkness.

"What's the report, Blink?" Peter took her sudden arrival in stride. "What diabolic defenses have they set up?"

"Do we need more camouflage?" Sal asked, reaching down and grabbing a fistful of mud in preparation.

Blink held Leroy in her hands like a baby and began to brief the others. "I don't think you'll need more camouflage. I ran some experiments to see if they could detect magic outside of the base. It looks like a school. It's not a normal jail place. I can't fly if I get too close to it. I think it might be dangerous for the fairies to go near."

"Is it safe here though?" Bard asked.

"Should be," she answered. Dillweed, Foxglove, and Hawkbit all nodded… They felt no ill effects of any kind of magic drain.

Bard pulled a spider-silk net out of her overalls' breast pocket. "We should set up a meeting place here, in case things go bad and we need to retreat or the fairies need to hide."

She passed the net to Newt, who put his bushwhacking stick between his teeth and held onto the silvery scarf as he climbed the nearest tree. He tucked it between branches and leaves, perfectly obscuring it.

"Remember this spot," Bard told everyone as the three fairies examined the hiding spot and made sure it would sufficiently obscure them above the heads of any magic hunting officers.

"How could you not fly?" Peter asked Blink. "You're the best flier I know—except for me."

"You might be able to fly, Peter," she conceded, "but something is wrong about this place. It doesn't want to let you do magic."

Gwen puzzled over this phenomenon. "How big of a radius is there where you can't fly?"

Blink blinked once and asked, "What's a radius?"

"How far away do you have to be before you can fly again?

She thought. "Like half a football field?" she guessed. "It's hard to tell with the forest."

"But *how?*" Peter demanded.

This made sense to Gwen, but it was alarming. "They must have an anomaly reduction device of some kind... but it would have to be *huge*." The simple keychain Dawn had carried around at the mall had been an intense magical drain and prevented any magic or perception of magic to crop up while they were in public. To create the same effect for such a large space of forest, they would need something much more powerful.

"What's an anomaly reduction?" Bard asked. The children all took a step closer to Gwen with curious wonderment.

"Anomaly is the grown-up word for magic," Peter answered, but he waited on her for a better understanding.

"The reduction device is basically a black hole that sucks up magic and creates a field where nobody normal notices anything that might be magical and nothing magical can happen. The one I saw was a personal-sized one, like a coin. It was really heavy. I can't imagine what the one inside their facility must be like."

Peter burst into a grin. The others were perplexed, but he was already scheming and ready to throw half a dozen questions at Gwen. Newt climbed down out of the tree and sat on the forest floor as he and the others watched their quick exchange.

"Is there a way to turn it off?"

"It's just solid metal of some kind."

"Would I be able to pick it up?"

"I don't think so."

"Would the grown-ups be able to pick it up?"

Gwen thought again about how heavy the keychain was. "Maybe a very strong one could... but I doubt it."

"Does it stop all magic?"

"I'm not sure. I think it sucks up what it can, and then just hides the rest. Things that are innately magical might not be affected—or at least, not as affected. The way it was explained to me was that it was an extremely magical object that puts all its magic into hiding and stopping other magic from people."

Peter snapped and got the fairies' attention. "Hawk, go with Bard and see what Blink is talking about. If anything feels wrong, you have her come right back with you. Stay in her reach."

Hawkbit saluted Peter like he was his commanding officer. Bard didn't question the order but marched off in the direction Blink pointed her. While they went to test the anomaly reduction field, Peter continued his line of questioning.

"So is this akin to a fairy field?"

"A fairy field?" Gwen asked.

"When enough fairies gather, they can use their magic to hide in plain sight. It happens all the time in Kensington Garden." Peter's grin was growing like a fern's unfurling leaves in the light.

"So it is a little bit like the spider-silk?" Blink asked.

"Yeah, a little. Only it works on unsuspecting adults, instead of drones."

"They won't expect us!" Sal cheered. The children were all sorts of nervous and excited, glowing in the spastic purple-green light of Dillweed and Foxglove, who were getting more fidgety in the air every second.

"But they know about magic, so they might not be so unsuspecting," Peter mused, putting his hand to his face and stroking an imaginary beard in thought. "Still, it is some advantage. This would explain why it took Piper so long to escape… did he tell you how he managed to get out?"

Gwen shook her head. "He just mentioned he hypnotized someone." She bit her lip, trying to force back the shudder that wanted to strike her spine. "But then that doesn't make sense with my theory that it only affects things that aren't innately magical…"

"Piper is magic," Peter assured her. "He could have done it if his guards got sloppy. This is good news. Blink, what's the layout like?"

In answer, she let Leroy down and got down on her hands and knees to pull up all the plants in front of her. She smoothed over the dirt quickly, the cold of the night never seeming to bother her or any of the lost children. When it was out of mind, it didn't occur to Gwen to feel cold either. It was only an occasional thought of reality that reminded her she ought to be cold during winter nights like this.

Leroy dragged a tiny rat toe along the dry and level dirt, limping along as he etched lines on the ground. Blink pointed and explained for him as he finished his diagram. "Whatever anomaly machine they have, Leroy isn't affected by it. And he must be at least a little magical because he's the smartest rat I've ever met. The entrance is here, and they have a lot of laboratories along this hallway. There's a basement, too. Leroy couldn't get into any of the rooms down there. There was a guard, and all those rooms needed keys."

"Easier to get to the experiments than the prisoners then," Peter surmised, staring at the simple dirt sketch. "Real keys or their magic card keys?"

Leroy squeaked. Blink somehow translated. "Magic flat keys."

His eyes went back to the dirt sketch. He squatted and picked up a twig, tracing small rooms in the basement Leroy had outlined. The rooms lined the walls, leading to a single room at the end of the basement's hall. "What I want to know," he asked, "is if there are experiments upstairs and locked cells downstairs… what do you think they have locked up here?" He placed a promising X on the cell at the far end of the hall.

"Do you think that's where the magic-stopper is?" Blink asked.

Something rustled in the bushes. The sound startled everyone, but the yellow glow of Hawkbit was an instant relief. Bard had returned and was happy to announce, "Hawkbit doesn't have a problem with the field. He said he could feel it, but he was okay to fly in it."

"Good." Peter rose and stood tall, flinging his twig away. He looked at the fairies, all hovering over Bard at the moment. "Everyone, dust up. We need at least one fairy to stand watch and signal Tiger Lily and the others back home in case our mission fails and we get caught." He took off the knapsack—Princess Charlotte's crown and the invaluable Never Tree root within it—

and threw it into the trees above. It caught on a broken branch and hung inconspicuously camouflaged above their heads. He announced to the fairies, "If all else fails, you need to get Leroy to bring Piper here for his payment and return Rosemary."

Gwen smiled. For someone who rarely thought more than a minute into his playful future, Peter was a masterful strategist, with all the right priorities.

Peter looked back into the tree above them. "Newt, get that spider-silk back down out of the tree. I've got a plan."

CHAPTER 38

THE MISCHIEVOUS BAND FOLLOWED BLINK AND LEROY TO THE FACILITY. Peter marched forward with such confidence Gwen would have thought he already knew where he was going. As soon as they were in the magic-reduction device's radius, they lost their ability to fly, but also their ability to be reliably tracked. At least, they assumed that when no officers came for them.

Peter was the only exception. Too confident to let anything interfere with his flight, he continued to bound into the air as if nothing was wrong at all.

Once they reached the building, they hung back in the bushes. The description Blink had given of it as a school seemed fitting. There were windows all along the walls, but they were high and out of reach, even for adults. The building was a single story, but it was a towering story. It was made primarily of brick, but concrete reinforced what wasn't, and two tall columns stood beside the doors of its only entrance. The windows were wide enough for children to fit through, but without their normal ability of flight, those would be useless.

A tall, razor-wire fence surrounded it—which also posed a problem to flightless children. The chain link fence's gate was clamped shut with a heavy padlock, but something was flying on the other side.

"What is it, Peter?" Newt whispered while his commander investigated with his spyglass.

"Drones," Peter answered, staring their little red lights down through his wooden periscope. "At least two of them, and probably four—one monitoring each side of the building."

"How are we going to get inside?" Sal hissed.

"Gwen has my lucky skeleton key," Bard told him, "but I don't know about the drones?"

Peter adjusted his spyglass, fixing his gaze on the door. "The skeleton key won't help us, except with getting through the gate. I don't think the door has a keyhole."

The six of them and their three fairies huddled together in a discussion of all their options. All plans were considered, even the impossible ones, until Sal fell upon the best solution.

"We should break a drone," he announced. "When grown-ups' things break, they always find out and try to get someone in trouble. When a grown-up comes out, we could attack them and get the key!"

Bard stared at Hawkbit and proposed, "Or maybe we could have a fairy steal it from him. He wouldn't even know then."

Foxglove volunteered, but recanted when she was informed she couldn't pinch, bite, or otherwise harm the adult. Dillweed decided to go instead.

Peter agreed at once with this course of action, and gallantly took charge. He pulled out his slingshot and loaded it with a steely marble before he hovered up over the fence and fired down at a drone rounding the corner of the building. They watched the red light fall to the ground with a crash, and then fade off. After that, they waited.

Gwen felt a tug on her jacket sleeve. Bard was staring up at her.

"Are you scared?" the little girl asked. How could someone so small read her like a book? Gwen nodded a bit and smiled as if she felt silly for it.

"It's okay to be scared. I just wanted you to know you don't have to be. Everything will be okay." She wrapped her arms around Gwen's hips in one of the half-sized hugs she was now so used to.

"Thanks, Bard," she whispered, feeling a little stronger for it.

In a minute, a dark-haired man in grey coveralls came out of the facility, grumbling. He had a set of keys and a plastic card attached to his belt. He wandered the building's perimeter until he found the collapsed bot. He wore a miner's light, and kneeled beside the broken drone as he examined it.

Dillweed shot between the chain links of the fence and zipped to the man's hip. With the drone down, he wouldn't have to worry about it finding his pixie dust trail until the man had finished fixing it. He worked industriously and inconspicuously to slip the key card off its metal clip. Once he had it, he flew back to the others and dropped it into Peter's hand.

Gwen, in the meantime, had been figuring out how to use a hundred-year-old iron key to open a steel padlock manufactured within the past year. To her amazement, the tip of the wide key shrunk down and melted into the lock. With a simple twist, she had the lock opened and quietly pulled the gate open. They flooded in, lucky that the drone engineer had his back to them and his focus on his machine.

The children swiped into the facility and flooded in, uncertain what they would find inside.

The building's interior reminded her of a doctor's office or small hospital. The tile was freckled with blue and silver, and the walls were a drab blue color, like a foggy sky. The wood doors were almost white in contrast. A stairway to their right lead down into a darker region of the building.

Their first move was to take out the cameras. Sal and Newt dug some raven tree fruits out of Gwen's satchel and pitched them straight into the cameras monitoring the entrance. Their twinkling eggshells cracked on impact and covered the camera lenses with a thick and goopy cream, leaving them nonfunctional.

"Let's get down to the cells and find Hollyhock," Peter

announced. "After that, we'll figure out which lab the pipe is in."

So they descended, following Peter's cocky confidence down the concrete stairs in unnerving florescent lighting. They tried to stay quiet, shuffling down the stairs until they got to the heavy locked door at the bottom. Peter swiped it open and it took all Gwen's strength to pull the door open for everyone. The children swarmed in, much to the surprise of the security guard.

"What the—you kids can't be here!" she exclaimed, almost as frustrated as she was surprised.

The door closed behind them though, and in the concrete basement, the children knew they no longer had need to be quiet. They ran screaming down the hallway, too many for the guard to apprehend. She grabbed a hold of Newt, but let go of him with a yelp when he bit her. In response, she grabbed the Taser at her hip as he ran off.

Only, it wasn't a Taser. Gwen didn't recognize the device, but she suspected it was an experimental product of magic and technology. "Stop! *Stop!*" the guard yelled, backing up toward a cell door before firing the weapon and shooting a streak of visible current—whether electrical or magical, they couldn't know—at Newt. He dodged her erratic fire the first time, but the lightning-like product hit him when she fired again.

The shock shot Newt's body up into the air, but when he fell, it was as if he were in slow motion. The boy's body had seized up, but drifted back to the ground in gentle paralysis. The guard began firing at other targets, and everyone dashed in a mad attempt to avoid her fire

Gwen met eyes with Blink, who pulled Leroy out of her cargo pants' pocket and cradled him in her hands. While the screaming, flailing children zigzagged all through the hall, Gwen snuck to the cell behind the guard woman with the key card. Foxglove maliciously tied the woman's shoestrings together, and Dillweed and Hawkbit worked together to lift her walkie-talkie off her belt. Once Gwen was in position, Blink then ran up to the guard woman and chucked brave Leroy right at her.

The guard screamed as she attempted to bat Leroy off her, but the friendly rat made a horrible show of snarling and snapping while he clawed at her uniform and held on. Gwen wrenched open the cell door and watched as the guard stumbled backward and fell into it in her attempt to get the rat off her chest.

Leroy sprung off her and dashed out as soon as she was securely inside, allowing Gwen to slam the cell door shut. The guard pounded on the thick glass of the door's slender window, but the sound was muted and signified her helplessness. "Sorry!" Gwen apologized before running off to see what condition Newt was in.

Lying on the floor, his body was all locked up, even his jaw. He could only manage mumbled "Uh-huhs," and "nuh-uhs," in response to questions.

Bard held onto his head and patted it as she reassured him, "I'm sure it's nothing a little fairy dust won't fix." All three fairies danced over him, dusting him from head to toe.

"Sal, I'm designating you medic," Peter announced. "See what you and the fairies can do for him while the girls and I search for Hollyhock. I need Newt up and in action when we storm the labs."

"Yes sir!" Sal exclaimed. He began doing chest compressions on Newt, but fortunately, he didn't know how, so no damage was done.

Peter swiped the key card from Gwen and opened the nearest cell door. Blink stole the key card from him right before he plunged in to investigate, and she opened the next. Bard and Gwen joined in this effort. There were only nine cells all total, and most of them were empty, including the one they'd locked the guard in.

Gwen opened a cell door, and a yowling cat came screeching out of the cell. It scampered off as fast as it could, not so different from her own beloved Tootles at home, except it wore a stately hat and a pair of black leather boots on its hind legs. It seemed almost completely ordinary, and Gwen suspected that what magic the sharply dressed cat had once possessed had been drained away in this institution.

She went to open the next cell, but Bard still had the key card and was on her tiptoes staring into an unopened cell. Bard pressed her wide-eyed face against the thick window and Gwen came to see what had the girl's attention.

Inside, a faint and foggy presence danced, fluctuating between gold and blue-green colors. It was ephemeral and seemed to suck all the light out of the cell in order to feed its own glow. The eerie darkness of the cell made a troubling backdrop for the amorphous creature within.

"I don't think we should open this one," Bard announced.

Peter's patience had run out with these cells; Hollyhock wasn't in any of them. He took the key from Bard and raced down to the last cell. "She's got to be in the last one then, right?"

The cell at the end of the hall was the only one that did not have a window to look into. The door was heavier and vault-like. Gwen looked back at the ghostly presence in the cell, and considered what the adults might have locked up in the biggest vault. "Peter…"

He was already pulling at the metal door, prying it open. They couldn't see anything inside, only darkness.

Newt and Sal came running over with the fairies. With the help of the fairies, the effects of the magical Taser had worn off fast enough. They hung back with the girls while Peter drew his dagger and stepped slowly into the dark chamber.

Gwen poked her head in, just enough to discover a switch on the wall. Flicking it, she turned on two rows of overhead lights, which began buzzing over the vaults many racks and strange objects.

The children were willing to wander in once there was light, and they found the storage room filled with everything from mundane household equipment to magical specimens of botany. Everything was tagged and labeled. "What is all this?" Peter asked aloud.

Gwen looked at a shelf with a pair of glass shoes and a rose bush cutting that shouldn't have looked nearly as bright or alive as it did. "Confiscated materials," she announced. "Magical contraband."

"I bet the Piper's pipe is in here!" Sal exclaimed. The children scattered, everyone searching the shelves for their target. Peter took to the air and scanned the topmost shelves, searching "But where's the magic canceler they're using? I want to destroy it!"

Gwen found an evidence tag seemingly suspended in the air. She reached out to touch it, but bumped against an invisible ball of thread—undoubtedly the one that her small spool of thread had been taken from.

In a matter of seconds, Sal had found the pipe—a large, purple-painted instrument that did not look anything like any flute Gwen had ever seen. Hollyhock was nowhere to be found, however, which meant she would have to be upstairs in one of the labs.

"But what about the magic canceler?" Peter cried.

Newt went running out of the room. "Maybe it's in the door you guys didn't check."

Gwen hated to break it to him, but said all the same, "That's just a broom closet. It isn't even locked or anything."

Still, Newt ran out to check. In absence of any other plan, the children followed after. Gwen convinced the children not to steal anything else besides the pipe. They didn't know what kind of unfamiliar magic these objects held, or who might get in trouble and be investigated if they disappeared.

The guard woman was still pounding on her cell door, but her walkie-talkie was going off where Dillweed and Hawkbit had dropped it on the floor. "Erica, pick up, dammit! I'm locked out! It's Andrew, come upstairs and let me in!"

Newt pulled open the one unlocked door in the basement. It was more than a broom closet. It contained the building's water heater and electrical generator. The fuse box was mounted on the wall, and other mechanical and electrical components that Gwen didn't know the function of. In the very middle, it also had a solid, black, block of metal.

Peter untied the spider-silk at his waist where he'd worn it like a sash. Gwen saw immediately what he was about to do, but her mind was also preoccupied staring at the generator, different from any she'd ever seen before and clearly enchanted by some grown-up technology. The anomaly reduction device couldn't simply be eliminating all the magic in the vicinity. The interplay between magical technology and this block of magic-sucking element was more complex than her present understanding of it. How were the two interacting in this room? How could the adults have laboratories in which they were experimenting with magic and also deprive the children of flight?

"Peter..." she began, cautious and confused.

But Peter shared none of her apprehensions. He spread the spider-silk like a fishing net and threw it high over the impossible block. The net drifted down, covering the monolithic black block in a wispy veil of silver netting. Everyone took several steps back on the speckled tile as the two enchantments—one magic canceling, the other magic hiding—came into contact with each other.

The technologies all around them started to short out, shut down, power off, and light up... it was a jarring series of reactions from the electrical systems that were calibrated to exist beside the anomaly reduction device. They began behaving anomalously, panicking as the supernatural aspects of their programming lost touch with the one thing that was wirelessly keeping them grounded in reality. The children found they could fly again, as the lights above began to flash, and electricity was delivered throughout the building in limited, frantic bursts.

This was no longer a stealth mission.

CHAPTER 39

Hollyhock had to be in the labs upstairs. If they had to encounter anomalous activity researchers, it probably would be to their advantage to short out all of their technology first. The children crept back upstairs, lighter than air as they flew up in the shadows of the stairwell. They heard the voices of researchers as they discussed this sudden power loss.

"Hasn't anyone seen Andrew?"

"I don't like it. I think we should call the officers."

"And drag the black coats out into this? That's the last thing we need."

Blink carried Leroy, Bard held tight to the pipe, and Newt had picked up the kitty cat in the boots and hat. They drifted up to the top of the ceiling, where only a few emergency backup lights illuminated the dim hall. As adults came out of their labs, they were looking for each other, not flying intruders.

"The system's completely down?"

"Is Richards running experiments on the anomalium again?"

"Does anyone have access to basement? Where on earth is Andrew?"

All the children pressed themselves flat against the ceiling. Peter waved his compatriots over and motioned for them as he inched closer to the unguarded, open door to one of the labs.

When he gave the signal, they dropped off the ceiling and flew into the lab in a furious rush. Peter pulled his slingshot out and immediately took a threatening aim at the researchers within with such confidence they backed up and put their hands up.

"Whoa, watch out there, kid!"

The children scattered in the room. Newt dropped the cat; it yowled but landed fine on its feet. Everyone searched for Hollyhock, but within seconds, it was clear she was not in this lab.

In the middle of the blue-grey laboratory and its speckled floor, however, a glassy, round object the size of the grapefruit sat on a lab table. It glowed red and blue in turn, colors dancing like weightless lava within it. So well acquainted with magic, the lost children knew an extraordinary object when they saw one. None of them knew what it did, of course, but from the shiny metal stand on which it sat, they knew it must be important.

Peter grabbed it.

"No, no, no, no!" a balding researcher yelled, running toward him.

Peter no longer had his slingshot out, but the giant marble was a better deterrent. The researcher kept his hands up and stopped.

"Be careful with that!" his lab partner yelled. Both men wore white lab coats and looked like the sad sort of adults who stayed late into the night at their work.

"What does that thing do?" Gwen asked. The researchers' fear seemed born of something more than concern for their creation. They were scared, and Gwen knew enough to know she should be scared too.

The children flocked around Peter while the researchers exchanged a glance. "We're not sure," the bald one admitted. "But the matter within is extremely volatile and suggests a highly combustible nature."

"What's that mean?" Sal asked, cocking his head.

Gwen understood at once. "*Peter, don't drop that!*" she cried.

"Why not?" Newt demanded, floating overhead and watching the colors dance inside it like living goop.

By this time, several other scientists had gathered at the doorway of the lab and were gawking in with the same horror.

"It's explosive," Gwen told him. "It is very dangerous."

Peter smiled and shook his head. "I don't think so."

"Peter," Gwen warned, terrified at the prospect of dying in a violent explosion over a matter of Peter's confidence.

"But," he continued, "if you're worried about it, you can have it back. We're just here for our fairy."

The researchers both began babbling: they didn't know where she was, they didn't have clearance, they couldn't—

Peter lifted the marble over his head and got ready to smash it to the ground, and the men acquiesced. Gwen didn't know whether to trust his confidence or the researchers' authority. On top of that, she couldn't tell whether Peter was even serious in his threats to smash it.

"Take us to the fairy," Peter demanded of the bald researcher. "And keep your hands in the air. Everybody else, stay put!"

Peter held tight to the marble, making sure no one would be able to snatch it from him as they exited the lab. Nobody would have dared though.

"Watch out, he's got the ammonia noctigen and acetic solium!"

The facility's lab-coated staff stood back in pale-faced horror. The brave ones whispered between themselves.

"Did the black coats get called?"

"Where the hell is Andrew?"

"Nobody move! This is a robbery!" Newt shouted, lifting his fingers up like a gun.

"No, it's not," Bard said. "It's just a rescue mission, and we're very sorry for the trouble."

"No, we aren't!" Newt objected.

Peter stayed focused. "Are you taking us to our fairy?"

"Yes, she's in the transportation lab," the researcher told them, not looking back at the children forcing him through the facility.

"It's at the end of the hall. You can have your fairy back. This isn't going to work out for you though. If you leave now, you might be able to escape. We've already called the Anomalous Activity Department. The black coats will be here in minutes."

"You are the Department of Anomalous Activity," Gwen accused.

"We're just research and development," he told her. "You kids don't understand what you're doing. We're trying to figure out what makes this stuff works, and how we can make it work for everyone. We're not the bad guys."

"Yes, you are," Sal insisted. He then pretended to shoot at him with his fingers too. "You're the ones who bombed Neverland!"

"No, we're not. We're just trying to help with what we have. It's the black coats who are after you, and you've forced us to call them."

The researcher turned to a door at the end of the hall and, very slowly, as to not alarm Peter, reached to his belt to get his key card and swipe them in. No one was left in the dim transportation lab, so Peter stepped in and let his fellow children fly in with him.

On one of the three lab tables in the center of the room, Hollyhock was trapped under a bell jar.

"Step away from the door," he told the researcher, who complied.

He did so, but asked, "Okay. You've found your fairy. Can you hand me our experiment back now, nice and easy?"

"No," Peter answered as he chucked the blue and red marble down the hall like a bowling ball. The researchers all ran in the opposite direction, screaming. Peter slammed the lab door shut. Just a second later, the entire building shook with a violent explosion. Tendrils of purple smoke began curling in from underneath the door.

"Serves them right for keeping pickled night and sun brine in the same jar," Peter declared before heading straight for the glass container imprisoning Hollyhock.

She had been railing against the bell jar with her tiny fists, but now she shook with unexpected joy and hope—Peter had come for her! Her little fairy heart swelled and beat more glittery blood through her veins than it ever had before.

"Secure the door!" Bard cried, clutching the stolen pipe in her hands. "Gwen, help, you're big!"

Gwen found the closest file cabinets and poured all her energy into pushing one of them against the door, and after that, another one against the door. It didn't matter. They didn't need a way out; they would be going through the windows now that they were free to fly.

Wanton destruction surrounded her. Blink and Leroy were both clawing pages out of books. Newt and Sal were shoving computers off their desks. Bard, too small to be of any help with her own idea of barricading the door, was flying up around cabinets and emptying them out onto the floor. Small prototype devices were smashed and breathed multi-colored sparks and fumes as their barely captured magic escaped them. They targeted the tiny, fragile-looking things. Had they known how to smash the strange standing scale against the wall or the prototype car frame in the center of the lab, they would have.

Peter was still trying to figure out how to break Hollyhock free. The bell jar was screwed to a copper plate embedded on the surface of the lab table. Hollyhock yelled to warn him, but her fairy words were muffled by the glass and surrounding chaos. Peter found out for himself that touching the plate or the screws resulted in an unpleasant electric shock—a feature that forced Hollyhock to continue flying and radiating the maximum amount of magic she was capable of producing. "We'll get you out of here Holly," he told her, looking around for something heavy that would be easy to swing into the base of the glass.

The lab was well trashed by this point, especially since Foxglove had summoned all her vengeful strength to balance scissors on the counter tops and cut wires connecting the internal machinery of devices plugged into the wall outlets. Peter grabbed a tablet computer from the lab table and warned Hollyhock,

"Watch out," before he bashed the base of the bell jar. It took several whacks to not only crack and break the glass, but also smash open a hole big enough for his friend to escape through.

Blink hurtled a brutalized book at the car frame, then loaded Leroy back into her pocket. Newt went to Peter's side, waiting to be of assistance in this final task. Bard thrust Piper's pipe into Gwen's hands as she flew up alongside Sal and began pushing open the wide windows. It took both of them to thrust the windows open far enough to escape.

They heard pounding at the door, but Gwen's barricade wasn't budging—yet.

Hollyhock exploded out of the bell jar, her fairy dust flinging everywhere in a cloud of joyful freedom as she bolted for the window.

"Foxglove, come on," Bard called from the window. Peter chucked the tablet against the scale for good measure, but everyone else was on their way up. When the over-eager fairy refused to leave her malicious pursuit, Bard zipped down to drag her away. Gwen took to the air, but stayed low to the ground as she went to the opposite side of the room. There was still yelling and chaos coming from the halls, and the lights continued to flicker even now that the children were done with their destruction spree.

She flew carefully with the pipe in hand. Newt was having a hard time getting through the window, so Sal was helping pull him through. Bard grabbed Foxglove and contained her between the cage of her ginger fingers. Blink was already out and gone with Hollyhock—back to their rendezvous point to fetch Princess Charlotte's crown and the Never Tree root—but Peter waited at the top of the window for the rest of his band.

Gwen saw Newt start to stagger before she felt the disorienting feeling hit her too. Fearing for the pipe, she landed as fast as she could. Her motion was more graceful than Newt, who all but fell to the floor, or Bard's awkward somersault as she was forced to release Foxglove and break her fall. Peter wobbled at the top of the window, but retained his ability to defy all laws—adult and physical.

As Newt slipped out of his hands, Sal fell to the ground also, but landed outside. Somewhere in the forest nearby, Blink's flight shorted out and she continued on foot.

"What happened?" Newt shouted.

"I can't fly!" Bard announced, startled by this paralyzing development.

Foxglove went to the children and powdered them in her fairy dust, but to no avail. Their flight was taken from them, and they were as grounded as any child who had never met a fairy.

Someone pounded on the door. The noise reverberated with an eerie metallic sound as it went through the file cabinets stacked against it. Someone was trying to shove their way in, and they were getting more forceful about it.

"Come on!" Peter yelled, but to no avail. They were stranded, far below the windows. Hollyhock, seeing that something was going terribly wrong for the children, flitted up to the window and came back in… her curiosity blending with her compassion for them.

The door edged open, just a crack. It was only enough to let the man's furious voice in. "You kids open this door! Come here!"

Gwen knew she had little time. "Hollyhock, Foxglove, come here, fast!"

The fairies answered to the confidence in her voice—they could hear she had a plan. They were heartbroken when they heard it.

She handed the pipe over to them—that all-important antique flute was just barely within their capacity to carry when they both held onto it. "Take this up. Now."

Their initial shock and frustration—they wanted to save the children, not some musical artifact—was dissipated by the sheer force with which Gwen commanded them.

The man at the door yelled again, and budged it another inch. "The police are coming! You're in a lot of trouble. Now start cooperating."

The fairies were slow to heft up such a weight with them, but there was no doubt they would make it.

"Gwenny," Peter shouted down. "We're going to get you out of there!"

"There isn't time," Gwen told him. The man at the door was yelling again. "The officers are going to be here any minute—you need to make sure you're gone by then."

"What about all of you?" he yelled.

"Just go!" Gwen yelled. She could feel fearful tears sneaking up on her eyes, but she ignored them. "We'll *live*."

"Oh no," Bard muttered quietly. "Oh no." Newt called out for Sal, well knowing the futility of his cry. The fairies reached Peter and heaved the pipe into his hands so they could catch their breath. "Take the pipe," Gwen demanded. "Use Leroy to find Piper." Biting her lip, she focused on the pain of her teeth digging into her skin instead of the horrible desire to cry. She wrestled her voice into forcing her last words out with conviction. "Get Rosemary back."

Peter stared at her. Was he awed by her compassion, or disgusted with her maturity? She would never know. Bard was curled up and sitting on the floor now. Newt climbed cabinets and pressed himself against the wall, hoping to move through it.

Gwen held Peter's gaze, their eyes all fear and sadness.

The door finally gave, and she could hear the man storming in. With no other option, Peter slipped away from the window. Gwen turned to see the man. She put a comforting hand on Bard's shoulder as she faced the adult, their spider-silk net clenched in his furious fist.

CHAPTER 40

THE ADULT HAD THEM ALL SIT DOWN ON THE LAB STOOLS AND KEEP their hands on the seats with them. It was still three against one, but there was no way they would be able to mischief their way out of this predicament. Even if they made it out of the lab room—and not all three of them would—there was still the matter of getting out of the building. The security woman was probably untied by now, too.

Unlike the scientists, this man was in a pale grey mechanic's work suit. He had a long, angular face, but it wasn't gaunt. His salt-and-pepper hair was more salt than pepper, but he didn't look much older than her own father to Gwen. He paced in front of the children, his large feet hitting the floor with heavy purpose. He had rough, dark hands, and an unfortunate hatred in his eyes, but the most frightening part for Gwen was the absolute certainty that she had seen him somewhere before.

When he was younger, maybe, with far fewer white hairs on his head, back when wrinkled creases had only started to take root in his face. Perhaps not even in person… on television or in a photo. She couldn't place him, and not even the sight of the embroidered *Andrew* patch on his suit jogged her memory. She simmered inside herself with her curiosity, afraid to draw attention to whatever strange connection they might have had. While she brooded on this, on either side of her, Bard and Newt were having a much harder time of regulating their disappointment.

"I want Sal!" Newt's plea was a pointless one, and he seemed to know the only thing he could do was slap his seat and make a grating noise on the metal lab stool.

"Stop fussing. This isn't a game," the man told him, wadding up the thin spider-silk and stashing it deep in the pocket of his work suit. "It never was—and it certainly isn't now."

"Who are you?" Bard asked, fighting back her timidness enough to get the three words of the question out.

Her reverent tone and unwillingness to make eye contact calmed him down. It was a sign she was giving up her antics. "I'm an engineer," he told her. "I make sure things work right, and I fix them when they don't. And right now, a lot of things aren't working because of you kids."

"We just wanted Hollyhock back," Newt mewed. His eyes were anxious and uncomfortable as they looked around the room. Gwen had never seen him like this. He'd weathered disasters before—not as severe as this, but in childhood, all disasters shared a similarity of scope. None of those had ever forced him away from Sal.

"Hollyh—oh. The fairy."

"She's our friend," Bard explained. "If we'd kidnapped one of your friends from here, you would have wanted to save them, too."

"These people aren't my friends, they're my coworkers." He tried to stifle his contempt, but it leaked into his voice anyway. He was a man who, when frustrated, was frustrated with the whole world and everything in it.

"And what are you doing here?" he demanded, facing Gwen. "You're old enough to know better—not that you should know about any of this in the first place."

He paused with his attention on her. His brow twitched up slightly and his eyes narrowed, almost imperceptibly. Gwen stared back.

Do you recognize me too?

There was a noise at the lab's door. "Anomalous Activity officers! Is anyone in here? Identify yourself!"

They pushed in, past the narrow squeeze of the file cabinets as the engineer answered. "Hey, I'm Andrew, the maintenance guy. I've got three of the kids in here."

The two officers—they always came in twos—approached. They wore black trench coats that buttoned all the way up to their necks. These were not agents undercover as ordinary law enforcement… they made no pretense of normality. They looked like secret police in all black combat boots and back-slanted berets.

The woman came forward, looking chillingly similar to every unflattering caricature of a business woman that Gwen had ever seen. Her hair was pulled into a dark knot of a bun at the nape of her neck and her face was painted with the sharpest and ugliest strokes of makeup. Her partner, a tall and stocky man with a thick neck and a thicker gut, walked slower but with just as much purpose.

"Has Pan been here?" she demanded, locking eyes on the engineer.

"I don't know. I didn't see any of the kids until I got in here and found these three. Erica said—"

"We know what Erica saw. Six of them locked her in one of the basement's holding cells."

"My God, did you get her out of there?"

She ignored him. Her partner continued to survey the room, disgusted with the destruction Peter and his comrades had left in their wake. "We have drones searching the surrounding forest for the others."

The fat-necked man spoke then. "You were the one who managed to get the power stabilized and detain these three?"

"Yeah. Everyone was evacuating. I headed to the utility closet and found it was an easy fix." He pulled the spider-silk back out of his work suit. He looked so strange, a handyman with a jumper and callused hands facing these two officers of some unmentionable law.

"What is that?" she demanded.

"Not sure. Some kind of fabric that cancels out the effects of our anominium. They draped it over the anomaly reduction device. All I had to do was take it off to—"

She snatched it out of his hands. "We'll take this."

"There's nothing like that anywhere in the lab. I'm sure the researchers—"

"It's evidence," she spat.

The thick neck's eyes moved quickly over all three children, as if that was all it took to comprehend the complexity of their characters. It was the first time either of the officers had spared a glance at them. "Did you get their names?"

"No, but the boy's been calling for someone named 'Sal' ever since I got here."

The woman turned to them. She spread a patronizing smile over her face as she leaned over and greeted them with shallow friendliness, "Hello, children."

The three of them were quiet a moment. Then Bard told her, "It's not polite to talk about people in front of them."

Her phony pleasure didn't falter. "What's your name?"

"It isn't polite to ask someone's name without introducing yourself," Bard told her. "For a lady who is so grown up, you don't act very ladylike."

The engineer snickered, and she shot him a deadly look. Her face looked natural again with the bitter frown back in place. "Well, why don't you grow up and show me how it's done?"

"I miss Sal," Newt moaned again.

"What about *you*?" the man asked, the veins in his neck visibly pulsing as he spoke to Gwen.

"Sorry," she said, "I don't talk to strangers."

"You think you're real cute, huh?"

The woman's eyes turned to furious and skeptical slits in her face. "How old are you?"

"I'm tall for my age."

"Is Pan finally realizing children are too inept to stand a chance against us?" Gwen's blood heated as the lady officer spoke. "He's smart to have you along to do his bidding for him. He doesn't mind losing you—so long as he never gets caught red-handed in a place like this."

Gwen held her tongue. Newt couldn't. "That's not true! Peter loves us! Peter's our friend! Peter—"

The Bluetooth piece in the woman's ear buzzed, and she pressed it to take a call. She listened for just a few seconds before replying, "We're on our way."

Gwen's hot blood turned to ice in her veins as she heard the chilling satisfaction in the woman's voice.

"They need us to do a full sweep of the building," she told her comrade. He nodded, and then they both extended their arms and flicked their wrists.

Nothing happened.

Their puzzled expressions watched the ground, and they repeated the motion several times with increasing frustration. The engineer looked on in bored apathy, eventually informing them, "You're in a controlled laboratory. Unless you have a magic more powerful than the hundred pounds of anomolium we have downstairs, you're not going to be able to shadow-cast."

"What? Why not?" the man barked.

"The only magic that works here is the experimental tech… you know, the things we're *supposed* to be using magic for?"

The woman's eyes narrowed in contempt, and she muttered, "You white coats."

"Hey," the engineer objected, holding his hands up, "I'm just maintenance."

The woman cast an unpleasant glance at the children before turning back to the engineer and announcing, "Officer Reyes and I will have to go after them ourselves then. Since you're so good at maintenance, you can stay and maintain these children in custody."

"What?" he objected, "I was only babysitting them until you got here—I've got a hundred or more issues to start repairing with the electrical system after what these brats did to it. Some of them are active threats to the facility's security!"

"That can wait. We've still got fugitives on the loose. We need to track them down before they leave the premises. Until then, you're on babysitting duty."

"There are serious security issues I need to deal with—our drones need to be manually rebooted after the anomolium surge and *multiple* cells were broken into downstairs—"

"We are aware," the woman officer curtly replied, cutting him off. "And once we locate the remaining fugitives, you will have time to address those issues before heading to the office of the CAO."

"What," the engineer responded, the word more disbelief than question. "You want me to go downtown to see the Chief Anomalous Officer?"

"I'm sure he'll want to hear from you exactly how these children managed to get past your drones and into the cells downstairs."

The engineer scowled as the woman attempted to shift the blame for this night onto him. "Don't you think he'll be more interested to hear your explanation for why Peter Pan and the rest of them were not apprehended before they managed to find our research facility?"

With patronizing confidence, the officer told him. "Everything is under control now that *we're* here. You don't need to worry about us."

The engineer folded his arms and watched as the two officers marched back out of the room, leaving him with his grimace and three captives.

The engineer stared after them for a moment, and the children were quiet with pensive apprehension. "You three and your little friends have made a real big mess of this place."

"What's going to happen to us?" Newt asked, his lip quivering as he pouted.

"They're going to take you home, back to your families, and your parents are going to ground you—in every sense of the term."

Grounded. Months ago, Gwen's mother had threatened to use that as a punishment. The word had taken so much shape since then. In the world of Neverland, being grounded was an overtly literal thing of even worse consequence. She couldn't imagine going back to a world where she couldn't fly. The act had come to feel like a human right and basic freedom to her. The only place she couldn't fly was this prison… this prison that spanned an acre in the woods and all of adulthood.

With a defeated sigh, she absorbed the reality that her story was coming to a completely unexpected and utterly unavoidable end. Her head spun in an attempt to adjust to this development and reframe her reality in such a way that she could accept what was happening. There was no denying Gwen had become ungrounded from her life and the reasonable track it had been on before Peter swooped into it.

Newt started to cry.

Bard bounded off her stool. "Hey," the engineer yelled. "Sit back down!"

She ignored him and climbed up Newt's stool. They were small enough to sit on it together while she hugged him. The engineer made no further objection.

"Neverland *is* home," Bard moaned, her frail voice revealing how close to tears she was, too.

The engineer turned away, averting his cold eyes to this scene and blowing his impatient breath in the other direction. "You're not going to get any sympathy from me, not after the mess you've made here. You're going back to your real homes."

Gwen started thinking through the ramifications of that. That was simple in her instance, but she doubted it would be as easy for the younger children.

"Bard, what's a memory you have from *before* Neverland?"

She had to think for a moment. "Once, my papa took me to

the five and dime and let me pick out a doll. He had them wrap it, too, with a pretty pink ribbon."

"I had a cap gun I used to shoot all the other kids with!" Newt chimed in, momentarily oblivious to everything else.

These answers visibly perturbed the engineer.

"It isn't going to be that easy," Gwen told him, and he understood. In all likelihood, Bard and Newt did not have families to return to.

"I'm sure the Magic Relocation Program will figure something out," he grumbled.

"Not before the others return for us."

He cast her a mean glare. "What do you mean?"

Newt caught the gist of her remark, even if he didn't understand the psychologically manipulative motives behind it. "Peter will come for us! He'll rescue us just like we rescued Hollyhock."

Their adult guard groaned. "Haven't you all caused *enough* trouble here?"

"Not by a long shot," Bard told him, still petting Newt's head. "We'll get out of here, when the others come. They won't stop until we're rescued."

"Which is a real shame," Gwen continued. "Since we already got everything we needed from here, and there wouldn't have ever been a reason to return, if you weren't detaining the three of us."

"Look here..." He marched over to Gwen as he spoke. "I won't stand for threats, and I know what you're trying to do. I'm not on your side, girl. Kids like you—you're the root of the problem, and I've got no sympathy for you."

"Why don't you like kids that go to Neverland?" Bard asked.

"I wouldn't mind you if you went to Neverland and *stayed* there. But you always come back, and bring all this magic hullabaloo with you... dragging anomalies and nonsense into a perfectly functional reality."

He was getting visibly frustrated in a way that suggested he would lose control if pushed further. Gwen didn't take him for a violent man though, and aside from physical injury, there didn't seem to be any way in which their situation could worsen. She kept prodding him. "If you're so opposed to anomalies and nonsense, why do you work with them?"

"You think this is my idea of fun?" he bit back. "You think I spent six years studying physics and engineering so I could get some sort of degree in magic? You think when I was learning about the great feats of innovation man was capable of, I dreamt of pulling enchanted spiderwebs off boxes made of imaginary metals?"

"Then how did you end up here?" Bard asked. It had been a long time since any of them encountered someone so staunchly opposed to fantasy and whimsy. He was bitter, even for a grown-up.

"I climbed the ladder and couldn't get back down," he grumbled. He stuck a finger in Gwen's face and leaned down to bark at her. "You'll know the feeling when you get home. That sense that whatever you do is going to be an absurd waste of time because somewhere out there, someone's going to be doing the same thing with magic. We've opened a door we can't close. I came here as a researcher, initially. I didn't know when I took the job. They told me I was joining a team of experimental scientists who were trying to engineer next-level drones."

"Did you build the drones that come to Neverland?" Newt exclaimed, terrified.

He shook his head, but didn't verbally acknowledge the question. His focus remained fixed on Gwen. He vented to her, perhaps because she was the exact amalgamation of sympathetic parts he would never encounter in anyone else. She was caught at a crossroads of fiction and fact herself; and she understood his. "I spent my whole life learning to be an engineer, wanting to invent something. I had a few jobs like that, but that just isn't how the world works now. They don't want engineers anymore, they want reverse engineers. Men aren't making things—they're just pulling apart the pieces to a puzzle someone else has already put together."

"That doesn't sound like it would be nearly as much fun," Bard remarked.

"No. It isn't." He cast his glance back over at the door out of the laboratory. When Newt shifted in his seat, he whipped his head back around at the noise. He wasn't going to let them out of his sight. For all his adult failings, he knew better than to turn his back on children any longer than it took to blink. "This information revolution… it isn't a real revolution. We're bringing to life the dreams of a few men, with means they wouldn't have wanted us to use, realizing technologies we're not ready to deal with. And what's the result? Kids growing up sick on social media, toddlers staring at tablets, and people thinking a search engine replaces an education. Citizens who believe their cell phones are going to make a difference in a revolution, and governments that want to listen to what we say in front of our smart TVs like some Orwellian state. It's all progress… but it's faster than we can keep pace with. Man shouldn't move faster than his own mind can carry him."

"Hasn't he always?" Gwen asked. Bard and Newt weren't following a word of this. The events and technologies were as beyond them as the language he was using to describe them. They were following his sense of discontent however, and Bard was emotionally intelligent enough to realize she didn't need to understand all of what was being said. She could see that some sort of plan was guiding Gwen through the conversation, and for the sake of that, she did her best to keep Newt quiet.

"We've always moved a little faster than we could reasonably manage, but never like this. The industrial revolution—that was a technological breakthrough. That was man's mind at work. Railroads, electricity, steel… everything from iron production to rubber tires and bicycles came out of that. We managed that ourselves, with no help from mad hatters or magic little boys."

"And then Peter showed up."

"Exactly." He pulled up a stool of his own and got off his feet, facing Gwen. His arms still crossed, he did not look comfortable in his coveralls. "So, of course, the first thing we did was figure out flight for ourselves."

"You mean airplanes?" Bard asked.

"Yeah." He glanced over his shoulder at the door again.

Gwen drew his attention back. "Has everything invented in the past hundred years just been reverse engineered from some kind of magic?"

"No… people tend to get wary of it when they realize that things like planes are going to be used to bomb civilians, and nuclear power is going to kill people a lot faster than we can think to save them."

Newt whispered to Bard, "What's nuclear?" She didn't have any better of an idea than he did.

"If there's magic out there, it ought to stay *out there,*" he lectured. "If children want to run off with that, fine. But don't come creeping back here and guiling the rest of humanity into playing with it too."

He kicked the remains of the broken bell jar with his foot and watched it skitter across the speckled tile as the sound echoed in the quiet laboratory. He continued to fume without another word.

Gwen took as deep a breath as she could without attracting any attention. "Then let us go, and we'll take our magic with us. "

"You're not getting out of here," he told her. "You've caused too much trouble for me and everyone else. You've stolen God knows what, ruined research, and destroyed this poor lab. You've caused too much trouble to get to just walk away." He picked up a heavy book from where it lay on the floor, its broken spine turning it into a lethargic bundle of paper. "Besides," he continued, "there's nothing I could do to help you get out of here."

"You could just let us go!" Newt exclaimed, pushing out of Bard's protective hold.

"Think again. The building is crawling with black coats and researchers. You wouldn't make it back out the front door before someone caught you."

"We could go out the windows," Bard proposed, swinging her

feet as she sat on the stool, her back now to Newt.

"You can't fly here—and you never will, now that the officers have your silver sheet. You're trapped."

Bard pouted, Newt scowled. Gwen, however, felt there was something more to this line of thought than was getting said. Was he really just bringing up this moot point to further devastate children? Or was he dodging some thought in his own mind, protesting verbally what he wouldn't say aloud?

"There's another way out of here." She didn't know where her confidence came from.

He eyed her, and she fought the urge to flinch. "If you kids didn't manage to destroy it during your rampage. And from the looks of this place, that's a pretty big if."

"Oh boy!" Newt exclaimed.

"Where is it?" Bard was shaking in her seat. "What is it?"

"It's none of your business—this is all top secret research. And do you know how much trouble *I'd* be in if I let you get away? You're. Not. Going. Anywhere." His sharp words matched his remorseless face. If he was sad, it was for the state of human technology, not their plight. He was no friend… but Gwen knew their only hope rested with convincing him he was an ally.

"I don't know," she told him. "It sounds like you're already in trouble, and if we escaped after the black coats left us with you instead of letting you patch up security… wouldn't that be more their fault than yours?"

"What, am I going to get overpowered by a teenager and two kids?" That prospect was unbelievable; they could all admit that. He was tall, and if he was half as strong as he looked in his coveralls, they wouldn't stand a chance. "And they'd know I told you how to get out anyways."

Thinking as fast as her neurons could fire, Gwen tried to imagine a strategy that would have the engineer believably compromised. There was no way to reasonably threaten or coerce him. She knew she had seen him before—that suspicion had turned to certainty over the course of the time she'd been trapped here—but it was still too vague a recollection to figure out what kind of leverage she might have over him. Peter and the others were gone, and could not be depended on... but the officers didn't know that. The lost children out in the woods somewhere could slip past their guard and aid in escape now. The fairies, the skeleton key, Leroy...

As soon as she thought of the means of their escape, the mechanics of it became perfectly clear.

"We could hypnotize you." She didn't mean to yell so loud. "The pipe—we stole the Pied Piper's pipe—it hypnotizes people. It would be the perfect alibi. Get us out of here, we never come back, and all you have to tell them is you heard a song and blacked out."

The engineer looked, for the first time, like he was on the verge of seeing their side of the argument. "You stole the pipe?"

"It was in the big cell. Behind the vault," Bard told him, corroborating Gwen's story.

"So you came here for more than just a fairy, huh?"

"Yeah, we stole it ourselves!" Newt exclaimed.

The engineer was quiet.

"Plus, we'll give you this back," Gwen announced, digging into her pocket and pulling out the key card the fairies had stolen from him.

She held it up and watched his eyes go wide with hatred as he realized where his keycard had gone. "Give me that!"

He lunged at her, but Gwen hopped off her seat and backed away, telling him as she did, "We'll give it back if you help us get out."

"Oh, they'll be real mad at you for losing that!" Newt exclaimed.

Gwen nodded, confidence filling her little by little. "So what do you say? Are we going to give you your card and help you get the black coats in trouble, or do you want us to stay here and cause more trouble for you?

The engineer was livid, but as a few rational thoughts trickled past his rage, he could see how well he was compromised. The stolen pipe gave him a perfect alibi, the keycard would mitigate his responsibility for the incident, and now that the Anomalous Activity officers were on the scene, they would be party to the fault, too. In a measured but angry voice, he asked, "You kids swear you'll never come back?"

"We swear."

"Pinky promise!"

"Cross my heart and hope to *die!*"

He glanced back at the door one last time, half-expecting the condescending Anomalous Activity officers to be on their way back inside. They were searching the building though, and would not be back to harass him for several minutes more.

"Let's go," he decided. "We'll have to be quick. You're lucky you ended up in the transportation lab."

Newt and Bard sprung off their stool like synchronized divers. They followed Gwen and the engineer as he went to the scale beside the cabinets. It was pressed against the wall, as close to the outside as they could get.

Newt was smallest and nearest, so the engineer plucked him and set him on the weighing machine. There were several unusual aspects of the scale that Gwen noticed as she examined it closely. The digital display kicked on as soon as it sensed Newt's weight. Against a blue LED background, numbers glowed and a touch pad sprung to life on the screen. The engineer examined the tiny symbols on each of the keys and began tapping away and swiping through settings, as fast as he could. "This is experimental technology… but I take it that isn't a deterrent."

"I'm a scientist now!" Newt exclaimed, happy to be a guinea pig.

It buzzed and chimed, almost as if its noises were the friendly reassurances of a robotic voice. The different tones seemed to signify specific settings, but there was no telling what any of it meant. "Hold still. Perfectly still," the Engineer told him. The machine began beeping, and the beeps increased in speed and volume at an alarming rate.

Gwen saw how serious the instruction was, but doubted Newt's ability to follow it. "Pretend you're a statue," she called, hoping that if she framed it in the playful terminology he usually functioned in, he would understand better.

He did his best, but being a hyper child, he drew in a deep breath with his gut less than a second before the beeping came to an abrupt stop. There was a sound like glass cracking, and then the boy was vanished.

"Newt!" she yelled.

"Wow!" His voice was faint, drifting in from the high windows.

"Relax," the engineer told her. "He's outside. This thing only has a range of about fifteen feet. You're lucky they have it operational at all. Now get over here."

Gwen grabbed Bard's hand and dragged her along, not even realizing that she was doing so until they were standing in front of the chrome-plated scale. Bard was wide-eyed with fear. She was more than reluctant—she was petrified after watching Newt disappear before her eyes.

"Come on, Bard." She gave the girl's hand a squeeze and her back a push. "Newt's waiting. He got through fine and so will we."

She didn't budge.

"Can we go through together?" Gwen asked.

"Not unless you're willing to come out conjoined at the hip, no."

She looked back at Bard. "I'll go first, okay? If I go first, you'll come after me, right? We're going to be brave girls. I know how brave you are, Bard."

Bard looked uneasy, but there wasn't time to fully dismantle her phobia. The only reasonable solution was to go and bank on Bard's panic reversing her decision once she realized she was left alone in this awful building. She felt awful for subjecting Bard to that, but she knew it was the best chance she had of convincing her to move quickly—and time was paramount.

Gwen stepped onto the scale and smiled at Bard. It was fortunate for her Bard was so scared—trying to convince the little girl there was nothing to fear kept her from realizing how frightened she was. She couldn't manifest the terror of throwing herself into an experimental teleporter; she couldn't even pause to feel it. She just kept smiling and heard her voice as she exclaimed, "Isn't this exciting!"

Bard remained silent in her overwhelming apprehension, staring at Gwen and clutching her own arms as if she felt a horrible chill in the room. Gwen looked to the engineer. "Make sure she comes through after me. Promise me you'll send her through."

"I'll do my best," he responded.

Gwen couldn't ask for anything better from him. She chucked his key card over onto a counter where he could get it after he'd finished sending them out.

As she stood on the chrome step of the scale and he leaned over the control panel, she was closer than ever to him. There was something familiar even about the way he smelled—as though he used a familiar deodorant or laundry detergent. Whatever it was, the similarity was something that felt manufactured, suburban, ordinary… and yet it ate at her as she pretended like it didn't matter that she would never see this man again without knowing where she had seen him before.

"Hold still," he told her. She took a deep breath and prepared to hold it as long as needed. The machine began its beeping countdown again, like a camera timer about to go off. She kept smiling, trying to communicate to Bard how simple and easy the process was. What Bard couldn't see was the raw fear keeping her frozen and pinning her smile to her face.

The beeps were approaching a single, sustained tone. Any second she would vanish. What would it feel like? She couldn't afford to think about it. The beeping was so incessant and loud from her position beside it, she didn't even hear the door hit the file cabinets again as someone tried to push into the room. She only saw, as a black-coated officer slipped into the room.

"HEY!" he yelled. He started sprinting for them. The engineer backed away from the device. Gwen's first response was to tense up—the best thing she could have done for the teleportation process.

The officer came running. He reached out. His hand extended toward Bard's little arm. She finally animated, trying to run, and wanting to escape this trap they'd been caught in.

"*Bard*!" Gwen yelled, forgetting everything as she reached out her right hand in a desperate motion to save her.

The beeping stopped, and a horrid ringing in her ears started. All the light in the room seemed to collapse in front of her into a single pinprick. Condensed into the brightest single point she'd ever seen, she closed her eyes and tried to blink it away. Her ears were screaming in themselves. Then the light disappeared altogether.

She was tumbling, collapsing, falling with a sob into the grass. Someone grabbed her arm.

"Run, Gwenny! Run!"

CHAPTER 41

PETER PULLED HER ALONG, BUT HE MET WITH UNTOLD RESISTANCE. Gwen had a vendetta against saving herself. She had to wait by the side of the building. Bard was going to come through the teleporter any second. Any minute. She would. She had to.

Bard was not coming.

She wanted to howl; she settled for sobbing, breathless and quiet. She felt weak at all her joints, and she clutched her hands and gritted her teeth. Her paranoia made her sense a definite weakness in all the muscles of her right arm and hand.

"Gwen-dollie, we have to get out of here or they'll catch us too!"

He had come back for her. Without a plan or any means of clandestine infiltration, Peter had still returned and poised himself outside while black coats combed the grounds. The Anomalous Activity Department's number one most-wanted fugitive had a better sense of self-preservation though.

"You stupid girl!" he exclaimed, his muttering words only audible to Gwen. She wanted to object—to defend herself and make him understand that wanting to save Bard wasn't stupid at all. Before she could, he bent down and swept her off her feet. He took to the air and got them as far away from the ground as he could. They still didn't know Peter could fly even within the radius of their anomaly reduction device. The black coats who accused Peter of knowing better than to get caught red-handed were right to think that Peter's strategic mind knew the value of keeping himself out of risk. They just underestimated his love of adventure, his draw to danger, and his unerring loyalty to his friends and fairies.

Strange drones whirled in the distance. The devices the officer had spoken of were still running wild in the woods, looking for traces of fairy dust. As Peter carried Gwen—slowed by her weight and the detriment of the uncovered anomalium block within the facility—he reassured her as best he could.

"Holly and Fox are in a spider-silk purse. The drones are only going to find what's left of their trails. Dill and Hawk are taking a very long route back home to throw the drones off everyone else. They'll be fine, always half a mile ahead where it's already saturated with magic. They can camp out in the trees too. The drones can't follow them as fast here."

Gwen cried into his chest, unresponsive. He kept talking, either oblivious to her sad silence or trying his best to keep it from consuming her. "Newt's on his way back too. I sent Blink for the knapsack. She'll be back to Tiger Lily's with her rat by now."

At last, they broke the perimeter of the Anomalous Activity hideout. Peter involuntarily lunged as his efforts became twice as productive. Almost whacking into a tree, he rose higher and adjusted their course amid the highest branches of the forest. "I've got you," he whispered.

Gwen unlocked her fingers from where they were laced around Peter's neck. With a deep breath, she thought of all the happiest things she could and pushed off him. She kept her arm linked with his, holding onto it as a safeguard against her emotional instability.

She wouldn't let them win. She wouldn't let the officers rob her of her joy.

Everyone, except for the fairies still running from the drones and the officers searching the woods, was already back at Tiger Lily's. Without the fairies, no trail of magic would lead back to their safe house. Dillweed and Hawkbit would continue to give the adults a wild goose chase until they headed back to Neverland with a report for Jam and Spurt.

The adults would have no trail to follow to Tiger Lily's home, and since they investigated just the other night, it seemed unlikely they'd come poking around again. When Dillweed and Hawkbit vanished to Neverland, they'd likely assume the children went too.

Even still, the children would arrange a guard shift for the night. At the first sign of adults, they would all flee and send Leroy to Piper with their plans for the invasion.

Peter and Gwen arrived at the safe house and hurried inside, the misadventure over at last.

She went straight to Tiger Lily, sitting down beside her on the couch and curling into her shoulder. She couldn't bring herself to interrupt the gleeful sense of victory that kept the lost children all rejoicing. Tiger Lily took one look at her troubled face, though, and knew to fold the girl into her arms as she sat down.

Blink was wearing Princess Charlotte's crown, tipped on her head so that the large crown wouldn't fall down to her neck. Sal was glued to Newt's side and talking a million words a minute at him—the chatter blurred into an almost consistent sound. Newt, shirtless, was too busy showing off his stomach to listen. His belly button was missing. Something must have gone wrong with the teleporter, because his belly button was now on his back. He was delighted as Hollyhock and Foxglove poked at it, marveling over the unexplainable anatomical change.

"Where's Bard?" Blink asked, the first to realize someone was missing.

Peter sat down, cross-legged, on the floor. The sudden shift in atmosphere drew the others toward him. The children stood, fixed like stars, as the fairies orbited their favorite boy and listened as he explained in no uncertain terms that Bard had gone the way of all other lost children before her.

He spoke with great praise and respect, a natural orator as he gave an unconventional eulogy for the freedom she'd sacrificed in order to return Hollyhock and secure the pipe they needed for Rosemary's rescue.

Gwen and Tiger Lily stayed together on the couch. The woman held Gwen's right hand, and the girl felt the hand was somehow different. She had reached out for Bard with it, moving it in an even more dramatic manner than Newt had flexed his stomach with a breath during his teleportation. She was too concerned with Bard to worry.

"She was sweetest of all the girls," Newt announced, tacking on, "No offense, Blink and Gwen."

Blink nodded. "She was a Taker-Carer."

Foxglove named her with a word that had no translation outside of Neverland—a word to mean that she had the soul of a mother. Tiger Lily, who had known Bard only briefly, in the long ago days that were her last in Neverland, agreed with the sentiment. "She was very motherly at heart. I think she will make as good of a grown-up as she made a kid."

"I'm going to miss her," Sal whined, sitting down and wrapping his arms around his knees.

"I wish she hadn't lost," Blink replied, taking the crown off her head as if it were a hat she needed to remove out of reverence.

Lost. The word struck Gwen in a strange way. *Lost what*? Bard didn't lose anything—they had lost Bard. Then it occurred to her how they were using the word.

They were playing a game. As always, as ever, they were playing… and Bard had lost.

There was great melancholy and even some tears that night, but the grief did not extend beyond that. The children knew the stakes of their game were high, but at the end of the day, it would always be a game.

CHAPTER 42

Newt and Sal slept, their limbs interlocked in the strangest way as they sprawled out on the couch. Blink wanted to sleep on the floor in Tiger Lily's room where her animal town was still set up, so they piled blankets and pillows in the corner so she could make a happy little nest on the outskirts of her imaginary village. Peter and Gwen were given the twin beds in the guest room since they were the biggest.

Gwen fell in and out of sleep so restlessly she couldn't tell the difference between anxious dreams and her tired thoughts obsessively replaying the past two nights' events. Her brain gravitated toward the same memories and fears, conscious or otherwise. First, Rosemary had been kidnapped, and now Bard was lost.

She thought back to the first day she arrived in Neverland and how welcoming Bard had been. She was the oldest, with a childish wisdom that served her well. Gwen still had the pink ribbon she'd tied into her hair that afternoon… making braids and small talk while the others plotted to drown her in the lagoon if she didn't tell a good story.

Tiger Lily's remark gave her the most comfort. It was easy to see Bard as a mother, especially with how she had looked after

Spurt and always searched for ways to make children and fairies feel more at home and safe. She'd knitted so many of their spider-silk nets with no substantive help from anyone else. She was destined for a loving adulthood. There wasn't a bratty bone in her body, and that would translate into a kindhearted temperament too few adults possessed. Reality would be a bit better of a place if she was grown up in it.

But who would take the place of the little mother of Neverland in the meantime? Gwen's stomach churned—should that responsibility have fallen on the oldest girl? Or the oldest child? Either way, she felt at once that she had shirked away from some innate responsibility she hadn't known to assume in Neverland. Bard had been so much better suited to it. Gwen was at last comfortable enough to admit that she was often more lost than any of the other lost children. She needed to be watched after in Neverland, not the other way around.

It's not such a terrible thing, she told herself. *It's what everyone in the whole wide world has ever done. All children grow up.*

Except one.

She wasn't sure she'd fallen asleep at all, but when she rolled over in her groggy haze and saw Peter missing from his messy bed, she knew she must have nodded off at some point. She waited a minute to see if he was only getting a drink of water and would be right back, but the window was open, and in her heart, she knew he was already gone.

She couldn't imagine where he would go. Fresh air didn't sound like a bad idea, so Gwen pulled her chic little jacket off the floor and put it on over her pajamas. It was still freezing cold in the middle of the December night, so she wrapped herself in the downy quilt of her bed. Half-crawling, half-flying, she made her way out the window and floated up in the makeshift robe. She didn't have to get very high before she spotted Peter.

He'd taken one of the sheets with him and laid it out like a picnic blanket on the unsloped roof of the mobile home. He was stretched out on it, hands laced behind his head as he stared straight up at the stars. He caught sight of Gwen and gave her a nod.

She floated over and sat down beside him on the sheet. "Was the bed too comfortable for you?" she teased.

"I don't like beds." He didn't move his eyes away from the stars. "First, you get a bed, then you have to have a bedtime, and it's all downhill from there."

"It's a slippery slope."

"Most real things are."

"Mind if I join you?"

Peter scooted over a few inches, leaving plenty of room on the sheet for Gwen to lie down. "Want some blanket?" she asked.

"Sure."

She spread the square-dabbled quilt over them with one sweeping motion. Nestled under the blanket, lying beside Peter, she at last was free to look at the stars.

After a whole life in suburbia where streetlights and house lights dimmed the brilliance of the stars, she couldn't help but marvel at these ones so much closer to Lake Agana and the forest. "They're beautiful… all of them."

Peter didn't share her perspective. "They're not as bright or many as they are in Neverland."

"True," Gwen acknowledged, "but I'm pretty sure Neverland has stars all of its own. As far as reality goes… it doesn't get much better than this." She remembered what Lasiandra had said about the strange stars that hovered over her home world, and how peculiarly they arranged themselves in the sky. She wished she understood the differences better.

"We've got better constellations and better stories for them, too," Peter bragged.

She smiled, imagining what stories must arise from stars in such a fantastic place. "You've never mentioned constellations there. What constellations does Neverland have that we don't?"

"I forget." Peter stretched under the cover, fidgeting like a little boy in bed. "But they're better. You should figure it out when we get back. You're the one with all the good star stories."

"We should go stargazing some night."

Peter smiled. "Everyone will love that. We could catch some fireflies and slingshot them up. See if any of them stick. That's how you make stars, you know."

Gwen laughed. She couldn't tell if he was pulling her leg or not. Peter lied to her so often that it didn't matter anyway. "I don't think that's how it works."

"I'll go with Rosemary then, when she comes home. She'd love it. She could get stars to stick."

"Now you're just trying to make me jealous." Peter didn't react, his face just held tight to his smile. He was so confident Rosemary would be home safe and sound soon. She couldn't help but share in the glow of that optimism. Gwen imagined the impossible pastime of shooting stars into the sky and felt encouraged. "I'd like to make stars with you." Her voice was soft, as if only now respecting that they were close and alone in the middle of the night, not needing to speak any louder than a whisper.

She stared at Peter, but his eyes never left the sky. He could have watched the unmoving stars for hours, for years… for lifetimes. Reaching out under the cover of the quilt, she took hold of his hand in hers where not even the stars could see it.

He finally broke his gaze and looked at her, a blank expression replacing his starry smile.

"Thank you for coming back for me today, Peter."

"Of course," he told her. "I knew you wouldn't make it home without me."

She laughed at his ego. He didn't care. "I owe you my life," she told him.

"No, you don't."

"I owe you my childhood then."

"Probably."

"What's left of it."

"There's plenty of it left in you," he told her. "Trust me. I'm a certified expert."

"Who certified you?" she chuckled.

"I did. I'm an expert, remember?"

The nonsense trickled away. They kept holding hands.

"You don't owe me anything," Peter told her. "Not your childhood, not your life. Everything you do, you do for you. Remember that."

"I suppose so," Gwen agreed, dismissing her usual argument that everything she'd done since meeting Peter was for Rosemary's sake. "I know I don't owe my life to you... but I might give it to you in Neverland anyway."

"There are far worse things," Peter told her, "than giving your life to friends and spending it down in Neverland." A silence lapsed over them before he asked, "You are going to come back with us, after the invasion with Piper? No back-and-forths about it this time?"

Gwen was reluctant to answer. How could she explain that her brain only functioned by going back and forth on everything all the time? There was no way to put that out of the process, but she thought she could for once foresee the end result of all her belabored confliction.

"Bard would want you come back," Peter whispered.

"I think everyone would," Gwen admitted, "even me."

When Peter didn't offer any continuance of the conversation, she looked over and saw his eyes closed. His breathing was deep, and his eyes raced under his eyelids. She imagined that Peter, no matter how long or little he'd been asleep, spent every unconscious moment dreaming of new adventures. His hand twitched, jerking out of Gwen's, and he turned away, as free and unconstrained as ever.

She made herself comfortable, tucked tight under the quilt and fortified against the cold with the warm magic Peter seemed to radiate. She closed her own eyes and, as she drifted off, she imagined the stars were gossiping in approval of the children's strange and wonderful friendship.

CHAPTER 43

GWEN FELT BARD SHAKING HER. HER DREAM HAD HER BACK IN HER own home, but not her bed. She was sleeping in Rosemary's room, in her bed, terrified, but slowly waking up to realize the girl had come back. Only this time, it wasn't Rosemary; it was Bard. She could almost hear the girl's voice, but the dream was giving way. The feeling of a hand on her leg, prodding her gently, was overwhelming her sense of dream. Her consciousness, barely alert, didn't want to identify the sensation, because in her heart, Gwen knew it couldn't be Bard shaking her.

In reality, it was her cell phone in the flimsy pockets of her polka-dotted pajamas, shaking with the exuberance of an incoming call at this late hour. Dizzy and groggy, she fished it out as she came to terms with her consciousness. She was on the roof, and it was cold. This didn't make sense anymore.

She saw the call just in time to miss it. *Jay Hoek's* name and contact picture was plastered on her cracked phone screen for just a second before the call went to voicemail. She didn't have a chance to answer, but opened her messages app and quickly texted him back.

Hey, sorry, people are sleeping here. What's up?

A moment later, after he'd left her a voicemail, he responded to her text.

Just wanted to know if you wanted to meet up tonight.

So much happened between her glimpses of Jay that it seemed like weeks had passed since she last saw him, not days. At least, that was how she justified her pounding desire to see him. She checked the time. Amazingly, it was just minutes past midnight.

Can you make it out to Lake Agana?

Gwen snuck down off the roof.

Not sure. Can you come over here? Or meet somewhere in the middle?

It was probably for the best that they didn't head into the forest tonight, even if they did stay in the state park. Who knew what the Anomalous Activity officers were doing, or where they were searching for the children.

Still, flying all the way across town to Jay's seemed like a lot, and Gwen was apprehensive about meeting him at his house. It had been wonderful, but almost too much so. She felt comfortable, she felt infatuated, she felt cherished and cared for... It was a lot to take in, and she wasn't sure she was ready for the intensity of that experience on a night when they weren't just going to watch a movie and fall asleep on the couch downstairs.

Davies Park?

She leaned against the pale blue corrugation of the mobile home's wall, her phone in both her hands. She clicked the screen on and off, waiting until the smiling message icon appeared again.

I can be there in fifteen.

She grinned, and took to the wind as she typed.

Same. See you then.

Davies Park was only a few blocks from the town center where Rosemary and she had summoned Piper. Having flown that way three nights in a row, she imagined it would be easy to make it to the urban park.

She flew at an enjoyable pace, grateful she didn't have to hurry. Nothing was after her, and no disasters were unfolding.

She was simply on her way to see her favorite man.

It was funny how until she went to Neverland, she had always considered Jay more or less a boy. Now, he seemed like a man if only because he was in the process of growing into one. It might be an honorary title at the moment, but Jay made growing up look good.

At the park, Gwen landed on the roof of the jungle gym. This late at night, no children were out, and few cars drove past the park on the ordinarily busy Howard Street. She waited on the plastic and metal structure, overlooking the uneven field of grass, swing set, and old merry-go-round spinner. She waited.

A bicyclist came spinning up Howard Street at a ferocious pace, and then pedaled fast along the paved path toward the play structure and picnic tables. He popped a wheelie before coming to a stop.

Gwen clapped, but also called out, "Show off!" as she drifted down off the jungle gym's roof.

"Says the girl *floating* over," Jay replied, unstrapping his helmet and turning off the bike lights. "Like I can even attempt to keep up in the arms race of cool with you."

She laughed and lingered in the air a tantalizing moment more before dropping to her feet. In almost the same motion, she bounced up on her tiptoes and kissed his cheek in place of a hello.

The kiss drew the corner of his lips up toward it; she watched as his smile spread on his face. "Thanks for meeting me here. Dad's got his car for work tonight and getting my mom's keys… it would have been hard to explain on a Wednesday night."

"No problem. I'm glad we could connect."

He took hold of her hand. "One of these nights I'm going to have to take you out on a real date."

They strolled around the park, hand in hand, going back and forth on a whole number of subjects. Gwen and Jay unraveled each other with a conversation that wove and twisted over every subject… and every topic was romantic, because they were in a blissful moment of intimate discovery. Every answer, every detail, and every memory they shared was another piece in the puzzle they wanted to build. Gwen could not comprehend that this was what was fleeting about young love; this was the transitory bit of new relationships that she would spend most of her life without, whomever or wherever she settled with. She could sense a divine energy imbued in everything they discussed, and she knew this was magical in its own right.

They talked about childhood memories, dreams, cooking mishaps, and everything in between. They discussed their aspirations, too.

"It's kind of exciting," Jay admitted as they wandered off the path they'd been walking loops on. "I got the last of my college applications off today."

"Oh my gosh," Gwen didn't know how to react. Sometimes, she forgot how much a year's difference made between her and Jay when they were in this transitional stage of life. She climbed onto the merry-go-round, giving it a little spin as she boarded. "Where did you apply?"

"A few safety schools—the U, Eastern, Arizona State—but hoping to get into an academy."

"An academy?"

"Yeah. I applied to West Point and the USNA, but I'm not sure about my odds. They're really selective." He came over to the merry-go-round and grabbed hold of one of its bars. With all his strength, he flung it. Gwen started revolving at twice the speed. "I think my best bet is with the Coast Guard Academy out in New London."

"London?" It was hard for her to hear as she spun away from him.

"New London, Connecticut."

"Wow," she responded. She couldn't imagine that far into the future. Jay graduated, going out of state—*joining the military?* "The military? Really?" she asked aloud. It had always seemed to her that the military was a place for people who didn't know what they wanted to do, needed the G.I. bill for tuition, or didn't have other options. As Jay pointed out though, West Point and the rest were selective, and prestigious. She tried to fathom what would draw him to that.

"Yeah," he answered. "It seems like a good idea. I don't know if I'll go for sure, even if I do get accepted. Of course my mom hates the idea... but I think it might be the right place for me." He kept spinning her with gentle pushes now that she was in motion. "Coach Wilson is always talking about the importance of training your body and mind as a unit. You shouldn't think of them as separate entities, and any good you do for one will be negated if you don't make sure to take care of the other. The idea of going to an academy that focuses on both seems like the richest experience I could have, you know?"

Gwen sat down, her movements cautious as the merry-go-round spun. Jay backed away. As he continued to speak, the device slowed a bit with every cycle.

"My uncle served in the army, so he always used to talk about it. It's not that he glamorized it or anything—far from it. But the one thing he said that really stuck with me was that every man needed to give to his country as much as he could. Not everyone can join the military, but if I *could* do it, if I could push myself through the ordeal of it... shouldn't I act on that? If those of us who can, don't, who will, you know?"

She stood up, holding to one of the many handles. "It's really hard for me to imagine you in the military."

He clapped his legs together, rigid as a board, and saluted her. "Private Hoek, reporting for duty."

"Yeah, see, I still can't really imagine it."

"That's okay," he told her, hopping up on the merry-go-round with her, pressing himself against her as he held onto the same handlebar. "It's hard for me to imagine you in Neverland." He kissed her forehead and studied her face, a blur of confusion and adoration on his. "Are you really going back? Is this just... what you're going to do?"

The merry-go-round spun her slowly back around.

"I guess so," Gwen answered. "At least for now. I can always come back. Everyone does eventually. There's not a lot of opportunity cost at my age. It's either leave my family and watch my friends scatter for college in the next year, or just put everything on pause."

"Gap year in Neverland, huh?"

"Yeah. Only the whole not-aging thing would make it easy to take a gap decade... if I wanted. I'm not sure how long I'd be there, really."

She hadn't stopped to think how long she would really stay in Neverland. Children could go half a century—she'd seen that in action with Bard—but she had cultivated and grown her mind into more complex an instrument. She didn't think she could be forever satisfied in an existential petri dish like Neverland. There was a massive world in reality, with infinitely more people and places to explore, even if Neverland's magic could generate a never-ending stream of new experiences. They would all be bound to the nature of the island.

"Maybe only four or five years," Jay suggested. "When I got back from West Point or New London, I could look you up."

"And help me study for my GED." She regretted the joke as soon as she made it. This wasn't like any other life decision that could take two lovers away from each other. This was a choice that would fundamentally begin reversing their ability to relate. Wherever they went in reality, they would continue growing and having a rich spectrum of experiences as young adults coming into their own as people. In Neverland, Gwen would simply be on pause. There would be no opportunity for intellectual or emotional growth, and as mature as she felt, she knew that a lot of personal development would happen in the next few years of their lives... If she chose to be there for it.

She kissed him. She didn't know what else to do. Did it cheapen their nascent romance to know it was a doomed affair? Gwen wished she could tell him that everything she felt was very real, very true, and she would give the world to explore every inch of their hearts together... but so much more than this mere world was on the line.

There would be other boys, other romances... she had one shot at Neverland, and it was already more like a second chance considering how old she was. She didn't want to believe that trivialized their feelings. High school sweethearts rarely lasted—couldn't the romance still mean something even if they acknowledged that?

"I suppose I should spare myself certain rejection and not ask you to be my girlfriend then, huh?"

Gwen winced and smiled, her heart feeling exactly what her face displayed in that moment. She hadn't known she could experience both with such simultaneous intensity. She wanted to say yes, just for tonight. Her desire had a desperate excitement to it, but the logistics of it wouldn't mesh with the decisions she was making in her life at large. The chambers of her heart once again were pulling away from each other—a single organ conflicted to the brink of civil war inside of her. "Yeah, probably," she squeaked.

"That's okay," he told her, yet again. "My ego isn't hurt if you're leaving me for *Peter Pan*," he admitted.

It sounded wrong to her when he said it like that. She wasn't *leaving him for* Peter, not in any sense that people usually used that expression. "It's just that..." She collected her thoughts and did her best to articulate them. "I've got my whole life to fall in love. I've only got this one last chance to run off and be a kid."

"I get it," he assured her. His understanding tone told her she didn't need to further defend herself. Who knew, maybe a year or two earlier, Jay would have made the same choice if confronted by the chance Gwen had. She appreciated him, she loved him. With this realization, all of her effort went into trying not to cry. It was so unfair. She wished Peter had never arrived in her life at that moment. She would be so happy to continue forward with Jay, unaware of any other option. Knowing her options, however, she knew she would never be able to live with the wondering and unfulfilled longing for a Neverland she might have had.

"Do you know when you're leaving? For… good?"

She nodded, biting her lip and hating that the conversation had come to this moment. "Tomorrow night."

"What!" Jay exclaimed, leaning back and almost losing his balance on the merry-go-round. "No, you can't—it isn't finished yet!"

"What isn't finished?"

"Your gift!"

More confused than flattered, she had to ask, "What gift?"

"I'm making you something, something I want you to have."

Gwen's heart sank another inch in her chest. It never seemed to get tired of falling. One of these nights, she knew it was going to fall right out of her. "I'm sorry, Jay."

He hopped off the merry-go-round and paced a bit. On the next cycle, Gwen stepped off too. She was dizzier, having spun for so much longer.

"I can finish it tomorrow," he decided. He smiled. "I'll stay home sick and work on it. I can get it to you tomorrow night."

This gave him a visible sense of relief, so Gwen was loath to squash his excitement. "I'm not going to be able to meet you tomorrow night."

"No—I can make it work. I can meet you wherever you need me to."

How could she explain that tomorrow she would be meandering all over suburbia with the Pied Piper and fleeing the authorities immediately after?

"I'll drive out to Lake Agana tomorrow night."

"No, you shouldn't—I don't think I'll be able to… no, I'm *certain* I won't be able to make it."

He picked up her face in his hands, lifting her eyes to his with the gesture. "I think you will. Tell you what, I'll be there. If you can't possibly make it, so be it. But I'll be there, with your gift. I don't want to miss the chance to give it to you, however slim it might be." He added, "I've put a lot of work into it."

"I won't be able to come." But her voice betrayed how badly

she wanted to, and Jay was banking on that desire to win out and worm its way into her agenda, whatever other obligations she had that night.

"I'll be there," he told her, his gentle smile making the promise as much as his words. "I'll be there for you."

Still holding her face in his hands, he brought her lips to his and kissed her again, by the light of the moon and in the shadow of the jungle gym. The merry-go-round spun to a stop beside them.

CHAPTER 44

LEROY WAS SENT FOR PIPER FIRST THING IN THE MORNING. GWEN TOOK a picture of Peter wearing the crown and holding the antique pipe and Never Tree root. Tiger Lily uploaded it and printed it on her desktop printer. Peter then scrawled a message to Piper, telling him when and where to show up with Rosemary that night. There was no communicating with the rat regarding Piper's whereabouts, but they suspected he was nearby, possibly even watching them in some capacity already.

Gwen slept in late that morning—still on Neverland's schedule or just nocturnal from all her late nights. She woke up in the last minutes of the morning, full of anxiety. Foxglove was waiting on the nightstand beside her bed.

Humming to herself, biding time until Gwen woke, Foxglove's purple shimmer was the first thing Gwen saw upon opening her eyes. The instant visual stimulus was enough to remind her with full force everything that would occur today.

Meeting Piper, rallying children, whatever face-off resulted with the Anomalous Activity officers, leaving again for Neverland… rescuing Rosemary.

On the other side of the bedroom door, she could hear a happy ruckus of discussion with everyone talking over each other.

She saw the quilt she'd left with Peter balled up on the floor. She was glad she'd crawled back into a real bed and fallen asleep fast and cozy after returning from her outing with Jay.

She dressed in the little blue party dress and long, purple leggings that Dawn had bought for her earlier this week. Outside the bedroom, she discovered that Blink's animal town had migrated like a small circus, and was now scattered around the perimeter of the living room's carpet. In the center, the children were clustered around multiple maps of the town. They perched with the wild excitement of wolves over a fresh kill. Tiger Lily sat with them, her back as straight as her face, offering strategic wisdom as a redskin tactician, and practical advice as a resident in this corner of reality. She held her head high and wore feathers in her hair. She'd smeared lines of bright red lipstick over her cheeks like war paint.

The afternoon was consumed by planning a route for the night. Peter's intention was to cover as much ground as possible. They would be on the move already when the Anomalous Activity officers responded. They charted potential routes with crayons, circling and coloring in advantageous areas. When the adult forces caught up to them, they wanted to make sure they had the higher ground. Blink rebuilt her animal town into a shoddy model of the neighborhood they intended on ending up in. Gwen helped—blowing the children's minds in the process—by saving and comparing routes on the map app of her phone.

"Zoom in! Further! *Further*!"

"How does it know the names of the businesses, too?"

"Is that little blue dot really us?"

"Is it a map of the *whole world?*"

Peter was blunt enough to take it right out of her hands. He had trouble with the accelerometer. No matter how he tried to tip it to get the screen to face up, it always reoriented itself before he could get a good look at the contents of the map. "This is the most marvelous compass I've ever seen!" he declared. "It's awfully big, but I understand now why you always carry it around with you."

Gwen took it and turned off the auto-rotate feature before handing it back to Peter. He was amazed to find he could get addresses and even pictures of houses with it.

"Does it tell you which houses have children in them?"

"No, definitely not."

She was surprised to find she, too, had trouble manipulating her own phone. Her hand seemed uncoordinated, as if it had forgotten basic motor tasks. She tried not to worry about what the transporter had done to her hand when she'd reached out for Bard. It wasn't until she tried to scrawl a note on one of the maps that she realized what had happened.

"Oh my God," she announced, staring at her hands. "I'm left-handed."

The children intermittently grew tired of planning an invasion and wandered off to play with the wide selection of toys contained in Tiger Lily's house. Their interest drew them this way and that, but at any given moment, there were always one or two children helping Peter plot. Once they had eaten the last of the bread and peanut butter, Tiger Lily smudged off her war paint and took the feathers out of her hair to go to the grocery store.

Dinner was served in installments—a pot of mac and cheese with hamburger mixed in stayed on the stove all evening, and grilled cheese sandwiches were made on demand. The children all took Tiger Lily's caring and cooking for granted, which she seemed to deeply appreciate. She was preserving their world—a behind-the-scenes actor who propelled their endeavors forward through acts of simple support. When she brought them popsicles, however, she received ample, excited gratitude.

The sky darkened. Night fell. The clock stayed still, but time passed in creeping seconds and slinking minutes. In order to avoid releasing any trackable magic ahead of their meeting with Piper, the five flying children and four fairies loaded into Tiger Lily's car and she drove them into town. The fairies sat in Peter's lap, and Newt and Sal double-buckled. It was a cozy ride, but the children were more thrilled for the novelty of being in a car than they would have been to fly.

They parked across the street from the Rotary Club's Rose Garden, and everyone sprinted for the rendezvous point after fast but heartfelt goodbyes to their wonderful caretaker. Gwen went with the children, checking half a dozen times for any oncoming traffic while the reckless kids ran across without looking.

Once they were safe across the street, Gwen finally looked back and saw Peter.

He was still in the car with Tiger Lily.

He didn't join the others in the rose garden until Jam and Spurt appeared in the sky. Tiger Lily's sedan putted away, its red taillights disappearing as it rounded a bend. Gwen wished she'd gotten a better goodbye. She remembered the feeling of falling asleep mushed up against Tiger Lily the night before… the woman had been unequivocally kind to her.

Time was passing quickly though. She checked the clock on her phone. It just past eleven, and if Piper was prompt, then she would see her sister soon… not that there would be any time for a proper reunion.

Jam and Spurt descended from the sky in a cloud of shining, flitting fairies, including Dillweed and Hawkbit. Left in Neverland, they had been charged with rounding up as many fairies as they could, a task second in importance only to fetching Piper's pay and pipe. Their past day had been a long exercise in tromping through the woods and recruiting as many as they could to venture back to reality and help draw new children to their cause. While some fairies were still against the children's crusade and the magic-hungering adult attention it brought to their home, plenty of others supported the children and knew their best chance of protecting themselves rested with the young ones who came to their island.

The sky was dabbled with a rainbow of shimmering fairies. Gwen hadn't seen so many since Bramble's wake at the willow tree. How they came through and escaped radar was a testament to the combined power of their magic. They settled among the rose bushes, glowing in place of the flowers that had been pruned away for the winter months.

Gwen kept her eyes glued to her phone while the others gave Jam and Spurt a briefing and tried to counteract Jam's desire to re-plan everything to her liking.

Right as the digits changed to eleven-eleven on her screen, the world went still.

The slight breeze, much like the distant traffic noise, hadn't been noticeable until it came to a jarring stop. The children fell silent. The fairies stopped buzzing. The world was without sound, without motion.

The wind came to life like a gasp for breath. The force of it whizzing by felt as though it would knock her over. Gwen held tight to her clothes and grabbed her hair out of her face. She watched the whirlwind that formed and the black mass that twirled into existence in the center of the garden. It took form, and all at once, Piper was kneeling in front of them. He stood up, stretching to his full, unnatural stature.

"Hello, Pan." His bitter voice matched his eyes. Leroy, running in ecstatic circles around his feet, was a comical contrast.

"Where is she?" Gwen screamed. The second she realized Rosemary wasn't with him, she prepared to tackle the man. She didn't know what she would do, but she would do it to the best of her ability to avenge Rosemary and find out where he'd hidden her.

"She can be here shortly." Piper's apathy was infuriating. "You have my pipe and payment?"

"I've got it," Peter said, pulling the enchanted flute and priceless crown out of his knapsack and handing them over.

Piper immediately placed the crown on his head and wore it with greedy pride. "What about the Never Tree root?"

Peter pulled that out, too, and the dark root with its rune-like patterns shot a satisfied look into Piper's eyes. Peter leapt back into the air and hovered out of reach, however, and Gwen told Piper, "Rosemary first."

Piper smiled, briefly. "Very well, *mäuschen*." He grabbed his cape in his hand, pulling it from its strange fluctuations. Shaking it out and then spinning it, the dark cloth seemed to expand into a small hurricane. He jerked it away with a flourish, and a poofy-haired little girl appeared in the middle of the rose garden. The fairies floating around all trilled with joy to see her safely returned.

"Rosemary!" Gwen cried, running to her as Piper slid away.

She collapsed to her knees as she flung herself into an eye-level hug with Rosemary.

Her little sister's skin felt cold, and her eyes were glazed over with a persisting confusion.

"Now give me the Never Tree."

Peter hesitated. "This isn't going to help you hide, Piper."

"That's no concern of yours. Hand it over," Piper demanded.

"It's only going to weaken the island. Let me keep it and graft it back, Piper. Not even Neverland can protect you from the deal you made with the mermaids." A discordant buzz surrounded them, as the fairies warned Piper against this as well.

Piper wasn't amused, and his dark voice intimated his dissatisfaction. "Do we have a deal or not?"

Peter took a breath, and then nodded. He threw the root to Piper, who caught it in one hand and snapped his fingers with the other hand.

Rosemary sprung back to life. Vivacious but confused, she hugged Gwen back and told her, "I had an adventure."

Gwen felt a happy tear run down the side of her face. "I want to hear all about it, Rose."

"Some other time," Piper told her, brushing his cape back and standing with his colorfully patched waistcoat. "First the matter of tonight's business. Where do we begin?"

Peter handed him the map with their final route. "This is our course."

Piper's straight teeth formed a crooked smile on his face. He adjusted his hat and tucked the map into the pocket of his loose trousers once he had a cursory understanding of their direction.

"We'll make this a night to remember. When we're done, they'll rue the day they ever tried to lock the Piper away."

The fairies drifted out of the rose bushes, clumping in orbit like multiple moons among each lost child. The kids themselves sprung into the air.

Piper lifted his ancient wooden flute to his mouth, for the first time in eight years. "Let the concert begin."

CHAPTER 45

Piper neither walked nor flew. He hovered, in the true sense of the term, less than an inch above the ground. Gliding as if on skates, he leaned to and fro as he pushed himself along at a speed to rival the children's quick flight.

He played his pipe whimsically, getting used to the instrument again after so long away from it. His fingers flew along the holes of the glossy, purple-painted pipe. It resembled a clarinet more than any other modern instrument, yet it was clearly its own musical species. It belonged to some family of woodwind that had died out long ago. Piper had a spectacular range, and the timbre of each note carried an earthy depth and a light airiness. This was not the tiny melody of her music box recalling a memory… this was what Gwen had heard when she was Rosemary's age. This was the sound that enchanted her to her window and would have taken her out of it, too.

The children hung in formation, flying forward in a massive ring as Peter flew ahead and kept them on course. Gwen hung close to Rosemary at the forward-most point of the circle. The familiar fairies orbited her—the new recruits clumped around the younger children, drawn to their youthful energy. They divided into small platoons of four or five fairies a piece.

After reorienting himself to his instrument, Piper pulled it down from his lips and stopped. He asked Rosemary, "Do you remember the song?"

"Yes!"

"All of it?"

"Yes!"

"Alright. Are you ready then?"

"*Yes!*" Rosemary cherished the word more with each utterance.

"Peter," Piper called, "I'll be off fast after this. It's a pleasure doing business with you."

"No hard feelings about last time?"

"No," he said. "You've made good on that. I don't pretend to have faith in this scheme of yours, but good luck all the same."

"Thank you, Piper."

He smiled, and Gwen recognized the expression. It was that sad, amused smile that Dawn had given her. He wasn't driven to help them… he was just caught up in his own nostalgia for a time when normal adults were powerless against the wonders of magic.

He nodded to Rosemary, and then began the song from the start.

There was only a measure before she began singing:

Come ye children with light heart and fast tongue,
Your silver is spoken in lands still young.
Wake up now, we sing for your ears alone.
Rise and come out, let our mission be known.

Rally your souls and bang hard your heart-drums,
Tonight is the night, before morning comes,
To make the great break that will set you free.
The stars have opened the gateway, come see!

The tune was not entirely the same as Gwen remembered it, but this did not disturb her. The song he played had changed with age and purpose. They had refined their mission, and Rosemary's voice lent a new energy, a new melody, to the cause.

The children peeled away from their circular formation, fairies following like fighter jets as they zoomed up and down the street, along the left and right, circling houses one after another, looking for faces. Peter rocketed off, the first to spot a tiny face in a second-story window. Gwen followed after and circled the house, peering in other windows.

The pudgy-faced little boy had a bowl cut as round as his glasses. He stared out, entranced by Peter. The flying boy signaled the little one to open his window, which he did, slowed only by his awe.

"Do you want to come to Neverland?"

The little boy's little round mouth could hardly form the words he sputtered out. "Are you Peter Pan?"

"I am," Peter assured him. "And these are all my friends." He gestured back to the street and all the flying creatures and children in it. "We're looking for children who want to come help protect Neverland."

"From *pirates*?"

"And worse!" Peter told him. The boy was spellbound as a fairy shot into his own bedroom and began examining him. "And this is Hawkbit."

The boy's mouth fell open, and yet somehow managed to retain the full extent of its enthusiastic smile.

All along the street, lost children prodded others awake… beckoning them to open their windows and meet the fairies accompanying them. Piper played on, depending on Rosemary to carry the melody and song when he took little pauses for breath. This was not the Pied Piper's song of ancient fairy tale. The adults were bound by the laws of its magic not to hear what was transpiring in the streets, compelled not to worry about what might be happening outside. If they were awake and struck by any impulses, it would only be to close the blinds or go to bed. The children came, not coerced, but easily convinced when confronted by the happy offer the lost children were making.

Look out of your windows, come listen here:
We are your friends and you've nothing to fear.
Our dreams fancy free and fairy feral
Are in danger and horrible peril.

Piper hovered fast along the street, and Rosemary kept pace in flight with him. Most of the lost children hurried with them. As soon as they got a child willing to come and covered in fairy dust, they zipped ahead to make up for lost time. Blink was in charge of staying behind with the new recruits, corralling all the children from the first few blocks and helping them all get comfortable flying together.

Two bubbly fairies stayed behind with Blink, and their silver and pink lights guided the children to her while the rest of Peter's ambitious brigade moved along their route through the city.

We're calling you in words you'll understand,
To help defend our beloved Neverland.
No spoiled old soul will hear this sweet plea:
We're building an army, come and join me!

When Rosemary got to the end of her song, she returned to the beginning. Between her singing and Piper's instrumentation, it sounded loud enough to wake the whole neighborhood, but only children went to their windows.

In the middle of suburbia, every other house had someone who wanted to come along with them.

"Can I bring my brother?"

"Of course!" Spurt laughed. "Bring all your brothers, all your sisters! You can bring your *cousins!*"

The freckled girl ran off to another room. She was covered in so much joy and pixie dust that she lunged into flight midway there.

Elsewhere, a timid boy in dinosaur pajamas told Sal, "I don't think so. I'm not supposed to go out at night."

"That's okay," Sal told him, waving goodbye. "Sorry to wake you!"

Newt, a more assertive recruiter, reminded kids that if they changed their mind they could get a flashlight and do Morse code with it out their window. "It doesn't even matter if you know Morse code! Just try!"

Children poured out into the street, gathering around Blink and her fairies, swarming and following the parade of lost children.

Gwen caught snippets of their conversation. She was amazed at how many of the children were unfamiliar with each other even though they lived in the same neighborhood. They were mere blocks away from each other, but differences of grade level, extracurricular activities, and their pre-existing playdate schedules, had kept them apart. Hadn't that been the reality of her childhood as well? Grown-ups had dictated her social circle. Knocking on neighbor kids' doors or bicycling aimlessly up and down the street was a thing of another generation's childhood. She'd forgotten this in Neverland, where the community and camaraderie with all creatures and other children had spoiled her.

As more boys and girls joined the herd of new playmates, they realized they could wrangle others into this adventure.

"Nick lives down this street!"

"I want go see Allyson and Hannah! Can I go get them?"

"Jessica's going to *pee herself* when she sees me flying!"

The new ones took to flight and magic like ducks to water and bread crumbs. Imploring fairies to come with them, they expanded the territory the lost children were planning on covering. Blink flew higher and higher, trying to keep track of the innumerable children their mission was fast compiling.

In intervals, Peter's brigade reformed, checking in to make sure everything was still going according to plan.

Blink zipped down during the third of these rendezvous. "I see lights. Like policemen, only… different."

Peter's face was full of stoic resolve and adventurous anticipation. "They're coming then."

"We're lucky they haven't shown up yet," Gwen reminded him.

"There's no way they were expecting this so soon, or able to prepare for it." Peter counted on his fingers, but for no discernible reason. "They probably haven't sent scouts because they want to launch a proper counter measure with all the forces they can assemble."

"Oh gosh, this is going to be the biggest adventure of my life," Newt exclaimed, bobbing and jittering. He added, "The biggest so far, anyway."

They split up again, determined to visit as many more houses as time would allow.

For some reason, none of the houses Gwen investigated yielded any children. What few children she had uncovered were not interested in taking off with her. She tried not to take it personally, and imagined it was all for the best. She didn't even know how she felt about being an active participant in this mass abduction. She'd gone along with this—as always—for the sake of getting Rosemary back and sticking close to her.

Out of the darkness of a bedroom, a boy approached his window and stared at Gwen. The whites of his eyes were vibrant against his dark skin, and they were transfixed on her. He didn't make any motion, or even display surprise. He looked as though he thought he was still dreaming.

Gwen flew over to his window and tried to convince him to open it so they could talk. He tried, but it was too heavy for him. From the outside, Gwen got some traction against the glass and helped push it up. It only budged an inch. She floated down and spoke through the crack. It was wide enough for Foxglove to fit through, so she did. Sitting on the window ledge, she waved and greeted the young boy. He looked like Rosemary's age—*not older than nine*, she thought. In her peripheral vision, Gwen saw lights in the distance, flashing like police cars, but oscillating between shades of purple and red she'd never seen before.

"We're going to Neverland," she told him. "Do you want to come?"

Foxglove cheered. The thin boy spread his chapped lips into a surprisingly small smile. "Yes," he said simply, desperately.

Gwen tried to get the window to lift higher. "How do you open the window?" she asked.

"I can't. Dad fixed it so it doesn't open all the way."

"Can you get out downstairs?"

His eyes, a happy hazel color, followed Foxglove as she danced and hummed over his head, showering him in granules of condensed, pure magic.He nodded, but he didn't seem in control of the wistful motion. "I can go out the back door?"

"I'll race you there." She laughed before they both took off.

If she hadn't been so focused on helping the boy out, she might have stopped to wonder what parent made certain their child couldn't open their window wide enough to squeeze out of at night.

Around the house, Gwen saw the sliding door into the garden and backyard. She waited, gazing into the living room and admiring the antique globe near the window. Ambient street light poured in from the expansive windows on the other side of the house. She could see a stained glass lamp on the coffee table and a sword mounted over the fireplace hearth.

The boy came down the stairs, lighter on his feet, thanks to the fairy dust. Foxglove accompanied him. He came running to the door so fast she thought he would slam into it like an overeager dog. Standing in his Spiderman pajamas, he unlatched the door and slid it open. The house's aroma of old books ambled out as Foxglove shot free and the boy put a cautious, naked foot out on the grass, still holding the door in one hand.

"What's your name?" she asked.

A subtle motion behind him caught her attention. Someone was on the stairs, silhouetted among many other shadows against the window. "Twill?"

The man's voice was familiar. The boy turned to face it.

Looking beyond his son, he saw the girl in his garden. "Gwen?"

He stepped down off the stairs and turned on a light.

She felt the full force of her worlds shattering as they collided.

She didn't have a voice. It was her sheer disbelief that spoke. "Mr. Starkey?"

CHAPTER 46

"So this is where you've been," he announced, staring at the fairy flitting by her side. "I'm glad to see you're not sick."

Gwen shook her head, flabbergasted. "Mr. Starkey…"

Her teacher was fully dressed in his usual tweed jacket. He must have already been awake, waiting up, reading, working… whatever grown-ups did at night. "I have to admit, I had a lot more sympathy for you when I thought you had mononucleosis. A very believable alibi, that was."

"I didn't—I don't—" She didn't know what compelled her to speak when she knew that she had absolutely nothing to say, no words with which to react.

He walked toward them, slowly. Foxglove tucked herself away behind Gwen, clinging to the collar of the girl's dress. *You know him*? the fairy buzzed, but Gwen couldn't hear anything but the sound of Starkey's footsteps as he walked across the carpet, one slow step at a time. He didn't break eye contact. His body was full of tension.

"You should leave, Gwen. Whatever the plan is, it can work without my son. Twill, come here. Come back inside."

Even as he spoke to the boy, he kept his eyes on Gwen. She backed away slowly.

Twill panicked.

"No!" he screamed. "Take me with you!"

His plea was irrelevant. With Foxglove's dusting, he had everything he needed to enact his own will. Running headlong into the garden and crushing a few hibernating begonia flowers in the process, he took to the air.

"Twill, no!" his father screamed after him. His eyes bounded back to Gwen. "I won't lose him," he declared. "I won't let you take him away from me."

Gwen realized what Mr. Starkey's slow approach toward her was distracting her from. His shadow, halfway across the room already, suddenly bolted for the fireplace. Up the wall, it reached for the shadow of the sword hung above the mantle. As soon as his shadow had hold of it, Mr. Starkey clapped his hands and flung it back to him. The shadow and its shadow sword warped back to him, bring the sword with it. He didn't even need to look at the oncoming blade. His shadow held its shadow, and when the two figures synchronized, the sword sprang into his hand naturally.

Gwen screamed and Foxglove pulled at her collar. She leapt into the air. She would have been too afraid to fly, but the sheer impossibility of her speech-and-debate teacher charging at her with a sword was enough to compel her belief in flight.

She went straight up like a rocket. Feeling only marginally safer once she was on the roof, she saw Twill zipping toward the others… and the approaching Anomalous Activity unit rolling down the street toward them.

"Twill!" Starkey screamed into the night. As he left his home, he grabbed a hat off his coat rack. The greyed tricorn was too modest and worn to be a costume piece. Twill's laughter sounded from the sky on the other side of the house, and Starkey bolted out.

She had to warn Peter.

Flying as fast as her faith would carry her, Gwen went to the head of the line where Peter and Piper where shouting the last of their conversation over the approaching sound of otherworldly sirens.

"I leave the rest to you, Pan!" Piper tucked his pipe into the shadows of his cape. There must have been a pocket somewhere in its cavernous folds, but the cape seemed to simply eat the pipe. He was grinning, his mustache and mouth twisted with vengeful pleasure.

"Take care, you crazy dog!"

"Give them hell for me," Piper told him. "And, if you happen to survive..."

He picked up his cape. Leroy scampered over to his foot and clung to the laces of his boot. His crooked posture made him look like a broken doll as he stood with his prized crown worn over his ratty hair.

"...don't ever try to find me again."

The cape swooshed, swallowing Piper whole and vanishing him altogether.

"Peter!" Gwen screamed.

"Ah, you're just in time! You are about to witness the greatest cunning of any general ever to take to air." His vanity bled out from between the teeth of his smile. He pulled out his spyglass and expanded it to get a look at the arriving adult forces before barking to Newt and Sal, "Get the new ones moving. The fairies know the way—they'll get them to Neverland!"

Blink was already shepherding them toward the stars, the moon, the horizon... every celestial plane or object that was willing to bend to the children's will. The sky was in a frenzy of delight, called upon after restless ages to perform great feats for the mortals it eternally watched over. They lent whatever power was left in them to the children, grateful to facilitate such a fantastic adventure.

The fairies and children dispersed, in twos and threes and fives. The night welcomed them through its doors to another side of life, another reality that wasn't real at all.

Twill was already fraternizing with Rosemary. The lost children themselves weren't going anywhere. They were bracing themselves for an unbelievable showdown. They needed to buy the others time, or this mass exodus would risk being compromised by trackers. Once they'd caused a big enough commotion, once they'd stirred up all the magic for miles, they would abandon the officers in a storm of enchantment that would leave their radars useless.

"We've got company!" Gwen screamed.

"Aye, I see them coming!" Peter yelled, not latching onto the unexpected fear that she was trying to communicate.

"No—not them! A pirate!"

She didn't know if it was strictly true, but she knew the word would command Peter's attention, which she desperately needed to draw to the man coming for them.

Peter laughed, his confidence swelling like a balloon. He enveloped the night as he drew his dagger from its sheath and exclaimed, "Even better!"

CHAPTER 47

The Anomalous Activity officers came in force. The unit looked like a SWAT team. Half a dozen patrol cars came to a screeching halt in the street below, along with two armored vans. By then, the lost children had made their way to the last leg of their route and were caught in a cul-de-sac. They appeared blockaded in by the officers, but it was all part of Peter's plan. Even the adults could see the brilliance of the perfect retreat he'd set up. If they needed to fall back overhead, no one would be able to follow the flying children past the street's dead end.

Almost half of the new children had been whisked away with fairies. Others waited impatiently, and a few were too excited to realize they shouldn't stay and see this conflict out with the others. As the black coats rushed out of their cars, the fight began.

An officer got out a megaphone. "Ground yourselves *immediately*. You are in violation of anomalous activity regulation and are hereby commanded to *cease and desist* all 'magical' activity. If you fail to comply, we *will* forcibly ground you and take you into custody."

No lights went on in any of the houses. Piper's spell—perhaps in conjunction with whatever magic-control technology the adults brought—kept the suburbanites calmly sleeping or otherwise occupied in their homes. A few awestruck children pressed their faces against bedroom windows, grateful not to be caught in this confrontation. Aside from those timid kids, there was no recognition from any of the neighborhood's residents.

"Never!" Peter howled, his voice echoing like a war cry. That single word signaled everything his comrades needed to know. The children scattered in the air with what few fairies were brave enough to fight with them.

In response, the adults raised their pistols. They looked larger than life, like toy dart guns spray-painted to look like sinister weapons. They began firing, and long, fast streaks of lightning shot from the barrels of their guns. The children's sporadic flight patterns were hard for them to target, let alone predict, but it made being in the air much more dangerous.

Peter dropped down, free falling to escape with the aid of gravity. He was already attracting the most fire. He did not expect anyone to be waiting on the street below him. Gwen wanted to scream, but he felt the attacker before he would have heard her. Low to the ground, he felt his foot caught in the grip of a man's hard hand.

"Peter Pan!" Starkey shouted, startling Peter and pulling him so hard he whipped him out of flight. With all the strength of his left arm—his right still clutched his sword—Starkey flung Peter to the ground. The boy only recovered enough to mitigate the impact, not avoid it. He rolled back and threw himself onto his feet again. "Why, Gentleman Starkey," he exclaimed. "What a sorry surprise to see you."

"I want my son back, Pan. I've no quarrel with Neverland if I have my boy."

"What—this fight doesn't concern you? Where have you been all these years?"

"Never you mind. I want my boy, Twill, and I'll get him if I have to run you and every one of your lost boys through to do it."

"Over my aged body," Peter replied, brandishing his dagger as he ran head on to his adversary.

Peter was comparatively safe from the officers while on the ground, or at least not such a clear shot for most of them. The children above continued to draw fire away from Peter and the new kids trying to escape into the night. Rosemary, her pockets stuffed with more fruit than they should have been able to physically fit, began egging the officers with raven tree fruit. The thin shells broke on impact and covered the officers in goop with the consistency of marshmallow spread and the stickiness of super glue. While she managed to jam guns and glue feet to the ground with this tactic, Foxglove lead her fellow fairies in a wicked campaign to jam guns, cut wires, and steal earpieces.

Newt screamed as he and Sal hurtled water balloons at the officers. Whatever liquid they were filled with, they seemed to force the opposition into slow motion upon impact.

"This one's for Bard!" they cried, avenging their comrade with all the passion their little hearts could muster… Which was a lot.

Gwen covered Peter. She avoided flying, but tried to take as much of the adult's fire as she could to protect him. After the first shot she'd unintentionally taken, Gwen had realized their fire was calibrated for children. While it grounded her all the same, she was not debilitated the way the children were. Or maybe it was just her belief that she was older and more capable that compelled her to power on. Maybe the difference was that she wasn't afraid of imaginary lightning guns the way children were. Every shot stung, but not in a painful way. Her spine tingled from top to bottom as she absorbed the electric shocks, like an acute and powerful dopamine rush she could feel moving through every major connection of her nervous system. The children above cooed in delight and awe, watching her bravery in action while they continued to skitter away from any fire. When the time came to fly, she would have her work cut out for her, escaping this onslaught, but her tactic was sustainable for now.

"I see the years have finally stopped being cruel to you," Peter told Starkey, slashing at him, one blow after another.

"Ah, but what they are doing to you," Starkey cut back. A line of sweat beaded on his forehead. He did not have the ability to break up his exertion with bursts of flight.

"What are you doing here?" Peter chuckled. "A schoolmaster again?"

"Nothing so ostentatious," he replied, able to banter and backslash as well as any self-respecting gentleman scoundrel.

"How far you've fallen since the days you sailed with Hook! You would have been better off if the crocodile had gobbled you up when you fell into the water."

"Ah, but then I would never have the chance to vanquish the infamous Peter Pan!"

The voice of the megaphone sounded again. "We've established a perimeter. There's no escaping. Surrender and ground yourselves!"

"Never!" half the children cried, echoing their fearless leader. The adults weren't bluffing though. As the ragamuffins soon discovered, there was no pushing past a certain height or distance. Somehow, the Anomalous Activity Department had put an invisible bubble over the battleground and trapped all fliers within it.

The children still had the advantage. They didn't need to defeat the Anomalous Activity officers, only escape them. Blink lead a team of children out to the backyard of a house on another street, her fast thinking giving her the idea that they might be able to make a run for it and pass undetected if they were on foot. She doubted the adults would trap themselves, and her hunch proved right. Adapting, she began ferrying everyone out on foot through the neighbor's yard. Whatever was working against them was a double-edged sword for the adults. None of the officers or special forces were shadow-casting, and Gwen suspected this was an inability created by their field.

It was not a long-term solution, and Peter's wandering attention convinced him he had greater adversaries to contend with than Starkey if the grown-ups were causing so much trouble. "If you'll excuse me," he said, launching up, bowing, and tucking his dagger away. "I'm needed elsewhere. It's been awful, Starkey. Awful as always."

All cocky and full of himself, Peter zoomed through the air. "On three!" he screamed. Everyone within hearing distance either panicked or prepared. "One… two… *three*!"

A deafening roar, even amid the clamorous chaos of their fight, erupted as Newt, Sal, Blink, Spurt, Jam, Gwen, and Rosemary all screamed with Peter, "OLLY-OLLY-OXEN-FREE!"

Nothing visible changed at first, but Blink found she could once again fly up past the bounds of the adults' perimeter. She gave an affirmative wave to Peter, and shortly thereafter, they noticed the engineers and flames that were pouring out of one of the armored vans. The device they'd been manipulating the environment with had short-circuited, and the ensuing electrical fire was spreading throughout their equipment and mobile tech lab.

Children were getting snatched out of the sky. The veteran children were too nimble in the air and familiar with flying to be taken down, but some of the others were sitting ducks with their disoriented reaction times. Various officers plucked them out of the sky—some officers undercover in ordinary police uniforms and others in their terrifying black coats. The lightning bullets did not zap them of their magic, only removed their ability to manipulate it. As if paralyzed and pulled by heavy chains, the children froze in the air and lowered, against their will, to the asphalt street below.

Once grounded, the children were captured by officers who loaded them into an armored van—the one that wasn't on fire. Locked away, there would probably be a nasty process of bureaucracy and cover up for the Anomalous Activity Department before the kids made it back into the homes they had left short minutes ago. Most of the children, however, were still making it away on the wings of the night alongside the fairies.

Gwen was dodging fire and trying to stay low to the ground. She was less confident in her flying abilities than the other children seemed to be. Pushing her insecurities out of mind, she did her best to stay clear of both the adult's fire and her teacher-turned-pirate. Starkey was still brandishing an impressive sword. He was chasing after Peter, but Gwen was now between the two.

"*Pan*!" he howled.

The scene was pandemonium. Officers were tripping over their feet or glued to the ground. Researchers were attempting to put out a vehicular electrical fire. Children were vanishing and darting through the sky while their fallen compatriots were loaded away. A suburban pirate was stalking down the street with blood lust written all over his face. When one of the black-coated officers pulled a bazooka out of the patrol car, it almost went unnoticed.

"Ready, aim, *fire*!" his commanding officer shouted. He aimed straight at Peter, and with the wide spread of its projectile, there was no escaping it.

The children's spider-silk net had been re-purposed by the adults they'd terrorized last night. Packed into the cannon and tied to weights along its edges, it came spinning out like a high-velocity fishing net. As soon as it hit Peter, it knocked him off his equilibrium and pulled him out of the sky. He dropped like a fly, and front-line officers marched forward in full SWAT gear.

Furious Foxglove didn't stop to think before she flew to the bazooka-wielding officer. Rosemary, familiar enough with Foxglove's vice to see the vindictive, pointless retaliation for what it was, flew after her.

It was too late. In her wrath, Foxglove bit the officer's ear. The uniformed man yelped, and dropped the bazooka as he slapped his hand against his head—missing Foxglove and whacking himself. He had a better weapon against her though.

"I don't believe in fairies!"

Like a candle flame, Foxglove's purple light was snuffed out. Her body drained of color, stiffened, and solidified... going through the stages of death and hitting rigor mortis in the blink of an eye. She dropped to the ground like a dead bird.

Rosemary slammed an egg into the officer's face, and then kicked him in the chest until he was down. Yanking the megaphone away from the woman holding it, she swept up Foxglove's body and shot directly up before retreating away from the density of officers.

"I do believe in fairies!" she screamed into the megaphone. It was too late for little Foxglove, whom she tucked neatly into the pocket of her dress for safe and reverent keeping until she could be returned to Neverland and buried on her native soil. "I do believe in fairies!" she continued to scream into the megaphone, counteracting any other utterances from officers attempting to suppress anomalies in their vicinity.

Foxglove had been so much more than an anomaly. As Rosemary shouted into the megaphone over and over, her tears turned to two constant streams down her face.

Several yards away, Peter was moaning under the net. If his impact were anything as hard as it looked, he would not be getting up on his own.

No, Gwen thought. Without Peter, there couldn't be a resistance, could there? This was his army he was building. They needed him to lead them. It was his vision of Neverland that inspired them all. He was the infallible, the unconquerable… the one too clever to ever be defeated.

He stayed under the trap of the spider-silk as the officers closed in around him. They formed a tight circle, and Peter was only visible from where children hovered above. No one dared take on the special forces surrounding him, and most of them had enough trouble defending themselves from the rest of the adult platoon. Gwen circled at a distance, dodging fire and waiting for an opportunity to help.

She should have known better and stayed away like the rest of the children. Peter didn't need her help at all.

"Hahahaha," he laughed, theatrically tearing through the spider-silk net with his dagger. "You daft fools! Spider-silk doesn't stop magic, it only hides it!" On his feet faster than they could react, he announced. "I'll fight you all at once! With an arm tied behind my back and my fingers tied in knots!" He jabbed one of them in the arm before leaping into the air above them.

"Leonard, are you okay?"

"My arm!" the black coat yelled. "The kid just stabbed me in the arm!" He wiped a thin trail of blood with his glove, amazed that Peter Pan was as reckless and lucky, as cocky and dangerous, as any and all rumors claimed.

Gwen's pride was quelled when she felt a hand on her foot. With the same trick he'd used to bring Peter down, Starkey now had a hold of her. He yanked her foot—it took far less to destabilize anxious Gwen. Toppling down, he half-caught her and pulled her into a hostage's position, his sword's blade inches from her neck.

"Peter!"

"Pan!"

They yelled simultaneously, but their tones conveyed wretchedly different sentiments.

Peter forgot his bravado and fight with the Anomalous Activity agents. In an instant, he was over Starkey's head and landed a good two yards behind him.

"Careful, careful, careful..." the pirate cautioned. "Another step closer and I'll slit her throat. That goes for all of you!"

The adults were at a loss. They weren't expecting someone sinister to show up to their carefully planned battle. As viciously as they wanted to suppress magic, they were not prepared to use lethal force against children. They didn't want anyone killed over this skirmish. Peter, however, was accustomed to high stakes and murderous pirates.

Gwen wrestled in his grip, trying to pry his arm off her. It was no use. The cagy teacher was older and stronger than she would ever be. "Peter!" she gasped.

"It's very simple. I want my son back." Starkey nodded up to the sky, but didn't let his eyes leave Peter. "Bring Twill down and I'll let her go. It's that easy. Then the rest of you can all carry on about your squabbles."

Starkey stepped aside. Gwen could see him now in front of her, but she still felt his grip immobilizing her. Glancing down, she saw the hands of his shadow on her neck and realized the hand she felt holding her was that of his dark double.

Starkey walked in the moonlight, but only his sword cast a shadow. "Have we got a deal? Or will I have to kill you and negotiate with one of your lost boys?"

Peter dropped his dagger to the ground. "I won't hold any boy back from Neverland. If you must kill me, kill me."

He held his hands out at his side, presenting himself for slaughter.

"Peter, no!" Gwen cried, but a shadow clapped over her mouth, and she was forced into silence.

Starkey was enraged by this response. His request was in every manner reasonable and mature, so he cursed the unreasonable boy who would sooner die than handle a situation maturely.

He raised his sword with a furious cry, but Peter didn't give him a chance to strike. Launching into the air, he sped full force toward the sword and grabbed Starkey's wrists, forcing the sword back and pushing it down. Gwen's lungs belted a horrible scream that remained trapped in her mouth and behind the shadow hand as the blade of the sword came inches from her. There was no impact. Not with the physical sword, at least.

The shadow of the sword slashed down and cut into the foot of Starkey's shadow. It recoiled like a wounded animal, and went back to its master's feet for protection and repair. Gwen was freed just in time to see her own shadow.

Her shadow had suffered much worse in the strike. Severed at the right foot and punctured at the left, it writhed in a pain Gwen couldn't share. She reached down and clutched at it, but there was no touching a shadow. It pulled and pushed away from her foot, and as Peter picked up his dagger and resumed sword fighting with one of his oldest enemies, Gwen watched her shadow detach from her altogether. It fled from the body that had allowed it to come to such harm, and she chased after it. "Wait, come back!" she called to it. Unlike the adults, she had no masterful manipulation of her shadow. She couldn't control it at all.

Rosemary defended the last of the fairies. On the ground, Blink ushered the few remaining children out of the perimeter on foot with Newt and Sal's help. From there, they were able to fly again and make their way to Neverland. Twill, at last, was escorted away from what remained of his reality. Spurt was roped into Jam's plan to divert the officer's attention from Peter while he finished his fight with Starkey—a pirate who had already lost his battle. As all of these glamorous roles were fulfilled and the evening drew to a heroic close for all, Gwen chased her shadow far away from the victorious scene and company of her fellow young soldiers.

CHAPTER 48

HER SHADOW SLIPPED OVER EVERY SURFACE IT COULD. GWEN RAN through the sky, wobbling up and down in an attempt to keep it in sight. Sometimes, it disappeared into other shadows, but Gwen kept flying toward it until it panicked and dashed away. The sound of the battle behind her faded, and the lights of fairies and patrol cars became an ephemeral glow nearer to the horizon than her, it felt. Everything was worlds away as Gwendolyn Hoffman chased after a part of her that—like so much of her—seemed to want nothing to do with the choices she was making.

There was an enviable simplicity to chasing her shadow. After so long trying to follow her heart, the act of moving after the two-dimensional and monochromatic shadow was in some ways relieving.

The stakes were too high for Gwen to appreciate this. She was busy avoiding telephone wires and house awnings. She didn't stop to wonder what life would be like without a shadow, or pause to consider it might make its way back to her eventually. Tonight was her last night in reality, and she didn't want to abandon a piece of herself, however frivolous, to grow old without her.

The shadow was unimpeded by the landscape of suburbia. It climbed the fences and walls of houses as easily as it raced across their roofs and swam through the broken surface of swimming pools. It moved on land as Gwen moved through air, and an onlooker might not have known the girl and her moonlit shadow were separated at all.

Obstacles became easier to dodge as they left suburbia. Houses became fewer, and the residential area turned to sparsely developed country. She knew they were heading back the way they had come earlier in the night, but her thoughts churned slowly as she focused on keeping her shadow in sight. If she blinked at the wrong moment, it would be gone. Was it trying to return to the perceived safety of Tiger Lily's house? Gwen couldn't imagine what motivated a shadow.

She lost it once, as it dove into the tall grasses alongside the highway out of town, toward the reservation. Cutting a path as the crow flies, the shadow made the shortest distance of a long trek.

Their route left the authorities further behind as well. A panicked Dillweed tried to keep up with her, afraid for what would happen if she got isolated without a native of Neverland to guide her home. The Anomalous Activity Department had no intention of letting her get away that easily. She was wounded—that made her an easy target. Sirens came screeching after her, but she was faster than fairy or authority. Blazing off on her own, however, meant she left a distinct magical trail away from the scene. Dillweed persevered, determined to catch up to her before the authorities did.

The shadow passed the reservation and wrapped around the edge of the forest to the entrance of the state park. Barreling down the path, it lost its shape among the shadows of the tree canopy stretching over the dirt trail. The abstract motion was all Gwen could track with her eyes. Why didn't it just dart into the forest? It could catch its breath—if shadows even had breath—or lose her for good in the totality of shade beneath the tree canopies. Did it *want* her to chase it?

The trail from the park's entrance to the lake was not long, and Gwen prepared to pounce on her shadow as soon as they hit the clearing around the lake. On open flat ground, she stood a chance of catching up, dropping down like a bird of prey, and hopefully trapping it under her.

How she would attach it again was beyond her. If she could only hold onto it until she was back to Neverland…

Her eyes glued tight to the shadow, she watched as it flew toward the maple tree and distracted her by putting a boy in her peripheral vision.

Leaning against the tree, Jay was relaxed in a handsome sweater as if everything was right with the world. "Gwen," he called, his face lighting up.

It was too much. The new stimulus brought too many thoughts and short-wired her single-minded purpose of catching her shadow. The consequences of her actions hit her as hard as the ground did when she toppled out of the sky.

"Whoa!" Jay dropped the giant sketchbook he had tucked under his arm. Approaching Gwen, he offered his hands. "Nasty fall. You okay?"

She put her fingers on his palms. He held her and helped her to her feet, pulling her into a hug. Over his shoulder, Gwen could see their shadows clinging to each other on the bark of the maple tree.

"Oh no," she muttered. She'd forgotten about Jay. In her blind desire to catch her shadow, she hadn't seen how she was trapping herself. The sirens in the distance weren't catching Jay's attention yet, but he would hear them soon. They were getting closer.

"You came," he said, smiling.

"It's a mistake, it was an emergency, I had to get to the lake… you shouldn't be here!" She felt like a crazy woman, babbling at Jay with her wind-tangled hair and dirt-smudged dress.

"It's okay. I know you have to go," Jay told her, grabbing her and steadying her. "I just wanted to give you a parting gift."

He let go of her and walked back to the tree where he'd left his sketchbook. Her shadow followed, clinging to his on whatever surface it appeared, its posture screaming, *Don't make me leave.*

"No, you're not going to be able to get out in time!" She put her hand to her mouth and bit her fingers between her teeth, trying to focus. "They're coming for me."

Her frazzled concern began to register with Jay as the product of a serious problem. "Who—the police? Like the ones at the party?"

"Yeah. They can follow my flight. They'll track it here."

She wished she could pick him up and fly him off somewhere far away. So many people who loved her protected her. Why couldn't she protect someone else for a change?

Anywhere he went on foot, they would be able to catch up. Anywhere he went with her, they would be able to follow.

"I'm only in a park after dark. It's a misdemeanor charge at worst, right?"

"If they find you while tracking me, I don't think it will be good, Jay."

"I can plead ignorance," he said and smiled. "I'm kind of surprised I haven't gotten in more trouble for running around with the unbelievable Gwen Hoffman."

This would make the second time Jay was found at the scene of Gwen's disappearance. Just because the black coats hadn't pressed any of their secret charges against him after the party didn't mean they would forget him. From a grown-up's perspective, Jay would appear to be aiding and abetting her escape every time she needed a hand getting away from them… and the Anomalous Activity Department would not take kindly to that. The sirens were audible to both of them now. Jay was no longer comfortable.

"I need to get you out of here," Gwen announced. Her priorities shifted. She could take whatever came of getting caught… she'd made her decisions. Maybe now life was making a decision for her.

The one thing she knew was that she couldn't let anything happen to Jay.

What were her options though? She looked around, but there

was so little around them… the woods, the sky, the lake.

Hiding wasn't an option. She'd seen just last night how rigorously adults could comb these woods. If they released drones again, then magic wouldn't even matter. They would be able to trace Gwen's magic to Jay like bloodhounds with a scent.

The woods. The sky. The lake.

There was no way for her to get him in the air. He was too far gone and grown up, and it would only make things worse if they found him covered in incriminating fairy dust. He was grounded.

The woods. The sky. The lake.

The lake was as still as glass. The stars floated in its liquid looking glass.

She knew what it would take to get Jay out, and she knew what the price would be… but she could not imagine the cost.

CHAPTER 49

"Come on," Gwen told him, striding toward the lake "We're getting you out of here."

"Where are we going?"

"I don't know." She rooted through her purse. "I can't go with you though. I have to get to Neverland."

"What's that?" Jay was as enchanted as anyone would be upon seeing a mermaid scale for the first time. Between its iridescent colors and the moonlight, the scale shimmered with a beautiful silver rainbow. "A calling card," Gwen replied, chucking it into the water. She threw it shoddily with her right hand—she still wasn't used to being left-handed.

Dillweed finally caught up to Gwen. His wings exhausted, he saw her and flew into her face. He didn't even care that a grown-up-ish person was standing beside her.

"Gah!" Gwen yelled, surprised by the stimulus of a bright green fairy shaking her face and yelling at her. Dillweed loved her too much not to yell.

"Get in my pocket, we'll leave soon." She pulled him away from her face, pinching his arm gently with her fingers. He continued to fuss at her, but went peacefully into the pocket of her satchel.

"That's a fairy," Jay muttered, transfixed.

Laughter and splashing broke the silence of the lake. "Don't tell me you've never seen one before," Lasiandra replied, propping herself up in the water, her hair still dripping wet. Jay's jaw dropped. "Next thing you know, you'll say you've never met a mermaid either," she teased.

The mermaid laughed and splashed her tail, letting it catch the moonlight and reflect it in a hundred new colors. She enjoyed the look of baffled wonderment Jay gave her, but promptly ignored him. "Who's this, Gwen?"

"This is Jay. We're in trouble, Lasiandra." The sirens had stopped approaching. They were in a static location, not far from them. She knew the patrol cars were stopped in the parking lot, and Anomalous Activity officers would be on the path to the lake already.

"How can I help?"

Gwen took a deep breath. "How fast can you get from here to warm waters?"

Lasiandra lifted a wet hand out of the water and snapped her slick fingers. "It wouldn't take more than two minutes, if I stay in the waters of this world."

"I need you to take him. The black coats are closing in. I can fly, but he's trapped."

She was grinning, and it was a concerted, failed effort to suppress it and feign surprise. "Oh, right now?"

"Yes, Lasiandra. This very second."

She looked down and back up. "I want to help, Gwen. I'm just not sure that I can without..."

The girl pulled her compact mirror out of her purse and snapped it open. Lasiandra saw her reflection... for once not in choppy waves or dim tide pools, but in a mirror. All cunning drained from her face as she was confronted by the key to her heart's desire.

"You can have it. It's a deal," Gwen told her. "Promise me you'll keep him safe, that you'll take him home... that you'll take care of him."

"Gwen, wha—" Jay didn't have words for the question he wanted to ask. His world was coming apart at its seams. His question didn't even exist, only an abstract sense of being without answers.

"I promise, of course," Lasiandra replied, lunging forward and emphatically uttering the words, as if insulted Gwen had to ask. But she wasn't insulted. She was looking at the mirror. She was elated.

"Do whatever he asks within those constraints."

"I will do anything within those constraints," Lasiandra swore.

A second's hesitation swiped at her heart, but it made no difference. Lasiandra had promised.

She tossed the compact mirror down to Lasiandra, who caught it in her hand as if she'd rehearsed her whole life for the chance to catch it.

"Take care of him. Don't let any harm come to him."

"I won't let anything happen to him, Gwen." She stared up at her strange landmaid friend, the first to ever endow her with so much responsibility, so much faith. "You've just given me a sky glass!" she laughed. "Don't you trust me?"

"I do," Gwen told her. "But I *love* him."

"And I, you, my friend," Lasiandra assured her.

"What's going on?" Jay asked, unable to process their conversation as it rushed by.

Gwen grabbed him. "You need to go with her."

"Where? In the water? It's freezing!"

"You'll be okay," she told him. "You'll be in Hawaii or something in seconds. She'll get you home once it's safe. Just hang onto her and let her do her swimming. She's the best friend I have in Neverland. She couldn't tell a lie if her life depended on it. Trust me." He shook his head no, but then heard the sound of people shouting and coming down the trail.

Whether it was self-preservation, the sudden awareness of this grand opportunity, or some combination thereof, he agreed, "Okay." He looked down, as if just now aware that he was holding his sketchpad. The water would ruin it and everything in it. He gave it a second's thought—there wasn't time for anything more. "Take this. Take it all and bring it back to me someday."

"I—"

He thrust the book into her hands. "Go to Neverland, but keep it safe, and don't forget me." She'd never seen Jay so serious. "Someday, you'll come home. Promise me you'll find me. Promise that at least someday, my friend Gwen will come home."

She didn't know she was crying until the tear was already halfway down her cheek. "Will you really still be waiting?"

"I want you in my life," he assured her. "If you can't be my girlfriend now, promise you'll at least be my friend in the end."

"I promise," Gwen whispered. "I promise—to the moon and back again."

As soon as he'd gotten the vow he wanted from her lips, he kissed them. She felt all his longing and regret as he squeezed her arms. She felt her tears freezing her face and blurring the sensation. There was something else between them though—excitement, wonder, the brilliant feeling of an adventure… hopelessly fantastic even if it was pulling them apart. At least Jay was a part of it now. At least he had seen and been and had a few nights of it with her.

In a fleeting moment of self-control, Gwen pushed out of his arms. "Go," she commanded. "I love you."

He smiled, that gorgeous smile that she had fallen for in between the equations and classwork of Ms. Whitman's third period math. They'd had an adventure. They'd had a romance. With a big breath, he leapt up and threw himself into the lake. Gwen's shadow followed him, but could not go beneath the water. The shadow rippled on the surface, broken by the water until it fled back to shore. It still would not come near Gwen.

Jay surfaced, his teeth chattering. Lasiandra already had a hold of him. "This is it!" she cried to her friend on the shore. "I told you—the stars promised we'd be great friends in the end! And this is it. This is the beginning of the end."

"Stay safe!" Gwen called to them, clutching Jay's book in both her arms.

"I'll see you in Neverland!" Lasiandra told her, swimming off. "Take care of yourself! This is only the beginning!"

Jay was still looking back at her when Lasiandra pulled him under. Just like that, they were gone. No new ripples formed. Wherever they were, they were far beyond the mortal reaches of Lake Agana.

"Hey you, stop!"

The black coats were halfway across the clearing, only now emerging from the dark woods. They raced toward her, but they were only running with their grown-up feet.

"Come on, Dillweed," Gwen whispered, rousing him from his rest in her pocket. He flitted up, his energy renewed. "Let's go home."

She did not need a running start. She did not need to crouch and leap up into flight. Gwen simply lifted into the air by sheer force of whimsy and love. Shooting like a star, she raced up toward the sky, a little green fairy twinkling at her side. Her heart decided, her mind as clear as the star-dabbled night sky, she left the world with only the beautiful possibility of the future in her thoughts.

She flew, without so much as a shadow to weigh her down.

About the Author

Author Picture by Margaret Hubert

Audrey Greathouse is a lost child in a perpetual and footloose quest for her own post-adolescent Neverland. Originally from Seattle, she earned her English B.A. from Southern New Hampshire University's online program while backpacking around the west coast and pretending to be a student at Stanford. She is easily excited and has grand hopes for the future, which include publishing more books and owning a crockpot. She can usually be found somewhere along the west coast, and at AudreyGreathouse.com

ACKNOWLEDGEMENTS

I AM EXTREMELY GRATEFUL (AND YOU SHOULD BE TOO) FOR CLAIRE Hanser, who got me through all the hardest parts of this book. Craig Franklin and Rosie La Puma both deserve a round of applause for helping me revise my lump of a manuscript into a wonderful book. I would like to thank, as always, the NaNoWriMo program. My gratitude and love goes to my Grammy DiVerde, for years of love, and all the support I could hope for with *The Neverland Wars.* Also I'd like to recognize my Uncle Jamie, for trying not to let his heart-attack interfere with my book signing, and my Aunt Jackie for actually taking him to the hospital.

And thanks to Zaq Whittington. For everything.